THE GATEHOUSE

AT BLUSTER HILL

LOIS KULP

THE GATEHOUSE
at Bluster Hill
by Lois Kulp

Copyright © 2024
All rights reserved.

Library of Congress Control Number: 2024945372
International Standard Book Number: 978-1-60126-955-3

Masthof Press
219 Mill Road | Morgantown, PA 19543-9516
www.Masthof.com

MORE BOOKS

by Lois Kulp

Amber of Steeplechase

Bittersweet Hollow

Dudley of Finney's Station

Heather

The Inn at the Mill

Lord of the Abbey

The Maid on Crow Hill

The Parson of Hunter Hall

The Village of Birch's Ford

I
dedicate this book
to the Sunday evening group on R.L.2
at
Souderton Mennonite Home:

Simone,
our Nova Scotian, who can talk non-stop, and if
she stops, she falls asleep.
Esther,
the queen of homemade chocolates.
Doris K.,
whose humor
does us good like medicine.
Dorothy,
her twin sister,
who shares her cookies
with us.
"Goodnight Irene,"
whose alertness and vigor defy her
ninety-four years.
Doris G.,
who keeps us informed of her newest
"great-grand."
Sara,
who quietly exudes a spirit of peace and calm
over the group.
Lois,
who is the proud great-grandmother
to one-year old twins.
Jim,
who animatedly challenges
our sluggish brains
as we struggle to
comprehend.
And finally,
John,
who supports Jim as the other
gander
in this gaggle of geese.

Thank you for being my new family.
We are not alone.
We face the sunset together.

PROLOGUE

It all began just one week before Christmas.

Trinkels, the city I grew up in, had enough little shops that it was worthwhile to wander down Main Street to see the Christmas decorations and gift suggestions in the shop windows. Mama, of course, was too busy to go with me and had very little money for gifts, but I had turned sixteen in September and although she had been very protective of me since Papa died a long time ago, she now trusted me to take care of myself. I looked in vain for some snow to be falling as I headed out, but instead, a cold, miserable rain was making the city look dull and gloomy.

But I was not deterred. I dressed warmly, held my umbrella firmly over my head, and stepped out into the cold rain, and made my way down to the center of town, some three blocks away. In due time, I reached the tall, dark buildings in the center square of Trinkels, which surrounded the fountain that I loved to hang out at in the summertime. However, today it looked so cold and unappealing to me that I barely gave it a glance.

I began my window shopping on the north side of the square. The bakery had extra large iced, gingerbread cookies in animal shapes and kris kingle and ribbon candies displayed in the shop windows. Other shops displayed dolls with porcelain heads and carved wooden toys. I was so intent on looking at some elegant crocheted doilies that I never noticed that the rain was now mixed with snowflakes.

After a while, I crossed to the other side of the square. In doing so, I walked right by the fountain. There were a surprising number of people scurrying around the square despite the weather, and just as I got to the fountain, two young boys chasing each other ran in front of me and one of them slipped on the ice that was beginning to form on the cobblestones. He slid into me and down I went and before I knew what was happening, I felt someone else fall on me, just like a row of dominoes.

The two young boys got up and ran away, but the person that fell on me quickly stood up and looked down at me.

"Are you hurt?" he asked, real concern in his dark eyes.

"No," I replied, embarrassed by my dirty, wet clothes. "I think I am fine."

"Let me help you up."

He did so. He was young, tall and skinny. Perhaps a bit older than me.

"I am afraid I have damaged your umbrella irreparably," he said. "It looks rather sad."

The smashed umbrella certainly did look ready for the junk pile. "It is no great loss. It is old and was already bent a bit. Anyway, it is now snowing and I do not need it anymore," I replied.

"Do you live here in Trinkels?" he asked.

"Yes, I was just looking at the window displays."

"Oh, I was, too. Were you looking for something special?"

"No, I just like to see what they have. I don't have much money to spend."

Somehow we kept talking and we looked at the window displays together and then he walked me home. We both enjoyed the afternoon and in the following weeks, we would sometimes meet at the fountain and wander around town. When the weather got milder, we saw each other more often. He lived on the opposite side of town and his name was Conrad. He was two years older than I was, and it made me feel very important that an older fellow was interested in me.

We were seeing each other nearly every week, when we hit a snag. A new family moved next door to my mother and me. And there was a boy named Mike in the family. Within the week, I got to talk to him a few times. He was very funny and he amused me. I was just sixteen and I found most boys interesting.

One evening, I set out to meet Conrad at the fountain. As I left the house, Mike, who was also heading downtown, joined me. I had already told him about Conrad and he knew I was going to meet him. As we walked, Mike amused me with his funny stories. His tales were so far out that I doubt they were really true, but they were hilarious. I was laughing merrily at one of his tall tales as we approached the fountain. I did not even notice Conrad right away, but when I did, his eyes were on the neighbor boy and he did not look happy. Mike waved goodbye to me and then went off in another direction and I walked up to Conrad.

"Hi," I greeted him. Conrad did not answer me. I wondered what happened that he was so gloomy. "Is something wrong?"

He took his time to answer. "Who is he?" he finally asked, a definite pout on his face.

"Who?" I wondered if I missed something. I had not seen anyone go past. Conrad looked at me impatiently.

"The fellow you were having such a good time with."

"Oh, him. That's Mike. He just moved in next to us. He is really nice and terribly funny. I just laugh till my stomach hurts sometimes."

Conrad's face was beginning to look like a thundercloud.

"Exactly how often do you talk to him?"

"I don't know. Often. When he sees me, he comes over to talk."

Conrad looked at me like I had spoken a blasphemy. "You are my girl," he said. His eyes were dark with anger.

"Maybe I am," I said, giving this new Conrad a good look, "but I can talk to whoever I want to talk to. Just because you are my boyfriend doesn't mean that I can't have fun with other fellas."

"Yes, it does." The answer came out very quickly. I gave Conrad a good look. He was serious. I was getting tired of his sour mood and I was not about to have him tell me who I could talk to.

"Who says?" I said, my dander rising.

"I do." His dark eyes were flashing.

"I am only sixteen. I am not married to you. If I want to talk to other fellows, I will."

"Not as long as you are my girl."

"Well, if that is the way you feel, you can forget about me. I won't have you telling me who I can talk to."

The conversation picked up heat and before I knew it, I was telling Conrad he could go get lost and he angrily began walking away from me. I watched him go with mixed feelings. I liked him but no way was he going to keep me from talking to other boys.

As I watched him walk away, he suddenly stopped and turned once more to me.

"Some day, June," he said slowly and forcefully, "you will come crawling back to me."

And that is how it ended.

CHAPTER 1

Ten years later

Someone was knocking on the front door. It was nine o'clock and dusk was falling rapidly. The street lamps were being lit and the sound of children playing outside in the summer evening was getting dim. I was not yet accustomed to being alone and I was not a person easily frightened, but recent events in my life left me feeling very alone. Before I could get out of the wing back chair, the knock came again. Louder. I eased myself out of my chair slowly and went to the door, opening it cautiously.

"Good evening," said the gentleman waiting at the door.

"Good evening," I replied, relieved that it was a man that I knew from my church. I knew he had lost his wife about a year earlier and I did not feel it was quite proper to invite him in at this hour, so I simply waited to hear what he wanted.

"Miss Merriweather." The man now looked like his words had escaped him.

"Yes?"

"I ah, heard of the death of your mother and I wish to extend my sympathies."

"Thank you."

The man must have a short memory. He had already spoken to me at the funeral. I remembered now that he had extended his sympathy a long time and I had been extremely relieved when he was finally finished.

"I ah, was wondering..." He cleared his throat. "I heard of your circumstances and would like to offer you a job. I lost my wife eight months ago and have six little ones."

I knew the family. There were many children and the oldest not more than ten. Among them, there was a set of twin boys about four years old and I remembered them as very busy little boys.

"I need help and I think you would do well in taking care of my family." He hesitated and gave me a hopeful smile. "I thought, if things work out well, you could perhaps have a permanent place in our family—as mother."

He looked a bit sheepish as he added this last bit. As well he should. He was probably in his late thirties and was not bad to look at but he coughed a bit self consciously as I stared at him in something close to horror. The man was possibly fifteen years older than I was and I had barely ever talked to him and now he was suggesting possible marriage. I found myself without words, which did not happen too often with me.

"I believe I surprised you. I hope it is a welcome surprise."

I could not believe what I was hearing. Yes, I did need to earn my own way in life. But raising some other man's children was not my wish at all. I wanted my own children. My head was reeling.

"I...hardly know what to say," I stuttered. Never in my life had I been so at a loss for words. He came to my rescue.

"Maybe you would like to think it over."

"Yes, yes. I must think it over," I gasped. I really did not need to think it over, but it would give me time to get my spinning head back on my shoulders where it belonged.

"In that case, I shall leave you and I will stop by again in the next couple days."

"Thank you, sir."

"Goodnight, June."

I did not like the way he said my name. He should have said Miss Merriweather. After all, I had just addressed him as sir. June from his lips was far too intimate.

I closed the door almost before he turned around to return to his carriage. I wondered if any of the children were in the carriage with him. Or maybe he put them to bed first and that is why he came so late. I somehow stumbled to the sofa and sat down hard. I took a deep breath and stared into space. *Was this to be my lot in life? Is this what God intended for me?*

I don't know how long I sat there, but after perhaps fifteen minutes, I began to think seriously about what the man said. How did the man ever manage being both father and mother to six children?

He was really to be pitied. And me? Maybe this would be my only chance at marriage. He seemed nice enough, but this was not at all what I wished for. How I wished for Mama! Or a sister. Someone to give me advice. But I had been an only child. For just a moment, I imagined a sister sitting next to me. Maybe she would have laughed with me over this offer. But right now, this was no laughing matter. I felt like crying. I felt like I had no one. No one at all. Oh, people from church and other friends had extended sympathy, but I needed someone to sit down and help me to sort this out. Someone to help me through the rest of my life. And my best friend had.... I did not even want to think of that.

As I stood up to get a glass of water, my hand slipped down the side of the sofa cushion and I felt something. I pulled it out and discovered it to be an envelope. An unopened envelope. I had sorted the mail here two days ago and this one must have slipped down the side. I looked at the return address, hoping it was not another bill. To my happy surprise, it was a letter from my Aunt Sarah Morgan. She was an older sister to my mother and was such a comfort to me at the funeral. I opened the letter quickly.

> My dear June,
>
> I did not get to talk to you very much at the funeral and now I keep wondering what you are going to do with your mother gone. I am sure you will not be able to stay where you are and I would like to invite you to come for a prolonged visit. Or perhaps even

make your permanent home with us. You have been here before and you know we have lots of work here on the estate.

Theodore had a heart attack last year and has really slowed down. He has promoted one of his trusted workers to general manager of the estate and now Theodore does what he feels like doing and lets the manager deal with the many problems and decisions. As for me, Theodore's sister is living here, too, and her mind is not quite what it used to be and her hearing is in yet worse shape. I have a cook that comes a few days a week, but she is leaving in about a month. I have a girl that comes in and cleans. But there are always errands that need to be run, mending to do, butter to churn and a whole host of things to do that I no longer get done. We have a big garden and the canning is waiting. It is nearly overwhelming. We have too much going and in spite of hired help, it doesn't all get done. Please do consider my offer. At least come for a long visit and we can discuss your options then.

Love and prayers to you from,

Aunt Sarah and Uncle Theodore

I remember my mother quoting the verse in the Bible "Before ye call, I will answer." I could not believe what had happened to me as I read the letter. It was like a burden rolled off my back.

Although my relationship with God was somewhat lacking after losing both parents, I felt like maybe God did think of me once in a while.

Three days later, the widower came to call. I was now ready for his visit, and with my plans firmly in place, I politely told him that I was moving from the area and I wished him well. I even wished him success in his search for help but as I closed the door on him, I breathed a sigh of relief that it would not be me.

CHAPTER 2

The train was dirty and I was hot, in spite of the partially opened window. I had been on the train for three hours now and the excitement of the trip was wearing a bit thin. I was, however, thrilled at the speed at which we traveled. It sure beat the coaches, but going across the countryside by carriage, one did not have all this black smoke from the engine finding its way through the partially opened windows. I would be filthy by the time I arrived at my uncle's estate. The white mustached conductor had just announced that the next stop would be Thackeray's Pond, which was the small town where my train trip would end. I had eaten my sandwich, my cookie and had already drained my bottle of water. And in this July heat, I was still thirsty.

Having nothing better to do, I looked around the train at my fellow passengers. A mother sat alone with a young child who had been fussing for most of the last hour. Two teen-aged girls, sitting close together, laughed and ate apples as they talked. At the last stop, two men in top hats and dark suits entered and appeared to be in serious conversation ever since they sat down. They sat about six seats in front of me and the one man spoke in low tones, but the other one spoke quite loudly and I could hear everything he said. It seemed they had been to a funeral and the conversation appeared to center around the deceased. The quieter man was partially hidden from my view by another passenger, but the one doing most of the talking was a middle-aged man with a thick, black mustache and he used many hand and arm gestures and seemed upset over something. I found myself being entertained by him.

Finally, the train slowed and with much screeching and hissing of steam, we stopped at Thackeray's Pond, which was just a few miles from Cobbler's Crossing where my relatives lived. I was more than ready to leave the train. I turned and exited the door behind me, and, bag in hand, waited for my trunk that was in another car. The young man who brought me my trunk carried it to the porch of the inn and I headed into the inn to check when the stagecoach would arrive. I was informed that I would have a twenty-minute wait. I drank a glass of cold lemonade at a table by the window and watched a few children playing ball in the park across from the inn. I also saw that the sky looked as if a storm was headed our way. I hoped it would hold off until I was at my uncle's estate. If I remembered right, I would have about a mile to walk once I got to Cobbler's Crossing.

When the coach arrived, I directed my trunk to be taken to the stagecoach and when that was taken care of, I entered the coach as the last passenger. I discovered that two of the passengers were the two men that had been on the train. Now I sat right next to the man with the black mustache and although I could not see the other man, by the tone of his voice, I judged him to be quite a bit younger. They now discussed horses and I no longer listened to them. I was busy looking out the window and watching teams going by with wagons loaded with hay. It was quite hilly here and the rolling countryside was dotted with cows and sheep contentedly grazing. The coach, pulled by four strong horses, creaked as it rolled down the sometimes steep, country roads, and now, nearing my destination, I was trying to envision a new life with my aunt and uncle. I had visited them with my mother a few times and knew they lived on a large estate. Would I be happy here? My passion in life seemed to be sewing. Would I have opportunity to do that here?

The coach had been slowly climbing a hill and now it rounded a bend and suddenly we were in the small village of Cobbler's Crossing. And right in the center of the small village, our coach came to a stop in front of a white plastered building where a weathered sign proclaimed it to be Shepherd's Inn. The building stood on a wide open crossroads with tall elms standing not only in front of the inn, but also on all four corners, spanning the road and giving much needed shade on this hot July day. It was a pretty village with just a few shops—the cobbler, from whom it probably got its name, the smithy, a small mercantile and another building which, if I remembered correctly, was the post office. And scattered around the village were perhaps twenty houses and a church with a high white spire.

I was the first one off the coach. I had written my aunt about coming, but did not know then exactly what day or time I would arrive, so I knew no one would be coming for me. That was fine. I needed to walk after so much sitting and I knew the way. I only needed to cross the cobbled street and head up the country road perhaps a mile. But first, I had to ask the footman to place my trunk on the porch of the inn, where my uncle could pick it up. That done, with a smaller bag in my hand, I turned to cross the street.

And only now did I see what I had failed to notice before. The village street was blocked by a broken down cart that stood in the middle of the dusty road. The horses that had pulled the cart stood there uncertainly, not quite knowing what to do. Several small pigs ran haphazardly and joyfully in all directions, squealing their delight over their freedom, as a gathering of amused villagers stood by enjoying the action. Some men, of course, were trying to catch the pigs, and as I watched, one pig ran into a young boy, knocking him down amid much laughter from the spectators. I did not watch long, since I had a mile to walk, and was eager to get to my destination, especially after hearing a threatening rumble of thunder. Black clouds were rolling in my direction. As I considered where best to cross to the other side, I saw a large flock of sheep heading down the middle of the road right where the broken down cart stood. No wonder the inn was called Shepherd's Inn if this road gave the right of way to the shepherd with his sheep. His flock took up the whole road. The pigs were not yet caught and with the sheep headed in my direction, I wanted to quickly cross before they passed. However, as I stepped into the street a voice called to me.

"Stand back until the sheep pass."

I stopped short and turned my head to see who had spoken. The words of caution were certainly for me as I was the only one thinking of crossing the street, except, of course, for the squealing pigs. I found myself staring at what appeared to be the younger man who had traveled with me. Perhaps he was at home here. At any rate, he still wore his top hat as he stood in the shade of the elm tree, and although I could not see his features, I knew his sober dark eyes were fixed on me. And for some reason, it irritated me. I had a mile to walk and now the sky had turned black and again I heard a rumble of thunder and it was louder this time. The storm was approaching rapidly. I looked away from the man for a few seconds and then I looked back at the flock of sheep coming toward me. I could still get across. I glanced at the man again. I could tell by the tilt of the hat that he was still looking at me. It seemed he did not trust me. However, when I saw someone begin talking to him, causing him to look elsewhere, I gave a last quick glance in the direction of the sheep and ran. It was a close call, but I made it. Well, I nearly made it. First my swinging bag nearly tripped me in the middle of the street and just as I reached the grass on the other side of the road, one of the stray pigs ran right in front of me and in my surprise, I stumbled and fell. I got up as quickly as possible but could not help but look across the street to see if the man had seen me. Now, of course, I was looking over a flock of woolly, baaing sheep and I was not a little embarrassed to see the same dark eyes focused on me. I could just assume his disgust at a woman not obeying him. My experience with men in the last ten years was not very positive and, in spite of my fall, I felt a bit smug at ignoring his warning.

I quickly looked away and lost no time heading down the road to Bluster Hill, my uncle's estate. I now not only had the dirt from the train on my clothes, I had green grass stains on my skirt from falling. I heard another rumble of thunder, even closer now and when I had gone the length of just one field, I felt the first drop of rain. It did not take long for that raindrop to transition to a downpour. I stopped walking long enough to reach into my bag for my umbrella. It was not a man-sized umbrella, but it would have to do. The wind began to blow stronger and I barely managed to open the umbrella and when I began walking again, it kept going inside out on me and in the end it helped not at all because of the wind. I put it back in my bag, wet as it was. When I had walked the length of another field, a carriage came by and stopped just ahead of me. As I walked up to it, a young man with a friendly smile and blonde curls looked down at me.

"I think you need a ride!" he shouted to me above the wind and rain. "Where are you going?"

"To Bluster Hill!" I hollered back.

"Give me your hand."

I gave it willingly. I needed a ride badly, even though his carriage was open and I would still get wet. I was a bit embarrassed though, because I certainly looked like a bedraggled rag doll. He flicked the reins as the thunder rolled and lightning flashed.

"My name is Brian!" he shouted. "You seem to be a stranger."

"My name is June," I replied. "I am visiting my uncle and aunt at Bluster Hill."

"Ah. Sarah and Theodore. I know them well. In fact, I picked apples for them the last three years. Reach behind you. There is a tarp that will keep you from getting soaked through."

I did so, and wrapped the small tarp around me and pulled it up over my head.

"Thanks," I said. And then fell silent as thunder crashed and the horse began to act skittish. No more was said as Brian's attention was fixed on the horse, but he soon turned off on a lane to my uncle's house. This entrance was what I always remembered best from the estate. Even in the downpour around us, I could see the gatehouse. It had always fascinated me. It was impressive and unique. It stood at the end of the drive and we now drove under a part of the gatehouse that arched over the road. There was a room over the arch we passed under, and the rest of the house was to the right. A wall went out on both sides of the entrance. Now, in the drenching shower, I could not see it very well, but I had to wonder if anyone lived in it. If no one lived in it, maybe I could. The thought excited me.

We traveled on down the lane, a field on both sides, and then entered a strip of elm and maple trees that spanned the road. Once under the trees, we forded a small creek and then rode uphill to the main house. It was a lovely stone house that looked over the meadows toward the village. I knew that behind the house and down the hill partway on the other side, was the barn and also other outbuildings. Beyond that, the orchard and fields and more meadows. It was a large, beautiful estate and I was glad that I had decided to come.

We pulled up to the side portico of the large house and I quickly exited the carriage. Brian's blue eyes smiled at me.

"Enjoy your visit."

"Thank you and thanks for the ride."

He drove off into the rumbling thunder, while I knocked on the door. My aunt came to the door and instantly broke into a welcoming smile.

"June! I am so glad you came. Come in, come in out of the rain."

"Please excuse me, I am wet and dirty."

"I don't care, let me give you a hug."

It felt so good to be hugged by my aunt. I felt very alone in the world since my mother's passing. I found myself blinking back the moisture in my own eyes and seeing my blurred eyes, Aunt Sarah blinked back her own tears.

"I am so glad you came, and I hope you came to stay," she said, standing back and taking a good look at me. I felt so grimy and imagined my dark hair hanging over my face in strings, while my aunt, her face wreathed in love smiles and wearing a crisp, clean apron, looked very well-groomed.

"I really don't know if I shall stay. But quite honestly, I have nowhere else to go. Well, I could have worked for a widower with too many children, but he was already seeing the possibility of me becoming the mother of his children, and he was too old for me."

"Oh, dear me," laughed my aunt. "You need someone younger than that!"

"By the way, I left my trunk at the inn. I hope someone can pick it up."

"No problem. Someone here is always running to the village for something. But now, come have some cold mint tea from our meadow. You are probably hungry and supper is a couple hours away. But I have a chocolate cake here and I'll cut you a piece of that. I think I shall have to light a lamp, it has become so dark in...."

She never finished her sentence. There was a flash of lightning and a terrible crack of thunder that was followed by the distinct sound of something breaking and then hitting the house. We stood for a moment, frozen with fear, but when nothing more happened, I followed my aunt to the back porch where we found a large limb from a tree close by, lying on the ground with part of it leaning on the roof of the porch.

"Thank God it did not take the whole tree," said my aunt. "That tree gives welcome shade these days when it is so hot. But it is another job to be done. There is no end of work around here. I've been canning beans all morning and the early apples are nearly ready and then there will be applesauce to can."

"I am happy to help," I said, taking a bite out of the chocolate cake and licking the sticky icing from my fingers. "I want to earn my keep."

We spent the next hour just talking. As we talked, a fluffy gray cat came into the room and took a good look at me from a safe distance.

"Oh, what a lovely cat! What is his name?"

"It is a she and her name is Misty."

"She is the right color for the name."

I called the cat to me and she came willingly. I never stayed a stranger long to cats. As I talked to Misty, I noticed a woman standing just outside the kitchen, in the hallway. She said not a word and just stared at me. When my aunt saw her, she called to her.

"Come in, Becca. This is my niece June, who has come, hopefully to stay. And June, this is Theodore's sister Rebecca, who lives with us. We just call her Becca."

I said hello, but Becca just stared at me and finally walked away. She was a thin, tall woman with distinct lines in her face, wearing a dull gray dress. Aunt Sarah informed me that Becca talked very little and was quite harmless although her silent stare could unnerve one.

Just then the door opened and my uncle came in, wet from the storm.

"Hello, who have we here?" he greeted me. "How did you get here in this storm?"

"I got caught in the rain but a young man by the name of Brian picked me up. He said he picks apples for you."

"Oh, Brian. Sure I know him. He is a fine young man and a good apple picker, too. I presume he will be picking apples for us again by next week."

"Did you see the limb that came down?" asked Aunt Sarah.

"Limb down? From the storm?"

"Yes. I don't know if it was the wind or lightning, but it fell right after a loud crash of thunder."

Uncle Theodore went to survey the damage to the porch. I remembered him as a man with his hands in several things at once. He had so many interests. But I could see the years had taken their toll on him, too. Or maybe it was the heart attack. His big frame was not quite as robust as formerly and he walked with a bit of a limp. He soon came in again.

"It is fixable." Then he turned to me. "I hope you came to stay, June. Sarah can use you."

"If you will have me, I'd like to stay for a long visit."

"That is good news. Did you bring a trunk or something to be picked up?"

"I did, but it is at the inn."

"I'll go get it. I do the easy things around here and let the others do the hard work."

———

By suppertime, I had my trunk and I was shown the room that would be mine. The high walls were covered with blue wallpaper with small pink and yellow flowers. The room had tall windows with a view of the front lawn and between the tall trees surrounding the house, I could see the stream we had forded and the village in the distance. I remembered a small foot bridge a short distance from the road, which was for those wanting to cross the stream by foot. My room had a bed and a small chest of drawers. There was a straight-back wooden chair in another corner by a small table and a wardrobe for my clothing.

The cook had left for the day, but she made us a savory chicken pie for supper and a salad straight from the garden. As we chatted around the table, Becca gave me long looks, but she said nary a word. Uncle Theodore chatted about all aspects of the estate, clearly still enjoying the work, although under doctor's orders to take it easy.

"My thumper does not want to behave anymore," he said. "And Sarah keeps an eye on me as well. I am blessed by good workers. We have cows and we raise a lot of beef cattle, some chickens, a couple pigs for our own use and a few horses. I'll walk you around the place this evening if it stops raining," he promised me.

The rain did stop and just as dusk was falling, Uncle Theodore took me for the promised walk. I met my uncle's dog Dusty, who accompanied us and who would come every so often to me for some sweet talk and a pat on the head.

We walked slightly down hill, past the barn, the chicken house, a corn crib and a couple other outbuildings. Off to the left was the apple orchard. Not far from the apple orchard were a few cherry, peach and plum trees. My uncle kept up a running dialogue of all his many interests on the estate.

"My grandfather bought the land and farmed here. My father added the orchard. I love the place. I love living here, but I can't do the work anymore. We always had help, but I do less and less." He sighed. "It is hard to slow down. I loved my work. I loved making money and fixing the place up. But..." he sighed, "I've come to the realization that when I go, I leave everything behind. All I worked for stays here. I should have spent more time on the spiritual. That is the only thing I take along. I'm trying to improve on that part of my life. But now I am old and...well, I am thankful for each day the Lord gives me."

We walked a short time in silence before he continued.

"Sarah likes to can and work in the garden. But there is lots of work to do here and I don't expect you to work for nothing. I will pay you. I am just glad you are here. We have a good manager who is in charge of the estate now. And we have a part-time cook and a girl for cleaning. The estate has done well so we are not hurting."

Later, sitting with my aunt on the back porch she asked again if I would stay.

"I want to say yes, but I love to sew. It is a passion with me. I have done sewing for other people and I hope someday to be able to do that for a living."

"Ah, you'll find a man and then you can sew for your children," said my uncle who came up to the porch, overhearing us.

"I am not thinking very kindly toward men at the moment. I don't seem to understand them."

"Oh, yes, I did hear your engagement was broken," said my aunt sympathetically. "I am so sorry."

"I don't know if I am sorry or not. I am planning to make my living without a man at this point."

After my uncle went into the house, Aunt Sarah leaned a bit closer to me.

"You have had some rough spots in your life. We all have to deal with them. The important thing to remember is that God is right there with you in the midst of your trouble. He does not leave you. It just feels that way because you are focused on your hurt. Your pain."

"I don't seem to make good choices."

"I don't remember who said this to me," said Aunt Sarah, "but it has helped me in life. And it is this. It is the journey that counts."

"What do you mean?"

"God is not so much interested that all goes well for you. He is interested in your spiritual journey. The spiritual is of uppermost importance to Him. It takes us a long time until it becomes of utmost importance to us. We need the trials to learn. No one goes through life without them. As to your poor choices, God knew you were going to make them. And He did not stand in the way. He let you make them and watched with love the whole time. But the important thing is, have you learned something?"

I sat in silence. She was not expecting me to answer. It was something to contemplate. She continued.

"There was a time that my husband only thought of the money he was making here. But since his heart attack, his priorities have changed. The spiritual is what is the most important and there are many ways we can serve the Lord right where we are. No one on earth loves you more than God loves you. Keep in contact with Him. I know it seems like a one-way conversation, but God will get through to you what He needs you to know. Someone put it well when they said, 'God is not really silent. We are deaf.'"

CHAPTER 3

And so began my life at Bluster Hill. At first it seemed like a visit, but soon I was canning applesauce, gathering vegetables from the garden and getting acquainted with the estate. I churned butter for the first time in my life and I learned to know Bella, the cook who came a few days to cook and bake. Bella was in her sixties and was single all her life. Now, her time here was nearly over and she was going to move to her cousin's in a distant town. Nettie, the cleaning girl came whenever needed. Not every day, but it seemed there was always something needing cleaning, besides the weekly cleaning.

I was surprised how many people came to the house in a day. Sometimes it was someone from church. Other times it was a worker that got hurt. Or a hired hand that came to do some work on the house. The tree limb was removed in record time the morning after the storm and in a few days, the damages to the porch were mended.

———————

"We will eat supper in the dining room this evening," said Aunt Sarah on Friday afternoon. "Our estate manager always comes for supper on Fridays. It is a good time to sit down and discuss any business or problems of the estate."

I had seen a couple men who worked the land and cared for the cows. I had not yet met any of their employees, but one day when looking out the kitchen window, I saw Sarah was talking to a gray-haired man out along the garden and when I asked her later who she had been talking to, she said it was the estate manager, Grayson. So this evening I would at least meet the estate manager. I set the table for five and was told to use the good china and goblets.

"I always like a nice table," Aunt Sarah said, "and Friday nights are always a bit more formal although our discussions are everyday problems. Bella always makes a special meal and usually enough for leftovers for the next day. But this is her last week. Do you enjoy cooking?"

"I cook, and I enjoy it, but sewing is my first love."

Supper was at seven. Bella had made a nice beef roast with potatoes and carrots and sliced tomatoes from the garden and applesauce from the orchard before she left for the day. It all smelled heavenly and I was hungry long before suppertime. Since we had company, we all dressed up for supper and even Becca was reminded to change her dress.

I heard the knocker shortly before seven and Aunt Sarah, who was slicing the meat, asked if I would please answer the door for our guest. I went to the door and swung it open.

It was not our supper guest.

This was not a gray-haired man. It was a young man with dark hair. I looked at the man and instantly thought of the man with the top hat on the train. The one who warned me about crossing in front of the flock of sheep. But I was not sure. At the same time, bells were ringing in my head. This man reminded me of a young man that I had not seen in ten years. Someone I had once known quite well. *Was it possible?* I was so shocked, I just stood there looking at him. *Why was he here? Should I invite him in?* He seemed a bit taken back himself. *Was this really Conrad?* We just stared at each other. I finally found my voice.

"I assume you wish to see my uncle. I'll call him," I spoke quickly, coming out of my trance. But I did not call immediately. I just kept staring at the visitor.

Conrad, if this was Conrad, did not reply, which added to my discomfort, but I thought I detected just a bit of amusement in his otherwise sober face. I was beginning to feel embarrassed and felt I needed to explain my hesitation.

"We are expecting someone else and I expected you to be that person." It all sounded extremely lame, even to me and I felt my face heat up. "I will get my uncle."

I turned, leaving him standing on the porch, as I went for my uncle. I had acted like a bumbling country girl and I was eager to hide. Fortunately, I met my uncle in the doorway to the hall.

"Someone is here to see you, but it is not the estate manager," I said quickly, and kept walking into the kitchen.

"Hello, Grayson," I heard my uncle say behind me. "Come on in. My niece seems not to know you."

I stopped in my tracks. *This could not be the manager of the estate?* It couldn't be. The manager had gray hair. I had seen him. And it could not possibly be Conrad although he held such a strong resemblance that I felt it was Conrad. I hurried into the kitchen.

"June, will you please put the vegetables on the table while I finish the gravy?" asked my aunt.

I somehow felt all thumbs. How did I manage to make such a dunce out of myself? What was the name my uncle had called him? I just could not put it out of my head that it was Conrad. Maybe Conrad had a brother. The likeness was too strong not to be related. And if it was Conrad, why was the name different? And although I thought he was handsome at eighteen, this man was a knock-out.

"Aunt Sarah, this week when I asked you who you talked to at the garden, you said it was the estate manager."

"When? Oh yes, I remember. I did talk to him there."

"That man had gray hair."

Aunt Sarah paused. "If he had gray hair it was the gardener, not the estate manager. I believe I talked to both of them that morning." She kept stirring the gravy, not noticing my confusion or red face. "Is Grayson here now?"

I swallowed hard. "He is."

I said no more. I wanted to run away, but I obediently picked up the bowls of vegetables and the salad and took them to the table in the dining room. Finally, the potatoes and gravy were ready to take in and then Aunt Sarah brought in the platter of roast beef.

"Oh, we forgot to pour the water in the glasses," she said. "Would you take care of that?"

I was glad to escape for a bit yet. I stood in the kitchen and stared into space for I don't know how long.

"The water pitcher is on the table," called my aunt, thinking I could not find it.

"Coming." I really did not hear what my aunt called to me. I was so lost in thought. I had come to the kitchen for something and could not remember what. Oh, the water!

I quickly brought in the pitcher of water, glad for something to do. My uncle and our guest were already in the room, waiting for me. My hands shook as I poured and my face felt hot. I kept my eyes glued to the table, trying to make myself as small and inconspicuous as possible as I filled the goblets but my heart was hammering and I hoped the pitcher of water would not slip from my trembling hands. I had been expecting an interesting supper, listening to the men discuss the work on the estate. Suddenly, I wished to be anywhere but here. Well, not quite. Just a mouse in the corner perhaps. Fortunately, the men kept a running conversation as I poured. The more I heard his voice, the more I was sure that this was also the man who had traveled with me in the coach and train. This was bewildering. But worse than anything else, if this was Conrad, it was the man I had spurned ten years ago.

"Now," said my uncle as I finished and Becca made her silent way into the room, "it seems we need to make some introductions." He glanced at me and then at Grayson.

"I don't think you two have met yet." He waited just a moment.

"We have not been formally introduced," said Grayson in a low voice.

I have to admit, he was looking very good in his riding habit. I was mentally comparing him to the boy I had known. There was a world of difference. Everything had improved. His manners, his looks, his whole bearing. And it shook me. It had to be Conrad. Or his twin.

"Grayson, this is my niece, June Elizabeth Merriweather and she has come, we hope, to stay here and make Bluster Hill her home. And June, this is Grayson Everleigh, our estate manager."

I was only a few steps from the man I knew as Conrad, and as the introductions were ended, Grayson took a step toward me and offered his hand.

"Pleased to meet you, Miss Merriweather," he said very formally, but he looked deep into my eyes as he spoke. It shocked me, but I took my cue from him. I would also act like we were strangers.

"Mr. Everleigh," I said, nearly stumbling over the formal name as I took his hand, knowing that we had indeed met before and even had a bit of history behind us. My face was burning. Somehow my aunt and uncle did not seem to catch on to our awkward meeting. They must not have been watching me, because I am sure the shock must have been evident on my face.

We sat down to eat. There were five of us. My aunt and uncle sat at opposite ends of the table and I sat with Becca on one side of the table and across from us, sat Grayson. I would have rather sat alongside of this man I knew as Conrad, rather than sit across from those dark eyes. However, after the blessing on the meal, and the food was passed, there was a continuous conversation between the men and I even learned something of the whole operation of the estate as I listened. Becca ate without talking and little was said between myself and my aunt because she was also involved in the conversation. The discussion included future improvements to the estate, the apple orchard and the coming harvest, and even some discussion concerning the employees.

As the men talked, I took the opportunity to send fleeting glances at the man I had known as Conrad. I had no doubt anymore about his identity. This was Conrad. And Conrad was also the man who had traveled on the train and coach with me.

About halfway through the meal, the gatehouse was mentioned. And in the next sentence, I realized that Grayson lived in the gatehouse. That surprised me so much that, before I knew it, I spoke.

"You live in the gatehouse?"

He looked at me, perhaps as surprised as I was, by my speaking to him, and after a slight pause and steady look, he said, "I do."

He said it without cracking a smile. This new Conrad had his emotions under tight control. I was now embarrassed by my outburst and wished I had not spoken. I had said nothing to him at all during the meal thus far. But I could not stop now.

"I love that gatehouse," I continued, but I looked away from him and included everyone at the table. "I remember it from when I was quite small and we visited here. I forget who lived in it then. I was never inside, but it is so beautiful from the outside."

"That was probably old Justin," said Uncle Theodore. "My grandfather wanted a gatehouse although there was no real need for it that I know of. I think he actually had a gatekeeper. After my grandfather died, my father let old Justin and his wife live in it. He was a faithful worker that stayed on even after his wife died."

As my uncle spoke, I glanced at Grayson's hands. There was no ring and no talk of a wife. I was now curious about the man I had spurned. He seemed to be a gentleman, and I wondered how I had not recognized his voice in the carriage or when warning me about crossing the road. But then, I had no reason to expect him here. I wondered if he found it amusing that I fell after crossing the road in spite of his command.

In a brief silence at the table, we heard someone knocking at the front door. I quickly offered to answer. It was another man I did not know. He had a pleasant face, was balding slightly and was perhaps in his forties.

"Hello," he said as I opened the door. "I am Pastor Stafford. Is Theodore in?"

"He is. Come in," I said. "I'll tell my uncle you are here."

My uncle soon returned with the pastor in tow.

"Sarah," he said, "this man's wife is on a mission of mercy and I've invited him to join us."

Grayson quickly made room beside him at the table as I went for another plate. Introductions were made between me and the pastor and the conversation shifted.

"So your name is June. I have a daughter Mary Lou who I know would like to make your acquaintance. My other daughter Jan, just got married about a half a year ago and Mary Lou is missing her. On Saturday is the church picnic. Be sure to come."

"We plan to be there," promised Aunt Sarah.

"And where do you come from, June?"

"I lived in Lehigh County in Trinkels."

"I am sure Sarah and Theodore are happy to have you. Just don't let them work you too hard. This is a busy place."

There was general laughter.

"I am guessing that your wife is with the Gables this evening," said Aunt Sarah.

"She is. The youngest daughter, Donna, has been caring for her mother all week and my wife thought she needed a break. So Lucille is there this evening, giving Donna an evening with her boyfriend."

"Mrs. Gable broke her leg two weeks ago," said Aunt Sarah to me. "Her daughter Donna is about nineteen and still at home, so she is taking care of her mother and the boys."

"I did not know there was a boyfriend," said Uncle Theodore.

The pastor sighed. "It is someone the family is not quite happy about, and therefore it has been kept secret. He is not originally from around here. She calls him Bud, whatever that may stand for. She met him at a town baseball game. The parents feel he is not quite open about his past. There are holes in his stories. The father wants her to stop the courtship. Bud does not attend church and I have seen him only once and not long enough to form an opinion of him. But Donna is quite thrilled to be with him. Pray for the family. Donna knows they have reservations and there are some hurt feelings."

I went for dessert then. I told Aunt Sarah to stay sitting and they continued to talk as I took the dirty dishes to the kitchen and eventually served them coffee and pie. I wanted to observe Grayson, but he was directly across the table from me and it was impossible. But the gangling lad I had known had developed into a handsome man with a shock of dark hair.

"Great cherry pie," said the minister.

"Thank June for the pie," said my aunt. "You know pies are not my favorite thing to bake. The cook did the main meal."

"Ah, I shall come by often for pie," said the Pastor Stafford. "What do you think, Grayson?"

"I never refuse pie," he said with a slight smile, but he did not look at me.

When the meal ended, the men went into the parlor and Aunt Sarah and I went to the kitchen. I persuaded her to leave the clean up to me and told her she should go to the parlor also since they had things to discuss. Becca had disappeared into her bedroom, and when I had finished in the kitchen, I too, went to my room. I walked to the open window and leaned out. It was now dark and I saw fireflies dotting the fields and the trees on the lawn sloping down toward the village. But I was barely aware of them. My life was flashing before my eyes. In the drama of the last couple years, I had almost forgotten Conrad. He must have recognized me also, especially after my uncle announced my full name. I remember having some real regrets in the weeks following our breakup, but I had never even seen Conrad since. Later, I met Gerald. We dated for about six months and then, for no reason that I could see, he abruptly quit me. Actually, he just never showed up again. I was hurt, although I wasn't devastated. That was yet to come.

Several years later, I met Alan. He had blonde, straight hair and blue eyes. In no time at all, I was head over heels in love with him.

This was going to be it. About that time, my mother fell ill. There was no cure for her. My father had died years before and I had no siblings. I was the caregiver for my mother and she needed more and more care and I had less and less time for Alan. After dating a year he asked me to marry him. I said yes. But when we talked seriously of marriage and a wedding, I told him I could not leave my mother in her condition. A short time after our engagement, Alan, realizing that I would not leave my mother, broke the engagement and began dating one of my close girlfriends. He gave her a merry chase and they were married at the end of six months. That was the worst time of my life. I had lost the man I thought I would marry and I lost a good girlfriend at the same time. About a month after Alan got married, my mother died. I was still getting over Alan and decided men and I did not get along.

I was still sitting at the window when the katydids began to sing. If you could call it singing. There must be a lot of them here and they made a real racket. Just as I was about to turn away from the window, I heard a door. I sat and watched in the gathering dusk to see if I could catch a glimpse of Grayson leaving. Sure enough, I could dimly make out his figure walking with giant strides out the lane, across the ford, and then get lost in the trees, as he headed for the gatehouse. I wondered if he remembered his last words to me. But if Grayson thought I was going to crawl back to him, he had another guess coming. I could live without men. I loved to sew. I was going to be a seamstress.

CHAPTER 4

In the days that followed, Aunt Sarah found more and more things for me to do. She liked working in the garden and hated mending. I loved to sew and mend and soon had a basket in my bedroom with all the mending to be done. When Bella did not get bread made, I made it. Aunt Sarah also brought me material that she had bought to make herself a dress and a new shirt for my uncle. She had a new treadle sewing machine that she could not bring into my room, but it stood in the wide hall upstairs. Becca, I discovered, took care of the laundry. Uncle Theodore heated the water for her in a huge pail and she took care of the rest.

I had yet to have a conversation with Becca. She spoke seldom. She said very short sentences and that only when talked to. She was also very deaf, which made conversation harder, almost impossible. Probably that is why she spoke so little.

Nettie, the cleaning girl, was a bit shy, but a good worker. She was nineteen years old and she was quite happy to talk.

"What are you sewing?" she asked me on her way down the hall on Friday afternoon.

"Aunt Sarah needs a new dress," I answered. "Can you sew?"

"I don't know if I can sew on a machine. We don't have a sewing machine."

"Do you live close by?"

"In the village. My father has sheep."

"Oh, I believe I saw him take them through the village on the day of my arrival."

"He goes through the village with them every day. I love the baby lambs. Sometimes we have to feed a lamb with a bottle."

"Do you have siblings?"

"Yes, a whole lot of them. I am the oldest." At this point she leaned close to me. "I have a boyfriend."

"Oh?" I said. "And what is his name?"

"Gary. He lives in the village, too."

"Is he cute?"

She giggled. "I think so, but my sister says his nose is too big." She giggled again. "He is real tall and skinny and he is very kind."

"That is the kind to have," I said, happy for her.

Saturday dawned clear and warm. The picnic was scheduled for six o'clock. The summer days were long and there would be lots of time for food and fellowship outside before the sun set. I had made potato salad and a large chocolate cake the day before, and we added pickles and fried chicken to the meal on Saturday. Everyone would bring more than enough food and I was looking forward to meeting the pastor's daughter. We packed the food basket, took jars of mint tea along, and left in good time so we could eat promptly at six. I was eager to meet everyone.

Uncle Theodore drove the carriage down away from the house, across the stream and up a slight grade and out the lane. As we drove past the gatehouse, I wondered if Grayson was inside. I did not want to look too hard at it in case he would see me and think I was looking for him. I would not give him that satisfaction after what his last words to me had been.

As we drove down the hill to the village, I had to remember my coming to the estate in the thunderstorm. This was my first time down the hill since my arrival. The day was warm, but the sun would soon be hidden by trees and hills in this rolling countryside. Across the fields, I could see farmers haying. The church was right on the edge of the village and this time, there were no sheep coming down the dusty road.

A good number of people were scattered around the church lawn when we arrived. There were tables set up with white tablecloths and many dishes of food waiting to be eaten. Before we were out of the carriage, the pastor and his wife walked across the shaded lawn to us.

"Welcome, Sarah," said Mrs. Stafford.

"Hello, Lucille," my aunt replied, "we have such a nice day for this picnic. I was so scared it would rain like it did last year. Please meet my niece, June, who has come to live with us. And June, this is the pastor's wife, Lucille."

"So glad to meet you, June. I heard of you from my husband and my daughter Mary Lou is eager to meet you, too."

Mrs. Stafford looked around and seeing her daughter, waved her over. I saw a blonde-haired girl in a yellow dress coming across the lawn. She was laughing and talking to people as she made her way over to us.

"Mary Lou, this is the girl your father told you about. Her name is June and she has come to live with Theodore and Sarah."

"Hi, June," she said. "Nice to meet you. Want to come with me and meet a few other girls?"

The girls I was introduced to were probably all a bit younger than I. They were older teens or early twenties. I guessed Mary Lou to be around twenty-five. I found out that her sister that married recently was four years younger than she was. The girls were friendly and curious as I was introduced. After the introductions, I glanced toward a group of young men standing close by, watching the girls. Suddenly a boy that I recognized came over to me. It was Brian, the young man that had brought me through the rain on my arrival.

"How are you doing?" he asked.

"Good."

"So you are staying around here?"

"I am."

"You did not show up to help pick apples yet."

I laughed. "I heard they were starting but my aunt keeps me busy in the house."

"It will be a busy week. And in September there will be more apples to pick. These are the early apples."

Mary Lou then pulled me aside and walked with me to a large maple tree where a few chairs were available to sit on.

"I hope we can be friends," she began. "How old are you?"

"I am sure I am older than you," I replied. "I am twenty-six and soon to be an old maid."

"Not with your looks," responded Mary Lou. "Anyway, I am glad you are single. I am twenty-five. My sister Jan just got married and I miss her so much. We used to do everything together. But tell me about yourself."

"What do you want to know?"

"Where did you live before you lived here?"

So I told her about my home and the loss of both parents. And just for fun, about the widower who needed a nursemaid for his children and a possible wife.

"Help the needy," said Mary Lou, "I would have slammed the door in his face. My brother has a four year old that drives us all bananas when we get together. Six children under ten sounds like a nightmare to me. But then, one never knows with whom one may fall in love. Unfortunately, there are few eligible fellas around here. The ones my age are my cousins."

I was wondering what she thought of Grayson, but decided I could ask her that another time. I had not seen him here today yet and wondered if he even came to church. But I would not ask. We were then called to eat, and Mary Lou and I served the drinks. It gave me opportunity to meet people and all seemed friendly with the exception of perhaps one girl named Lillian. She smiled until she heard I lived at Bluster Hill with my aunt and uncle. Then the smile faded and she watched me with a wary eye. I decided that Lillian had her eye on Grayson.

Mary Lou and I were among the last to eat, since we served the drinks, but finally we sat down at a long table where the singles had congregated. The food was delicious and plentiful.

It wasn't till we were almost finished eating that another carriage arrived. To my surprise, it was Grayson. Mary Lou made no comment, but I saw Lillian was aware of his arrival. I had a hard time not watching Grayson as he parked his carriage and came to the food tables. But I wanted our former acquaintance not to be known. Grayson glanced around the picnic area, nodded to a few people, filled a plate with food and then sat with a couple young men who soon engaged him in conversation. We were no longer serving drinks, but I saw Lillian quickly get a glass of lemonade and take it to him. I watched as she handed it to him, but could not see his face because she stood in the way. But she came right back to the table.

Later, some of the younger youth played croquet and Mary Lou and I drifted off by ourselves.

"Do you have a boyfriend?" she wanted to know.

"No, and I am not sure if I want one."

"Why?"

"I have bad memories. Either I choose wrong or they do."

"Tell me."

So I told her all about Gerald and about Alan. It still hurt to talk about Alan and she was very sympathetic.

"Be glad you are rid of him," she said finally. "He doesn't sound like someone who would stick with you through thick and thin."

I wanted to disagree with her. I had liked him a lot. And how long could I really expect him to wait for me? He had had no idea when I would be free to marry. In that sense, I could not blame him. But it felt good to talk about it with her. I never told her about Grayson. It would have made a good story and she would have been wide eyed. But it was safer not to tell. Stories could get out and I didn't think Grayson would have been happy about it.

"And what about you?" I asked.

Mary Lou shook her head. "I have no such story to tell. The only fellas that ever asked me out did not interest me. They are brainless and one cannot have a decent conversation with them. I was sort of interested in Ralph, before he showed his preference for my younger sister! That was a bit hard to take at the time, but I am happy for her."

"So are there any fellas around here that interest you now?"

"Not my age. Well, I am not sure how old he is, but there is this fellow at market that talks to me if he sees me. But he is always busy and I don't really know him and at market we never have time to talk."

"You go to market to sell things?"

"Yes. We have a big garden and sell the vegetables there. Here in the village everyone has their own garden, but in town they don't. So they buy from us. The market is in Thackeray's Pond. Have you been there?"

"Yes, I got the stagecoach to Cobbler's Crossing from there."

"Well, it is a pretty big town and we take baked goods and produce from the garden. Some jam and preserves, too. But you will maybe come with Sarah to sell apples. They come to market, too, in September and October."

As we talked, two other girls came across the lawn to us. They had been playing croquet and now sat down with us.

"June, this is Jeannie and Annelie. They are cousins to me and we have great times together. And you can bet your boots they were playing croquet because Bill and Fred were playing."

"Don't even say Bill's name. He was flirting with Isabelle," said Jeannie and we all laughed at her expression.

"What about Fred?"

"He never even saw me," said Annelie with a friendly smile at me. "He has no idea I exist."

"We must all get together sometime," said Mary Lou. "Have a girl's party."

"That sounds like fun," I replied.

The evening was very enjoyable. Before we went home, everyone gathered to sing some hymns together and it was twilight before we headed to the carriages. After saying goodbye to Mary Lou, I looked for my aunt and uncle and I happened to see Grayson, who was talking to another man by the carriages. The man had his back to me but Grayson faced me and I was certain his dark eyes were on me. I had to wonder what he was thinking. He merely nodded when our eyes met. I went home happy to have met Mary Lou. I was sure we would become friends.

But in the coming days we did not see each other too often. As for Grayson, I really did not see him often either. He came on Friday evenings and I tried to act like he was simply the estate manager, but it was hard. The Conrad I knew had become an astute businessman and gentleman. He never gave me reason to think that he remembered our dating. Which of course, was not possible. But he put on a good act. He was polite to me, and I to him. But nothing personal was exchanged. At the supper table he talked business always with Uncle Theodore and I listened. Once the meal was over, they went to the parlor and I to the kitchen. Just once in a while if I would suddenly look at him I would catch his eyes on me, and I felt sure he was remembering.

CHAPTER 5

July slid into August and I helped with canning, which took up most of my time. The garden vegetables, the early apples, the tomatoes and beans all needed to be preserved in some fashion. The summer kitchen was used heavily and at night we fell exhausted into bed. But I was happy here with my uncle and aunt. Once in a while, I got an afternoon off and I would sit by the pond and read a book under the weeping willow trees. And I often mended evenings, while sitting with my aunt and uncle in the parlor or on the back porch. My uncle had lots of stories and I was learning a whole lot about their lives. We had only seldom visited them as I was growing up and I had many questions for them.

One afternoon while working on apples with my aunt, I asked about children.

"You never had children, did you?"

"We had a little girl who would have been about two years older than you," was the surprising answer.

"I don't remember anything about her! Why do I not know of her?"

"That is because she died before you were born."

"Oh, but my mother never mentioned her. It must have been terrible."

"It was just when she was so cute and fun to interact with."

"And you never had another child?"

"No. It seemed we could not have another. However, a few years later, we adopted a little boy."

"Oh, I sort of remember that you had a son."

"That was Roland, but he died of influenza at the age of thirteen."

"Oh, how sad!"

"That was a huge blow for Theodore. He wanted an heir. He wanted to pass on the estate to a son. But it was not to be."

As we talked, Aunt Sarah wiped a tear from her face. "When one falls in love and marries, all seems so rosy. We don't expect trouble. But it comes. It comes to everyone. But God gives us strength for the day."

One Sunday afternoon, Mary Lou and her cousins Jeannie and Annelie came for a visit. After showing them my room we then walked down to the pond and sat under a weeping willow tree. The conversation soon turned to boys. Jeannie, I discovered, could be rather grumpy and always saw the negatives in life. Her sister Annelie seemed quite the opposite and got disgusted with her sister's pessimistic outlook. But I enjoyed them both.

"Jeannie," said Mary Lou, "you were out with Marvin lately, weren't you?"

She brightened. "Yes, and he took me for another ride last weekend but I don't think things are moving along. He doesn't seem really interested. And he did tell me that he has other plans for this next weekend."

"Did he say what they were?"

"No, but I talked to Joe, his best friend, and Joe says Marvin is going to Thackeray's Pond."

"What is at Thackeray's Pond?" I asked.

"Who knows?"

"Oh," said Annelie, "I bet he is going to the Harvest Festival. That is always a big thing."

"Is that this weekend?"

"Yes. Shall we go?"

"Isn't that just for farmers?"

"Not at all. The theme is agriculture, but there are lots of vendors selling things and there is always food. Anyway, if the boys are there...."

"I say let's go. We can go and spy on Marvin!" said Annelie jokingly. "That is where all the boys will be this weekend."

"So why didn't he invite me there?" wailed Jeannie.

"Actually, there is someone I would like to spy on, too," said Mary Lou. "And I am sure he will be there. How about you, June?"

"I can't think of anyone I would like to spy on, but if you are serious, I would go. I just need to clear it with my aunt. She may have something that she wants done."

It took a lot of planning but till it was all said and done, one thing leading to another, it was decided that Mary Lou would ask her brother to take us to the festival, leaving right after lunch on Friday. The cousins would come to Mary Lou's house and hopefully Uncle Theodore could take me to the parsonage to meet them all. The girls left with the promise to let me know how the plans worked out. The next day, Mary Lou came by with the carriage to tell of the change in plans.

"Hi June," she called as she stepped from the family carriage. "I came to tell you our revised plans. We hit a snag when my brother said he would not bring us home again. He has a date that night."

"Oh dear. How will we get home?"

"After much thinking, I remembered that Mama's sister Laura lives in Thackeray's Pond and she is a widow and her children are all grown and out of the house. And she loves company and Mama says she will write her a note and tell her we would like to stay for the night."

"Oh, that is the best plan yet," I said. "That way we can stay into the evening. Do you really think it will work?"

"I am sure it will. She had seven children and still has lots of energy. She also has empty bedrooms. Mama says it will do her good to have us. Her husband just died a year ago."

It was all very exciting. When I shared our plans with Aunt Sarah, her response was immediate.

"Of course you may go. You do so much for us. You deserve a weekend with the girls."

I was suddenly eager for the weekend. I had pretty much had my head to the grindstone ever since I had come and this sounded like fun.

For some reason, Grayson could not be at supper on Friday evening, so he was there on Thursday evening for supper. In the course of conversation, the Harvest Festival got mentioned.

"Are you going to the festival, Grayson? Is that why you are gone tomorrow?" asked my uncle.

"Not this year. I hate to miss it, but I have plans I cannot change."

"Well, maybe June will be our representative this year. She and a group of girls are going and they will stay overnight at a relative of one of the girls."

Grayson gave me a studied look. "That sounds dangerous," he said, with just a hint of a smile. It was the first time he did anything close to teasing me. And the first time he was really addressing me that I could remember.

Uncle Theodore laughed. "They probably will not get into as much trouble as you and I would have at their age."

I had to smile to myself, knowing our real reason for going was to spy on the boyfriends or would-be boyfriends of the girls.

"Since when are girls interested in harvest festivals? That is a farmer's paradise. Or is the attraction the farmers?" said Grayson, looking at me. I was, for the moment, speechless at his teasing.

"At the Harvest Festival they have quilts and crafts and jams and jellies and who knows what," said Aunt Sarah for me. "I always found it interesting. And," she gave Grayson a significant glance, "it is also where all the boys will be."

Grayson was still looking at me.

"You think these country girls are to be trusted, let loose in a festival town?"

"You forget, I was a city girl," I said.

I almost swallowed my tongue. Had we ever talked about me being from a city? Of course, Grayson knew, but my aunt and uncle did not know that we had known each other.

My uncle and aunt both laughed, not catching my mistake. "Well, Grayson, it is too bad you have plans. Otherwise, you could have gone as their chaperone," said Uncle Theodore.

"I have a feeling they will need one."

If he would have laughed, I would have laughed also. But he kept a straight face and I was left to wonder if he still thought of me as the immature seventeen year old.

———

Right after lunch on Friday, Uncle Theodore took me to the parsonage. There I met Mary Lou and her cousins. Ronny, a brother to Mary Lou, was commissioned to take us the five miles to Thackeray's Pond.

"Mary Lou," said her mother as we were going out the door, "I think the broom man is usually at these festivals. I've been waiting for him to come around here and he hasn't been here in a long time. I need a broom and he has the best brooms I've ever used. So if you see him, buy one for me."

"Fine," said Mary Lou.

It was mid-afternoon when we arrived at the festival and the town was teaming with people. We spent the day eating food from a few different food stands, listening to a group of old men playing fiddles and mandolins, and mostly talking among ourselves and watching the people. Particularly the boys. There were farmers displaying their root vegetables and apples, and artists and woodcarvers showing their creations and tables of homemade fudge and other goodies. There were helium balloons for the children and games for the older ones. We finally found the broom man that Mary Lou had been told to look for.

"Young lady, what can I do for you?" asked the man wearing a wide brimmed hat to keep the sun out of his eyes.

"My mother needs a broom and told me to look for you."

"Well, take your pick. I have all shapes and sizes. You will know what your mother wants."

As Mary Lou looked over the brooms, I saw the man eyeing her.

"You related to the minister's wife in Cobbler's Crossing?" he finally asked.

"She is my mother," said Mary Lou with surprise. "You remember coming to our house?"

"I don't remember you, I remember your mother. And you look like she did. She was in my class in school and I was sweet on her."

"Oh my," said Mary Lou smiling and taking a closer look at the man.

"When I got older, I was just about ready to ask her out and then didn't that preacher man come along and that was the beginning and the end of it."

Mary Lou laughed heartily. "I will tell my mother. She will enjoy the story."

"That's the truth and she is still a good looking woman."

"I'll be sure to tell her that—when my father isn't around," said Mary Lou, still laughing.

He laughed too then, and they exchanged money and we were off. However, ten minutes later, Mary Lou was complaining. "Why on earth did I buy this broom already? I shall have to carry this thing around all day!"

I was very interested in the quilts and sewing crafts and I talked a long time with another woman whose passion was sewing. On her table, among pillows, handkerchiefs and doilies, were sunbonnets. These were not ordinary sunbonnets. They had such a wide brim that when I tried one on, I had only tunnel vision. It was impossible to see anything on either side—only straight ahead. The girls found it hilarious. One was a natural color with little red cows printed on it and I ended up buying it just for laughs. At another booth, a woman was selling knitted scarves and shawls and Annelie bought a beautiful blue shawl.

An hour later, sitting on a bench at the edge of the park and eating ice cream, we watched the activity at a church across the street. It appeared to be a wedding. We saw the bride and groom come out of the church and ride away in a decorated wagon pulled by two white horses. I think we all looked longingly after the carriage, each one of us imagining ourselves as the bride.

By evening, the atmosphere had changed. There was a bit of a coolness in the air and the vendors had gone home. Now, there were many well-dressed people strolling around the park, mixing in with the more rowdy teenagers and children. I watched a lamplighter place his ladder against a lamp post and climb a few steps, open the glass and light the lamp. Then he came down the ladder and walked to the next lamp. As we passed the band stand, we saw a group of perhaps ten musicians assembled there, tuning their instruments. It was a lovely evening and the park looked very romantic in the lamplight. Promptly at eight o'clock, the music began, followed by a short speech by the mayor and when the music began again, the people began to dance.

During the afternoon we were too engrossed in our sightseeing and shopping to think of our reason for being here. But now, it was evening and boys came that could not come in the afternoon. The girls were watching each boy that went by, looking for Marvin.

"Is there any reason for me to know who Marvin is?" I asked, wanting to help search for him.

"Probably not. Oh, he has red hair and he was at the church picnic," said Jeannie.

"Is his hair straight or frizzy?" I asked.

"Straight. Do you remember him?"

"I think I do. I remember seeing a redhead drop his glass of lemonade at the picnic."

"Sounds like something that he would do," said Jeannie.

Annelie admitted that she was also looking for someone that she liked, but did not expect him to be there. The four of us strolled around the park and finally Mary Lou saw the fellow she was interested in, but he was with another girl and she would not tell us who he was. Jeannie was so sure that Marvin was with another girl that she was almost sick over it. She was already feeling unwanted although we had no proof that he was even with someone else. I have to admit, although I said I had no one to look for, my thoughts went to Grayson once in a while, but simply because I was not interested in anyone else. I was not interested in him either, I reminded myself. I would not come crawling back to him. I wondered where he was this evening and if he had a date. At some time his name had come up, but the girls had assured me that he did not date at all. They never knew him to date. He was considered, at least by them, to be a handsome, but contented bachelor who probably enjoyed all the attention he got from single girls.

There were more and more people in the park and many were dancing. We just kept strolling around, the girls looking for the boys they were interested in, sometimes even going outside the park. Finally, we went back in the park and strolled around the area where people were dancing. An hour went by when there was a gasp from Jeannie.

"Annelie! Look over to the right of the band. Doesn't that look like Marvin? And if it is, he *is* with someone else."

"What is he wearing?" asked Annelie. "There are a hundred people to the right of the band."

"Oh, I am sure it is him. He is wearing a light top and blue pants. And a blue cravat. He is close to the bandstand and he is standing real close to her and..."

"I see who you mean. Now they are dancing. It sure looks like him, but in this dim light...."

We all watched them dance. The lighting was poor, but I could believe it was Marvin. Not that many boys had such red hair. When there was a pause in the dancing, the couple walked over to a bench and sat down. Jeannie was not only heartbroken. She was angry.

"I'd like to walk right up there and sit down beside them," she said, spitting her words out with force.

"Oh, Jeannie. You would spoil all chances for him. He would not thank you for that. And maybe he will some day come back to you," I said, trying to soothe her.

"I need a spy," she said sullenly. "Someone he does not know. I want to know what he is saying to her." She looked at me with a thoughtful look in her eyes. "June, you could be my spy. You could sit on the bench with them. He does not know you as well as the rest of us. Go! Please?"

"But I am sure he will remember me from the picnic. I was the stranger there, remember. The only new person. He will remember me."

The others were enjoying this and joined in Jeannie's request.

"You could put on your sunbonnet," said Mary Lou with a twinkle in her eyes.

"And the shawl that I bought," added Annelie.

"And carry my broom and everyone will think you are a cleaning lady on her way home from work," added Mary Lou laughing. "You could hear what sweet nothings he is saying in her ear."

First we laughed, but Jeannie was serious. "Do it. Go quickly before they dance again."

"You really should," said Mary Lou. "And dress up. Just for fun. We could at least get a laugh out of it."

I can't believe I let them talk me into such foolishness. But I could not fight all three of them. We were out to have fun. So we walked into the shadows and I pulled out my sunbonnet. Then Jeannie put the shawl around my shoulders and Mary Lou handed me the broom. At the same time, we kept an eye on the bench. We did not know how long they would sit there. I had to hurry. Probably no one knew me, even without the bonnet, but at least Marvin could not see my face. I carefully made my way to the bench. As I walked, I leaned over a bit with my face more to the ground than looking straight ahead, and to the accompaniment of snickering from the girls behind me, I finally arrived at the bench where Marvin and his girl were sitting and talking. The bench was really not very long but there was a bit more room on the far end. So I walked just past them and I sat down quietly on the very end of the bench. And listened. Marvin and his girlfriend took no notice of me whatsoever.

"You are a great dancer," said the male voice. "I'm not very good."

"Oh, yes you are," came the ultra-sweet soprano voice. "Anyway, who cares? It was fun. Are you glad I invited you to dance?" Her voice dripped with honey.

A slight hesitation. "Yeah."

"I'm glad I did, too. You are very handsome. Do you think I am pretty?"

"Yes. You are very pretty." There was giggling.

"Where have you been all my life?" she asked. He mumbled something I could not understand. "Do you have a girlfriend?"

There was some hesitation. "Not a steady girlfriend."

"Is she here, too?"

"No. I don't think so. I hope not."

"Are you going to kiss me?"

There was silence for an extended time. Then some soft mutterings. I did not dare look at them because I would have to turn and look directly at them, due to the long brim on the sunbonnet. I had absolutely no peripheral vision. For the sake of Jeannie, I finally coughed and the couple got up rather quickly and walked away. I did not have very good news for Jeannie. But I had been successful as far as spying was concerned. I had been so intent on listening to them that I forgot how strange I might look. But I had not even looked at anyone walking down the path by us. Now I turned to see where the girls were. I had to turn completely because I could only see straight ahead. But first, I had to wait for someone to pass by so I bent my head down as I waited for the person to pass me. I could just see his feet and trousers as he walked past. He seemed well dressed for the Harvest Festival and I wondered if he was from the wedding party across from the park. Just when he should have been safely out of my sight, he hesitated, took a couple steps back and sat down where the couple had been. I did not want to take my sunbonnet off in his sight and as I contemplated what to do, I felt, rather than saw, that he turned slightly to me. Certainly he would not talk to me! I was supposedly looking like a British char woman. However, when he cleared his throat, out of sheer panic I quickly adjusted my shawl, ready to leave the bench as soon as I could see if the girls were still at the same place, waiting for me. And in that moment the man spoke.

"Excuse me, madam, but could you possibly tell me what time it is?"

I hesitated only a moment. He had a strange voice and although he appeared well dressed, I was now sure he was drunk. Maybe he drank too much at the wedding. No, he did not act drunk, but there was definitely something weird about his voice and it scared me. I promptly got up, grabbed the broom and nearly stumbling over it, walked away from the man. I did not look for my friends. I simply went off the path into a darker area close to where I had left them, and tore off my sunbonnet and shawl in the process. Then, standing in the shadows, I carefully raised my head and looked around for my friends. I soon saw them and promptly hurried up to them. Annelie and Mary Lou were laughing at me and Jeannie looked anxious.

"Here is your broom, Mary Lou, I nearly fell over it coming back. And here is the shawl, Annelie. What a relief it is to be rid of them. Some weird man came and sat on the bench and started talking to me just as I was leaving. He scared me."

"I guess we were watching Marvin," said Mary Lou. "I didn't see the man."

"I sort of remember seeing someone sit down there. From here he did not look weird. What did he want?" asked Annelie.

"To know what time it was. What an old trick. He had a really weird voice, but I got out of there."

"Did you hear anything that Marvin said?" Jeannie wanted to know.

"Yes. Nothing very good." I hated to disappoint her, but she deserved the truth.

"Tell me everything you heard."

Although I knew she really did not want to hear it, I told her all I remembered.

"That girl is downright disgusting and he is so stupid to fall for her. When he turns his head she will start on the next guy."

"Which he seems to have done to you," Annelie reminded her.

"Well, I am through with him. But I would first like to wring his neck," threatened Jeannie, with fire in her eyes.

Now that we had tracked Marvin down, we asked Annelie who she hoped to see. She did not want to tell us, but finally gave in. It was a fellow from church and about a half hour later we bumped into him hanging out with some other fellas at the edge of the park. Annelie and Jeannie immediately began to talk to him and we stood there for a good half hour before we realized it was late and we had to walk a couple blocks to Mary Lou's aunt's house.

"We have to head there right now," said Mary Lou. "Otherwise she will be in bed before we get there."

"How do we get there?" I asked. "Is it far?"

"We walk. But it is only about four blocks. We'd better get going."

Although it was getting late, there was a lot of activity yet on the street, due to the music in the park. Already on the first block, some young fellows came by in a carriage and slowed as they reached us. Jeannie immediately turned a smiling face in their direction and thus encouraged, they stayed alongside of us, finally offering Jeannie a ride. She declined a bit sadly, I thought, and they finally left us. After walking another block, another young lad came slowly by. Again, Jeannie turned a smiling face to him and then, to her happy surprise, found it was a boy that she knew from school days. He kept on going, but soon he came by again and offered her a ride. To my astonishment, she promptly agreed. I stood in shock as he helped her into his carriage.

"Jeannie," called Annelie after her sister, "we are not going to stand here and wait for you. He can bring you to Mary Lou's aunt."

"Where is that?" asked the young man.

"Just down to the next corner and then right for two blocks. Number twenty-five on Turtle Lane."

"Got it," said the young man with a smile and they were off.

I looked at Annelie.

"I can't believe she did this to us," she said, thoroughly disgusted. "She is just mad at Marvin."

"Do you know this boy?" Mary Lou asked.

"Actually, I do, but not very well. I knew him from school, too, but he was in her class. But Mama and Papa would have not allowed this. And now I feel guilty."

"She would not have listened to you," I soothed her. "Let's just hope she gets to Mary Lou's aunt soon."

When we turned down Turtle Lane, we suddenly found the street much darker and almost no one on the road. This was no longer Main Street. The street lamps were lit, but rather far apart and now I was eager to get to our destination. Behind us, I heard the clop of a horse and carriage. Was it those first boys again? When it did not pass us, I became a bit anxious and just when I was about to say something to Mary Lou about it, we arrived at her aunt's house. I was relieved and happy to have arrived. We made our way up the walkway to a brick house with a wraparound porch. Mary Lou knocked at the door. It was opened almost immediately by a gray-haired, but spry woman with a welcoming smile.

"Hello, Mary Lou. Bring your friends in. I was beginning to get worried. I did not know if you could find the way."

"Oh, I knew the way, but we were having so much fun that we didn't notice how late it was," she replied as she introduced us all to her Aunt Laura.

"I thought there were four of you," said her aunt.

"There are, but a young man from Jeannie's class in school just drove by and offered her a ride and she took it." Seeing Aunt Laura's concerned face, she added, "I know the boy, too, and I think it will be all right. But I could not stop her."

Aunt Laura showed us the way up a curved staircase and down a short hall to two bedrooms. There we deposited our bags and then followed her back downstairs where we sat around the kitchen table with a cup of tea and some shortbread cookies.

"Tell me about your day," said Aunt Laura, as she poured our tea. "I used to go every year with my husband, but my walking is not so good anymore, and it is not as much fun alone, so I stay home. Did you see the quilts?"

"We did and all the other crafts. Besides that, we saw all sorts of big pumpkins and other vegetables and there was a flower market also."

"I always bought black raspberry jam there. I knew the lady that made it. We had black raspberries at home and I miss them, so I would buy it at the Harvest Festival."

"I bought a broom for mom and had to carry it around all day," lamented Mary Lou.

"And I bought a lovely blue shawl. I'll get it and show it to you," said Annelie.

"Oh, and I got an interesting sunbonnet that you must see," I said, close on Annelie's heels.

But when we got to the room, I looked in vain for the sunbonnet. How had I lost it? *When* had I lost it? I remembered taking it off as I walked away from the bench in the park but did not remember having it since. Had I dropped it? I returned empty-handed and sad to the kitchen.

"Did any of you girls see my sunbonnet?"

"No, not me," said Mary Lou. The others said the same.

"Did you see it since I wore it?" They all shook their heads.

"I saw you taking it off as you walked away from the bench," said Mary Lou.

"I can't believe it. I must have dropped it. None of you hid it as a joke?"

"No."

"You needed a sunbonnet in the park this evening?" Laura asked curiously.

We ended up telling her the whole Marvin story. She thought it was funny how I got dressed up to eavesdrop on the conversation and laughed when the gentleman scared me away.

"The young boys don't know what they want when they are so young," she said to Annelie. "He will grow up sometime. But he does not sound like the kind of boy I would wish on your sister."

"I wish she would get here," said Annelie, looking at the clock in the kitchen.

But I was thinking about my lost sunbonnet. I could not go back tonight anymore, but I would go back before we left town the next day and see if I could find it. I knew approximately where to look. If I dropped it right after I took it off, it should still be there. It would not be on the pathway, but up on the lawn where I took the sunbonnet and shawl off.

When Aunt Laura stifled a yawn, we got up from the table.

"Please go to bed. Jeannie will certainly be here soon and we will wait up for her," Mary Lou assured her aunt.

"Are you sure? I hate to go to bed before you do."

"We will wait up and let her in. You just go to bed."

The old woman must have been very tired, because she agreed to go to bed. In the meantime, we stood at the window, looking out at the dim lamplight in front of the house, hoping for some sign of Jeannie. Maybe they could not find the right house. Maybe they could not see the house number. I could tell that Annelie was very concerned and also angry at her sister for doing this to us. We were tired also. Where was she?

When the clock in the dining room chimed the half hour, I spoke up.

"This is too long. It is eleven-thirty and I think we should go looking for her."

"In the dark?" asked Mary Lou.

"There are some street lamps along here but let's go up to Main Street. I know my way a bit around here from coming to market."

"I do, too," said Mary Lou. "We won't get lost, but what about Aunt Laura? Can we just leave her in the unlocked house?"

"I don't think we have much choice. No, we will lock up and take the key along. And I think it is safer if all three of us go looking for Jeannie."

They agreed. We had to take action. Before we left, Mary Lou stood at Laura's bedroom door and heard her soft snore. Then we very, very quietly went down the stairs and walked out the front door, locking it behind us.

It was just too dark on this street and the quietness was unsettling. Not even the bark of a dog. We walked briskly to the brighter lights of Main Street. It was cool now, and I shivered in my light wrap. Once on Main Street, we found that it, too, was dismally deserted. We walked toward the center of town. One would hardly know that just an hour or so before, all was still music and dance. Now nothing. We walked quickly, always looking for someone who might turn out to be Jeannie. I could tell Annelie was close to tears. She was scared. Finally, we heard the clip clop of a horse coming up the street behind us. Hoping it was Jeannie and her friend, we stood and waited. However, it was no carriage. It was a man on horseback. A sheriff, no less. He stopped when he saw us.

"Good evening, ladies," he said. "May I ask what you are doing out so late?"

Annelie immediately spoke up. "My sister went for a ride with a boy that she knew from school days. But she has not returned."

The sheriff looked us over carefully. "Where do you live?"

"We are not from here. We were here for the Harvest Festival and we are staying with someone we know on Turtle Avenue."

"I will help you, but I need to know your names."

Oh dear, I thought, *now we are written up and are on the police records.* One by one we dutifully gave our names and addresses and and the sheriff took a good look at each one of us before writing them down.

"Follow me," he said when he was finished writing, "I have a good idea where she might be."

We followed the sheriff and his horse down another block where he had his headquarters. He let us in the building and then came around with a carriage. We climbed into the carriage and he flicked the reins and we went rapidly down the street a block or so and then he turned left onto a dark side street. There was a dim lamp by a door about halfway down the street. That is where he stopped. He got out of the carriage and walked into the dimly lit bar. In no more than five minutes, he led Jeannie out the door to the carriage. The Jeannie that came in the door was not the same confident one that had left us earlier.

"Jeannie, what is going on?" asked Annelie almost beside herself with relief.

Jeannie said nothing, but she smelled of smoke and alcohol. And then she started to cry. "I was so scared," she sobbed.

"Why didn't you come home?"

"He didn't want to leave yet."

"What were you doing?"

"Just sitting in that bar with a bunch of his friends. Girls, too, but they were all drinking and smoking and...it was awful and they wanted me to drink. They wouldn't take no for an answer."

"Did you?"

"Not much. It tasted terrible. And they were getting drunk and..."

"Were you there ever since you left us?"

"No, we drove around a bit. That part was fine. But then this."

"Did he...were you all together all the time?

"Yes, but..."

And then we were back at the house. The sheriff helped us out of the carriage. He had a few words of wisdom for Jeannie and he waited until we were inside the house before he drove away. We went as quietly as possible up the stairs, tiptoed past Laura's bedroom door and fell exhausted in our beds. Our Harvest Festival had a bitter ending.

———————

The next day dawned in an amazingly short time. I was not ready to get up, but we had to get the stage by eight, so Ronny could pick us up at the appointed time in Cobbler's Crossing. Annelie asked us to keep Jeannie's story to ourselves and we agreed to it. After a substantial breakfast of eggs and bacon and toast, we headed to the stagecoach stop. But first I made a quick stop at the park. I walked into the park until I was sure of the bench I had sat on. There was no bonnet anywhere around the bench. I then walked across the lawn, trying to remember just where I went, as I shed my bonnet and shawl. But alas, my wonderful sunbonnet was nowhere to be found.

CHAPTER 6

September arrived, and the apples were ready for picking in the orchard. I do not know how many trees Uncle Theodore had, but he had men picking and sorting and when market day came, they went to the closest town, which was Thackeray's Pond, to sell apples. Aunt Sarah enjoyed going to market and usually helped to sell the apples there. So on market day, Uncle Theodore hitched up the wagon of apples to two horses and the three of us went to market. Uncle Theodore, Aunt Sarah and I. It was fun. Thackeray's Pond was a big enough town to have a good-sized market. We were not the only ones selling apples and there were other farmers there selling potatoes by the bushel and house wives were there with their canned goods and home crafted items. I was excited to see Mary Lou there with her mother, selling jam and preserves and homemade pies. The market was a busy place of people selling, buying, chatting and shouting to call attention to their wares. We did not all have to be there to sell our apples, so we took turns walking through the market and seeing what others were selling. When it was my turn, I spent some time talking to Mary Lou and then strolled through the entire place finally coming to a young man who was displaying his woodcarvings.

"May I help you?" he asked.

"No, I am just admiring the carvings. Are you the craftsman?"

"I am," he replied, smiling broadly. "I've been interested in woodwork since I was a little boy. I learned it from my grandfather."

He proudly showed me a chest he had made with flowers carved into the top.

"I'm impressed," I said.

"My name is Wesley Hastings," he said. "I think I saw you at the church picnic."

"Oh, I did not realize you were from our church," I replied. "My name is June Merriweather."

"Actually, I am not from your church. I live here in Thackeray's Pond. But I was at the picnic with a friend."

"Oh, I see."

"But you did not play croquet," he said.

I was surprised he remembered. "Oh, I was just getting acquainted with Mary Lou, a new friend. I had just moved to the area. We were too busy talking to play croquet. So you probably know Mary Lou also?"

"Yes, I see her here at market."

Just then someone came up to ask about a cedar chest he had made and I thought I should make my way back to the job of selling apples.

"I hope you sell lots of your woodwork," I called as I turned to go.

"Thanks. Maybe we will see each other again tomorrow."

As it was, I did not have to go the next day, but I did go again the next two weekends and each time I saw and talked to Wesley. He was easy to talk to and before I knew it, I was telling him about living with my relatives. He was a nice young man, quite tall and thin with frizzy brown hair, but very nice.

One thing I discovered, was that in apple season, apples took precedence to everything else. It was just apples, apples, apples. The whole month we went to market with apples. At home, neighbors and people from the surrounding area dropped in for apples. In the meantime, we dried apples, we canned apples and we made pies and dumplings and you name it, it was apples. Uncle Theodore was in his glory. The apples were his pride and joy and he loved the whole process, but evenings he looked totally exhausted and Aunt Sarah kept telling him to let the others do the work.

———

On my last day of selling apples at market, Wesley came by again. I knew he came by just to see me and I was pleased. We could talk so freely and he was always interested in what I thought or had to say.

"Hi June," he said now, as he strolled up to me. "Looks like you are about sold out." He sat on the end of a wagon that was parked close by and made himself comfortable.

"We are. Uncle Theodore is quite pleased with our sales and this is the last day here."

"I don't see him around today."

"He was here but he was not feeling very well and so Aunt Sarah took him home again at noon. He has been pushing it with the apples. But he enjoys it so."

"So how are you getting home?"

"Aunt Sarah said she would tell the manager to send one of the boys. We have a lot of boys helping just now with the apples."

A customer came up at that point and bought the last of the apples. Wesley stayed and we chatted since I had nothing else to sell. As I was speaking, I noticed Wesley watching someone behind me.

"Hello Grayson," he said. I turned to see Grayson just approaching our stand. I had not expected that he would pick me up and suddenly, as always, I was very self-conscious.

"Hello Wesley. How are you?"

"I am just saying goodbye to June. Looks like she sold everything you brought."

"That was her duty," said Grayson without a smile. "How is the woodcarving coming along?"

"I am happy with it. I would have liked to sell more, but that is life. I am about ready to leave, too. Goodbye, June. I've enjoyed our chats. Maybe I'll see you around."

After Wesley left, I handed the money that we had earned to Grayson and we were soon on the way home. He was not a big talker and I expected it would be up to me to start any conversation we might have. I had not seen Grayson much in the weeks of apple picking. While I was scrambling for something to talk about, he spoke.

"So you learned to know Wesley?"

"Yes. Nice fellow," I answered.

There followed a bit of silence as we waited in town for a horse and carriage to cross in front of us. When I thought back to our dating days, this was a very strained conversation. We had talked more freely then. I wondered if it was as strained for Grayson as it was for me. I almost thought so. And I wondered why it had to be.

"So, this being your last day at market," Grayson resumed, "I now have another job for you." He glanced at me. I waited.

"Have you ever made a frankfurter bun?"

"No, but I've seen them."

"I need at least fifty for next Saturday."

"Are you having a party?"

"A corn husking," he said. "We have it every year. Not a big deal, just a fun time for the youth from church and from the surrounding area. Some young married couples might come also. Do you think you can do it?"

"I think so. Has Aunt Sarah ever made them?"

"Actually, up till now we had hot chocolate and doughnuts. But I would like to try something a bit different this year and your aunt and uncle agreed to it."

"It sounds like fun. I'll see what I can come up with."

He nodded, and for a full minute no one spoke. We were going past a church sitting at a crossroads, when he suddenly pulled on the reins and the next thing I knew, we were driving into the lane at the church and then he parked by the cemetery under a big maple tree that was turning yellow. I looked at him, wide-eyed.

"I want to talk to you without being interrupted by traffic," he said, by way of introduction. I waited, wondering what was so important to discuss. He dropped the reins and propped one elbow on his knee and looked at me.

"Do you have acquaintances here in this area from Trinkels?" It was the first he mentioned the town where we first met.

"No, certainly not that I know of. Why do you ask?"

He did not answer right away, but looked off in the distance. It made me think he was hesitant to say what he felt he needed to say. But he finally looked back at me.

"This past Sunday, I was eating at an inn some miles from here. I was there with a friend, and sometime during the meal, two men took the table behind us." He paused again. "I had my back to them and was busy talking with my friend, so I did not pay them any attention. But suddenly I thought I heard one of them say your name. Your name is not the most common around here, and I half cocked an ear in that direction at the same time as I was listening to my friend."

When he paused again, I spoke.

"Well, there must be another June, because I know of no one that knows me from Trinkels around here. It could not have been me that they were discussing." I felt no qualms and sat back and relaxed, surprised he was telling me this.

"There is one problem," Grayson said slowly, his eyes on mine. "I later heard the word Trinkels."

My eyes opened wider. "You are sure?" Grayson nodded. "Could you hear anything else that they were saying? It must be coincidence."

"I can't tell you the exact words anymore, because my friend was talking at the same time. But from the conversation that I could pick up, it sounded like something was said about wanting to find you."

"What did the other fella say?"

"He mumbled a bit. I could not hear him, but I do not think he knew you. Or this June he was talking about. It was the other man that was looking for you."

I did not know what to say. I sat silent, wondering who it could be.

"Did you see the man?"

"Well, I finally let my friend know that I was trying to hear the man behind me and when the two men got up to leave, I stood also.

They were still talking, so I knew which voice belonged to which man. He was the taller man, wearing a mustache and smoking a cigar."

"It does not sound like anyone I know," I said. "I know of no friend who smokes cigars. What color hair did he have?"

"Brown. Nothing special about the hair. A bit messy and perhaps a bit of a wave to it."

"It is certainly no one of my acquaintance. It must have been coincidence that they mentioned Trinkels," I said. But even I could hear the question in my voice. *Was it really coincidence?* Grayson said no more. He flipped the reins and we headed home.

CHAPTER 7

There was a lot of preparation for the corn husking party. Of course, Grayson had most of the work, but it was fun planning and getting ready for our part in the event. We just hoped it would not rain. There was to be a full moon and they would need the light of the moon to husk the corn. I experimented with the buns two days before the corn husking party and now I felt confident that we were ready.

Saturday dawned with morning clouds, which disappeared before noon. I began kneading the dough right after breakfast. Aunt Sarah was enjoying the challenge as well and stayed by my side to help. We let the dough rise, and then punched it down and made strips of dough that would form the rolls for the frankfurters. We had pans setting all over the kitchen, close to the heat and when they had risen, we shoved them into the oven, pan after pan until we had not fifty, but sixty rolls. We were happy with them.

I was secretly glad, somehow, to be able to prove to Grayson that I could make the rolls he wanted. He was always a bit stiff and formal around me and true to form, when he stopped in the kitchen mid-afternoon and Aunt Sarah proudly showed him our rolls, giving the credit to me, he looked pleased but only gave me a glance and a nod. The plan was to have the frankfurter roast after the corn husking and the hot chocolate would be prepared in the house over the range but then it would be taken to the barn on a cart and Grayson would have a fire and a place to set the container of hot chocolate to keep it as warm as possible on this cold night.

"Were you ever at a corn husking party?" asked Aunt Sarah as we worked on the buns.

"Never. I was a town girl. But I am excited about seeing it."

"You must take part. Not just observe."

"I think I will be busy here with making hot chocolate," I said.

"I will not let you do all the work. And all the cups we gathered, they will have to go out, too."

In the midst of our talk, Grayson came for an early supper. We knew he was coming and had the food waiting. We would eat later.

"June, set a plate for Grayson in the dining room," said Aunt Sarah.

"No need," replied Grayson. "I'll grab a bite here in the kitchen."

"June should be helping to husk corn," said Aunt Sarah as soon as Grayson sat down at the kitchen table. "She was never at a corn husking party and she needs to be there. She needs some fun."

"In that case she should be there," said Grayson, not looking at me.

"But...."

Grayson cut me short, this time looking at me. "Your Aunt Sarah is quite capable of making the hot chocolate. She's been doing it for years. Theodore and I will have everything under control out in the field and barn. As your employer, I am assigning you to corn husking."

Aunt Sarah laughed out loud and Grayson himself had to smile, though he tried to look sober.

"But you might want to wear gloves," he added.

"I have a good pair of gloves for corn husking," said Aunt Sarah. "I'll let you have them. I don't expect to husk corn anymore."

I was secretly pleased to be able to join in the corn husking and I assured her I would stop and help with the food when the time came.

––––––––

Darkness fell early these days, and the huskers began arriving just as the moon came up over the horizon. Aunt Sarah shooed me out the door, her gloves in my hand, wishing me an exciting evening. I saw Mary Lou arriving and I went out to meet her. From what I knew, she did not have a boyfriend but on this night, anything was possible. I remembered the time I was talking to Wesley at market, she walked by and she had had little to say to me after that. But I never said anything to her about it. But I wondered.

"Hi, Mary Lou!" I called.

"Hi, June!" Her eyes were shining and she looked excited as she walked up to me.

"Ready to husk corn?" I asked.

"Sure! Are you husking, too?"

"I am. Maybe someone will ask you to be his partner."

"I doubt it."

She was looking around while I was talking to her, and I wondered who she was looking for, but did not ask. Suddenly I saw Wesley. He saw me at the same time and came over to say hello to both of us and then he just hung around. Mary Lou chatted with him also and I no longer saw her looking around at the other fellas. The girls and boys stood in separate groups and looked shyly back and forth at each other. When most had arrived, Grayson got them all quiet and Uncle Theodore spoke.

"Welcome everyone. The moon is our only light this evening and we will need to keep working to stay warm. Remember about the red ears. If you get one, you get to kiss your partner."

There was excited laughing and the pairing up began. It was my first corn husking experience and I was a bit disappointed not to have a partner and found myself wishing Grayson would take part. I was shocked at myself, but he would definitely make it more interesting for me. The other fellas just looked so immature to me. However, there were others there without partners and since Wesley said nothing to me or Mary Lou about husking corn with him, the three of us simply walked to the nearest corn shock together.

"Hey, let's husk corn," he said to both of us.

Mary Lou and I joined him, one on each side of him and the husking began. There was a lot of laughing and talking as the husks began to fly. I could see, out beyond the corn shocks, Grayson gathering wood for the bonfire. I wondered if he would help husk corn at all. I saw several single girls watching him and whispering about him. But for most of them, he would be considered too old.

I heard Jeannie's voice at one time and in the bright moonlight I saw her busily husking corn with someone who looked suspiciously like Marvin. Could it be? Could she forgive him so easily? I saw Annelie standing with some girls and as I looked, I saw a young man come and step in beside her. I wondered who that was? Between chatting with Mary Lou and Wesley, I kept an eye on Annelie. The boy seemed to be talking to her. But he was a stranger to me. It was not long before the first red ear was found. It was not at our shock, but we all heard the whoop and the squeals. There was a lot of talking around the corn shocks and the moon was rising higher all the time, giving us needed light.

After perhaps an hour of husking corn, I suddenly found Grayson at my side.

"June, there is a young man looking for you," he said, watching me closely.

I looked at him quizzically. "Are you sure? Who is it?"

"Maybe you should come and see for yourself."

He looked so serious, but didn't he always? My thoughts went back to the conversation we had on the way back from Thackeray's Pond. I had to wonder if it was possibly the same man he had seen at the inn. I wondered if Grayson recognized him as the same man. He stepped back as if to lead me to him, but I was not quite ready to go. I just could not think of anyone who would be asking for me.

"Did you ask him his name?" I asked as I threw down the corn I had just husked.

"I did." I waited for him to tell me, but he remained quiet.

"And?" I urged.

"He evidently wants to surprise you."

I hesitated. "Surprise me?"

Grayson observed me silently. In the background I heard a shout and knew someone had found a red ear. I hoped it was not Marvin.

"I'll take you to him," Grayson said again.

There could not possibly be anyone here looking for me that I knew of, but I followed Grayson with slow steps as he led me to the bonfire. As we approached, I saw a man standing silhouetted against the fire but I did not recognize him. At least, not at first glance. When we reached him, he said nothing, but just looked at me. I noticed that Grayson stood there, too, waiting. I was beginning to realize that Grayson was a good person to have for protection. He was coming across like a faithful watchdog.

"Hello?" I said.

The stranger leaned a bit closer to me. "Don't you know me, June?"

I caught my breath. "Gerald?"

He smiled. "Do I look so different?"

I just stared at him in disbelief. This was the boyfriend who dated me for a good six months and then suddenly just did not show up again. Till now, years later. He looked nervous now that I stood silent, and I saw he had a smoldering cigar in one hand.

"What brings you here?"

"I am nearly your next door neighbor. I live only about six miles from here. My brother moved here and invited me to this area. I just got work in a carpenter shop."

"Oh," I said. I somehow did not know what to say. Gerald looked different somehow. His hair was messy and partly down over his face. "I did not know you were invited here tonight."

"Actually, I wasn't, but my neighbor knows you and told me about you being here."

"Your neighbor?"

"Yeah, Brian. He picks apples here sometimes."

I stood flabbergasted. After years of not seeing him, here was Gerald again. I noticed Grayson had moved farther away but was still within hearing distance. As Gerald and I stood facing each other, I was remembering my embarrassment and disappointment when he stood me up after months of being close friends.

"You are a little late for our date," I said quietly, hoping Grayson could not hear.

"Our date?"

"Remember?"

"Oh." Gerald laughed a bit self-consciously. "Is that what happened?"

"I don't know," I said, a bit irritated and speaking a bit louder. "What *did* happen?"

"Can't we just let the past be past?"

I did not like what I was seeing or hearing of this former friend. He seemed not to have moved forward in any way since I had last seen him. I had never been in love with him, but he had hurt and embarrassed me the way he had let me stand.

"You know," I said slowly, "I really don't want to know what happened. And you are right about letting the past be past. You are in my past and I would like it to remain so."

He just stood there, looking at me trying to understand what I had just said. I did not blink an eye, but looked right at him. I knew I could never again be even his close friend, and certainly nothing more.

"Goodbye, Gerald." I turned and walked back to the corn shock where Mary Lou and Wesley were laughing and talking. Just as I got there, Wesley got a red ear and let out a whoop that let everyone know what he had found.

I looked at him, wondering who he would kiss, but he had eyes only for Mary Lou. I watched as he a bit awkwardly reached out to her and gave her a hurried kiss while others around us whooped. I felt just a bit left out. I had really thought Wesley liked me and that it was because of me that he was husking corn with us. Now I knew better. I remembered we had talked a bit one day about Mary Lou, and of course, she was at market, too. Maybe he had talked to me about her to gather more information about her. That happened sometimes. I wasn't really hurt, just confused by all that was happening around me. And I guess I was feeling a bit alone. I had just rejected Gerald who held no appeal for me, and Wesley had chosen Mary Lou.

I continued to husk corn, eventually chatting with those around me. And then, all too soon, Uncle Theodore came up to me and reminded me of my work with the hot chocolate. In my confused thoughts, I had almost forgotten my duties. The moon had climbed higher in the sky and the corn shocks were a lot smaller and the piles of corn were growing. I discovered I was cold and was ready to go inside. I took off my gloves and put them in my pocket and headed to the house. I had a lot to think about. As I passed the bonfire, I saw Grayson watching me leave.

A half hour later, we brought out the hot chocolate and cups. Grayson helped me set up on a makeshift table where we set mustard and homemade ketchup. The hungry crowd was slowly gathering around the glowing fire to roast their frankfurters. I saw no more of Gerald and hoped he had gone home. I had fun filling the cups of hot chocolate for the youth as they came through the line. It gave me a chance to see everyone. Mary Lou and Wesley were still together in line and her eyes were sparkling. I was happy for her, but I was already hoping this would not be the end of our girl time together. She was a good friend. Toward the end of the line, Brian came by.

"Brian, I did not know you were here. How did the corn husking go?"

"It would have been better to have found a red ear of corn," he said softly to me. I then noticed the girl who had picked up her drink just ahead of him.

"You could have bought one and brought it along," I teased.

"Good idea," he laughed. "Next year."

"Would you like me to roast a frankfurter for you or would you like to do it yourself?" asked a voice close to my ear. "We are keeping you rather busy here."

I looked up at Grayson who stood by my side.

"You know what? I would like to do it myself."

"Go. I'll take over here."

It was kind of Grayson and I quickly found a stick and put a frankfurter on it. Most of the group had already roasted their frankfurters and I found myself nearly alone at the fire. As I stood there, Brian came back to me.

"June," he began, "I found out that my neighbor knows you."

"Oh?"

"I think he was a former boyfriend of yours," he said carefully. "He was really excited to hear you lived around here. When I told him about this evening, I thought he might show up although he was not really invited."

"He did show up."

"Gerald? You saw him?" Brian's eyes grew wide. "Is he still here?"

"I really don't know." My frankfurter had caught fire and I pulled it in and blew out the flame. "I hope he left." Brian just looked at me curiously. "Did he say why it ended between us?"

Brian thought a bit. "I think he said he started dating someone else."

"Yes, without a word of explanation to me."

"Maybe it will spark again," he said, seeing my sober face.

"No, Brian. It is past and I hope he is gone. It is over."

"He doesn't seem to be your type," he said.

"He has gone downhill, in my estimation, but maybe I've set my ideals higher."

"Not a bad thing."

Brian walked away and I went to find a bun for my rather black frankfurter. I found a cup for my hot chocolate, which Grayson politely poured for me before going back to the bonfire.

As I stood and ate my snack, I saw Lillian, the girl from church that seemed to like Grayson, go up to him at the fire. She stood and talked to him for maybe five minutes. I wondered what they talked about. When he kept moving around the fire, she finally walked away. I suddenly realized she was walking over to me.

"Hello June." She had never talked to me and I was mentally scrambling to think what to talk about with her.

"Hello. I think your name is Lillian?"

"Yes. How do you like living around here?"

"I am quite happy here."

"I thought you were just here for a visit." That is what she probably wished. I did not particularly like this Lillian.

"I plan to stay here. I have no family except for this aunt and uncle."

She was silent a bit.

"What do you think of Grayson?"

"What makes you ask me about Grayson?"

"Well, he's single."

I did not answer her right away. It was a very personal question and I did not really know Lillian. I was pretty sure what she thought of Grayson. When I did not answer right away, she spoke again.

"Do you like him?"

"I do not dislike him. How about you?"

"Oh, we have been friends for a long time. We get along really good."

"That is nice," I said, looking around for Grayson and hoping he was not hearing what we said. I did not like discussing him with anyone, especially with him close by. I finally saw him talking with Uncle Theodore. It looked like he was looking in our direction, but I could not see well.

"What do you do here?" asked Lillian.

"I help my aunt. There is a lot of work to do here with the farm and the orchard."

"Do you think Grayson is handsome?"

I was getting really tired of this. "Yes, I do. Do you think he is?"

"Oh yes. Would you go out with him if he asked you?"

I really wanted to tell her that we had already dated, but I did not.

"Would you?" I asked, hoping to evade the question.

"Of course."

We stood in silence a bit. I never gave her an answer and she finally walked off.

The night was drawing to a close. I saw people returning to their carriages and knew the party was over. I said goodnight to Mary Lou and a few others, then I began putting the empty cups in the cart to take back to the house. Uncle Theodore and Grayson were putting the fire out. The moon was still shining brightly over the fields and suddenly the warmth of the party was diminishing. Thinking about the last couple hours, I had mixed feelings. The party was the most fun for those with partners. I wondered how many had been kissed by their dates. As for me, who would have thought that I would ever see Gerald again? I thought he was long married to the girl that had wooed him away from me. Or maybe he simply had a roving eye. But I had no interest in him anymore. For some reason, he seemed much less desirable than back then. Or maybe I had changed.

"I'm back, Aunt Sarah," I called as I entered the kitchen. I took off my coat and went close to the stove to warm up. Then reaching into my coat pockets for the gloves my aunt had kindly given me to use, I could find only one.

"Oh, don't tell me I lost a glove!"

I searched again. I looked on the floor. Had I dropped it? Certainly not in here. The glove was missing. What was wrong with me? First I lost my sunbonnet and now Aunt Sarah's glove.

"I'm going right back to find it. I know where I was when I put them in my pockets out there. Evidently one glove never made it into my pocket."

"Wait till morning," said Aunt Sarah.

"No, I may forget it," I replied, putting my coat back on.

I ran out the door and across the lawn. How could I have been so careless? The moon shone colder now and the ground was hard to my feet. The last carriage had made its way down the lane, across the ford and up to the gatehouse. The only people out anymore were Grayson and Uncle Theodore, still trying to get the fire to stay out. Amazing how there can be so much life in one spot one minute and so cold and empty the next. They both looked up as I ran past them.

"What's up?" Uncle Theodore called after me.

"I lost a glove!" I called back as I ran to the corn shocks.

The area where I had been looked a bit different now. The corn shocks were no longer standing. Instead, they were strewn about. I looked around, trying to figure out where I had been when I took off my gloves. Here and there was an ear of corn left on the hard ground. Although I had no trouble seeing, thanks to the bright moonlight, the dark blue glove did not stand out at all against the dark ground.

"Here, let us help you look," said Uncle Theodore as he and Grayson joined in the search. "Are you sure you are at the right place?"

"I think so, although it looks different with the shocks down. But it has to be somewhere in this general area. Maybe someone found it and picked it up."

"I doubt it," said my uncle. "Whoa, Grayson, what did you find?"

I looked up to see Grayson holding a red ear. When I saw him looking at me, my heart seemed to stand still.

"Well, Grayson," said Uncle Theodore with a delighted chuckle. "You know the rules."

I stared dumbly at Grayson and who knows what he may have read in my eyes. He was not laughing like Uncle Theodore was, but there was a look in his eyes that I could not decipher. I felt a blush coming on and made a pretense of searching for the glove, although I would not have seen it, even if it had been hanging on my nose.

"Grayson, don't disappoint, me," said my relentless uncle, beaming in the moonlight and not even pretending to search for the glove. He was waiting for results.

I wanted to act like I was unaffected by what was going on, and tried to keep my eyes on the ground, but when I gave a quick glance in Grayson's direction, I saw him take a step toward me.

I stood up straight and looked at him, not daring to think what might happen. My eyes must have been wide. He kept coming in the moonlight, the cornstalks crunching under his feet. My heart began pounding. He would not kiss me. Not Grayson, who was ever so careful not to even smile at me. And then, he finally stood very close to me, and never losing eye contact, he took my shoulders ever so gently and turned me slightly, so his back was to Uncle Theodore. Then he lowered his head and just brushed his lips against mine. He did not move right away. He just looked down at me, our eyes just inches from each other. Then he backed away and I silently prayed I would not drop in a dead faint at his feet. I could hardly breathe.

"Hot diggity dog!" I heard my uncle say in a pleased voice. "You are a fine man, Grayson."

I looked down, having to smile at my uncle's words and turned to pretend at least to keep searching.

"Is this the glove?" asked Grayson, holding a glove out to me. I did not look at him, because I was still smiling. Instead, I looked at the glove in his hand. I wondered that he found it so quickly after the kiss and wondered briefly if he had found the glove before he found the red ear.

"Yes, I think...thank you," I stuttered, not meeting his eyes.

"Good, now for a warm house and a bed," said my uncle. "I'm about shot." But as he walked by Grayson I heard his voice. "You will lie awake awhile, of course, remembering."

I nearly ran to the house. I was wide awake and all sorts of things were flying through my head. I could barely believe what had transpired. And I was exhilarated. I did not dare think what I was thinking. And last of all, I wished Lillian had been here to see it!

CHAPTER 8

It was on the last day of October when the hurricane hit. Two days earlier, Uncle Theodore had been sitting at the breakfast table, reading the weekly newspaper and announced it was suppose to be coming up the coast and there was the certainty of rain and wind for us although the worst would be along the coast. And, sure enough, now two days later, the clouds were rolling in with a rather humid air. It was starting to get windy and Uncle Theodore checked to see if we had anything around the house that might fly away and at suppertime, Grayson stopped in and made a report to my uncle of what he and his men had done at the stables and other buildings, in preparation for the storm. By the time we went to bed, the rain was hitting the windows hard and forceful winds were whipping around the house, making loose shutters bang and causing a howling in the eaves. I actually liked storms, as long as everyone was safe, but there was also the fear, accompanying the excitement, that something bad could happen. And that fear kept me from falling asleep right away, and I prayed there would be no damage to the house or trees around us. Eventually, however, sleep overtook me.

I do not know how long I slept, but something woke me in the dead of night. At first, I thought it was the storm raging outside because the wind sounded like it wanted to tear the house from its foundation. The rain was beating against the windows and a tree branch, now bare of its leaves, sometimes hit the shutter outside my bedroom window. Is that what woke me? I lay there a few moments, listening to the storm. But why was this terrible feeling of dread in my body? I felt stiff with fear. What had the storm done? What had caused me to waken? It seemed, as I continued to lie there, that there was something else accompanying the wind. I listened closely, feeling sure that something was terribly wrong. Then I heard it. There was a keening that was not the wind.

My fear increased tenfold. I could not move. The keening came again. Stronger. I jumped out of bed and opened the bedroom door. I could see the glow of a candle down the hall in my aunt and uncle's bedroom. Again I heard the keening. I hurried in my bare feet down the hall and stood at the door. Aunt Sarah was sitting by the bed in her white nightgown, looking down at Uncle Theodore. She seemed to be holding his hand, and she was crying. I hurried into the room.

"What's wrong, Aunt Sarah? Why are you crying?"

"He's gone, June. My beloved Theodore is gone." I looked in horror at the form on the bed.

"But that can't be. He was fine this evening."

Aunt Sarah blew her nose. "I think he must have called my name or at least made some sound. At any rate, I woke up and asked if he was all right. But he did not answer. I got up and lit a candle and went to his side of the bed. But when I saw him, I knew he was gone."

She broke down crying again and I knelt by her side and took her in my arms. I could not believe that my uncle was gone. Maybe he was not dead. Maybe he just looked that way.

"Shall I go for a doctor?"

I waited for my aunt to get control of herself.

"He is gone, June. A doctor cannot help, but we need to go for Grayson. He will know what to do. I hate to send you, but we have no choice. Get dressed and take a lantern."

This was a real nightmare. I had to go out in the driving rain and wind and wake Grayson in the middle of the night? Waking Grayson in the middle of the night at any time was scary enough. But I had to go out in this weather? I glanced at the clock. One thirty-five. No one in their right mind would go out in this weather. No one. But I knew I had to do this. For Aunt Sarah. I returned to my room and dressed hurriedly, my mind barely taking in what was happening. I had just been sleeping in a warm bed, glad to be safe from the weather, and now I was getting dressed and planning to go out in this wild storm? Unbelievable. But even while I was thinking these thoughts, I continued to put on my clothing. Once I was dressed, I went downstairs. I got a lantern in the enclosed back porch and with trembling fingers, held the match flame to the wick. There was no reason to take an umbrella. It would fly away or turn inside out. I looked at my uncle's mackintosh hanging on a peg close by. It was much too big for me, but it would keep me dry. Hopefully. I had no time to grieve for my uncle and no time to wonder if it was right for me to be using his mackintosh. I needed to go a quarter mile up the lane to the gatehouse where Grayson lived. And I had to ford the stream. How could I ever do that? It scared me to bits, but I mechanically kept moving.

Once in the mackintosh, I grabbed the lantern and pulled the hood over my head and headed for the door. Wait. I needed boots. I went back to the enclosed porch and found my boots. I put them on and headed once more for the door. I hesitated just a moment, taking a deep breath, then opened the door.

The wind hit me hard and my first struggle was to get the door to close behind me. That done, I began walking across the lawn to the driveway, wondering if I was in my right mind. I felt like I might blow away. I wanted badly to return to the house, but I had to do this for Aunt Sarah. I was fighting every step and I had no time to think ahead to the gatehouse or the person I would be getting out of bed. I had to walk carefully, lantern in hand, and find my way out the muddy drive, through the trees and eventually, across the stream. That feat seemed equal to crossing the Red Sea with Moses. But he had walked across on dry ground.

As I struggled against the wind, I wondered about crossing the stream. How deep could it be by now? Up till now, I had always easily gotten over it. But with this rain? But there was a walking bridge that I had never had to use. It stood maybe fifteen feet from the driveway.

Could I find my way there in the dark? But walking across the stream at night was not a welcome idea either. The stream was probably the halfway point to the gatehouse. The loose mackintosh whipped around my legs and the sleeves were too long and too wide and rain found its way in and my arms were wet. I picked my way carefully, following the drive but it seemed like forever till I got to the trees that stood on either side of the ford. The wind was whipping small twigs and some last remaining leaves off the trees and bits and pieces were hitting my face. I remembered the branch that had come down on my arrival and hoped no big branches would fall on me.

As it was, I came upon the black stream suddenly. The stream was wider with the heavy rain. One moment I was on land and the next I was stepping into the water. It surprised me and I pulled back out of the water. It looked like it was rushing too fast although it could not be terribly deep yet. But the longer I looked at the water, the more I hesitated to step into it. Instead, I raised my lantern to the soggy lawn and made my way carefully in the direction of the footbridge. I had never walked over it since I came, and hoped it was stable. I could barely see, even with my lantern but I followed the stream, looking for the bridge.

When I got to it, I breathed a sigh of relief. It seemed sturdy. I quickly stepped on it and holding on to the railing with one hand and carrying the lantern with the other, I made my way across, hearing the rushing water below me. But alas, as I neared the other side of the bridge, I saw that a large branch of a tree had fallen and firmly blocked my exit from the bridge. There was no way I could climb into that tangle of twigs and branches. I choked back a sob and turned around. What a nightmare this was turning out to be. *How was I ever to get across?* I felt completely alone and lost in a storm that scared me badly. I was scared at the force of the water even though it probably was not more than six inches in the middle of the stream. There was another exit far on the other end of the property. But that was far, far away. Actually I was never at that entrance. I had just been told about it. And I needed to get to this entrance. To the gatehouse. To Grayson. I made my way slowly back across the bridge. Once off the bridge, I held the lantern up and looked at the water by the footbridge. Maybe if I held onto the the bridge, I could make it. I took a deep breath and sent a frantic prayer heavenward and then, with one hand on the bridge, and the other hand holding the swinging lantern, I stepped into the water right next to the footbridge—on the side where the water could only push me against the bridge and not away from it. Very slowly and carefully, step by step, I made my way across the rushing stream. Just one cautious step at a time. And very slowly. I felt the water slosh into my boots. It was cold water and made my steps heavier. Harder to raise my feet. Step by difficult step, I crossed the stream, the water pushing me against the bridge.

When I was nearly across, I came to the fallen branch. I could no longer hold on to the bridge. I had to take a step against the current to get around the fallen branch. I held the lantern high. I had to go around the branch, but I could not see the bank. It had to be here because I'd come to the edge of the bridge. I looked at the branches. Were they strong enough for me to hold on to? If I took a quick step and hurled myself to the bank, I might make it. The water was rushing around my legs, trying to throw me over. I had no time to think. I simply acted. I hurled my body toward what had to be the bank. It almost worked. I made the bank with my body but not my legs. The water swirled up to my waist and the lantern went out. I dragged myself up the bank and sobbing out loud in sheer fright, I stood up. I was soaked all over and I had no light. I lifted my legs, hoping to let the water run out of my boots. I was cold and wet. And miserable. And very frightened. But I was across the stream. I had to keep going and not think about how miserable I was. I forced my way alongside of the rushing stream in the direction of where I thought the road should be.

"God, I need your help," I prayed out loud, feeling ashamed for praying now in my need and too seldom thanking Him for the blessings He sent my way through my aunt and uncle. I stumbled, cried and prayed as I headed in the darkness for the road, watching that I did not step into the black, swirling water. And then I was off the soggy lawn and on the driveway.

"Thank you God!" I cried out into the storm.

The night was black and there was no light anywhere. If there had been light, the rain would still have blinded me. I turned right on the road, staying close to the grass so I would not weave back and forth on the road. I needed to go straight. I needed to make it to the gatehouse. My movements were sluggish with my wet clothes. I set the dark lantern down and tried again to empty my boots. By now I was so cold my teeth were chattering. It was too dark to see anything, but the gatehouse went across the road. I would feel it if not see it. It seemed like forever. I could barely walk with my wet skirt and soggy boots. I would sometimes step into the grass at the side of the road and had to step back onto the driveway. Still carrying my dark lantern, I finally felt the stone of the archway across the drive.

"Thank you, thank you, thank you, God!" I cried out into the darkness and howling wind.

I crossed the drive and found my way to the door under the arch. I was exhausted and shivering with cold, but I banged on the door as loud as I could. Here, under the arch, there was finally some protection from the rain and wind. There was also a knocker, which I used. But I doubted Grayson could hear it above the storm. Finally, when there was a bit of a lull in the wind, I shouted as loud as I could. But the wind was so strong how could he hear? In desperation I just kept hammering on the door for what seemed a very long time.

And then, suddenly, the door opened, and I saw in the light of his lamp, a very surprised and disheveled Grayson. I think he did not recognize me at first but when he did, the door swung wide and he reached out to help me inside.

"What is wrong?" he asked, as he slammed the door, and then, without waiting for an answer, he pulled me with a strong arm over to the dying fire.

"I'm wet all over," I sobbed now in relief. "I fell in the stream."

I heard Grayson say something under his breath, but I did not understand it. He took the mackintosh off of me and disappeared for a few minutes and brought back a blanket. I believe he pulled the blanket off of his bed because it was warm when he wrapped it around me. He then sat me on a chair and stoked the fire. All this time, I was too cold to think. I was still recovering from my nightmare. Glad to be alive and under roof.

"Why are you here?" he asked when my sobs lessened, his eyes wide with curiosity.

I had almost forgotten, so centered I was on surviving the storm.

"Oh, something terrible has happened," I stopped to get my breath. "Uncle Theodore is dead. Or, at least, Aunt Sarah thinks he is dead."

Grayson just looked at me in shock, trying to comprehend what I had just said. It may have been thirty seconds of complete silence.

"What happened?" he finally asked, his eyes reflecting the light of the hearth.

"I don't know." I shivered. "I got awake...and heard her crying and...when I went to her, she was sitting by the bed and holding his hand. He...looks dead." I took a deep breath. "She said I should come for you. That you would know what to do."

Grayson sat in silence a few moments as he considered what I had told him. He then threw yet another log on the fire and went for his own mackintosh and a pair of boots. Then he returned to me.

"How did you get across the stream?"

"I tried the bridge but on your end it is blocked by a large, fallen tree branch. I went back and..." I shuddered, just remembering, "I stepped into the stream and held on to the bridge and then...I jumped and I made it to the bank except for my legs. That is why I am so wet."

Grayson just looked at me in horror for few minutes.

"Thank God you are safe," he finally said and sat silent, staring at me.

"June," he said as he got up to take action, "you must stay here. You cannot go out as you are. My horse is here in the stable and I will go for a doctor. We will need a doctor to pronounce him dead. While I am gone, I want you to go to my washroom and remove your clothes and towel yourself dry. Hang them on chairs in front of the fire and wrap yourself in the blanket. When I come back, I will stop for you and will take you back to the house. Do you understand?" I just nodded, sniffing, needing a handkerchief. "I do not know how long I will be gone."

Grayson left the room and came back with the needed handkerchief. He handed it to me silently and left the room again. When he returned, he was fully dressed.

"Stay inside. I will return as quickly as possible," he said as he reached for the doorknob.

He left quickly. He evidently had a horse here at the gatehouse. I did not know. I faintly remembered that there was a stall. I was glad I had warned him of the branch at the footbridge, in case he had to walk back. He would need a carriage. Or would he? Maybe he would just ride his horse to the village. It was not a night to be out in. As I looked at the closed door, I suddenly realized I was alone in Grayson's house. In the gatehouse I loved.

I got up quickly and walked, blanket wrapped around me into the kitchen, which led to the washroom. There was a candle burning on the kitchen table and another in the washroom. I found a clean towel and gratefully removed my wet clothing. The blanket he gave me was partially wet from being around me but it would have to do. I would sit close to the fire and turn the blanket so that the driest side was against my skin. Wrapping the blanket around me, I took my clothes to the fire and placed them on two chairs. I doubted they would dry in time, but when he returned, I would put them on again, wet or dry. It was not far to the village, but in the storm it would take longer. I then sat on a wing back chair sitting close to the fire. I wondered about this strange, scary night. I prayed for Grayson's safe return. I waited and watched until sleep claimed me. I slept soundly there next to the fire and did not waken until the door opened. I sat up dismayed that I was still wrapped in just a blanket.

"I will take you now," said Grayson, not looking at me directly. "I'll wait for you here."

Embarrassed at having slept, I carefully got up with the blanket still wrapped around me and without a word, I grabbed my damp clothes, and walked to the washroom. I dressed as quickly as possible and returned to the sitting room, where I draped his damp blanket on a chair by the fire.

"Did you get the doctor?"

"Yes, he is on his way." Grayson held out the mackintosh for me and I slipped into it. Silently, he led me out the door and helped me into the carriage. It was still raining, but the wind had died down some.

"What time is it?" I asked.

"Nearly three-thirty. The doctor was treating a stranger at the inn and I had to go for him there."

"Did you take the carriage to the doctor?"

"No. I got it now, to take you back."

We splashed through the roaring stream and Grayson left me off at the portico and then took the horse and carriage to the stable.

I walked into the house and changed clothes once more before going to my aunt. In the meantime, the doctor had arrived. I entered the bedroom and stood by my aunt while the doctor pronounced Uncle Theodore dead. I then left the room and went into the kitchen to make coffee. We would not get much sleep and maybe the others would be glad for coffee. I could barely believe this night. Now I was making coffee and setting cups out when we should all be sleeping.

While making the coffee, I heard Grayson come in the kitchen door. He said nothing but disappeared up the stairs. A short time later, the doctor, Grayson, and Aunt Sarah returned to the kitchen where I had coffee waiting. There was not much said. The doctor and

Grayson talked in low tones and I sat with Aunt Sarah who was too stunned to say much at all. I was glad to see her drink some coffee. The doctor then left and about an hour later the undertaker arrived and Grayson helped him take the body out to his conveyance.

It was a short night.

The rain was over by dawn and it was good to see the sun trying to chase the clouds. The fact that Grayson had already taken over the management of the place was a big plus with my uncle gone, but throughout the morning I wondered just how things would continue here. But there was barely time to think of that. The minister was notified and he came mid morning. He sat a long time with Grayson. Nettie arrived and cleaned the downstairs. My uncle was a well-known man and many people from the community would come in support of my aunt and mourn his passing. Aunt Sarah kept to her room until people began coming. Neighbors and friends dropped in bringing fresh loaves of bread, breakfast cakes, potato salad, chicken soup and much more. We almost did not know what to do with all the food. We shared coffee and cake with the people who came by. It lasted all afternoon.

At suppertime, I put out some of the hot food that was brought to us. Grayson ate with us. Aunt Sarah was in a daze. I knew the feeling. It was less than a year since my mother had died. Grayson gently announced that the funeral would be held the next day. I asked Aunt Sarah whether she had a black dress. She did. I had my dress from my mother's funeral. At least I did not have to scramble for black clothing. I fell into bed exhausted. Tomorrow would be a long, hard day.

CHAPTER 9

Early the next morning, Grayson and some other men from church, came to set up for the viewing. The kitchen was full of women preparing the refreshments we would have after the funeral. I hardly had time to think. People came before noon already to view the body. That lasted until two-thirty, when the body was taken to the church, where the service was set for three.

The church was full. I had the feeling Aunt Sarah would not remember any of the service. She was just in a daze. Pastor Stafford was hit pretty hard himself with Theodore dying so quickly. Following the service, there was the burial in the cemetery next to the church. I stayed by Aunt Sarah, as did Grayson. He could not have done any more than a son would have done and I was pleased how well my aunt held up. I could tell she trusted Grayson as a son.

The ground at the cemetery was still soggy from the rain, but thankfully, the sun was shining, though the air was brisk. I held onto my aunt's arm at the grave and felt her tremble. It was a terrible shock for her. Becca stood with us, as did some relatives that I did not know. After the burial, many people came to the house for refreshments and to show their support and to give comfort. I was busy making coffee and tea and pretty much stayed in the kitchen. When the last person had left, it was nearly six o'clock. Then the house had to be put to rights once more. We rested for an hour and then I heated up a supper of hot vegetable soup and biscuits. It was a relief to have no visitors in the house. We were exhausted.

While washing the dishes, I heard a knock on the door. Aunt Sarah called to me that she would get it, as she was expecting someone. I heard voices. It was Grayson with a stranger. They disappeared with Aunt Sarah into the library. I had the feeling this could be the attorney for the estate. I suddenly wondered what would happen now, to the estate. Would it be sold? I finished the dishes and, too tired to do anything else, went to my room. Aunt Sarah would know where to find me. Becca had already disappeared. I had watched her because this was her brother who had passed away. But I was not sure she really comprehended it. She looked confused rather than sad.

I am ashamed to say it, but I went upstairs and fell asleep. When I awoke, it was nine o'clock and when I checked on my aunt, I found her in bed, sleeping.

Aunt Sarah seemed preoccupied at breakfast, but I did not force her to talk. As we finished our eggs and bacon, she spoke.

"Grayson is coming over in a few minutes to talk to us," she said in a subdued tone. "We will meet in the library."

"Should I make coffee and bring over some of the doughnuts from yesterday?" I asked.

"Yes. Grayson will be glad for it." She said no more.

I was washing dishes when Grayson arrived and Aunt Sarah let him in and followed him to the library. A few minutes later, I took the coffee and doughnuts to the library. As I entered, I softly greeted Grayson who looked very sober. But then, did he ever smile? I immediately poured coffee, feeling self-conscious. I would have rather not been there, but it seems I was requested and I felt a certain fear about the subject for this meeting.

The library was bright with sunshine pouring in the tall windows, and I was a bit embarrassed that it was Grayson who was now building a fire in the hearth. I could have done it but had not thought of it. It seemed that Aunt Sarah was letting Grayson take complete charge. No wonder, she was still in shock and as manager of the estate he would know what to do about whatever had to be done.

"Please take a seat," said Grayson to me, motioning to the sofa in front of the fire where my aunt already sat. He then sat on a wing chair and put a sheath of papers on the small table by his side. Once seated, Grayson looked at my aunt.

"Have you shared anything with your niece?"

My aunt did not look at me. "No."

I was surprised at his question. Was this meeting about me? Immediately a host of questions filled my brain. There could be big changes now and I suddenly realized that I may be losing my home. My aunt could not run the estate and would have little interest in it without her husband. I felt myself go pale. Where would I go?

"June," my aunt said, turning to me, "a few years ago, Theodore and I made our will. We have no children living and Grayson is like a son to us. He has been working here for the last ten years and we are greatly indebted to him. We have left the entire estate to him with the stipulation that I may live here as long as I live."

I looked at Grayson, my eyes wide. I had never thought that Grayson would inherit. I thought it possible that the estate would be sold, or maybe continue as it was. I found Grayson's dark eyes on me, clearly watching to see my reaction. Did he think I would have expected something from the estate? I know my eyes showed my surprise, but I said nothing. There was too much to consider. Then I had another thought. He said Aunt Sarah could live here for as long as she lives. But I was her guest. She no longer had the authority to say whether I could live here.

"I can move somewhere else," I said quickly, but the thought scared me.

"I want to assure you, June, that you may remain here with your aunt. I know she would like you to. For now I need to know if you would be willing to stay on and be hired by me."

For some reason I blushed. Hired by Grayson? I just looked at him for a moment. "What do you mean?"

"There are jobs that need to be done. You are a big help to your aunt. I may have some errands for you to run. Can you drive a carriage?"

"I have already, but not often."

"Well, you can learn."

"Do you ride?"

"I did one time," I hesitated, then added, "I am a bit scared of horses. I had a bad experience."

"That can be remedied also," replied Grayson. "Would you be willing to stay on?"

"Yes. Yes, of course. I...have no other place to go right now."

Grayson's eyes rested on me for a few moments as if trying to understand something. "If you had another place to go, would you go or would you like to stay here?"

"I think I would like to stay."

I deliberately looked at my aunt when I said that. I did not want Grayson to think I was staying because of him. I could not quite forget our last date. Although he never gave any hint of the scene, he had to remember that he said I would one day come crawling back to him. This was just a little too much like that. I hoped he had forgotten the incident. But now he seemed to be all business.

"Good. Now that we have that settled, I suggest you continue on here as you have been and if I have something special for you to do, I will contact you."

At this point I was dismissed but the two sat together for another hour or so. At noon Aunt Sarah had more to say.

"There will be some major changes here now that Grayson is the owner of the estate. One of these things will be that he will move here from the gatehouse. It does not make sense for him to be a quarter of a mile away from the action here. He will move into the attached little house that he had already been using as an office along with Theodore.

The upstairs is now storage, but we will need to clean that out as he will use it as a bedroom. He will also be taking his meals with us."

"He does not want to move into the main house?" I asked.

"Not at this point, but, of course, he will someday."

Part of what Aunt Sarah said was lost on me. All I heard was that Grayson was moving out of the gatehouse. Oh, how I wanted to move in there! But I said nothing. The permission would now have to come from Grayson. And that would be a little tricky. And now we would always eat together? Aunt Sarah had no idea of our past connection. It would be hard for me to live this close to Grayson. One more reason for me to live in the gatehouse.

The following day, Aunt Sarah and I went over to the little house that had been added on to the main house at some point. It was connected at the hallway leading from the kitchen, but it had its own entrance from the lawn to the north of the main house. We entered now by way of the kitchen, and I was surprised at the amount of room in the little house. I had never been in here. Besides a desk, there was a table, a couple arm chairs and a hearth. Aunt Sarah informed me that Grayson planned to add a washroom and an enclosed back porch to it.

"Aunt Sarah, why couldn't we move to the gatehouse? Doesn't he want the big house for himself? In case he would someday marry?"

"I already offered that we could move into the part he will use, but then we have Becca and we can't leave her in the main house with him. And furthermore, this is what he wants."

"What will he do with the gatehouse?"

"I did not ask, but we do need him here with us. He is like a son to me. I feel safe with him here."

I said no more. But I did some thinking. Someday I would ask Grayson if I could move out into the gatehouse. It should not stand empty. But right now, there was too much to do. Later that day, we began our work in the storage area. Aunt Sarah really did not help much. We were often interrupted by kind neighbors and long-time friends who kept stopping by to offer condolences. Some brought a pie or a container of soup. They meant well, but it took her away from the storage area and I was left alone, not knowing what to do with the things stored there.

It was Nettie who finally helped me clean the upstairs room.

"Where did all this stuff come from, anyway?" she asked.

"Over the years, it collects. And my aunt and uncle have been here a long time. And Theodore's father before him and his grandfather before that."

"Goodness," said Nellie. "Don't they ever throw things away? Who wants this old baby carriage? If Mr. Everleigh ever marries and has a baby, it would fall screaming right through the bottom."

I had to laugh. Nettie was a good worker. The dust would fly when she got busy, but she seemed daunted by the baby carriage, old broken chairs, boxes of old dusty jars and other objects that I could not identify.

"Whose baby carriage is it anyway? They don't have any children," she continued.

"But they did," I said. "They had a baby that died and later adopted a son. I do not know how old he was when they got him, but I think he was still a baby. They would have used the carriage for him."

"Where is he now?"

"He died when he was thirteen. From influenza."

Nettie was quiet a bit after that. "You know," she said softly, "that must be really hard, losing babies and small children."

"I am sure it was. And there are many other people who lose babies also."

"My parents lost a child, but it was before I was born."

"Do they ever talk about the child?"

"Never."

We continued working in the dust and cobwebs.

"We'll just push the junk into one corner and tell Mr. Everleigh he can burn them. It won't be anything he would want as remembrances because he is not a relative." Nettie paused for a breath, then continued as she shoved the baby carriage into a corner. "Isn't it something that he got this whole estate just plopped in his lap?"

"Well, it sounds like he was a good worker. Aunt Sarah thinks of him as a son."

"Boy, don't you wish Mr. Everleigh was sweet on you. Then it would be yours, too."

I was horror struck by her statement. If Grayson would have heard her, I would have been mortified.

"Nettie, please don't ever say anything like that again. What if he had come up the stairs just then and heard you?"

But Nettie was not very repentant. "Maybe it would give him a good idea," she said in almost a whisper, as she glanced to the stairs. "Don't you like him? I wonder why he isn't married. He is old enough. And handsome enough. He always reminds me of a prince."

"How is that boyfriend of yours?" I asked, to change the subject.

"He is the finest man in the county. I hope to marry him and the sooner the better."

I laughed and wished her well. She simply stated the facts and was not shy about it.

Eventually, there were boxes of things that had me stumped and I had to have my aunt here to tell us what to save and what to burn. So I went down in search of her and brought her back with me. It was pretty simple although Aunt Sarah's thoughts were in an upheaval. Her brain was not working as usual. She looked like she had a headache. But she was evidently one who could part with what was not useful and most of the boxes joined the junk in the corner.

The next step was to get Grayson to get rid of the boxes. He had promised to stop in and a short time later, he came with two hired hands. They carried the boxes of things to be kept to the main house attic, and they took the others out to be burned. Then Nettie and I cleaned the room. It was a lot of work. There was only one window at each end of the room and the November day was cloudy. When the room was finally cleaned, and Nettie had gone downstairs with the last bucket of dirty water, I gave one last look at the room. It needed curtains. It needed more than curtains. I was just wondering how we could make the room nice for Grayson, when I heard heavier steps coming up the stairs. It was Grayson without the boys. I stood and waited for his entrance. I was ready to leave and planned to do so immediately. However, Grayson stopped at the head of the stairs and therefore blocked my exit. I was somehow very self-conscious being alone with him in the room. Why had I not gone down with Nettie? What did he think I was doing in the room? He glanced at me and then looked around him in silence.

"Looks good."

"Thank you." He said no more, but made no move to leave. And I could not get past him to leave without difficulty. I never could stand long silences and in my nervousness, I took the plunge.

"Grayson, what are you going to do with the gatehouse?"

He looked at me without answering for so long that I was inwardly kicking myself for asking.

"I have not thought that far," he said slowly, and I felt he was studying me rather than thinking about the gatehouse. It made my own thinking difficult.

"You won't just let it stand empty?"

"I don't know."

"Would you rent it out?"

"I...don't know. May I ask why you're interested?"

"I would love to live there." His eyes widened and in the dim light they looked darker than usual.

"You would like to rent it?"

"Eventually."

"No."

His answer was immediate. I was a bit chagrined. He did not even have to think before he spoke. He had no wish to rent the gatehouse he knew I loved, to me.

When he said no more and began looking at the room again,

I spoke again. I had started this conversation and did not know if I would ever have the nerve to bring it up again.

"Why not?" He looked almost shocked that I asked.

"It would not be appropriate." His words were clipped and he barely gave me a glance. Like I should know better.

"I am twenty-six years old." He stopped looking around the room, put his hands in his pockets and nailed me with his look.

"I know exactly how old you are." That was his first acknowledgment of our past connection. "And it does not come into question."

His answer left nothing to be discussed. I had stuck my neck out and my head had been duly chopped off. I dared to say no more. I know my mother would have given the same reason as Grayson, but I wanted this badly. I hoped my face was not red. But how I wished for a place of my own. Grayson continued to look at me until I felt awkward. I thought how strange this was. I had thrown him away so easily when I was young and too sure of myself and now here he was telling me what I may or may not do.

I looked away, disappointed. Did he realize how hard it would be for me to live this closely to him? I was finding the new Conrad intriguing. I was not indifferent to him although I wanted to be indifferent to him. I did not trust men. I had not forgotten Alan. Now I was in this awkward position with Grayson. I had no reason to remain in the room and to argue was fruitless. He was in charge. Not me. I was fortunate that he did not send me on my way without a home. I slowly made my way toward the door and stairs. He remained in my path.

"What would you do there all by yourself?"

Oh, he had not pushed the idea out of his mind completely. He was ready to listen. I took hope.

I suddenly thought of my passion for sewing.

"I love to sew. Maybe I could work part-time for you and instead of paying me, you could let me live in the gatehouse. There I could sew for people. Make dresses and all kinds of things. I could earn my own keep, perhaps. I could pay you rent." I know my eyes brightened at the thought.

"You will one day marry and then you will have little time to sew for others."

"I seem to have reached twenty-six without marriage. And," I added, feeling miffed at his refusing to let me live in the gatehouse, "I am less impressed with the male population all the time."

Grayson's head lifted a bit and his eyes opened wider in surprise. "Why the sudden anger at males?"

"I'm not angry."

"I think you are."

I had no answer. I realized I was angry. I was angry at Alan. I was angry at Gerald. And I was angry over the silly argument with Grayson so long ago.

"If I am angry, I have good reason to be angry," I said stubbornly and turned just a bit away from him. There was a moment or two of silence.

"I am sorry." His voice was low and serious.

"What are you sorry about?" I could not figure this man out.

"I am sorry that you are angry."

"I am not looking for pity." I said it with a bit of force and I was feeling that I was putting on a very sorry performance during this discussion. Again the silence. I could not look at him. I was embarrassed for all I had said.

"Don't let your anger consume you, June," he said quietly. "It will not help you."

Somehow his words, or perhaps it was more the soft tone, or even my disappointment in my own words that brought moisture to my eyes. I blinked rapidly and although I had to walk around Grayson to leave, I did just that. By the time I reached the bottom of the stairs, I heard him following me down and then he left the house.

CHAPTER 10

An hour later, Aunt Sarah wanted to see how the room looked now that it was cleaned.

"There should be curtains on the two windows," she said. "Maybe Grayson or one of the other men can take you to town to get material. I somehow do not feel up to it. Everything takes more energy than I have just now. I am still in shock that my husband is not coming back." There were tears in her voice.

That afternoon when Grayson dropped in, Aunt Sarah talked to him about it.

"Is anyone free to take June to the village to get fabric for curtains for your bedroom?"

Grayson looked thoughtful. "Maybe we can take curtains from the gatehouse and hang them there."

"Oh, no," I said without thinking. "They should remain in the gatehouse."

His dark eyes held a challenge. "For whom?"

"Well, surely you won't let the gatehouse go to ruin. It needs to be used and it will need curtains," I added, realizing that Grayson would perhaps think I was overstepping again.

"Oh, yes, Grayson," said my aunt. "What are you going to do with the gatehouse? Someone should live there."

Something in me got brave. One last chance. "I could."

I did not dare look at Grayson. I was hoping for Aunt Sarah's approval but of course she no longer had a say in it.

"Oh no," she replied after a short hesitation. "That would not be appropriate. You living out there alone. No, that would not work."

I could not help a quick glance at Grayson. He had a very smug expression on his face. Here was proof that I was wrong. Aunt Sarah had sided with him. Then he turned once more to my aunt.

"But I am remembering something. I know where there is a stack of fabric in the gatehouse. Maybe a couple piles of it."

"In the gatehouse?"

"In a box in a small cubbyhole. It has been there a long time, I suppose. It is in the little room directly over the driveway."

"Oh," said Aunt Sarah. "I remember that Justin's wife, Margaret, did a lot of sewing. I think that little room over the drive was her sewing room. And you say there is fabric there?"

"Yes, quite a bit of it."

"Could you bring it to June? Or maybe June could get it."

I bit my lip to keep from smiling. Grayson gave me a quick look. Did she really think that Grayson would trust me in his gatehouse? In his private living quarters now that he knew I wanted it? I was a bit surprised that she even mentioned it. Grayson's eyes answered me before he spoke.

"I'll bring it to you tomorrow."

Grayson, with the help of one of the hired hands, rearranged the downstairs room so the desk was in one corner and a table and chair in another. The rest of the room could be used for a sitting room with a couch and another upholstered chair. Since the building was attached at the kitchen, he could help himself in the kitchen for whatever he wished. Nettie was asked to come an extra half day to clean the downstairs and the room was about ready.

The following day, Grayson brought the fabric. There was quite a bit of it and I asked him if he had a preference for color and he gave the choice to me. There was a nice blue fabric that I thought was good for a man's room and by the next day, I had the curtains finished and Aunt Sarah and I hung them. The bedroom was now furnished and Grayson would be sleeping in his new quarters that evening. I found the room sparse and needing something to brighten it up. On this dull November day, it did not look welcoming at all.

"What can we do to brighten up this room?" I asked. "And it is cold in here."

"If he keeps the door open in the evening it will be warm enough, but the room does need something," replied my aunt. She looked at the bed. There was a brown, warm blanket on the top of it. I recognized it as the one Grayson had given to me on the night of Uncle Theodore's death.

"I have a quilt of many bright colors that would look nice on the bed," said Aunt Sarah. "I will give it to Grayson. I have more quilts than I need and have no children to pass them on to. Let's go get it and you can bring it up and put it on his bed. He will have a nice surprise when he comes back."

Aunt Sarah had a whole chest full of quilts. Brand new ones. I knew immediately which one she was talking about when I saw the colorful quilt.

"Perfect," I said. "That will add color and the blue in it will compliment the curtains."

"I hope he likes color. If not, he can exchange it for one of these other quilts," said my aunt.

———

So began a new chapter in my life. Uncle Theodore was gone and at the table in his place, was Grayson. It was an adjustment for all of us, but surely the hardest would be for Aunt Sarah. I admit to being relieved when I discovered that Grayson would only eat with us evenings, and on occasion, not even then. If Grayson was hampered by our past, when I knew him as Conrad, he did not let it be known. It was never mentioned. In the meantime, I was well aware of this new Conrad. He was a completely new person except, perhaps, for his self assurance and sober personality. We made only small talk at meals and I was generally glad when they were finished. Grayson stayed pretty much in his house, although he had access to the kitchen.

One day, Aunt Sarah had a question for him about a broken window, and as a result, he came up the hall where I was sewing. There really was no place for a sewing machine elsewhere and I was in the way for what he wanted to do. I was aware of his scrutiny of my makeshift place to sew. And a part of me wanted to say, "Yes, here is where I must sew and the gatehouse is empty." But I knew better than to say it. Men do not like to be pushed.

One evening, soon after that, when we had finished our dessert, Grayson turned to me.

"You seem to be the seamstress here."

"Such as it is."

"I have a shirt that has a seam that opened. Would you sew it for me?"

"Of course."

"Do you always sew in the hallway?"

"Yes. I have the most room there."

He said no more, but just before we left the table he turned to me again.

"June, I would like you to meet me at the horse stables tomorrow morning at nine." I waited for an explanation, since this had nothing to do with sewing. He gave no explanation, but instead he added, "I assume that you are free?"

"I am," I said, wanting to know more. But he simply stood up and turned to walk away.

"Grayson," called Aunt Sarah from the kitchen, "don't leave yet. I want to show you something."

I stayed sitting at the table and she brought in a small box.

"Sit down, Grayson, I want you to look at this." They both sat and Aunt Sarah proceeded to open the little wooden box.

"I found this box in the bottom drawer of Theodore's desk. When I opened it, I found some things he just did not want to throw out but they were not really useful anymore. Like this old watch that belonged to his grandfather. However," she continued, laying a few odds and ends out on the table, "at the bottom of the box was this paper."

Aunt Sarah handed Grayson a folded bit of very old paper. In fact, some of the edges broke off as she handed it to him. Grayson unfolded it and looked at it. Then he looked up at Aunt Sarah.

"I hope this says something to you, because it surely says nothing to me. Maybe your son's scribbling?"

"Not at all. The paper is much older than that. And I do know what it is."

Grayson handed the paper to me so I could see it, too. On the paper were the initials G H and then there was a drawing. I could not figure out exactly what it was, but it looked like it could be a small round box. But at first glance to me, it resembled a knitted cap such as a little boy wears with a round ball made of the same yarn on the top. Or, it could be a cake sitting on a flat plate, but then what was the round ball on top?

"So what is it?" asked Grayson.

"Well," began Aunt Sarah, "it is a long story. Theodore's grandfather bought this land and he is the one who gave it the name Bluster Hill. He built this house and the big barn and the first stable. However, I am told he was an obnoxious kind of person and made enemies easily. So he had the gatehouse built as a protection against his enemies. He always had a gatekeeper in it. But he died fairly young and had only one son, which was Theodore's father, so he inherited the place. He is the one that really made it a financial success. But Theodore's father did not trust the banks. So he hid his money. Not all in one place. He made notes to himself that really only he could understand. He did share his secrets with his wife, however. But he was killed in a carriage accident leaving Theodore the only son, and four daughters, among them, Rebecca and Lizzie. Theodore was twenty and had just married me a year earlier. His mother lived here with us until she died. But she is the one that told me about the notes and secret hiding places for the money. She had five or six notes. I don't remember exactly anymore. And she could tell us what the notes meant. And we discovered them and put the money in the bank. However, there was a note discovered later in another place after she died. We never really knew if it was a real note, or if he was thinking of making one and it got misplaced. I don't know. I just know, this is the note and we could never figure it out."

"So there could be money hidden somewhere yet?" I asked, since Grayson was silent.

"Maybe. Just maybe. But we do not know for sure. It seems strange it was not with the other notes."

"What does the G H stand for?"

"Well, this was always called the Great House. Of course, there is the gatehouse as well. And to make it more confusing, Theodore's father's name was George Horace and it could simply be his initials on the note."

"Did you ever spend time looking for it?" asked Grayson.

"We spent a lot of time looking for a container that looked like that picture. That seemed to be the most important thing on the notes. The pictures. And we never found any container like that. I don't know from the picture how big it is."

"That is exciting," I said, looking at Grayson who was not talking much. I could not tell if he thought it exciting or not. He seemed good at hiding his emotions.

He finally grinned and looked at Aunt Sarah. "Just watch, June is going to be searching every cranny of the house for the supposedly missing money."

"I just might," I said with a smile. "Is it finder's keepers?"

The next morning, shortly before nine, I headed out to the barn, wondering what he had for me to do there. It was a cold, chilly day with a few snow flurries in the air so I dressed warmly. Once at the stables, I looked around but did not find Grayson right away. I finally discovered him down at the stall of a chestnut-colored mare.

"Good morning, June," said my employer, his eyes taking in my attire.

"Good morning, Grayson."

"I want you to make friends with this mare, June. Her name is Star."

"Make friends with her?"

"Yes. I seem to have understood that you are scared of horses. We must change that. If you spend time with her, you will make friends with her, and then she will be your mare when you take the carriage to go to town."

I said nothing. It was important that since Uncle Theodore was gone, that my aunt and I be able to go to town without asking Grayson. I understood that, but it scared me.

"And eventually, you will learn to ride her." Grayson watched closely to see my reaction and I am sure my eyes widened.

"Ride? No thanks," I said with a firm shake of my head. "I really have no wish to ride."

"I wish you to ride."

I looked up quickly. The words were spoken low. Grayson was looking steadily at me and by his tone of voice, he was offering no options. He was now my employer. I did not argue. But fear gripped me. I really was scared of horses. As a small child, a neighbor man meant well and sat me on a horse and the horse promptly threw me off and I broke my collarbone. I had never had the wish to get on a horse again and thankfully never had to. But I said nothing now.

"For now, I wish you to feed Star and spend time with her. Brush her coat and talk to her, so she gets used to your voice. She is a gentle horse and you need not have any fear of her." Because I said nothing, he added, "Do you understand my instructions? Do you have any questions?"

I shook my head but did not look at him. He was not satisfied. "June?"

"I understand."

He showed me the brush and showed me how to brush her and explained the food and water to me. And then he left. He had not told me how much time I must spend with the mare, but I stayed with her for perhaps a half an hour and then left.

That evening, at the supper table, Grayson informed me that Rick, one of the men that worked with the cattle and horses, would be spending time with me and Star each morning at ten. I was relieved that it would be Rick rather than Grayson. Grayson made me nervous.

CHAPTER 11

And so began my relationship with Star. I quickly began to look forward to seeing her and I chatted aimlessly as I brushed her. Soon Rick, who was a lanky man in his thirties, had me driving the carriage around the house and down the lane. And then to the village. Always a bit farther. It was now December, and the air was brisk, but I was beginning to enjoy the challenge of driving the carriage.

And then one morning Grayson appeared as we were eating breakfast. "I need to go to Thackeray Pond this morning for some business," he announced. He paused and looked at me. "And I would like you, June, to drive me there."

I must have given him a very startled look, because he almost smiled, but caught himself.

"I don't know if I can drive in town," I stuttered.

"Then we shall find out, won't we?" he said quietly, his eyes not leaving mine and the slightest hint of a smile on his face. I felt my face heat up and my breakfast suddenly stuck in my throat.

"How soon?"

"I'll meet you under the portico in twenty minutes if that is alright with you."

I quickly finished my breakfast and drank my coffee. Then I changed my dress and took my purse. If we were going to town, I wanted to take money along just in case I had the chance to shop.

Aunt Sarah promptly ordered some hairpins, some hankies, and a few other items.

Grayson was punctual and so was I. When Star saw me she gave me a little nicker that pleased me. I patted her head and talked just a wee bit to her. Grayson looked on with a satisfied look and then helped me into the enclosed carriage and sat next to me. Sitting this close to Grayson brought back many memories. But this was no longer the Conrad of old and I was very self-conscious with his nearness as he handed me the reins. My hands suddenly felt clammy. But I was determined not to let him know he made me nervous.

The mare and I had become friends and so I gave the reins a flip and to my relief she moved. We went out from the portico into the cold December air and down under the bare trees to the creek, which we forded without incident. Then a bit upgrade to the gatehouse. Not a word was spoken and I wondered if the whole ride would be in silence. As we passed under the gatehouse arch, Grayson spoke.

"Have you done any sewing recently?"

"No, I've had to spend too much time with Star to sew." I let the sentence hang and bit my lip to cover my smile. I was aware of Grayson turning his head a bit and knew he was looking at me.

"Well, this is your test today. If you pass, you will not need more lessons on driving. Then you will have more time to sew and in the spring you will learn to ride."

"Pardon?"

"You heard me correctly."

"Con... er Grayson, you know my wishes regarding riding."

"And you know mine."

It seemed I had no say in the matter. I let it drop. Spring was a long way off.

———

We got to the village and after a short stop at the post office, we were off again to Thackeray's Pond. I remembered the day of my arrival and that I had been in the coach that day with Grayson and had no idea who he was at the time. As if reading my thoughts he spoke.

"So you did not recognize me when we rode the same coach on your arrival?"

"No, I did not and I believe we were in the same train as well. I kept hearing the man with you but you spoke too quietly."

"That was for your benefit."

"What do you mean?"

"I did not want you to recognize me."

"You knew it was me on the train?"

"I did." I let that sink in a bit. I wondered what he would say if I asked him why he did not talk to me. But I did not.

"You had been to a funeral," I said.

"We were. I suppose you heard John talking."

"Is that the man you were with? He had a loud voice and was complaining about something."

"He was left out of the will."

I had to laugh. It just slipped out. I was relaxing a bit as we drove through the bleak countryside. "Really? That was what he was complaining about?"

"Yes. He was a cousin to the man and hoped to inherit. But the man had too many relatives."

"You were more fortunate," I said after a brief hesitation.

"And I am humbly grateful," he said softly.

I was surprised at the wording. I did not associate humility with this man. But then, I did not know him anymore. He was far different than the teenager I had known. We rode a while in silence.

"So what have you been doing these past ten years?" he asked finally.

The question came suddenly and I was unprepared. So he wondered about those years between. And he was suddenly leaving the employer-employee relationship to cure his curiosity. I did not answer right away. I still felt the hurt and humiliation of the broken engagement with Alan.

"I nursed my mother for the last year," I said finally.

I felt Grayson's eyes on me. "I read you were engaged. And rather recently."

"Yes," I said. But I said no more. After a few moments of silence, he continued.

"What happened?"

I took a deep breath. Did he really care? "I could not leave my dying mother and he got impatient."

"And?"

"I have heard he is now married to a good friend of mine. At least I thought she was a good friend." I should not have said that last part. It revealed my hurt. There was a short pause.

"I'm sorry," Grayson said softly.

His words of sympathy brought sudden tears to my eyes and I looked away from him as I blinked them back.

"Were you in love with him?" I would have resented his question except for the tone of his voice.

"I thought I was."

He said no more and to get past the hurt, I turned the table on him.

"And you? What have you been doing?"

He did not answer right away. I gave him time to think.

"My dad gave up his work on the railroad and moved here to Berks County to work for his brother who is a carriage maker. And when I heard of the opportunity to work for your uncle, I took it."

I wanted to ask about his personal life, but it seemed if he was with my uncle that long, there must have been nothing along the line of girls. At least nothing permanent. Yet, I wanted to know.

"I've been a contented bachelor," he said, as if reading my un-voiced questions. Was he telling me he was no longer interested in me? Was he regretting his determined words to me as he left me that day ten years ago?

"Why did you change your name?" I'd been wondering a long time and now I thought was the chance to ask.

Grayson smiled a bit at the question. "My name is Conrad

Grayson. From childhood on, I was Conrad. In school I was sometimes called Con for short or worse, Connie. There was a girl in our school whose name was Connie. After a while, I felt like I had a girl's name. When I moved away, I simply started going by my middle name. I don't know any girl by the name of Grayson."

We were now coming into the town of Thackeray's Pond. We passed the pond from which the town got its name and on this December day it looked cold and uninviting. I thought I could see a thin layer of ice forming on the top. I watched a hawk fly to a bare tree and sit on a broken branch while scanning the ground for a possible meal.

"Just follow the street to the center of town. There you will find a place to pull in by the inn," instructed Grayson.

After a few blocks we arrived at the inn. I led Star to the hitching post and Grayson took the reins from me.

"You passed the test," he said without a smile. "Go do whatever you wish. Just a few shops down you will find a mercantile and they have fabric that will interest you." He helped me down from the carriage. "I will meet you back here in an hour."

I went gladly down the street to the mercantile. I felt a bit of elation at being on my own and doing what I wished. I walked briskly past the shops with a curious eye to the display windows I passed, until I came to the mercantile. My excitement mounted when I entered and saw all the wonderful fabrics. I wanted some of each. But, of course, I could not. However, I was glad that I had brought a bit of money along. It was not long before I had chosen fabric for a good dress. While nursing my mother, I had had little time to sew and I needed a good dress badly. I found a lovely rose-colored fabric printed with darker roses. I fell in love with it and took it to the counter. The woman was quite talkative and we chatted about fabrics as she cut my length of material. I then looked for thread and buttons, and also Aunt Sarah's hairpins, hankies, and a bit of ecru lace. I was so engrossed that I completely lost track of time. When I went to the counter, I stopped to look again at a lovely blue fabric. I wanted it badly, but I would wait. One dress at a time. I heard someone come in the door and to my chagrin, it was Grayson.

"Oh, am I late?"

"No, but it is snowing and we should get back."

I looked out the window. It was indeed snowing. I quickly paid for my purchases and went out the door with Grayson. On the way out of the store, I saw a display of Christmas cookies. Christmas! I suddenly realized it was only a week away and I had given it no thought. Of course, with Aunt Sarah in mourning, she would not feel like celebrating. I thought back to my last Christmas. There had been very little celebration then also, with my mother sick.

It gave me a strange feeling, walking down the street once more with Grayson and I wondered what his thoughts were. I thought how we had first met and then gone window shopping together. But again, it was a completely new Grayson. It seemed our past and angry words were completely out of his mind and memory. And he almost had me convinced that it had never happened. I found myself walking rather proudly by his side.

When we got to the carriage, Grayson helped me in and then he took the reins. With a soft clucking and a flip of the reins we were off. The snow was beautiful. It would probably not be a big storm, but the flakes were large and falling steadily. As we drove down Main Street I looked around at the activity around me. There were women with baskets under their arms, others coming out of the bakery and I could catch the smell of bread and cookies as we drove past. The carriages on the street all seemed to be traveling a bit slower in the snow and I thought it all beautiful. Once we were out of town, Grayson turned to me.

"So you got your shopping done?"

"I did. And I was reminded that Christmas is only a week away and with Uncle Theodore's passing, I nearly forgot it. What happens here on Christmas?"

"I hardly know," said Grayson thoughtfully. "I always go home to my folks. I think Theodore and Sarah generally had company, but I can't say for sure."

"How far away do your folks live?" It was a bit scary asking about his folks. I had never met them and I could not really remember who was in his family.

"They live about ten miles away. I take the train from Thackeray's Pond."

"Do you have siblings?"

I held my breath. I was sure he did but did not remember any particulars. Grayson hesitated just a moment and I sensed that he turned his head just a bit in my direction.

"I do. I am the oldest and my brother David is married and living close to my parents. My sister Brenda came on a bit behind us and she just turned twenty-one."

Wow. I could hardly believe Grayson was giving me some information about himself and his family. I sat in silence a bit, enjoying the snowy countryside and musing on the information that he had just offered to me.

"And how do you celebrate Christmas?" he asked.

I sighed and did not answer immediately.

"Over the years, Christmas was never a big celebration. I only have vague memories of my father, but we sometimes had a meal with an uncle and aunt on my father's side. Last year there was almost no celebration." I sighed again. "But Alan came for supper on Christmas Eve and the next day I went to his place for an hour or so. I could not leave my mother for long."

There was silence for a few moments and I found I was enjoying the ride through the snow with Grayson. It was even nice sharing some of my sad memories with him.

"And," I added softly, "this year Aunt Sarah is in mourning."

"What can we do for your Aunt Sarah this year?" asked Grayson, after a comfortable silence.

I was surprised. But maybe I should not have been surprised. He had inherited the farm. They had treated him as a son. Although he had his own parents, he was obligated to Aunt Sarah.

"When will you go to your parents?"

"On Christmas Day. Just for the day." Suddenly Grayson turned to me. "Do you think she would come home with me?"

I looked at him in astonishment. He was looking directly at me. He knew what I was thinking. He would not take Sarah without me. I did not answer right away. I had to think this through.

"What about Becca?"

"It seems to me that she generally is picked up by a niece of hers for Christmas. And it would be better for Sarah to be away from memories on this day. She has never been to my home and she would have no time to miss Theodore, since he was never there either."

"Do you think your parents...."

"My mother would love it. They both would."

I did not answer. It was a lot to think through. As we turned in the lane and passed the gatehouse, Grayson turned to me.

"And you? What do you think?"

"I think you should talk to Aunt Sarah about it and let her decide. But you better do it soon because if she says no, I will try to make the day nice for her here."

No more was said. Star stopped under the portico. Grayson stepped out, helped me down and handed me my packages. The snow was now a couple inches thick and it looked like a fairyland. Aunt Sarah welcomed me with a savory potato soup for lunch and then I happily showed her my purchases. That night at the supper table, Grayson brought up Christmas.

"Oh, is it almost Christmas already? I had not noticed. I really don't even want to think of Christmas this year," Aunt Sarah said with a deep sigh. "It just won't be the same. I have no wish to celebrate. But I guess that is selfish of me."

"Certainly understandable," said Grayson. "But I have an idea. If you stay around here, your thoughts will all center on the fact that

Theodore is absent. We could all go to my parents' home. They would be very happy to have you."

"Oh, I couldn't go away. I never go away at Christmastime. We were always here."

"That is why you should come with me. No matter where you celebrate Christmas, your Christmas won't be the same without Theodore. If you spend it with my family, you will have other people to occupy your mind. It would be good for you."

Sarah looked at me and I said nothing. I was not sure about it myself, but I did appreciate his offer and thought for Aunt Sarah it might be the right thing.

"Let me think about it," said Aunt Sarah.

The next day I began making cookies. Even if we went away, we should take something along. I even got Aunt Sarah and Becca involved. Becca cracked the nuts and Aunt Sarah kept her eye on the cookies in the oven for me.

When the mail came, Becca got her invitation from her niece who would pick her up the morning of Christmas Day. And that evening, Aunt Sarah agreed to go away for Christmas.

On the day before Christmas, I woke up to four inches of new snow. It was still cloudy, but the sky did not look threatening. Grayson hitched up the sleigh and drove the three of us to church at four o'clock for a service of carols and scripture. The service was well attended and on the way it began to snow softly again. Becca usually did not attend church with us, but on this evening she went along and now, in the church, she sat on one side of Aunt Sarah and I sat on the other, and Grayson sat beside me. I am not sure how that happened, but I was thrilled to sit next to him. We sang carols and he had a wonderful tenor voice. I saw Mary Lou for a few minutes after the service but we did not hang around. Our supper of scalloped oysters lured us home quickly. After supper we sat in the parlor together. We just never did this, but it was Christmas Eve and a time for family, such as it was. It was somehow nice. We talked about Uncle Theodore. I think it was good for Aunt Sarah. She talked a lot about him. How they met, about the loss of the children, and the happy days on the estate. There were tears, but I could tell she was happy to talk about the love of her life. I made popcorn and hot chocolate and we had a cozy evening. During a lull in the conversation, Grayson looked at me.

"Well, June, have you found the missing money yet?"

I smiled. "Did you?"

"I really did not look, but I keep my eyes open for the shape of the container. But you did not answer my question."

"You don't trust me, do you?"

He had to smile. "I shall not answer that."

"I have not found the money, but I admit, I have plans at some point to check every nook and cranny in the gatehouse. I am just waiting for my chance. After all, GH could mean the gatehouse."

"It could, but that old man was living in the gatehouse. I don't think George could have hidden it with a permanent resident there."

Eventually Becca went to bed and Aunt Sarah followed her out of the room.

"I'll play you a game of checkers," said Grayson as Aunt Sarah went out the door. I looked up in surprise. But this was Christmas Eve and it was a holiday.

"You'll be sorry when I beat you," I said smiling.

The look on Grayson's face was enough to make me laugh. We ended up playing three games. Every one of the games a hard battle. Grayson won two and I won the last one.

"You didn't give me that game, did you?" I asked as I gloated over my hard won collection of Grayson's black pieces. When he did not answer right away I looked at him. He held my gaze.

"You'll never know."

"Grayson! I don't want you to give me the game. That takes away the joy of winning!"

He chuckled, his eyes twinkling in such a manner that I loved. Then he stopped smiling. "Do you think I would be that kind to you?" It was a bit strange the way he asked. He was not laughing and joking. He was looking at me with a very serious expression. I hesitated, his look throwing me off.

"I...don't know."

He said nothing. And then I broke the gaze and stood. Grayson stood also. I heard the clock strike midnight.

"Merry Christmas, Grayson."

"Merry Christmas, June."

—————————

Christmas morning dawned gray and cold. I was afraid Aunt Sarah would want to stay home, but she was up and doing well. Becca was picked up at ten. We left soon after, loaded down with cookies and two pies. Grayson, probably due to the day it was, acted quite cheerful and did not hold himself so distant from me as he so often did. We took the sleigh all the way to Thackeray's Pond where Grayson put the horse in the stables at the station and we took the train to Forrest End where his parents lived. The house was on the edge of town and we were picked up by Grayson's father. He was a fairly tall man who stood like a soldier and greeted us with some reserve, so much like his son. He was friendly though and after introductions we were on our way to their home.

It was noon by the time we arrived and the whole house was a potpourri of savory fragrances—the roasted goose, the stuffing and all good things that accompany such a meal, including the sweet desserts. Grayson's mother met us at the door. She was on the chubby side and had just a few strands of gray in her hair, but had a sweet smile for us. She and Aunt Sarah had met before at Bluster Hill and after greeting my aunt she turned to me. A thoughtful look seemed to come over her face, and I saw her give a quick glance at her son. I had never met any of Grayson's family that I could remember. She welcomed me warmly and by then Grayson's sister came into the room and she introduced herself.

"June Merriweather? What a lovely name. I am Brenda, Grayson's sister. So nice you could come today. The more the merrier as far as I'm concerned."

Brenda had some resemblance to Grayson, although her hair was lighter and more wavy. Her outgoing personality was in sharp contrast to Grayson, but I found her delightful.

Just then the door opened and in came a three-year-old little girl accompanied by her parents. This then, was Grayson's brother and family. Introductions were made. The brother's name was David, his wife was Janet and the little girl was Susan. David shook hands with me and then looked pointedly at his brother who ignored him, talking to Janet. I wondered what that look was about. Grayson took a chance bringing a single girl here that he was not dating.

We were soon seated at the dinner table. I was glad to see Aunt Sarah looking pleasant and talkative, which was more her normal self. Grayson's father said the blessing and the food got passed around the table. Little Susan was occupied with her relatives who showered her with a lot of attention. Every so often, she would turn her eyes to me, but she said nothing.

Later, after dishes were washed, we sat in the parlor. At one point, Mrs. Everleigh was chatting with my aunt, and Grayson was talking to his father and brother, and Janet and Brenda were talking. I sat quietly observing. Little three-year-old Susan must have seen that I was free to talk. She came quietly over to me on the couch and sat beside me, not talking, but holding her doll. Then she looked up at me shyly, not talking.

"What is your baby's name?" I asked quietly.

"Molly," she said with a small smile. "Do you have a dolly, too?"

I had to think for a second. "No," I answered. "Wait, yes, I do, but I did not bring her along today. Actually, she is probably in a drawer in my room because I don't play with her anymore."

"Does she like being in a drawer?"

"Oh, I think it is quite cozy in there."

She looked at me a moment. "You are big now."

"Yes," I answered. "But her name was Sarah. I named her for my Aunt Sarah who is talking to your Grandma just now because she is the one who gave her to me."

She contemplated that a moment. "Is that lady your mama?"

"No, she is my aunt. She was a sister to my mama."

"Where is your mama?"

"She died."

She looked at me for a moment in silence. "My kitty died, too." She thought a moment. "I cried."

"Oh, I am sure you did. That is very sad."

"Did you cry when your mama died?"

"Yes," I said, suddenly remembering my loss and realizing that this was my first Christmas without Mama. I found myself blinking back sudden moisture in my eyes.

"Well, you are having quite the conversation with June," said her mother, observing us, and I realized that it had gotten quiet in the room. Then looking at me she added, "She is usually very shy with strangers."

"Her dolly's name is Sarah," said Susan to her mother.

Now my aunt Sarah looked up and began talking to Susan and I noticed the men glancing in our direction. While the women chatted, I heard David talking to Grayson.

"Did you say June's last name is Merriweather?" Grayson must have nodded. "Didn't you date a Merriweather long ago?"

There was a hesitation while I held my breath.

"That was a long time ago and far from here."

"Yeah, I guess it was. You were a sad sack for a while afterwards."

I did not dare look in that direction but began concentrating on Susan. I noticed, however, that Grayson abruptly changed the subject.

The afternoon went by quickly. Shortly before four o'clock, Mr. Everleigh took us back to the train station and after a full day, we were home by seven. Becca soon joined us and life was back to normal.

CHAPTER 12

I woke up with tears on my face. It was the first day of the new year and my mood was certainly not the best way to start a new year, but I had dreamed of Mama and it was so real. In my dream she was not sick at all and she was so kind and caring and when I woke up and found it was a dream I could not hold back the tears. As sometimes happens, the dream was so real I could not get it out of my head. I was just homesick for Mama. Aunt Sarah was wonderful, but she was not Mama. And suddenly, my life appeared very fragmented and empty. What was I doing here? I had lost Alan because I would not leave my mother and now I was with a widowed aunt and my uncle's sister who was just a bit strange. How long would I stay here? My mind went to my employer. He paid me but I did not do much for him. I was charity for him and for Aunt Sarah. I almost panicked as I took a good look at my life. And what about Grayson? He intrigued me but gave me no hope of a future with him. And why should he? I was the one who turned my back on him. He was, according to him, a contented bachelor. And if I showed interest now, he would think it was for his money.

I finally got out of bed, still hanging on to the dream of my mother. I ached for the days before she got ill. I just wanted so badly to talk to her again.

"June," said Aunt Sarah after breakfast, "are you all right? You seem quiet today."

"I am fine," I replied. I was afraid if I would talk about Mama I would cry and upset her, too.

"Listen, June, I promised Pastor Stafford that I would visit old

Mrs. Lawrence this morning. She wants to talk to me. He will pick me up in about a half hour and I will probably be gone for most of the morning. Becca is doing laundry and maybe you can make lunch for us. You are sewing this morning aren't you?"

"Those are my plans. I will gladly make lunch."

Pastor Stafford came with his carriage not long after that and I was suddenly alone in the house. Somehow things had changed since Uncle Theodore had died. Or maybe it was just much busier in the summertime. But now there was no gardening, no canning, and not so many people stopping in since my uncle's death. Becca was here, but certainly not good company. She seldom talked and almost never started a conversation. And then my thoughts returned to Mama. I just could not get rid of my somber mood. Why was I still here with Aunt Sarah? Not because she had too much to do. Things had changed since Grayson was in charge. The chickens and egg gathering was done by a hired hand. We still churned butter sometimes and we did all the cooking since Bella left, but it was mostly just Becca, who ate very little, Aunt Sarah and me. And evenings, Grayson, who ate well. Nettie still cleaned for us, but not as many days. We could keep up with things better since Theodore was gone. But there was something missing in my life and I was pretty sure I knew what it was. I wanted to sew. I had made a couple shirts for my uncle and a dress for Aunt Sarah and one for me. I had mended Grayson's shirt and did any other mending that needed to be done here. But I wanted to sew as a way to earn money. I did not really earn my keep here. I hated being charity. Grayson forgot to tell me to do things. Just once he did have me do some paperwork for him, but it did not take more than an hour. What I really wanted to do was sew. It was something I could do. It was a gift from God. I wanted to use it.

As I glanced out the window, I saw it was beginning to rain. Not a storm that I could enjoy, but just a steady, chilly rain that froze me on the inside and made me wonder if I would ever get to do what I really wanted to do. Picking up a book that belonged in the library,

I slowly walked there to return it to its shelf. The library felt cold, although there was a low fire in the hearth. I added a log and then stood by the window and looked out at the bleak landscape as the rain hit and ran down the windows. Before I knew it, I was thinking again of Mama and now, alone in the library, I let the tears run down my face as the rain outside was running down the windowpanes. I don't know how long I stood there, lost in my despondent thoughts. I had not closed the door of the room since I was the only one around, and suddenly I heard footsteps in the hall and heading to the library. I turned quickly and locked eyes with Grayson who looked at me in surprise. Remembering my tears, I wiped my face with my hand. Grayson did not look away. He slowly closed the door and came toward me until he stood directly in front of me.

"What is wrong?"

I was embarrassed at him finding me at such a low moment. I shook my head and took a deep breath. "Nothing," I said, wiping my hand across my face once more. "Really nothing."

"You were crying," he said, not budging an inch.

I looked out the window at the blurred image of the distant village.

"I'm just...I dreamed about Mama last night...." my voice became strained as I fought fresh tears. "And I...miss her."

I should not have added the part about missing her. That made it impossible to say anything more. Grayson did not move. His voice was very soft and gentle.

"I'm sorry you lost her."

His sympathy made it worse. I could not hold back the tears. He remained standing beside me. He did not touch me, but seeing my wet handkerchief, he offered me his own.

As I took it, I fumbled to put my wet handkerchief in my dress pocket. "I'm fine, I really am."

"Let's sit down and talk," he said.

I wondered if he was going to refer to our past. We had never discussed our former dating. He motioned to a couch in front of the fire and once I was seated, he sat down beside me and leaning front looked at me.

"Are you happy here?" he asked after a moment.

"Yes, of course."

"Not of course. Is this what you want with your life?"

I had to think. I did not want to sound ungrateful. I had it good here but then why was I so unhappy this morning?

"Not quite."

I think he sensed that I was beginning to be honest. He softly questioned me.

"What is not quite right?"

I hesitated again. Could I really say what I had just been thinking?

"Well," I said slowly, "for one thing, I am not earning my keep and I feel guilty. I would like to be more useful. I do not like living off of charity, and that is what is happening here. I like being independent."

"A career woman?"

"I don't like the sound of that. Independent, as in not living off of charity."

"Would you like to milk the cows?" His suggestion was so ridiculous that I had to smile. He actually smiled also. A real smile. Not a forced one. "What would make you happy?"

I glanced hesitatingly at the handsome man sitting beside me. Did he really care what would make me happy? I could not see behind his now expressionless face.

"Tell me. You are thinking of something."

He looked like he really meant it and I somehow took heart. Maybe he would help me find my way to do what I yearned to do.

"I love to sew," I blurted out. "I would like to sew things that challenge me. Not just plain work dresses. I would like to make gowns for people for special occasions. Jackets, coats, vests. Garments that give me opportunity to be creative." I paused, embarrassed at my telling him my secret wishes. "I believe God has given me this talent and

I just...." I stopped a moment. "But don't worry yourself about me. I will find my way. For now Aunt Sarah needs me."

Grayson just looked at me for a long moment. I could see his mind was working. I wondered if he was surprised by my admission. Would he think me foolish? Watching me closely, he spoke very slowly.

"If I would let you use the gatehouse for a place to sew, would that make you happy?"

My eyes grew bright. He couldn't really mean that. "You mean...?"

"Not to *live* in," he said quickly, perhaps trying to stifle a smile, "to *sew* in."

I had to think this through. It was so sudden. I had never thought of it like this.

"How...would that be? Could I rent it?"

"Well, you wouldn't have the money to rent it from me since you would no longer be working for me. But when you start your business going...then we will talk about rent. What do you think?"

"I'd *love* it. But Aunt Sarah?"

Grayson gave me a contemplative look. "Let me think it over and talk with her."

"Is the gatehouse completely empty?"

"Empty? No, not at all. There is a fair bit of furniture in it. It will need a cleaning, but I think it would be a good solution for your sewing."

"When can I see it?"

Again, he seemed to try not to smile at my eagerness. "Anytime. I can give you the key when you want to see it."

He got up to leave. "Con....I mean Grayson, I am...grateful."

He did not comment on the fact that I had nearly called him Conrad. He just looked a moment at me and I wanted so badly to know what he was thinking. How could he be so kind to me after I spurned him? He was all I could ask for. He could provide a living for me, he was kind and considerate. The Conrad I had known no longer existed.

"You are grateful," he replied slowly, "but you are also happier. And that makes me happy."

And with that he turned and left the room.

———

To say I was excited is to put it mildly. I could think of nothing else. True to his promise, Grayson talked with Aunt Sarah. She was hesitant when she realized I would be out of the house so much, but she was happy for me and gave her consent.

We went to see the gatehouse the next afternoon. Grayson was going into town and dropped Aunt Sarah and me off at the gate. It was a very exciting moment for me. We entered the door leading from the portico, which brought us into the sitting room. Beyond this room was a small kitchen and off of that, a washroom. The water pump was outside and all water had to be brought in. Between the kitchen and sitting room was a stairway. Upstairs was the bedroom. In this particular gatehouse, there was a room built right over the drive that had a window in all four directions. The room had a cot in it and a few shelves plus a small cubbyhole where, I presume, Grayson had found the fabric. This room was a bit higher than the room Grayson had used as a bedroom and there was an enclosed walkway on the roof from the lower bedroom to the room over the drive, which ended in a few steps to the upper room.

"Oh, Aunt Sarah, I am so excited. It is almost like having my own house."

"I don't think it will ever be your house—unless you marry someone who would be willing to share this tiny house with you."

"No married man would want to live in the gatehouse unless he were the gatekeeper. And that does not seem necessary at this point," I added. "When was the gatehouse built?"

"Oh, it goes back to Theodore's grandfather, Isaac. He came into some money, I forget the details and he bought this land. I think I told you he was a rather obnoxious man and had some enemies. He liked gatehouses and decided he needed one to keep his enemies off his land. He built the gatehouse and he even put a man in it. And ever after that, there was a man in there. Just about ten years ago, old Justin died and then Grayson came and needed a place to live. So there you have it."

"I never thought I would be inside this place," I said, taking in every nook and cranny.

"I would want you to be with Becca and me at night. But you could have a quilting or crocheting party here sometimes."

"What a wonderful idea!"

Aunt Sarah laughed. "Your eyes are sparkling. It is good of Grayson to offer this to you. We will need to get Nettie to help clean it so it gets done quickly."

"Sarah, I forgot to give this to you earlier," said Grayson that evening as we were seated around a meal of roasted chicken.

"A letter? I don't seem to get too many letters. Oh, this looks like it is from Catherine. That would be a niece of Theodore's. I'll eat my supper and then read it."

At the end of the meal, while I went for our dessert of cherry cobbler, she opened the letter. When I came back to the table she and Grayson were sitting in deep thought. The letter lay opened on the table.

"Is something wrong?" I asked.

"Well, we have a problem," answered my aunt. "Lizzie, who is a sister to Becca, has been staying with her niece and husband. Now they are moving to Ohio and Lizzy does not want to move to Ohio. Catherine wants to know if we can take her in. She forgets I no longer own this place."

I looked at Grayson. Yes, this was actually his problem. This was not Sarah's house anymore and it was his decision. All kinds of scenes flipped through my head. Grayson could simply say no. But he was given the estate by Sarah and Theodore. This was Theodore's sister. He would not say no. I hoped he would not give them the gatehouse. He would not dare, would he? On second thought, they would be too isolated there.

"When are they moving?" I ventured to ask.

"In two weeks. Lizzy was planning to move along and suddenly changed her mind. Catherine says Lizzy is also deaf and is sometimes not very pleasant."

We ate our dessert in silence, each lost in our own thoughts and fears. Grayson was saying nothing. Finally, finished with his dessert, he stood.

"I would like to look around the house. In each room." He looked at me.

"Go ahead. It is your house," said Aunt Sarah. "I think my room is presentable."

"Let me go and check my room first," I said.

I quickly ran up the stairs and made sure my room was presentable. Then while I did the kitchen wash up, Aunt Sarah put the food away. We were quiet with our thoughts. Another person here? An unpleasant person? How would she and Becca get along? But they were sisters.

Grayson made his tour of the house. When he returned, he called us to the parlor.

"I have a suggestion," he said, looking at my aunt. "If you, Sarah, are willing to take your sister-in-law in, I will try to make it possible. I am thinking of the little house where I live. I know it was just fixed up for me, but I think it would be good for them to have their own space. And they would have good access to the kitchen. Furthermore, I have discovered that most people who come here to see me, generally come first to this house. That is always an interruption for you. If I would give the little house to them, I would like to live in the side rooms coming in from the portico. The library could be my office as well as the library. And the guest room across the hall could be my bedroom. What do you think?"

"It is your house. It sounds fine to me if that is what you would like," replied my aunt.

Grayson looked at me. "And you?"

"I have nothing to say. It is your house."

"I would like your opinion." Why did he always look so serious?

"It sounds good to me. But would you be cramped? You own the house and have the least space."

"The bedroom is my personal space. It is large enough for a chair or two. And the library, although it is open to you both, will be my office. I will claim free access to the parlor and I already have access to the kitchen and dining room. That is good for me."

He looked back at Aunt Sarah. "And if anyone thinks it is inappropriate for me to be in the house with you two ladies, we can assure them that we sleep on different floors."

———

Two days later, Nettie and I went up to the gatehouse. I was so excited. I was going to be living at least part time in the beloved gatehouse. While Nettie cleaned the downstairs, I worked upstairs. But first, I simply prowled around. Not that there was all that much room to prowl, but I looked out each window and just imagined what could be done in each room if I did live there.

Knowing that Grayson had taken everything he wished to take out of the house, I felt free to look in some boxes in this upper room that Grayson used for storage. I was thrilled to find more fabric. When I thought I had finally gone through everything, I saw another seemingly empty lower shelf. I took my dust cloth and gave it a swipe and found it was not completely empty. I pulled out a piece of cloth and gasped, not believing what I had found.

The sunbonnet!

My mouth fell open. The sunbonnet looked exactly like the one I had lost. I just held it in my hand and looked at it for a long time. Could the woman who had sewed in this room have possibly made a sunbonnet exactly like the one I lost? Had she perhaps made them and sold them? And one was left? But she lived here pretty long ago. It did not seem possible. Grayson was the only one who lived here since she did and she had died before her husband. Grayson had heard about my losing the sunbonnet. He had heard it described. Had he possibly looked for one for me to replace it? That seemed impossible, too. What would he care about a sunbonnet? Even one that I lost. I did not know if I should take the sunbonnet or leave it. It was a mystery to me and after staring at it in wonder for several minutes, I finally put the sunbonnet back on the shelf where I had found it. I needed to think this through before I said anything about it.

In the meantime, every still moment, I was dreaming of having my friends over for a handwork afternoon. I wanted to share this gatehouse with Mary Lou especially. I had decided that I would keep the main room downstairs for the sitting room. Or, in my case, a room to have a party. I would have my sewing machine upstairs in what had certainly been Grayson's bedroom. Since I was not to stay overnight there, I would not need a bedroom. There was a cot in the room over the drive that could be used in an emergency. The little kitchen would come in handy for snacks for myself and the girls. Aunt Sarah said if I would do all her sewing and mending, she would not need the sewing machine. It was mine. The gatehouse was now cleaned, and Grayson and one of his men took the sewing machine up to my new sewing room. I was so thrilled. I could not wait to start sewing.

The next thing was to get supplies. Fabric, thread, needles, buttons and all sewing notions needed to be bought. Of course, I had some fabric, but I wanted new fabric for gowns that I hoped to sell to the upper class of our society. Someday I wanted to go to the stores in Thackeray's Pond, but for now, the village store would do.

"What will you sew first?" my aunt wanted to know when she saw me making a list of things to buy.

"I think I will first sew a few dresses and hang them in a store to let people know that I sew. Not just here, but in Thackeray's Pond. Then I hope to get orders so I can get into things more challenging."

"I have an idea that might be challenging for you," said Aunt Sarah.

"What would that be?"

"I know Grayson has been looking for a new suit and vest. You could try a few vests and if he likes them maybe he will order a suit from you."

That made me excited and scared at the same time.

It was a cold, damp January day and the sun was hidden in light clouds, but in spite of the weather, I took the carriage and Aunt Sarah and I went shopping in our little village. The store clerk was a woman from our church, whose name was Doris. She and her husband owned the store.

"Hello, Sarah and June," she said with a smile. "Come in and look around. I don't see you much in here anymore, Sarah. Well, I guess it was Theodore who generally came in. Too bad he is gone. But he is in a better place. I hear the manager now owns the estate. That was a big gift to him. But I guess he will take good care of you, Sarah. Is Becca still there?"

The woman finally could take a breath and Aunt Sarah chatted a few more minutes with the woman while I began looking around the store. Behind me, I heard Doris telling Aunt Sarah who in the village had a baby, who broke a finger, and who was out with a fellow she should not have been out with. While I was looking at fabric, Aunt Sarah told Doris what I was planning to do. The news of my new venture would soon be known. I could have spent all day looking at fabric, but I was limited in what I could buy. I did purchase fabric for a dress and also for an evening gown. I probably would not find a buyer for the gown here in the village, but I wanted to try making it. I also, with help from Aunt Sarah, bought fabric that would make a possible vest for Grayson. She had gone into Grayson's room the previous day to check the size of his vest, and now, equipped with patterns and all the notions I would need for my sewing, we headed back to the gatehouse. Once there, I deposited my goods and then took Aunt Sarah home. After lunch I would walk back out the lane and set up for sewing. But before leaving the gatehouse, I built a fire in the hearth. I would need heat in here and the house was cold.

I ate a hurried sandwich at noon, too excited to eat much. I was even too much in a hurry to eat any dessert, which was a wonder to both Aunt Sarah and myself.

"Go on," said Aunt Sarah, "I will clean up and then take a nap. That cold air made me sleepy."

The walk seemed long and cold to the gatehouse, but it was just because I was so eager to get there. The fire was still good and it looked like someone had added wood to the fire. Had Grayson been here? He knew I planned to work here today.

The afternoon flew by. I had to get organized, and by the time I had that done, it was time to head home. The daylight hours were few and although there was a window to the west, there was too little light. I set out to look for more lamps and was soon happy with the light they gave. But I did not have time to sew.

Just before leaving for home, I heard a horse whinny. Looking out the window, I saw a young man that I knew worked for Grayson, arrive with a load of wood on a wagon. I watched as he pulled in behind the gatehouse and then unloaded the wood close to the back door. In my excitement, I had forgotten that wood would have to be brought in for the fire. I had, in my selfishness in wanting the gatehouse, not thought of the extra work for Grayson.

I went to the door and called out to him. "I don't know your name, but thank you for bringing the wood."

The young man stopped working and smiled. "Glad to do it for you. My name is Marley."

"Well, thank you, Marley. My name is June."

I carried a few logs into the house before leaving and then placed some more on the back porch where they would be easy to get in bad weather.

I headed back to the house while Marley was still straightening the pile of wood against the house, but I had not gone far, before I heard the wagon coming behind me. I turned to wave as he drove by, but instead, he stopped.

"Do you need a ride?" he asked.

I hesitated. It was nearly time for supper and I was running a bit late. He seemed very nice.

"Sure."

He gave me a hand to help me up and soon we were driving in the lane together.

"Are you living in the gatehouse now?"

"No, I am trying to get established as a seamstress, and this is where I work."

"Did you just move here?"

"I've been living here at Bluster Hill since last summer. Have you worked here long?"

"A couple years. I live in a small cabin on the property here."

We were crossing the low stream, which was now ice. "Have you gone skating on the pond yet?" he asked.

"No. I did not even think of it. Is it frozen enough?"

"Sure. I often skated on it other years. You should try it out."

"I might. But I must find some skates first."

We were at the door and I thanked him and jumped down.

"Anytime. Anytime at all. Don't forget the pond."

At supper that evening, I asked Grayson about the pond.

"I hear people go skating on the pond here. Is it frozen yet?"

"Who told you that?"

"The young man, what was his name, oh Marley, who brought the wood."

"You talked to him?"

"Yes, he brought me back. I was just leaving."

I thought it took Grayson a long time to answer. "Yes, we do use the pond for skating in the winter. I suppose it should be well frozen now. Some of the villagers used to come. Haven't seen any skaters yet, but they know they are welcome. Marley just asked me about it today. He offered to build a bonfire for any night skating."

"Oh, that was always fun having the church youth and some of the villagers here," said Aunt Sarah. "Sometimes we made a party of it. But you are the boss now, Grayson."

Grayson looked at me. "Do you have skates?"

"Not anymore. I had some but I really don't know what happened to them."

"We should have some around here. You just need the right kind of shoe to fasten them to. It seems over the years we somehow got a collection of them," said Aunt Sarah.

"There are some hanging in the shed," said Grayson to me. "Go check them out."

CHAPTER 13

ut life seemed to get ahead of us and I did not get to go skating. I did see a few villagers on the pond the next afternoon, but that was the day that Lizzie arrived and Grayson had not yet moved into the house. There was nothing to do except put her in a guest room upstairs until Grayson moved out. Grayson's men had started trimming the apple trees in the orchard and Grayson was needed there. Lizzie seemed to take it in stride that we were not quite ready for her and for that, I was grateful. Of course, in the end, it made us more work, putting her in a temporary bedroom and later the big move to the little house. And the day after Lizzie arrived, Grayson had to go away for two days on business. Besides that, he had to move all his office work into the library, which had ample room, but we needed the men to do it. So we had Lizzie, who turned out to be much more noisy and grumpy than Becca in our living space until we got them moved.

To my amazement, I found out that Becca had no trouble talking, she just was not outgoing and now with a talkative sister here, there was a lot of talking between them. This would have been all right, but Lizzie who was very deaf, shouted to Becca, and Becca, who was equally deaf, shouted back, because otherwise, Lizzie would not hear her and she would have to shout it a second time. The whole rigamarole of moving people from one bedroom to the next was too much for Lizzie to understand and she tended to complain easily. I sure hoped it would change once they were in their own space. We spent a lot of time trying to tell Lizzie the whys and wherefores of it all and in the end we were shouting at her because that was the only way she could understand. But it left Aunt Sarah and me plum played out. Aunt Sarah and I eagerly awaited Grayson's return after just one day of Lizzie in the house. The move had to happen as soon as he came back.

When Grayson arrived late the next afternoon, we saw he did not come alone. He had been to a meeting regarding the raising of beef cattle and it seemed this man wanted to see the estate and see his cattle. They arrived right before supper and we quickly added a plate to the table. Now we had Becca, Lizzie, Grayson, his friend Abram, Aunt Sarah, and me all at the table. Six of us, and that should have been no problem. With just Becca it would have been fine. But Lizzie was another story altogether.

When the men came to the table, we were all waiting to sit down. All except Lizzie who had taken a seat immediately and seeing us still standing asked loudly why no one else was sitting. After a whole day of shouting at her, we just ignored her and introductions were made and then the rest of us took our seats. Grayson said the prayer and we commenced to pass the food.

Grayson sat at the head of the table, his guest at his left, then Becca and finally Sarah at the other end of the table. That left Lizzie next to Sarah and me to Grayson's right and his friend across from me. We were a strange assortment of people. Grayson had, over the ten years of his time here on the estate, met Lizzie a couple times, but Lizzie evidently had no recollection of him.

"Who are these two men eating here?" demanded Lizzie as soon as the prayer was said although introductions had just been made. She had understood nothing.

"You remember Grayson," Aunt Sarah said too quietly. "He worked a long time for your brother."

"Gray what?" Lizzie demanded. "Talk louder."

Aunt Sarah did not repeat herself. It would not have helped. I tried to get Lizzie's thoughts on the food and quietly passed her the potatoes. But that lasted only a few seconds. Her eyes went back to Grayson and then to me. The men bothered her.

"Who is he?" she asked, looking at me.

"Grayson works here," I said loudly, hoping she would be satisfied. I hoped Grayson did not care that I did not say he owned the estate. I just did not want to get into an argument with her about that. She then glared at Abram who was trying to hold a conversation with Grayson."

"Who is he?" she asked, looking at me. I looked directly at her and hoped she would read my lips.

"His friend," I said, although I had no clue if they were friends.

I must have talked loud enough, because she took the time to eat a few bites before she took to studying Grayson again. He tried to keep up his conversation, but I could see he was distracted by Lizzie and I did not blame him. We should have made the two sisters eat alone in the kitchen.

"Are you his wife?" she asked me, jabbing her fork in Grayson's direction.

I think I must have turned a bit red, but I tried to remain cool. This supper was a disaster and I vowed this would never happen again. I looked directly at her and shook my head.

"What?"

"No." I said it louder.

"Why not?" she asked taking a bite of meatloaf.

I was not aware of it, but no one was speaking and I was completely frustrated with Lizzie.

"Because he never asked me!" I shouted.

After a shocked silence that lasted just a second or two, everyone burst into laughter. Even Lizzie joined in. Our guest had a rather high voice for a man and it came out more like a cackle. He laughed and laughed and in my peripheral vision I could see that Grayson had joined in the laughter. My face felt like it might explode and I even thought Grayson's face looked a bit red. The conversation was clearly out of control and somehow, when we all burst out laughing, the tension evaporated. There was no trying to make this a formal meal with a visitor. This was, God bless her, Uncle Theodore's sister, and she was not only deaf, she was not quite up to par on social graces. I was beginning to doubt her mental facilities. I felt Grayson's eyes on my red face. I gave him a quick glance.

"I'm sorry," I mumbled quickly and then did not look at him directly anymore during the meal.

Lizzie finally began to enjoy her food and she made some noises while eating that were not very pleasant, but I was happy to see her enjoying her food and not talking. Once we were finished eating and the men went into the library to talk, I took a deep breath. Lizzie and Becca took over the parlor and Aunt Sarah and I washed the dishes and did a sad review of our meal. What a night. After the clean up, I got a guest room ready upstairs for Abram. I did not see our guest again.

The men were out of the house before breakfast and I did not see Grayson until the evening meal. This meal went far better than the previous evening and after dessert, Becca and Lizzie went into the parlor to knit and Grayson asked Aunt Sarah and me to come to his living quarters to talk.

"I think it is clear that Becca and Lizzie need their own space," he said, "and I would like to see them over here in this part of the house as soon as possible."

"I am sorry for last night's disaster," I mumbled, not looking at Grayson.

"It all turned out fine after we laughed," said Aunt Sarah. "There was no need anymore to try to put on any airs. It was a bit like an evening with the loonies but your guest seemed to take it in stride. What do you think, Grayson?" asked Aunt Sarah.

"I would not want to repeat the evening, but I do think June saved the day." He looked at me. "Thank you for your good intentions with her."

Grayson really was a gentleman, I had to admit. He was tiptoeing around my terrible statement and frustration and even thanking me.

The next day we spent serious time rearranging the rooms Grayson would occupy and by evening he was in. He had help from his men to haul the furniture. And then we moved Becca and Lizzie. Becca sort of took it without a grumble. She was the one who should have been upset. After all, she had been in her bedroom for a long time. But I think the move to the house extension was interesting and new to her and they were both reminded that they would have use of the kitchen. We did not add that when we had guests, they would be served either in their own space or in the kitchen. We would not take the chance on another fiasco like the last one.

"Well, June," said Aunt Sarah to me at the super table that evening, "are you set up to sew in the gatehouse?"

"I am. And now that everyone here is finally in their stationary quarters, I think I shall have time to sew, and I can hardly wait."

Just then I remembered the sunbonnet. With all that was going on, it had slipped my mind.

"There is the weirdest thing that happened," I said. "I can't make head or tail out of it. But when I was cleaning the upper room in the gatehouse the other day, I was wiping down the bottom shelf, and I felt something under the dust cloth. When I pulled it out, I couldn't believe my eyes."

"What did you find?" asked Aunt Sarah.

"A sunbonnet."

"Well, that is not so surprising. It probably belonged to Justin's wife who lived there."

"But it is a new sunbonnet."

"Well, she did a lot of sewing. My guess is that she made many sunbonnets."

"But Aunt Sarah, this sunbonnet looks *exactly* like the one I lost."

I sat back and let that sink in her head.

She did not seem rattled by it. "Well, it is amazing that it is the same material and color, but I don't see it as impossible. It isn't like it was a century ago."

"But Aunt Sarah, it also had this extra long brim. I bought it because I thought it was *funny.* Most sunbonnets have a short brim. When I put it on, I couldn't see anything but straight ahead."

Before she had time to respond, the knocker sounded and Grayson, who had just listened to my rantings without a comment, got up to answer the door. Since he had moved in, most of the time the knocks were for him. He came back with Pastor Stafford.

"I seem to come when there is food to be had," said the pastor, as Grayson pulled out a chair for him and I went to the kitchen for another plate.

"I hope it is just a friendly visit," said Aunt Sarah.

"I only wish it were," said the pastor with a sigh. "But how is everybody here?" he asked, looking at Becca and Lizzie, whom he had already met a few days before.

"Good," answered my aunt. "Becca and Lizzie now live in the extended house and Grayson has his rooms at the side entrance."

I saw the pastor's eyes go from Grayson to me, but he said nothing.

"He sleeps downstairs and June and I have our rooms on the second floor," offered my aunt.

"There are always adjustments," said the pastor, taking a bite of meatloaf, but I had the feeling his mind was not really on us and our living arrangements.

There followed a bit of silence while we waited for we knew not what. The pastor finally put down his fork.

"I wish things were as well at the Gables as they are here," he said finally.

"Is someone not well?" ventured Aunt Sarah.

"Donna is missing."

"What do you mean, missing?"

"It seems she and her boyfriend eloped. Or so were their intentions in the letter they found."

We sat in stunned silence.

"Since when?" asked Grayson.

"Since yesterday."

"Poor, poor girl," said Sarah. "Why? Why would she do such a thing? I presume it is with the boy she's been dating?"

"Yes it is, and he remains a bit of a mystery. He seemed nice enough, but Donna's parents did not like him. Felt he was covering something up. He was too quiet about his past. He is a few years older than Donna, and she was hurt by her parents' rejection of her friend and you know how youth are. Impetuous. Not realistic. They think they can overcome all odds. They do not want anyone telling them what to do." Pastor Stafford sighed.

"The parents must be frantic," said my aunt.

"They are. I tried to calm them. They are thinking the worst. Hopefully the couple will come back, whether married or not and we can work on rebuilding relationships."

The pastor's eyes now fell on me.

"I have come tonight to talk to you, June. I have a favor to ask of you." He just looked at me a moment and I wondered what he wanted with me.

"I have every reason to believe they will return. I have met the fellow and do not find him a dangerous person. I believe they love each other. I don't know how soon they will return but I think the family is feeling anger along with anxiety. Donna may need a female friend outside of the family. Someone who has not been hurt by this deed. Someone mature enough to be able to speak honestly and lovingly to the girl. I thought of you. When that time comes, would you be willing to reach out to her?"

"Of course," I said rather hesitantly, "although I don't really know her well. I have spoken with her a few times at church. Not much more."

"You seem to be the person God laid on my heart in thinking about this. Keep her in your prayers. I will try to keep you informed. And thank you for your willingness."

Pastor Stafford left soon afterwards. I was left with a feeling of helplessness. But at the same time, I had a strong feeling of wanting to help this girl and her family. I was unmarried myself. Could I really help her? Would she want my help?

I was washing up in the kitchen as I mused on what the pastor had said, when I happened to look out the window. I saw a glow. I went to the door. There was a bonfire at the pond. Suddenly I wanted to go skating. I did not know when I had skated last. In Trinkels, where I grew up, we had a river that usually froze up in the winter. However, sometimes it was too rough to skate on and somehow, I rarely got to skate. Now I wanted to. I wanted time to think about Donna. I wanted the fresh air in my face. I wondered if Marley had built the fire. It seemed I had heard he had offered to. As soon as I finished the clean up, I told Aunt Sarah where I was going and got dressed. It was cold and I bundled up. I had not yet gone to the shed to look at the skates, but I knew which shed they were suppose to be in. I took a lantern and hurried out the door. I had no trouble finding the skates. There were a few pairs hanging on the wall of the shed. Finding a wooden box to sit on, I tried fastening the skates to my shoes. It worked! I took the lantern and headed down to the pond.

Once at the pond, I saw there were maybe a dozen youth skating already. I was not there long before Marley found me.

"Hey! You came!" he greeted me. He twirled around a few times in front of me and then stopped in front of me and held out his hand.

"Skate with me?" He had a broad smile.

I simply put my hand in his. "But I have not been on skates for a couple years, so start slowly," I cautioned.

He was accommodating. It did not take long before we were flying around the ice. I slowly managed to find a few others on the pond that I knew. Brian was there. I looked around carefully, but did not see Gerald. I sure hoped he would not come. Finally, a few from our church showed up, among them Mary Lou and her brother. Soon Annelie showed up although Jeannie did not. I had made several rounds with Marley and now I told Marley I wanted to stop to see friends. He brought me to the bonfire and then he skated off again.

"Who were you skating with?" Mary Lou asked. "I don't know him."

"He works for Grayson. I just met him the other day. He brought wood to the gatehouse."

"Oh. Are you sewing there already?"

"No, but one of these days I shall. And then we must have a sewing afternoon with Annelie and Jeannie. Do they do any handwork?"

"Sure. Crocheting and knitting. Of course you will be sewing, right?"

"Right. But we shall have parties there and I just can't wait."

"Neither can I. But let's skate, shall we?"

And we were off. It wasn't long before Annelie was skating with other boys and later Mary Lou skated with Marley.

"Nice guy," she said when he brought her back.

"Seems nice. I really don't know him."

Mary Lou came closer to me. "Did you hear about Donna Gable?"

"Yes. I feel so bad for the family. And for her. I think she will regret it."

"How could she be so stupid?" asked Mary Lou.

"I don't know. We all make mistakes. Some mistakes are worse than others."

It was getting cold. We stood too long without skating. Finally, Marley came by again and asked me to skate. He was a good skater and I enjoyed skating with him. As we skated past the bonfire, I saw a tall dark figure that had not been there before. Grayson. I had not seen him skate all evening. I really don't think he was there, until now. He watched us skate past but did not make a move to get on the ice. After a few more rounds with Marley, I called it quits.

"It was fun, Marley, but I'm done. It is getting too cold for me."

"I better call it a day soon, too. I hope the ice stays a while."

"I hope, too."

He skated off. I removed my skates. Since the shed was on the way, I dropped my skates off there. I went into the house and found Aunt Sarah at the stove making me some hot chocolate.

"Oh thanks, this will hit the spot. I am half frozen."

"Who was out there tonight?"

"I did not know everybody, but Mary Lou and her brother, Annelie and a few others from church were there."

"And who did you skate with?" she asked with a twinkle in her eyes.

"Marley. I skated pretty long with him. He works here. Do you know him?"

"Yes. I think he has worked here a number of years. Seems like a nice sort of person. Was Grayson out there?"

"I saw him standing at the fire, but did not see him on skates."

Just then the door opened and Grayson came in. He looked at me but said nothing.

"How about some hot chocolate?" asked Aunt Sarah. "June was just about frozen when she came in."

"How was the skating?" He was looking at me.

"Good. Smooth ice."

"And Marley is a good skater?"

I found the question strange. Marley had skated here long before I was here. Grayson knew he was a good skater. I hesitated just a second.

"Very good. Were you skating?"

"No." He said no more. I wanted to ask why, but did not dare, somehow. Sometimes he was a closed book. A closed book with a rubber band around it. He took a sip of his hot chocolate.

"Why didn't you skate, Grayson?" asked Aunt Sarah. "I thought you liked skating."

Grayson swirled the hot chocolate in his cup and shrugged. He gave no answer. When he finished his chocolate, he glanced at me.

"I wish you all a good night," he said, and without another word, he left the room.

CHAPTER 14

It was Grayson's birthday and the occasion would be celebrated with his brother David and his wife Janet and his cousin Dale and his girlfriend Shanna. David and Janet I had met at Christmas, but the cousin and his girlfriend I had never met. They were expected in the early afternoon.

I spent the morning sewing, but I had promised to stay home and help with the birthday celebration in the afternoon. Having finished what I was working on, I was just ready to leave my sewing room, when I remembered the sunbonnet. Aunt Sarah had not thought it so strange that I found an exact replica of the one I bought, but I did. I decided I would take it to her, although she had never seen the one I bought. I quickly went to the shelf and reached down for it.

The shelf was empty.

I got on my hands and knees. It was gone. Shaking my head, I walked down the stairs and out the door. Now I was really frustrated. I had not dreamed it. Had I done something else with it? No, I had let it there where I had found it. I was not sure why I had left it.

My head was still spinning when I got home, but when I tried to tell Aunt Sarah about it, she only half listened to what I was saying. We had work to do.

Soon after lunch, Grayson's guests arrived. We met them shortly thereafter. I found both Shanna and Janet easy to relate to. They spent the afternoon going horseback riding with Grayson. A part of me wished I were going with them. I was looking forward to suppertime. I was living with three old women and I always enjoyed it when other young girls visited us.

Aunt Sarah and I spent the whole afternoon trying to make it a special occasion for Grayson. Besides the food, we also had the vest wrapped up to present to him after the meal. We had special candles on the table and used Aunt Sarah's best china, which were decorated with blue flowers and gold trim. I thought the table looked fit for a queen. No, for a king, for it was Grayson's birthday. Just a half hour before the meal, I went upstairs and changed into my best blue dress. It was one I had recently made and I was secretly well pleased with it.

We had the beef roast and all the vegetable dishes on the table before we called Grayson and his guests into the room and I was quite happy when I saw a very pleased expression on Grayson's face as he entered. He hid so much of his emotions that I felt I had scored a point when he glanced over the table and then looked at me. He could not completely hide his pleasure. I saw his eyes slide over me and hoped he liked the dress that I wore just for him. The meal was eaten and enjoyed with gusto. Cold weather makes for good appetites and the food was consumed with much laughter. His guests were talkative and spoke often of people and things I knew nothing about, but it was fun just to listen to them talk. Even Grayson talked more than usual. He could be so silent sometimes.

"So you live here with three women," said his brother during a lull in the conversation. "Just when are you planning to cut that down to one?"

I held my breath. I was the only young person in the house and I concentrated on my food and did not look at anyone.

"Why switch to just one when I can live with three?"

"That does not cut it, Grayson," said his cousin Dale. "You, too, will need an heir. It isn't too early to think about that."

There was silence. Grayson took a sip of water before he answered.

"Any suggestions?"

"Yes, I have, but I'll keep it for later."

I did not dare look at anyone. It seemed they were done eating and I was eager for a change of subject.

"We will serve coffee and pie in the parlor," announced Aunt Sarah, probably sensing my discomfort, "but first, Grayson, I think it is time for you to open your presents."

We all made our way to the parlor. I had to smile. Grayson was clearly not at ease with getting gifts and I had to wonder how he would react to the vest I had made for him. Once we were seated in the parlor, his sister-in-law, Janet, handed him a gift.

"For you on your twenty-eighth birthday, Grayson."

"Twenty-ninth," I corrected without thinking.

"Twenty-ninth? Are you really twenty-nine?" she asked, clearly surprised.

In the meantime, I looked at Grayson and I am afraid I had scared eyes. Grayson looked steadily at me. I had goofed. I should not know how old he was. Janet looked at me.

"Are you sure he is twenty-nine?"

"Am I wrong?" I asked Grayson.

"I am twenty-nine," he replied, looking at Janet.

"How did you know how old he was?"

I looked at Janet, scrambling for an answer. "He must have mentioned his age sometime," I said with a shrug.

"Well, Grayson, back to our conversation, in that case, it is very high time for you to think of matrimony. Bachelorhood is all right for a time, but we are tired of waiting for you to find a wife."

"Past time," added his cousin Dale. "Soon you will have no choice but to take an old lady with missing teeth."

We all laughed and even Grayson smiled but made no comment as he unwrapped his gift.

"Can we still hope?" pressed Janet.

"I need to find the right woman."

A part of me went silent. If he was still looking, it was not me. Had I spoiled all chances back when I was too young to know better?

I tried my best to keep cheerful, but I had to work at it. I felt like I had been rejected in front of the whole group. I tried to concentrate on the gift he was opening.

It was a new blue shirt. The discussion ended as this gift was followed by a pair of gloves from his cousin.

Aunt Sarah then looked at me. "Will you get our gift? I believe I left it in the dining room."

I had hoped she would give it, but I could not refuse. I got up, picked up the package that had been lying on a table and seeing another package next to it, I picked that up also. It was very small and light. It was not wrapped too well, and I wondered if it was a joke gift and wondered who had brought it.

"Here, Grayson, I don't know who the smaller package is from, but this one is from Aunt Sarah and me."

He ignored the smaller package and slowly unwrapped the larger package. He took a long look at the vest while the others looked on. Then he looked at me.

"Is this your work?"

"I made it and Aunt Sarah paid for the material."

There were instant exclamations about the vest. I was secretly very happy with it. I had seen vests that had extra stitching on the front and I liked it and tried to duplicate it. It gave it more style. I could see that Grayson was very pleased although, as was his way, he tried not to show too much. However, he thanked Aunt Sarah and me sincerely and I was happy, assured that we had pleased him. My spirits lifted a little bit.

He then looked at the other package, took it in his hands as if to open it and abruptly stopped. He then looked at me.

"This package has your name on it."

"What? It can't possibly be for me."

"See for yourself." He got up, crossed the room, and handed it to me. I was dumbstruck. There, on a little slip of paper was my name. I had not even noticed the name on the gift. When had this arrived and why on earth was I getting a gift? I looked it over carefully. I did not recognize the handwriting. In fact, I still thought it was a joke gift because the handwriting looked somehow as if it had been purposely scribbled.

"Look, I do not know where this package came from, but I am quite sure it is not for me. There is no reason that I would receive a gift and since it is your birthday, Grayson, I think you should open it."

"It is not for me if it has your name on it," he replied, not budging from his seat.

"Open it," said Aunt Sarah, clearly puzzled. "It wasn't on the table when I put our gift down, or at least I did not notice it, but it seems to have your name on it. Maybe you will know once you see the gift."

"You don't know anything about it?" I asked her.

"No, of course I don't. I don't know how it got here although several persons stopped in today."

Almost reluctantly, I opened it. I hated to. I was sure it was really for Grayson and I did not want to open a gift meant for him. It was wrapped loosely and it was soon opened. And when I saw what it was, it was clear to me that it really was for me. For inside the package was none other than...the sunbonnet.

I gasped and stared in disbelief at the sunbonnet for several long moments. This made absolutely no sense. Finally, I looked blankly at the group watching me. I was dumbfounded.

"I can't believe it. It is the sunbonnet! This is just impossible. I can't figure this out. I think there must be a friendly ghost having fun with me. There is no rhyme nor reason why this sunbonnet should be here."

The others looked at me blankly. Finally Shanna asked, "What's with the sunbonnet?"

"I lost it in Thackeray's Pond where I bought it. Then I found it in the gatehouse. When I went back for it today, it was gone and now here it is. I do not understand it and I'm beginning to think I am losing my mind."

The others laughed, clearly enjoying the tale, but I was too confused to laugh.

"Did any one of you bring this package this evening?" I asked the guests, determined to know what was going on. I knew it was not Grayson, because he had nearly opened it himself. And Aunt Sarah was clearly in the dark about it also.

Everyone gave me a negative answer. I was sure they were telling the truth because they were showing amusement as well as curiosity. They found it funny and odd, but I found it mind boggling.

"Who was in this house today?" I asked, looking at Aunt Sarah.

"The pastor stopped in to see me," she began.

"And Nettie came to clean," I added.

"And a man came to see Grayson, but he simply came in the door and was soon out again. And Becca and her sister were in and out sometimes." I could think of no one else.

No one had any clue how the gift arrived.

"I wonder if it could have been Nettie? Did I tell her I lost the one I bought? I don't remember," I mused to myself.

"This sounds interesting," said David finally. "But what is the story about the sunbonnet? Whose sunbonnet is it and why did you take it to Thackeray's Pond?"

"I *bought* it there. I did not take it there."

"And you lost the package there before you got home?"

"Not the package..."

"Or did you wear it there?" he asked jokingly and the others laughed.

"Well," I hesitated, "sort of."

"What do you mean sort of?" asked David.

"Well, I ...used it for a short time."

"What do you mean you used it?" asked Aunt Sarah, whom I had not told about its use. "Did you actually wear it?"

I hesitated. "Yes, but just for a short time. Sort of as a joke."

"Maybe if you tell us just exactly how you used it, we could understand your story better," said Grayson, looking soberly and steadily at me. He was the one I would be most embarrassed to tell.

"I....well, I can't tell the whole story but..."

"Aha. This sounds like there is something to cover up," said David. "We want to hear the whole story."

I looked around at the others. They were wanting a story and I was sure they would enjoy the tale, but I kept thinking of Grayson. He would think I was still that silly fifteen year old.

"We need the whole story to solve the problem," urged Dale.

"Well,...I put it on for a short time."

"You said that before. Tell us what you are keeping back," said Grayson.

I still hesitated. It just sounded so silly.

"She has a guilty conscience," said Grayson with a sober face. "I told you, Sarah, that the girls would need a chaperone." His eyes were still fixed on me. "I want to know why you wore a sunbonnet at the park."

"Well," I said slowly, not looking at him and aware that Aunt Sarah was also listening with big ears, "one of the girls had a boyfriend and he was there with another girl. We saw them dance together and then they were sitting on a park bench, talking. So this girl begged me to put on the sunbonnet as a disguise and sit on the bench with them to hear what was said."

"And you did it?" asked David.

"It was dark and as you see, the sunbonnet looked just like this one and if you put it on, your face is really hidden unless you look directly at someone."

"Put it on now," said Aunt Sarah.

I did.

David hooted and I could tell that Grayson's eyes never strayed from my face and the others laughed and waited for more. I removed the sunbonnet. I did not look directly at Grayson, for fear I would see...what? Disappointment that I stooped to eavesdropping? It now sounded terribly rude. Or that I was so silly? At the time, it was an adventure.

"So you actually did it?"

"It was a joke. I wore a shawl and had the broom that Mary Ann bought and was suppose to look like a cleaning lady on her way home."

"And when did you notice the sunbonnet was gone?" asked David.

"Not until we were at Mary Lou's aunt's house. I wanted to show it to her."

"So you lost it in the park?" asked David, intent on solving the mystery.

"Yes, and I went back to look for it the next morning. Gone."

"Well, someone must have known it belonged to you or you would not have gotten it back. Was someone close enough to steal it?" asked David.

"No. Well, the couple on the bench, but I still had it on when they left. I don't think they ever really looked at me. And maybe this isn't the exact same sunbonnet. But it looks exactly the same. The maker of the bonnet probably made more than one like it."

"Was anyone else around that could have stolen it?" asked Dale.

"No one. Another man sat down on the bench, but I know he did not take it."

"Who was that?" asked Grayson.

"I have no clue. After the couple left, and before I had a chance to get off the bench, someone was coming past and I ducked my head to wait till he passed the bench. But instead, he sat down beside me. And then, before I could get up, he asked if I knew what time it was."

"Did you know him?" asked David.

"Of course not. I only saw his shoes and the bottom of his pants, because I kept my head down and I would have had to look right at him under that long brim, but he had a strange voice and it was dark, and anyway that question is an old trick. So I quickly got up and as soon as I walked away into the shadows, I took off the shawl and sunbonnet and joined the others. Oh, I do remember taking it off after leaving the bench, so it was not stolen by that man."

"And you never saw the sunbonnet again?"

"Not that one, but I found one just like it in the gatehouse. That was really strange. Made just like it and it must have belonged to the lady who lived there long ago."

"That sounds fishy to me. Exactly like it? From years ago? Who had access to the gatehouse?"

"No one. Just me. Grayson, of course has access, but he does not come in. And anyway, he was not at the park that day. And he thought the gift was for him until he saw the name."

There was a bit of a pause. Grayson no longer participated in the query, but David was on a roll and I was glad to think it through with him.

"Where were you that day, Grayson?"

I looked at Grayson. Why was he asking him?

"At a wedding."

Grayson was watching me. A memory of a wedding across from the park flashed through my mind.

"Where?" asked David. There was a slight hesitation.

"In Thackeray's Pond."

I kept my eyes on Grayson whose dark eyes were studying me. It seemed everyone got quiet, but I was trying to understand Grayson. He was not denying anything. He was just watching me as he answered David. Was it possible that he was in the park? And that he had found the sunbonnet? But how did he know it was mine? And why did he keep looking at me now? He was not smiling.

I was scared to think further than that. Did he think I was the stupidest person in the room? I tried to remember the well-dressed gentleman. He certainly could not have been that person. The man had a very strange voice. A *false* voice. Yes, it was a *false* voice. I felt like I might faint and then I got hot all over. Hot with embarrassment. But Grayson had never said he was there on the bench. And why would he sit on the bench? The man had nearly gone by and then had turned back to sit down. Why? But no, I would have known if it was Grayson on the park bench. Of that I was sure.

"Were you in the park that day, Grayson?" asked Dale, before David had a chance to ask another question.

"I was."

"Did you see June?" There was a slight hesitation.

"I saw her friends, but June was not with them."

I breathed a sign of relief. He had not seen me.

"Did you find a sunbonnet in the park?"

A moment of hesitation. "I did."

Grayson was not denying anything. As he answered the questions, he just looked at me, a slight smile now on his face. Everyone else in the room seemed to understand Grayson except me and now they shouted with laughter.

I sat without a smile. I don't know if I really could not understand what was clear to the others, or if I refused to believe what they seemed to know. I could not put the pieces together. Why couldn't I laugh with them? I still had pieces missing. He saw the sunbonnet and picked it up. Why did he pick it up? I was not a poor sport. But the fact was, I was not getting the whole picture and I could not see anything to laugh about. I must be really stupid if everyone else was understanding this and I was not.

I was so embarrassed over my stupidity that I realized I was very close to tears. Now I knew what "embarrassed to tears" meant. If I did not care so much what Grayson thought of me, it would not be so bad. But I felt so terribly foolish.

I forced a laugh so that I laughed with the others, then I shook my head at Grayson who was still watching me but not laughing, and quickly left the room, saying I would bring in the dessert. But when I got to the kitchen, I just stood a bit in the middle of the room and stared at nothing. Why couldn't I laugh with them? I brushed away the threatening tears and took a deep breath. They thought it was funny and entertaining. I had to get over my crazy emotions.

After just a few minutes, I began taking the dessert, plate by plate into the room. Some of them were talking about other things by now and I offered the dessert first to Grayson, since it was his birthday. I gave him only the barest of glances, and waited for him to take the plate from me. He did not take it. I was forced to look at him. And then he took it, but he seemed to know I was somehow distressed. He said thank you and I went to the next person, just making small talk to anyone around me to cover up my emotions. No one mentioned the sunbonnet again, and I finally went back to the kitchen, leaving Grayson and his friends to visit, while I washed up the dishes.

"Well, we finally got the sunbonnet mystery settled," said Aunt Sarah as she came into the kitchen.

"Finally," I said, and then quickly changed the subject. She did not seem to notice my reaction to the whole sunbonnet story and she chatted of other things and finally said she was tired and would go to bed. At the same time, Janet came to the kitchen to call me in to help play charades. I went back into the room and I tried to forget my stupidity and eventually I could enjoy the game. I think Dale's girlfriend, Shanna, felt a bit out of the loop here with us, and she talked a lot to me, which helped.

Finally, the evening was finished and Grayson helped the ladies with their wraps. As they walked to the door to leave, I said my goodbyes and backed away, planning to escape to my room while Grayson saw his friends off. But he, seeing my intent, touched my arm with a restraining hand.

"Stay here."

Grayson stepped out the door a short time to bid his guests goodbye and then stepped back into the room. I had retreated to the hearth, feeling like a country bumpkin.

"Please sit down, June," said Grayson, motioning to the wing chair by the fire.

When I was seated, he sat on the sofa close by and leaning front, just looked at me a few moments. I barely knew where to look.

"I see now that I somehow hurt you."

"It is nothing," I replied, now more embarrassed than ever. "You did not hurt me, and I don't know *why* I couldn't laugh it off. I was embarrassed, mostly. First for doing such a silly thing, then for being so naive about the sunbonnet. I was only *extremely* embarrassed at my own stupidity. But quite frankly, I still do not quite get the whole story."

He hesitated. "I did not plan to go to the Festival, but the wedding took place at the church right across the street from the park, and knowing you were there with friends, my curiosity was aroused." Grayson put his hand through his hair, evidently not quite at ease about admitting his part in this story. "So after the wedding, seeing that there were still activities in the park, I decided to walk around." Again he paused. "I recognized your friends but you were not with them. They seemed to be in a huddle looking and laughing at someone on a bench a short distance away. Since you were missing from the group, I stayed out of their sight, and tried to see what they were looking at. What I saw was a rather strangely-dressed woman on the bench. Somehow, I guessed it had to be you, and you were up to something. I watched as you sat there next to the couple that seemed quite absorbed in themselves."

At this point, I was not looking at Grayson. I was mortified. I put my head in my hands and bowed my head.

"Then they abruptly got up and I saw my chance at a bit of adventure for myself."

I raised my head and looked at an almost mischievous Grayson, beseechingly. *"Please* tell me you were not the man on the bench with me."

Again, just a momentary hesitation and a keen look. Then he spoke softly. "I was."

"I am so *stupid!"*

"No, June. You are *not* stupid. And you were having fun. There was no reason for you to know it was me."

"But I should have known the voice was fake. I just thought it strange. And I could see nothing but your shoes and trousers. I did not dare look you in the face."

He grinned. "I wish you had."

"I would have fainted on the spot!"

Grayson chuckled. There followed a moment of silence. Grayson did not sit back. "Am I forgiven?"

I looked up at him in surprise. He meant it.

"Of course. It is past. Maybe sometime I will be able to laugh at it." I managed a weak smile. "I am mortified at my stupidity as well as for wearing the sunbonnet and being caught by you."

I caught my breath. For some people I would not have been so embarrassed. Just for Grayson. Had I made a simpleton of myself again?

"Thank you for your forgiveness," he said. I thought his eyes fascinating. "And again, many thanks for the vest. It is a work of art."

I was so happy for the change of subject. "Thank you, it was fun making it." My heart swelled with joy. At least there was something to be proud of.

Grayson stood and in spite of my confused feelings, I found that I was sorry he was leaving. I was now enjoying talking to him. Just before he exited the room he turned once more to me and bowed slightly.

"I wish you a good night and thank you for your part in the party."

And he was gone.

I sat there a while afterwards. I watched the fire and I thought of the man who had cared enough to come and seek peace with me tonight and had he known, I would have forgiven him anything. Anything at all.

CHAPTER 15

I was up at the gatehouse doing what I loved best. Sewing. It was wonderful having so much room. Over the next days I finished a dress and took it to the mercantile in our village. I really wanted to get clothing to the dress shop in Thackeray's Pond, but I wanted to get something in a store close by while attempting something more involved. I bought more dress patterns and fabric. Now I would soon have to sell before I bought more fabric. I also had the fabric to look through that had been left by the former tenants of the gatehouse.

Three days later, I took a gown to a dress shop in Thackeray's Pond. The storekeeper seemed impressed and willingly took it and even promised to put it in the window. I had hopes as I drove home again. A few days later, I received a letter from a woman in Thackeray's Pond. She wanted to see me and could I come to her house?

This was exciting. I shared the letter with Aunt Sarah and she was happy for me but I sensed her reservations. I knew she was missing me in the house and I tried to spend more than meals with her. But I was finally doing what I wanted to do. The letter informed me when the lady was available and I planned to go the next day. I could hardly wait. I did not know where Rosemary Corners was, so that evening at the supper table, I asked Grayson.

"Rosemary Corners? Why do you want to know where that is?"

"I must go see someone there." He looked at me, waiting for some more information. The silence got too long. "It is a Mrs. Forbes and she wishes to see me regarding some dressmaking."

Grayson was silent while he digested this information. "Do you know where Rosemary Corners is?" I asked him.

"It is in the better section of town." He gave me a long look. "Are you sure you want to do this?"

"Do you doubt my ability?"

My hackles must have gone up. He actually smiled a bit.

"No. But you may get more business than you wish for, if she likes your work."

"Isn't that the idea?" He studied me and I had to wonder what was going on in his head. "If I get business, I can pay you rent for the gatehouse."

"The rent just went up." There was a hint of a smile again.

"Are you going to tell me where Rosemary Corners is?"

"Do you need a ride there?"

"Is Star not well?"

I felt, for some reason, Grayson was having second thoughts about me in the gatehouse. At least as far as the business end of it.

"Star is well and probably could use some attention from you. But I don't know how good you know your way around the town."

"I certainly won't find my way unless you tell me." I was being a bit impertinent but I was enjoying the conversation and had to wonder why he was hedging.

"I need to go there this week sometime. You could go with me."

"I need to go alone. I must learn to find my way. I do not know how long it will take and I must go when it suits her, not me. You made me learn to drive, remember?"

"And this spring you will learn to ride. Make sure you leave time for that."

"I have no wish to ride and since I am no longer...."

"Miss Merriweather," said Grayson, his eyes holding mine, "you *will* learn to ride this spring."

At this point Aunt Sarah, who had listened with a smile to the conversation, chuckled and Lizzie looked up from the potatoes she was eating, and looked a bit fearfully at Grayson as he spoke. It is possible that she understood or heard very little of the conversation, but he said the last words sternly and louder. To my amazement, she leaned a bit in my direction and spoke.

"Are you scared of him?"

I could not hold back a smile but before I could give answer, Grayson spoke.

"She should be."

I felt myself getting red and I changed the subject by asking my question for the final time.

"And where, sir, do I find Rosemary Corners?"

A brief hesitation followed. "Drive to the center of town and turn right. Go two blocks and you will be in Rosemary Corners. It is a better section of town. You will be dealing with rich people. You may not want to deal with the rich."

"I do want to deal with the rich. I want to earn money and the rich have it. I don't want to be dependent on y…charity." I almost said I don't want to be dependent on you, but I was finding a part of me would like to be dependent on him.

Grayson was finished eating and sat back in his chair. "Do you know the house number?"

"I have it somewhere."

"And the name?"

"Forbes."

"Forbes, as in Thomas Forbes?"

"I don't know. I think the name was Estelle Forbes."

Grayson whistled softly. "Your rent just went higher. Thomas Forbes owns the biggest clothing company in the area. And is one of the wealthiest men in our county."

"Well, that is interesting," I said. "Do you know where their house is?"

"Actually, I do. It is a large white house on your right when you go through the crossroad. You can't miss it. But I think I should take you there. You will get lost or get in trouble. You need me…."

I was laughing. I don't really know if he meant what he said, but I was enjoying the banter.

"Thank you, Grayson. I shall enjoy the adventure."

But the next day, when I walked out to the stable, I was nervous. Rich women were very often snobs. I was a poor working girl, unmarried and trying to earn my keep. Besides that, would I really find my way to the rich section without problems? One of the workmen led Star to the carriage and soon we were off. I enjoyed new adventures, even if they were scary. Star seemed happy to be out and we went cautiously over the frozen creek and up to "my" gatehouse, as I had begun to call it. It was now February, but the day was rather mild as we headed out on the open road. I was enjoying riding alone out in the country. I liked the feel of independence. I would earn money and make it on my own. I tried not to think of the possibility of the woman looking down her nose at me. I met a few carriages on the road and gave a friendly wave. There had been a few snows, but nothing really harsh and with the sun shining brightly, I wondered if we were getting an early spring. I saw a red-tailed hawk sitting on a leafless tree, keeping his eyes fixed on the field around him, looking for his lunch.

All too soon, I was passing the pond for which Thackeray's Pond was named, and then Star was cantering down Main Street. When I got to the center of town, the sheriff was standing in the center of the intersection, where there seemed to be congestion. I wondered if it was the same sheriff that had helped us girls the night of the Harvest Festival. I gave him just a passing glance, wondering if he recognized me, as I made my right turn. After going two blocks, I stopped at another intersection and true to Grayson's word, across the street was a large white house. I just sat in the intersection for a few moments and took a deep breath before crossing the street. This could be my big moment. Once on the other side, I tied Star to the hitching post and made my way to the door, my heart in my throat.

There was a gleaming knocker on the door, which I cautiously lifted and let drop. In a short time, the door was opened by a maid with a white dust cap on her head.

"I am June Merriweather and I am here to see Mrs. Forbes," I said, as she looked at me questioningly.

"Please come in. I shall tell her." She came back shortly, relieved me of my cloak and led me down a wide hall. Opening a door, she led me into a bedroom suite. Mrs. Forbes was sitting on a handsome chair by a window, but got up as I entered. She gave me a bit of a smile and shook my hand, barely touching it. She was dressed in an emerald green dress with a string of pearls around her neck. She was polite, with reservations. She looked me over as if to see if I was worthy of coming into her house. My first impression was not so positive.

"I am so glad you could come," she said. "I saw the gown you made and have on display downtown and I am interested in a similar gown." She took a pattern packet from her table. "Here is the gown I would like you to make for me." She paused, as she handed it to me and let me take a look at it. "Do you think you could sew such a gown for me?"

"I have never done this particular pattern, but I am confident that I can," I replied. "Do you already have the fabric?"

She went to a closet, and handed me a heavy bag in which was the fabric. The necessary notions were included. "What do you think?"

"It is very beautiful fabric and I am sure I can do this."

"Good. How soon can we have a fitting? I will need the gown in two weeks."

"Could you come in a week?"

"Whenever you say, but where do you live?"

"I live at Bluster Hill. But I would meet you in the gatehouse where I do my sewing."

"I know Bluster Hill. Does Theodore Morgan still own it?"

"He died just a few months ago and it is now owned by Grayson Everleigh. Theodore Morgan was my uncle and I live there with my aunt."

We made the necessary arrangements. I tried to sound confident, but her manner made it difficult. But I was very excited. This is what I wanted to do and who knows what would become of my dressmaking?

I walked out of the house with a spring in my step and with the bundle of fabric in my arm. My heart was singing and I was elated. This was what I wanted to do and although she was not overly friendly to me, I did not consider her a snob. I unhitched Star, and rather than turning around, I decided to go around the block. I went down to the next intersection, which was now on the back edge of town, and turned left instead of right because I decided to see this section of town before heading home. I was feeling free, alive and adventurous. I admired the big, grand houses and then turned back toward Main Street. Now I was getting to a decidedly poorer section of town and at the next crossroads, I turned right to get out of this section.

After driving a couple blocks, I was slowly passing the park where the Harvest Festival had been held and was remembering the sunbonnet story, when I saw a girl sitting on a bench in the park. She was not facing the street but I could see her from the side and she looked sad and somehow familiar. And then it hit me. This was the missing Donna! The one who had eloped! I had to think what to do. I did not want to chase her off. But she was alone and looking decidedly sad. I pulled Star up to a hitching post and tied her fast. Then I walked back to where I had seen Donna. She looked very dejected and I saw a small suitcase on the ground by the bench. I was nearly up to her when she suddenly looked up. Her first reaction was relief. But immediately, her expression changed to fear and distrust. I almost thought she might run.

"Donna," I said softly, walking up to her. "I am so glad to see you." When she did not answer, I sat down beside her. "I am your friend. Don't be afraid. I saw you sitting here and I know your family is hurting badly, not knowing where you are."

Donna did not look at me. She had a very guilty look on her face, and I suspected the worst.

"Where is your husband?" I decided I could ask for her husband, since she said they were eloping.

She began to cry. First it was just blinking back tears. Then she just lost it and I put my arm around her and held her while she sobbed. When she finally got her crying under control, she asked if we could go someplace in the carriage. I agreed. Some people had already walked past us and had stared at the sobbing girl. We walked quickly to the carriage and I drove to the edge of town where I found a church. I pulled in there and parked along the cemetery.

"Now tell me your story," I urged her. "Are you married?"

"We are not married yet. But we will be. Bud said he had everything arranged, but when we drove away that evening, he said..." she hesitated, "he said maybe we should go to the inn and think it through first. He...I don't know if..." she hesitated, "maybe he just was not sure or...."

I did not say what I thought. Maybe she was scared to say what she feared. She blew her nose and continued.

"He said there was a problem and we had to do some planning. I was scared to go home. I had left a note. And I thought I loved Bud. I *do* love him. He wanted to stay at the inn for the night and the next day we would figure out what to do. He promised we would get married."

Here she began crying again. I waited. What was I going to do? It must be nearly a week since they were gone.

"So you spent the night in the inn?" Donna just nodded. "And you still aren't married?" She shook her head, crying. "Where is Bud?"

"At work."

"Where are you staying?"

"We are or were, staying at the inn. But it is too expensive. Last night was our last night."

"What about his promise?"

"He says he is still working on the plan."

"And where will you meet him, when he gets home from work?"

"Here in the park."

I wondered if Bud would show up. She was left to wait in the park, a suitcase by her side. He clearly had failed to think this through before deciding to elope. Where had he left his brains?

"Where is his family?"

"They live far away someplace. He never talks about them. He was living with some relatives." We sat in silence a few moments.

"This isn't exactly the way you imagined your marriage, is it?" I said softly. She began crying again.

"I can't go back to my parents. They will be so angry."

"They are hurt, but they are very concerned about you."

"I won't go back. I'll...I'll go with Bud to his relatives."

I was sure she was very embarrassed by what had happened. And the guilt must be heavy. I understood her not wanting to go back home, but I did not trust the so-called relatives. Did he really have relatives? I had no reason to trust this boy. If his family lived far away someplace, why would he have relatives here? I had to say the hard truth.

"His relatives probably know nothing of you. They may not want you."

"I won't go back home. Bud will think up something."

I did not say that Bud should have put a lot more thought into this before eloping. She stood up. I was afraid she would jump out of the carriage. This was going nowhere. Suddenly I thought of the gatehouse. Did I dare?

"Donna, would you go home with me?"

"My parents will find me there."

"I use the gatehouse to sew in. No one lives there. I could take you back there and give you time to think about your life. You may stay overnight and tomorrow we will talk again. I can't hide you forever and I can't let your parents keep wondering where you are."

"Does anyone come into the gatehouse?"

"They won't if I don't invite them," I replied, hoping that Grayson never came in there since it was my space for sewing. Donna sat in silence. "You know you will be safe. You know nothing of Bud's relatives." I wanted to add *or even if they exist.* "And you can't stay in the park overnight."

I think that last thought helped her decide. She finally gave me a hopeful look. "You won't tell anyone?" I hesitated. This was almost over my head.

"I will not tell anyone before we talk again tomorrow morning. I must get home for lunch. I will let you off at the gatehouse. I must get back before they ask questions."

I flicked the reins and we were off. I breathed a sigh of relief. As we drove, very little was said. We were each with our own thoughts. I noticed that if a carriage came toward us, she put her head down. Poor girl. She had made a hasty decision and was now cowering in misery. I found myself holding my breath as we approached the gatehouse. But all was clear. I tethered Star, and led Donna into the house. Before I left, I gave instructions.

"If someone comes to the door, don't answer. No one really comes, because they don't know I am here. I will try to bring you some lunch. There is no food in the house here, but there is a pump out the back door for water. There is a cot upstairs in the little room above the drive. Rest there if you wish."

I built a fire and with a quick wave, left Donna. It was at least better than sitting on a cold park bench. When I entered the house, I tried to act like all was well, but it was very difficult.

"You were gone a long time," said Aunt Sarah. "Did you find the house without trouble?"

"I did."

"How did you like the lady?"

Frankly, it seemed that my appointment with Mrs. Forbes was days ago. I had to adjust my thinking from Donna to Mrs. Forbes.

"Oh, she was not much of a talker, at least not to me, but I think, or at least hope, that all will go well. She is definitely an upper-class woman, but I hope I will have no difficulty in pleasing her."

"Is the fabric nice?"

"Yes, very. I left it at the gatehouse on the way back. It is a deep wine satin and she wants no bustle, rather the new princess line style. Instead of a horizontal waist line, there will be long body tucks and darts to create a very slim waistline. I am eager to get at it."

Somehow, although my mind was on Donna, we got through lunch and I helped Aunt Sarah to plan supper before I was off again. When she went off for a nap, I quickly made two big sandwiches and took a jar of milk and a couple apples for Donna. I felt like a thief when I smuggled it out the door. At the last minute, I remembered some canned soup in the basement and returned for a jar of that yet. Someday, I would tell Aunt Sarah, but not today.

When I returned to work on the gown for Mrs. Forbes, I found Donna sleeping on the cot. I let her sleep while I got my things in order to sew. I was eager to begin and was mildly put out that I had to spend time with Donna, but I was glad she was here with me. Safe. She was probably able to sleep a bit better, now that she was sure of a hiding place. But this hiding place could not last long. I did not like this at all, but, I kept reminding myself, it was better than leaving her in the park.

After perhaps an hour, I heard Donna stirring. She got up and wolfed down a sandwich and an apple and half of the milk while I was cutting fabric. When she was done, I stopped my sewing and sat in the sewing room with her.

"We must talk," I said. "I brought food that I sneaked out of the house. I do not like to do that. I am here at Mr. Everleigh's mercy and I do not want to make trouble. I would like to talk very seriously with you about Bud. Do you really believe he will come up with a plan for the two of you? Before you answer, do you really want to go on with this?"

She did not answer, so I went on. "You come from a loving family. Right now, you want to be on your own, but that is not possible. You see that now."

"But Bud…"

"He hasn't come up with a plan yet and…I am sure you feel guilty for the way you have been living together."

I did not know how she would take that, but she went to the same church as I did and she knew what the Bible said about marriage. And fornication. It was time to talk straight.

"Donna, I would like to help you get out of this mess. I know you are afraid to go home. But somehow, you did come here with me and you know Bud will look for you in the park this evening. I think you do not trust him anymore. And you should not. I don't know if he claims to be a Christian, or not. But this eloping was not what God intended."

I paused. So far, she was listening.

"Do you know, I think God sent me past the park today to find you. He cares about you. And Pastor Stafford is concerned about you. I would like to ask him to talk to you and for you to hear what he has to say. He is very kind and gentle."

The tears were rolling once more, but she was listening. "Just think about it. Right now I must start working on this gown that I have been commissioned to sew. Just relax and listen to what God has to say to you about your situation."

When she did not answer, I went back to my sewing and I spent the rest of the afternoon at the sewing machine. No one disturbed us. Most people did not know about my sewing in the gatehouse. When I went home for supper, Donna still had the soup and a sandwich to eat.

"If you hear a carriage coming in the lane, make sure no light shows. Maybe close the curtains. I will come as soon as I can tomorrow morning and see what you have decided. Will you be all right here alone? You may come with me to the house and eat supper with us. You do not need to hide."

"I will stay alone. This is better than with Bud's relatives whom I don't know."

Grayson was not at home for supper, which was wonderful. At least I did not worry about him asking me about my trip to Thackeray's Pond. Not that it would have mattered, but I was just glad for less stress. I kept up a running conversation with Aunt Sarah while Lizzie and Becca shouted to each other between bites of food. I went to bed praying that Donna would allow me to bring Pastor Stafford to her. If I was distracted at the supper table, no one seemed to notice.

I rose the next morning with Donna on my mind and as I walked into the kitchen for breakfast, I came to a complete stop when I saw Grayson was present. I was so surprised to see him that I simply looked at him in silence a moment. Unfortunately, he studied me with a look so keen that I could not hide my surprise. He had a very sober face and mumbled a good morning, to which I responded with a mumbled reply.

"Well, Grayson, you are usually out of the house by now," said Aunt Sarah as we began eating.

"I've been out already."

"You just forgot to eat breakfast first," teased my aunt.

"I got home at midnight."

I stopped eating and looked at Grayson. His sober eyes were fixed on me as if that should tell me something. I was a bit confused. That was all he said, but he looked so solemn that neither one of us commented on his words. We continued to eat and after a considerable pause, he focused on me.

"Did you find Rosemary Corners yesterday?"

I was thankful that he was being sociable in spite of his solemness. But my mind went back to all that had happened in Thackeray's Pond and I hesitated a bit, trying to focus on my visit with Mrs. Forbes. I was so focused on Donna that Mrs. Forbes was far from my mind. It almost seemed that it was days since I was at her house.

"Yes, thank you. I found it without incident," I replied, trying to think of something else I could tell him about the visit. When he said nothing, I continued. "I was a bit scared to meet her, but she seemed nice enough in spite of being a part of high society."

Grayson made no comment, but Aunt Sarah was chatty and kept the conversation going and it was not long before the meal was ended.

"Would you like more coffee, Grayson?" I asked, before taking his cup.

"No, but I would like to talk to you in the library. Now."

I looked at him quickly. His words were spoken low but commanding. I had no inkling why he would want me in the library without saying why. And when he added the "now," I instinctively knew that he was more than a little displeased with me. I followed him obediently to the library where he stood outside the door, facing me, with his dark eyes steadily watching me. I walked in the door he was holding open and he immediately followed me in and closed the door. He went to the small fireplace and added a log and then curtly told me to sit down. There were two chairs facing the hearth, and as I sat down, I found my heart beginning to pound. For some reason, Grayson was angry. And it was at me that his anger was directed. I had no clue what his problem was, but I did not have long to wait. He chose not take a seat, but rather, stood by the fire and fixed his dark eyes on me. I tried to look at ease, but I am sure that I looked much more like a scared rabbit, which probably pleased him. Finally he spoke.

"Miss Merriweather, when I make a vocal contract with you, I expect you to abide by it."

He let that sink in. My mind went to the gatehouse. It was the only "contract" I had with him. "I would like to know why you have not honored that contract," he continued.

"I do not know how I have not honored that contract," I said, but my voice trembled.

"You deny it?" He looked surprised.

"I do." I looked him straight in the eye. He stared so long at me that I felt heat rise in my face, and I finally had to look at the flames instead.

He took a step toward me. He'd been close enough already. Now he seemed to tower over me.

"I would like you to tell me where you spent the night last night."

My thoughts took flight. He said he came home at midnight. I had warned Donna about light if someone drove in or out of the lane. Had he seen a light?

"I await your answer, June."

"I was here in my own room." I swallowed nervously. It was not lost on Grayson. I knew that he thought I was lying and I did not look at him. I could not face those dark, angry eyes. I remembered the angry eyes of the young Conrad.

"In that case, I would like you to tell me whose light I saw in the gatehouse at midnight last night."

The picture was getting clearer. Donna probably thought no one would come in at midnight. And her light was seen. I had to think this through. I could not let Grayson think I had broken my word. But I did not want to wreck my hopes for Donna's reconciliation with her family.

"You seem to have a problem explaining the light to me." Grayson's scowl had darkened.

"I can explain," I said, still not looking at him and my voice shook.

"Then please be so kind to look at me and explain the phenomena. When someone cannot look me in the eye, I suspect deceit." I took a deep breath and looked at him.

"Donna Gable slept in the gatehouse last night."

I must say, my words took the wind out of Grayson's angry sails. He looked at me a long time in silence, not blinking an eye.

"Tell me more," he said finally, in a much more subdued voice.

So I told him the story. How I found her, what her situation was, and my hopes to get Pastor Stafford here to talk to her. As I talked, I saw the anger leave him and I continued.

"I feel so inadequate, She needs someone who will be kind and gentle with her. She made a mistake. We all make mistakes. She carries a lot of shame. I was just glad she agreed to come with me. I took some food to her. I will repay you. I would like to take her something for breakfast, too." I hesitated. "I am sorry for what happened. I did not wish to anger you."

I looked again to the flames of the hearth. There was utter quiet in the room for a few moments. Grayson retreated to the mantle and looked at me.

"I apologize. I jumped to conclusions. You did right." He thought for a moment. "What are your plans?"

I took a deep breath of relief. "I hope she will talk to Pastor Stafford today. I have not thought beyond that and I do not know even if he is at home right now."

"We must get Pastor Stafford in this and her parents must be told yet today. They must be terribly anxious," said Grayson. He paused and looked at me. "May I contact Pastor Stafford for you?"

This was a wonderful turn of events. I had help. "Yes." And I did not feel guilty for calling for Pastor Stafford. I had warned her about the lights and now Grayson had seen them and knew her story.

"I will go to her immediately, if I may," I said. "I must tell her what has happened."

"Do so and take what you want from the kitchen and do not speak of repayment. I am glad you found her."

When I stood up, Grayson came to me and offered his hand. When I gave him mine, he held it tightly as his eyes searched mine. "Forgive me. I had no reason to distrust you."

I blinked back tears. I was so relieved. The stress of yesterday and this morning melted away. I found I could not talk. I just nodded.

I left the library and went in search of food. Aunt Sarah was in the kitchen and I had to say something.

"Aunt Sarah. I must take some food with me to the gatehouse. I cannot tell you why right now, but later today, I will tell you."

She looked at me in surprise, but she trusted me. "Let me help you. What would you like?"

"Let me take an egg, a piece of that leftover ham and some bread and butter. That should do it."

Aunt Sarah made no comment as I gathered the food. Before I left, she added a pint of milk to the basket of food.

"Thank you for your trust," I said as I went out the door.

I could tell Donna was glad to see me. She had been there alone all night And surely thinking of Bud and how he must wonder where she was. I wondered if Bud was glad she was not around. He should have felt relieved because he certainly was not able to keep a wife at this stage.

"I brought you some breakfast, Donna. I'll help you make it in the kitchen. How was your night?"

"I woke up often. I love Bud, and I don't want to go to his relatives. But I am scared to meet my family."

"I have some bad news as well as good news," I said. "Last night Grayson saw your light when he came home. He thought I was here overnight, which I am not permitted to do, and I had to explain who was here. He was very understanding and since I said I think you should talk to Pastor Stafford, he will ride there and ask him to come. You need not fear. You know the pastor is a compassionate man. He will do his best to help you."

Donna said nothing. But she was not arguing about the pastor coming and I took that as a good sign. I saw Grayson go out the lane and by the time Donna had eaten breakfast, Pastor Stafford was at the door.

"Pastor Stafford, please come in."

The pastor came in. Donna was in the kitchen, but I called to her. She came with downcast eyes.

"I will let you two talk. I will be sewing upstairs and if I can help in any way, let me know."

I left the room. I felt a great relief at his coming. She was no longer my responsibility. I went upstairs and concentrated on the gown I was sewing. It was so much fun that I almost forgot the hard conversation in the sitting room. About an hour later, Donna came upstairs for her suitcase.

"Pastor Stafford is taking me home," she told me. Then she gave me a teary hug. I felt the crisis had passed. I prayed her family would be forgiving.

"You are doing the right thing," I said, hugging her back.

Three days later, Mrs. Forbes came for a fitting. She was pleased. She said she would go for more fabric and when the gown was finished, she had another for me to make. I was so thrilled that on Sunday, when I saw Mary Lou, I suggested that we have a girls' sewing party sometime in the coming week. We found Jeannie and Annelie and we decided on Wednesday afternoon, which happened to be Mary Lou's birthday.

"We'll have a birthday party and if we don't get to sew, it will be fine also," I said. "It is time we have a gatehouse party and Mary Lou's birthday is the perfect time for it."

CHAPTER 16

My life was getting busier. Evenings I took time to help make supper and chat with Aunt Sarah. During the day, I was mostly at the gatehouse, sewing. I was making a few items to put in the village store as well as in Thackeray's Pond. I wanted more than one customer. I was home so seldom that even Misty, the cat came running when I came in, and rubbed my legs with her silky fur. Aunt Sarah evidently did not give her the attention I did.

When Wednesday arrived, I did not go to the gatehouse in the morning. I spent the morning baking and icing a birthday cake for Mary Lou. I also made potato salad, fried chicken and packed a basket and added a loaf of bread and butter and a jar of pickles. I wrapped up a scarf I had knitted and found a blue ribbon to tie it with. We would have lunch at the gatehouse in style. At eleven o'clock, I loaded my things on a small hand cart that I found in the shed, to transport the cake and basket to the gatehouse. Aunt Sarah kindly packed six small plates, cups and saucers for me and said I could keep them in the gatehouse, as she had another whole set of dishes of her mother's. I knew there were some cups, saucers and a few other odd dishes in the gatehouse, but there was nothing suitable for a party. The air was chilly and the creek was low and frozen and I walked over the ford with care. I wondered if there could be snow in the air. We had not had any big snow all winter. It wasn't long before I was at the gatehouse and setting up for the party. The girls arrived before I was finished setting up and before we did anything else, I gave the girls a tour, such as it was, of the gatehouse.

"Oh, I love it!" said Mary Lou. "It is as cute on the inside as it is pretty on the outside."

"And it is bigger than I expected," added Jeannie. "A sofa, two chairs, a fireplace and small table and bookshelf. You should live here."

"I would love to, but Grayson and Aunt Sarah both say no. Inappropriate, they declare, for a young girl living alone. They forget I am now a spinster, unloved, unwanted and forgotten. I would be utterly safe here with the doors wide open."

The girls laughed as I took them into the kitchen and then upstairs. As I put my hand on the stair post, it felt like it wiggled. By the time Annelie put her hand on it, it fell off.

"Oh help, I think this post needs some repairs," she said.

I went back down, and to my surprise, the post seemed to be hollow and the top just did not quite fit right. No wonder it wiggled.

"I shall have to tell Grayson," I said, but I doubted I would. What would he think of damage to his property the first time I had the girls here? I tried to jam the top back into the hole and then forgot about it.

"And here is where I sew," I said, proudly, showing them the sewing room. "Just perfect for me. I had no place but the hall in the house."

"This is so exciting," said Jeannie as she climbed the short stairs to the room above the drive.

"Wow, this is also bigger than it looks from the outside. A lovely bedroom. Too bad you can't live here. That would be exciting looking out the window to see who was coming in the…oh, someone is coming out the drive right now. It must be Grayson. No, it is someone else and he is stopping here! Hey, he is a cute guy! June, come quick. Who is he?"

We all hurried to the upstairs window. It was Marley, coming with another load of wood.

"Oh," I said. "Don't you know him? He was skating on the pond that night you were here. Or maybe you were not here. Mary Lou, I think he skated with you."

"What is he doing here now?" Mary Lou asked, looking excited.

"Bringing more wood for the fire."

"Could we invite him to the party?" asked Jeannie.

"I don't think so. And I think he sees us watching him. We better get to our lunch."

Annelie finally dragged her sister from the window and we trooped downstairs to our birthday party. The kitchen was too small, so we sat in the sitting room at a small table close to the fire, and for the next hour we enjoyed our meal. The cold air outside made us hungry and we feasted on our fried chicken and potato salad. Finally, after pouring the tea in Aunt Sarah's blue flowered tea cups, we cut the cake and somehow the discussion came back to Marley.

"Do you see much of him?" asked Jeannie.

"Almost not at all. Our paths don't cross."

"Is he the one you skated with so much that night?" Annelie asked.

"Yes. We were just getting acquainted. But I've not seen him since, until today."

Just then someone knocked at the door. When I went to the door, it was Marley. He grinned his friendly grin.

"Just wanted you to know that you got more wood," he said.

I was sure he had seen the girls all watching him from the upstairs window, and he was probably curious who they were.

"Thank you so much. We are in the midst of a birthday party...."

Just then Jeannie, true to form, called out, "Give him a piece of cake for his trouble."

"Well, you may as well come in and meet the girls," I said, opening the door.

Marley suddenly looked shy. But he stepped inside. The girls suddenly got quiet. Marley really was a nice looking fellow with blue eyes and an endearing smile.

"This is Marley," I said to the girls, not able to hold back my own smile. "He works here on the estate. And Marley, this is Mary Lou, whose birthday we are celebrating, and Annelie and Jeannie who are sisters, and cousins to Mary Lou."

"Here, have a piece of cake," said Mary Lou, cutting a piece for him.

Marley could not stop smiling. This was perhaps the highlight of his day. Unless he already had a girlfriend.

"Thank you."

"Would you like some tea?" asked Jeannie, always wanting to accommodate.

"Thank you, but I better go before the boss finds me at a birthday party instead of stacking wood. I've got work to do."

And with a slight bow of his head, he turned to the door. Just as I was closing the door, a carriage came out the drive. It was Grayson. Poor Marley. He got caught with a piece of cake in his hand. Grayson just nodded his head to me and kept moving.

"Who came in the drive now?" asked Annelie.

"I believe it was Grayson."

"Now he is a man that I can't figure out. Why doesn't he court anyone?"

"He must be about the cream of the crop, with his looks," said Jeannie. "I'd take him any day. He carries himself like a king."

"Jeannie," sighed her sister. "You are *much* too young for him!"

"Maybe he likes them young. Maybe he is just waiting for me," she said with a twinkle in her eye. "Exactly how old is he?"

"He just turned twenty-nine," I said, "and I agree, you are too young."

"A hardened old bachelor, if you ask me," said Annelie. "But he seems like a real gentleman. Maybe he was hurt by someone. Or maybe he is too busy. He just inherited this place, didn't he?" She looked at me. "Sounds like quite the catch. Don't you think him handsome? You are more his age."

"He is handsome," I said trying not to betray my real feelings. And I thought it better that they didn't know that we were more than friends as teenagers.

"And?"

"You have to realize," I said slowly, "that we live under the same roof and I am really at his mercy for my home. I try to live cautiously around him. I do not flirt."

"Is he much fun? I seldom see him laughing, but of course I generally see him only at church functions, but he has a very sober look. I think...I believe, well, one would have to do things his way."

I tried not to say much. I was afraid they would see how very much this man affected me. I really did not want to discuss him. It felt demeaning to him, somehow. Like we were discussing a pork roast deciding whether it was too fatty and if it would be tender.

"What is he like at home? You sort of live with him."

"He has his own rooms and most of the days I see him only at suppertime. Some days he is gone all day and so I do not see him at all." I wanted us to talk about something else. "Let me clean up our dishes and then we can do some handwork here in the sitting room. I have some to do also, so we can stay right here by the fire."

"What is going on with Donna Gable?" asked Mary Lou. "I heard that she and her boyfriend eloped but something happened and they did not get married."

"And I heard she came back and her father really flew off the handle when he heard she was not married after having lived with him for several days. Maybe even a week," said Annelie. "What a scandal."

"And I heard that she still loves him. But she has probably heard the last of him."

I remained quiet. They evidently had not heard any of my involvement and that was good. I felt sorry for Donna and I believed she had learned a valuable lesson.

"What do you think, June?" asked Mary Lou, noting my silence.

"I feel sorry for her. She made a big mistake that she will always rue."

"But she says she still loves him. That is what I was told she said to her father, when he lit into her," said Jeannie.

"Maybe she does," I said. "And who knows, maybe if they get their lives straightened out, they will still get back together."

"Well, she surely made a big muddle of her life and I bet she thinks everyone is talking about her," said Jeannie.

"Including us," I could not help from saying.

"Why do you stick up for her?"

"She probably needs a friend," I said slowly, "and if you think about it, any one of us could have made the same mistake. We just were not given the temptation to do so."

"I wish I were as merciful as you," said Mary Lou. "I am sure she is sorry for what she has done."

"Where is the boyfriend? What is his name, anyway?"

"Bud. That is what she calls him, but wait, I did hear his name. Bud Russel, I think. I don't know of any Russel family around here."

"That name rings a bell for me," said Annelie. "Somehow I connect it to the covered bridge that got burned down last year. That was a group of boys and I think one of them was a Russel."

"Well, I hope it wasn't him," said Jeannie, "but it probably was."

"Ouch!" I said. "I just stuck my needle about a half inch into my finger. Well, I guess not quite, but it felt like it."

"Have you seen Marvin again?" Mary Lou asked Jeannie.

"Yes, and when he started talking to me, I told him he could go back to the girl he was smooching with at the Harvest Festival. He got all red and walked away. What do you know about Marley, June? He seems like a decent fellow."

"I think he is. I don't see him often, but I think Grayson thinks highly of him. I have heard him compliment him in conversations at the supper table."

There was a knock at the door and I got up to see who it was. The afternoon had gone so quickly that we did not realize that it was already three o'clock. It was Ron, Mary Lou's brother who was there to pick up the girls. After cutting him a piece of cake, the girls left with him and I was eager to return to my sewing machine. There was still enough light to sew a bit yet and since I had not had the opportunity to sew on it all day, I set to work on it. It seemed the light was getting dimmer, so I lit a lamp and set to sewing. I had talked enough and now it was just fun to sew. I busied myself with my work, reviewing the day's conversation in my mind as I worked the treadle with my foot.

I don't know how long I sat and sewed. I got so involved that I forgot everything else. But at some point, I was aware of wind that rattled the windowpane. I should have looked out the window, but I had to keep my eyes on sewing a straight seam. When I later looked at the window, I discovered it was completely dark outside. I turned down the lamp and pressed my face to the window. I could see nothing. But how could it have gotten dark so quickly? And what was that blowing against the window? Was it snowing? How could I have been so engrossed in my sewing that I was unaware of what was happening outside? I looked at my watch. Six o'clock! Where had those three hours gone since the girls left? It seemed more like a half hour to me.

I realized the house was cool and I went downstairs and lit a lamp and considered throwing another log on the fire. But I needed to be going. I did not know how long this storm would last, but I was not looking forward to going out in it. I packed the food in the basket as quickly as I could, and I finally blew out the lamps, lit a lantern and with the basket in my hand, opened the door. It was indeed snowing and it was blowing furiously. Even here under the arch, which was sheltered a bit from the worst of the wind, the snow was flying through the air and stinging my face. I was surprised at the strength of the storm because even here, I saw a few inches of snow already on the ground. I was not sure I could even make my way home in this storm! The cold cut through my clothes and in the light of the lantern I could see the wind was carrying the snow horizontally across the lane. I caught my breath and never took a step outside the door. There was no way I would dare to head out in this blizzard. I backed away from the door, frightened at the intensity of the wind, and closed it with effort. Once in, I immediately went back to the fire. I added two logs. Then I just stood still and looked around me. I would have to stay here overnight. Would Aunt Sarah worry? Would Grayson think that I had planned it? Well, there was no way I would go out in this weather and I would have no fear of unwanted visitors during this wild night.

I went to the kitchen and set my food basket on the table. I felt a mounting excitement in me. What an adventure! I was not scared. I felt safe here. At least I would not go hungry. But I did need water. The pump was very close to the house, but I needed to go outside to get it before the snow got too deep and the storm worsened. I would fill a bucket, as well as a pot to heat water for tea. I did not suppose any coffee was in the house. I quickly put on my coat and wrapped my scarf around my head and neck. I lit a lamp and set it in the window-sill. I would need that light outside. Then I went to the door, bucket in hand and opened it. I was nearly blown back into the room. This storm was angry! I finally had to force my way out into the raging wind, glad for the dim light coming from the lamp in the kitchen window. In a few faltering steps, I was at the pump. I set the bucket down and pumped, but had to stop and reach into my pocket for my gloves. My fingers were already aching from the cold. Then I contin-ued pumping, sheltering my face from the flying, stinging snow by burying my face in my scarf. When the bucket was full, I took it into the house and came back with my pot for the stove. It was all in slow motion due to the force of the wind. I fought for every step I took and every movement with the pump and container. The door blew open just before I got to it. A reminder to close it tightly against the storm. After slamming the door behind me in the safety of the kitchen, I just stood there a bit, shivering.

"God," I breathed, "please protect anyone who has to be out in this storm."

Then I took off my coat and snowy scarf, took them to the fire and draped them over a chair. I would have to keep this fire going. Wood!

There were only two pieces left. I needed to bring in wood. I quickly donned my coat and once again put on gloves and scarf as well. I had to do this before I thought about it too long. Before I got too scared to go out again. The wood was stacked close to the house, thank God. I had to do this. I *could* do this. The snow was not deep yet.

Once more I opened the door and faced the storm. I could not think of what would happen if I fell and broke a leg out here. I knew where the wood was stacked. I just had to go a bit farther than the pump. Once there, I found the wood almost frozen together from the cold and snow that was already packed into the wood. I threw a half dozen pieces toward the door, then added a few more. They did not go as far as I would have liked. I had to walk then to that pile and threw it piece by piece to the side of the door. Finally, I went to the door, pushed it open and threw it piece by piece into the kitchen. With thanks to God, I went in and slammed the door. I would not go out again in this storm.

I went back to the hearth to get warm and then gathered the wood and stacked it by the fire. It would easily be enough to keep me warm overnight. The house got cold easily with the door opening. I wished for hot chocolate, but I had none. But I could make hot tea to keep me warm.

The storm howled around the gatehouse and I thought how much more fun this would have been if the girls had been here with me. Now, alone, with this wild stormy wind screaming and attacking the gatehouse, I felt a bit of fear. What if a tree branch fell and broke a window? Or worse, came through the roof? I had to think of other things. For one thing, I was hungry. I stoked the fire in the stove and set the water on the stove for tea. Thank God I had made food for the birthday party. If I had just been sewing, I would have had no food. Tea would warm my insides and as I waited for the water to get hot, I ate half of the leftover potato salad. The chicken was gone. I buttered a slice of bread and ate a small piece of cake. The tea hit the spot. That was it for my supper.

My thoughts went again to Aunt Sarah. I found myself praying for her. I had seen Grayson go out the drive. I had not seen him return, but then, I had been sewing. But I prayed for him also. I feared for anyone caught in this storm. My thoughts returned to Grayson. Would he worry about me? He would surely know that I would not attempt to come home in this weather. Or would he be angry with me for not coming back sooner? Would he sit at home and wonder if I was attempting to come back? Or would he feel he had to come to find me? The more I thought of it, the more my mind imagined.

It was nearly eight o'clock when I finally went upstairs to the bedroom above the drive. I had nothing to do and I may as well go to bed. The room was not warm at all. I went to the window to look out. Of course I could see nothing. Then I realized the window was steamed up. Actually the steam was frozen on the pane. I scraped it off, little by little with my fingernail. Then I peered out into the blackness. What did I expect to see? There were no gas lamps lighting the entrance to the drive. Maybe at one time there were, when the gatehouse was first built. But now, no more. There was only the dimmest of light reflected on the snow from the lamp in the sitting room. I turned and went to the opposite window that looked out to the road. Again, utter blackness with the snow flying against the pane. Total oblivion. I could have imagined I was on the North Pole all by myself. Here, with the snow pelting against the window, there was not even the glimmer of reflection from the sitting room window. I went back to the other window, scraped more frost from the window and looked once more. I was looking toward the house, but even in good weather one could not see the house from here. Too many trees. But I looked anyway. Nothing. I was just turning away when I stopped. I peered hard through the window. Blackness. I thought for a moment that I had seen a light. Barely a light. It must have been a reflection from the downstairs window. But I kept my face nearly pressed against the window and kept it there till my forehead hurt from the cold. There! I saw it again! It looked like a lantern! Not so far away. Then it was gone again.

I fairly flew from the room and down the stairs. It could only be Grayson. It had to be him. I raced to the door and opened it. The snow swirled inside as I looked intently into the storm. But I could see nothing. I went for the lantern and my coat and scarf. I set the lantern outside the door then raced back to the kitchen. Someone was out there and what could they see? Just flying snow. I grabbed a wooden spoon and a large metal pan that was hanging on the wall. Then I stepped out the door and banged the spoon against the pan. I was freezing, but I kept at it. My heart was pounding with each clang of the spoon on the pan.

"Come here! Come here!" I did not know what else to call, because I did not know for sure who it was. And then I saw the lantern again. The person moved very slowly. I could now see him. He was totally exhausted and seemed too tired to lift his feet. And suddenly he went down.

And he did not get up again.

I threw the metal pan and spoon down on the floor and put on my gloves. I could barely see him in the snow, but the lamp gave a wee bit of light. I had no boots, but I had sturdy shoes. I kicked the metal pan out of my way before I stepped into the storm. Here, under the arch, I had a bit of a break, but as I left that area, I faced the storm in all its fury. I groped my way toward the flickering lantern and was frightened like never before. I had to get this person, whoever it was, into the house. I almost did not see him. In fact, I almost stumbled over him. I leaned down and brushed the snow and his scarf from his face. It was Grayson.

"Conrad! Grayson! Can you hear me? You must get up!" I saw not even the smallest movement. I knelt in the snow and put my face against his frozen face, cheek to cheek. "Wake up, Grayson!"

I was now crying for sheer fright, but I was not about to let him freeze in the snow. I shook him. I called his name. I stood up and grabbed one arm...and pulled. Then I pulled again. The snow made it possible for him to slide. I pulled some more. Each time he moved just a bit more. Once my feet slid out from under me and I landed on my seat, my shoes nearly in his face. I was nearly numb from the freezing cold. It would be so easy to give up. I scrambled to my feet and pulled again until finally, I was under the arch and nearly at the door of the house. And here was less wind and less snow. It was a bit easier.

"Grayson, you have to help me! I can't do it alone," I sobbed. "God, don't let Grayson die! Please, not Grayson!"

Once more I knelt down and put my face against his. I did not think about what I was doing. Only that I had to save this man. I had to get some warmth in his face. I put my face on both of his cheeks. I even pressed my lips across his. And then he moved his head. Just a bit. He must be alive.

I stood and put my snowy, cold, gloves on his boots and pulled him toward the door. I could get a better grip on his boots. I finally got him to the door. Thank God there were no steps. I dropped his boots and opened the door, set the lantern that had been setting by the door inside and pulled once more on his boots. I somehow got him inside the room and got the door closed. It was harder pulling him here, but the door was shut and the house was warm. I stamped the snow from my shoes and shook my skirt before the snow could melt on it.

"Grayson, do you hear me? Please wake up!" I was crying again. Was he dead? Had I imagined the slight head movement? I thought I saw a flicker of an eyelid. I brushed the snow from him, took off his gloves and rubbed his hands. "Grayson, wake up, please wake up!"

I felt his pulse. Praise God, there was one. He was breathing. I opened his coat to let the heat get to his skin. I removed the boots from his feet. That was hard, but in my despair, I managed it. I rubbed his feet in my bare hands. They were so very cold.

And then Grayson opened his eyes. He gave me a long look, but said nothing.

"Thank God! Oh, thank you, God!" I said, and not thinking of what I was doing, I brushed a bit of snow off his face and pressed my hands to his cold cheeks. I hovered over him, my face just inches from his and then, finally, he spoke.

"June."

"You are alive! You are safe!" I wiped the tears from my eyes so they would not fall on his face.

Grayson slowly sat up. I took his coat from him. I pushed a chair closer to the fire. "Can you get up? Or sit on the couch here in front of the fire. I can help you."

He slowly got up by his own strength and walked to the couch.

"I will get you some tea," I said, now embarrassed at what I had done when I was so frantic. I hurried to the kitchen and poured a cup of tea and I brought it to Grayson. I stood beside him. It never entered my head to sit down. I felt like I somehow had to keep him alive. He was quiet, but he was not big on small talk. I let him sit there and thaw out for what seemed to me a long time. I wanted him to talk. He finally looked away from the flames of the hearth and turned to me.

"Did you have supper?" I asked. He did not answer my question.

"Sit down, June." He pointed to the seat beside him. As I did so, he took my hand and held it, putting his other hand over it. I never saw such a humble Grayson.

"You saved my life, June. I would have frozen out there." His voice was not quite steady and I blinked back tears.

"I was so scared, Grayson," I said, my voice trembling. "I was never in my whole life, so scared."

He was still holding my hand between his. "I owe my life to you."

"I would do it again," I said, the tears in my throat making my voice thin.

"How did you know I was out there?"

I had to think a bit. "I didn't," I answered slowly, remembering. "But I was worried about anyone out in the storm...and I hoped you would not try to come, because I was safe. But for some reason, I went upstairs and looked out the window. I did not see you at first. There was just utter blackness. Then I looked out the other way. I had to scrape the frost from the windowpanes. And then, before going down, I gave one last look toward the house...and thought I saw a wee bit of light. When I was sure, I came downstairs."

"I heard the clanging," he said slowly. "I was going off in another direction. I may have zigzagged the whole way out here. The clanging helped me. But I was so exhausted. And so cold." He squeezed my hand. "I would not have made it without you."

The tears were running down my face, but I did not care. He had tears in his own eyes.

"God heard my prayers," I said softly.

"You were His angel," he said heavily, "and I thank you."

I didn't ever want to take my hand from his. It felt so good. His hands were warm now. But eventually, I had to slip my hand from his and blow my nose. This was a hallowed evening. Actually, a most wonderful evening. And thank God, Grayson was safe. I went to the kitchen and brought him the rest of the potato salad and a slice of bread.

"Oh," he said, "Sarah knew you had bread, so she sent some sliced beef to eat with it. You will find it in my coat pocket."

I found his coat, brought it to him and he handed me the sliced meat.

"Let me make you a sandwich. There is also birthday cake. I might even make myself a sandwich, although I already ate. The cold air gives me an appetite."

He sat in silence at the fire. He was recovering from a near-death experience. I could honor that. I was also digesting the fact that he held my hand so long and attributed his being alive to me. There was much to ponder. My innermost being felt warm.

After refilling his tea, I handed him the sandwich. I realized that though I had "saved" him, I was also, in part, responsible for him being out in the storm.

"When did your friends leave here?" he asked as we ate our sandwiches.

"They were picked up at three. I do not think it was snowing then. At least I did not see any flakes here under the arch. I cleaned up and then I thought I still had time to sew. And when I sew, I forget all else. I am neither cold nor hot. I have no thought of time. I am sorry to have worried you. But the time went so *fast*. I suddenly realized it was dark, and then, hearing the wind and something on the window-pane, I went to the door and looked out. That was the first I knew of the snowstorm. I quickly got dressed and I was ready to step out the door when I realized it was just too dangerous. So instead, I brought in wood and water. That was scary enough." He made no comment. "How long do you think you were out in the storm?"

He thought a bit. "I really don't know. We talked about you. Sarah thought you would stay here. But I wondered if you may have started out and then found it was too hard to see. I really do not know what time it was. I had just come home a bit before that. But I came in the other entrance because it was shorter. When I came into the house and Sarah said you were not home yet, I knew I had to come to find you, otherwise we would worry all night long. I ate a quick supper and I really thought I could make it, but the wind kept getting worse and I could barely see, even with my lantern. The storm had intensified just in the time since I had come home with the carriage."

"It is my fault you were even out in it. I am so sorry. Thank you for being concerned." I was feeling very guilty. "Oh dear. I never picked up your lantern. It is out there under the snow."

"We will find it eventually. How was the party?"

I was glad for the change of subject. I also noticed a change in Grayson. He was getting over the shock of nearly losing his life.

"Wonderful. Lots of fun. Of course it was girl talk. You would not have enjoyed it."

"But you did have one male among you."

I looked at him perplexed. "Oh! Marley brought wood and stopped in to tell me."

"I don't suppose you knew till then?"

I looked at him. Was he thinking Marley had no business coming to the door? But no, he was hiding a smile.

"Actually, we did see him, but he brightened the day for at least one of the girls when he came in, and for that he got a piece of birthday cake. Oh! Are you ready for cake?"

"Anytime."

After he ate his cake, he got up and stoked the fire. He added a log.

"It looks like you brought in enough wood. And water? Do you need more?"

"No. Let's not go out anymore tonight."

"I think there should be blankets upstairs somewhere," he said. "I did not remove them all when I left.

"Yes, I think there are some."

"I'll let you have the cot. I'll stay here and watch the fire...if I don't sleep too soundly."

"Let me go up and see what blankets are up there. You will need some as well."

I left the room, thinking again what a strange day it was. The man who said it was not appropriate for me to live here alone was now here with me for the night! Of course, we slept in the same house every night, but this was different. Here it was only us and it felt a lot different. I took the lamp and went up the stairs to the sewing room. And then up the stairs to the bedroom above the entrance. Sure enough, on a shelf I found two thinner blankets and several old, heavy quilts. Who knows how long they were sitting there, but tonight they would be used. I carried one thin blanket and a quilt down for Grayson. He would be by the fire and would be warm.

When I got downstairs, I discovered Grayson closing the front door.

"It is wild out there and a lot of snow has fallen."

"Are you sure I brought enough wood in?"

"For the night, yes. I wonder how long we may be here. I don't think there is a shovel in the house, but I believe there is one in the shed. If I can get the door open."

"Can we wait until morning? Maybe the sun will shine. Or at least we will have daylight. It is so scary out there in the dark." I could hardly think of going out in the storm again.

"When did you bring this wood in? Wasn't it already dark?"

"I put a lamp in the kitchen window. But everything took so long and now there is more snow."

"I really have no wish to go back out in the storm myself. We'll wait till morning."

I stifled a yawn. It was only nine o'clock but I was tense here with Grayson in spite of the open talk we had had. I thought he looked weary also.

"I think I will head upstairs," I said. "We are both weary."

First he just nodded. Then he turned to me. "I wish you a good night."

"I wish you the same."

I started up the stairs and turned. I had to know something. But I had to think how to word it. Grayson saw my hesitation and waited.

"You know, I...thought you might be dead out there in the snow. You were unconscious, weren't you?"

I sensed the slightest clenching of his jaw as if trying not to smile. His eyes strayed from mine for just a second. "I was too cold and exhausted to think, much less talk."

It was not the answer I wanted. Being unconscious is one thing, but just too cold and tired to answer is quite another. Did he know I had put my face against his, trying to put some warmth into him? Trying to bring him back from "the dead?" I quickly looked away and hurried up the stairs where I kicked off my shoes, jumped into bed, and pulled the blanket over my head. I had wanted reassurance, but I had received nothing of the sort. He had tried not to smile. I had the awful feeling that Grayson knew all too well about my cheek against his. Oh! And my lips pressed against his!

I did not sleep right away. I was up in the room above the arch. I had wind and snow beating on all sides of the room I was in, and it seemed almost like there were no walls. It was cold and it felt like my little room sitting on the arch could just blow away with the next strong gust. It was frightening. Could the windows blow in? Was it possible that the whole room could blow away? I could not go back downstairs. No way was I going to a sleeping Grayson because I was scared. So I hunkered down with the blanket over my head to keep my nose warm, and out of sheer exhaustion, I eventually fell asleep.

———————

Once I slept, I slept. I never got awake until long past daybreak. I listened for the wind, but could not hear it. I sat up in bed. I felt a bit of warmth coming up the stairs, but this was certainly not the best room in the house to heat. I looked to the window closest to me. It was frozen shut. I used my fingernails once more. It was still snowing but no longer blowing. Thank God for that. I looked at my watch. It was eight-thirty! I never slept that long! I wondered if Grayson was up. I was already dressed, so I put on my cold shoes and went downstairs. Grayson was in the kitchen adding wood to the stove. I saw he had a cup of tea on the table.

"Good morning," he said with a slight smile. "You must have slept good."

"Only after I assured myself my room would not blow away in the wind. It was scary up there!"

He grinned. "I did not think of that. I never slept up there because I did not need that room. But yes, I can believe it was frightening with the storm just on the other side of all four walls."

"And you? Did you sleep?"

"I did. Soundly. I woke up cold because the fire was nearly out."

"I no longer hear the wind."

"The storm is ebbing. There is a great deal of snow but it is letting up. Maybe Marley will come with the sleigh, if he knows we are here."

"He lives on the property, doesn't he?"

"He stays in the little cabin and when there is a snowstorm, it is good to have someone on the property. I can always count on him."

"So he deserved his piece of cake," I said.

Grayson grinned but made no comment.

"I waded through the snow to the shed," he said. "Then I had to find a place to shove the snow from the door. But I found the shovel, which will come in handy because I must soon go after more wood."

"I will help you. It will go better with two."

"No, you have no boots."

"Oh, I forgot. Well, you can throw the wood on the stoop and I will bring it in. And," I added, "breakfast will be birthday cake, tea, and any bread and butter we have. Oh, and there is a bit of roast beef left over yet from Aunt Sarah."

"A feast. We could be here with nothing. Good that someone had a birthday. By the way, did you find anymore sunbonnets upstairs?"

He had a nasty glint in his eye.

"I did not. And I never did hear how it was here and then it was not here."

"Very simple. You found it. I did not mean for you to find it. So I took it again. And then you did not find it until I wrapped it up for you."

I just shook my head.

––––––––––––––––––

After we got the wood in, I went up to sew. We had to wait to be rescued and Grayson had a firm trust that we would be rescued by Marley. And we were. In the meantime, Grayson got the shovel and managed to make a path through the snow to the woodpile and I helped him bring in some wood. It was fun working with Grayson. I tried to forget the embarrassment of the evening before, and hoped he was too cold and tired to realize what I had done.

Marley arrived shortly before noon with two horses and a sleigh. He skirted around drifts in the field and arrived triumphant. I took my now empty basket and we headed for the door. The sun had just appeared and it was dazzling white and beautiful outside. I had come without boots and although there was some snow shoveled at the door, I still would have to walk a few steps in some deep snow to the sleigh. As I stood and looked at the beautiful countryside, Grayson took the basket from me and handed it to Marley. Then he turned around and with a glance at my bootless feet, he scooped me up and carried me to the sleigh. I'm afraid I gave him a quick, shocked look once I was in the sleigh and was met with a steady look as he watched me blush.

When we got home, Aunt Sarah had an early lunch for us and Marley also stayed. After Marley left, Aunt Sarah wanted to hear the whole story and at the end of it, suggested that if we did not have to tell about spending the night there together, we should not. But Marley was already gone and who knows what would be said. But most likely, Marley had been given the same advice by Grayson.

Later that week, I took a few staples to the gatehouse. Coffee, sugar, salt, some dried noodles and a few jars of fruit and veggies. And a nightgown. I would not take a chance of getting stuck there again.

CHAPTER 17

We got an unexpected visitor a few days later. Vesta, a cousin to Becca and Lizzie came to the door, all smiles and with plans to stay for a few days. She was a big woman and evidently neither blind nor deaf and was in rather sound mind. I say rather. She arrived as a ship with her sails full blown and filled the house with her presence. I was home at the time she arrived, and hearing of her intentions to stay a few days, I quickly got a room ready on the second floor since there would be no room for her with her cousins. Vesta, I learned, lived in a town about twenty miles from us, and was a widow. She was at least ten years younger than her cousins and had dark eyes that missed nothing and hair that was on the frizzy side and seemed to form a halo around her round face. She was a jolly soul and meant well, I presume, but she was a lot to get used to. I was not sure how long she would stay, as she had not given a definite time, but I somehow knew our lives would not be quite the same with Vesta in the house.

The first day she was here, I did not go to the gatehouse. I thought Aunt Sarah needed me. Vesta was a big person and in seemingly good health. She would need food. So we baked bread, a pie or two, put on a big pot of stew and finally made a chocolate cake and a batch of molasses cookies. By the end of the day I was eager to leave the kitchen and get back to sewing.

Shortly before supper, Grayson, who had been gone all day, came home and announced that we would have a guest for supper. We had learned our lesson regarding guests with Becca and Lizzie shouting to each other, so now, whenever we had visitors, we had Becca and Lizzie eat in the kitchen. It was just better than all the shouting at the table with a bewildered guest sitting there. When I relayed this to Vesta, she wasn't sure she liked this idea. I think she enjoyed being in the thick of things and felt left out. We finally told her that it was someone doing business with Grayson and they would certainly talk business during the meal and with the deafness so rampant in our midst, it was best if the three of them stayed in the kitchen to eat. I promised her I would see that they were properly served.

Grayson and his guest arrived promptly at six and after getting the three cousins eating in the kitchen, I went into the dining room where Aunt Sarah and the two men awaited me. Before we sat down, Grayson introduced us to our guest, Winston Chambers, a big man with an air of authority about him. As soon as the food was passed, the two men began talking about horses and Aunt Sarah and I just mostly listened in. Partway through the meal, I began to notice a lively discussion drifting in from the kitchen area.

"I can't hear you!" shouted Becca, who now talked much more with both her sister Lizzie and now her cousin here.

"What?" shouted Lizzie even louder.

"She can't hear!" said Vesta, bellowing at both of them.

"I know that. I can't hear either," said Lizzie.

"What?" shouted Becca.

"She can't hear either!" shouted Vesta. "I think it is in the family."

I stopped eating, wondering how to stem the uproar in the kitchen.

"Who is that big man that came for supper?" It was Becca again.

"He is talking with Grayson."

"What about?"

"Who knows? You couldn't hear anyway."

"Ouch," said Vesta. "I just kicked my bunion against the chair."

"What?"

"She kicked her onion!" shouted Lizzie. "What are you doing with an onion down there anyway?"

"A bunion! Not an onion!"

"How did you get that?" It sounded like someone's mouth was full.

"What?"

"I said how did you get a bunion?"

"Don't know. Just growed there."

"Did you go to the doctor? Maybe he can cut it off."

"He can't take it off. So I wear slippers."

"Flippers? What do you mean flippers?"

I silently prayed the guest did not hear the comedy in the next room. I was wondering if I should close the door between the rooms. I was, of course, listening because I was conscious of the visitor being there. Was Grayson aware of all the noise coming from the kitchen and did he think I should quiet them? I looked anxiously at the men, but decided they were quite animated about the horses they were discussing and probably did not hear it. I tried to relax. I gave Mr. Chambers another look. Every time I looked at him, I had a feeling I had seen him before. But nothing came to mind and I decided he just resembled someone I knew. When I saw that the plates were empty, I thought maybe the food should be passed again in case someone wanted more. That proved to be a mistake, because as I began passing the bowls around, there came a lull in the conversation. And in that lull, Vesta's voice came clear and strong from the next room.

"I always have such trouble with my bowels!" she announced in her trumpet voice. "Nothing helps."

That did it. I unceremoniously shoved back my chair, and with a mumbled apology, left the table, went to the kitchen and shut the door behind me. It was just too much. The talk ceased immediately and Vesta loudly announced to her cousins that they should finish eating as we were now getting dessert.

I did take time to cut the pies before I returned to the dining room again. I needed time to forget what the guest had heard. I returned to the table and when we finished our meal, I took the used plates to the kitchen. I had made cherry pies for supper and as I approached the table with the pie, it seemed the horse conversation was ended.

"So, are you keeping everything under control in Thackeray's Pond?" asked Grayson.

I thought it a strange question and took another look at the stranger.

"So far so good. Well, we never seem to have enough sheriffs at the Harvest Festival. Whenever we have a lot of people from out of town there is the potential for problems. There were two fights that we had to break up and several instances of thievery. We were kept busy till late at night."

When Winston said sheriff, I stopped mid stride and took another look at our guest. And then I knew why he seemed familiar. Without his uniform, I had not recognized him. But this was the man who found Jeannie for us. I quickly caught myself and put the pie on the table, nearly dropping it in my nervousness. Would the sheriff mention the girl he had to find? And did he recognize me? I hoped Grayson did not see my hesitation. There was little that he missed. I did not dare look at him but I was aware of his eyes on me and it was hard to ignore his scrutiny. I know he saw me nearly drop the pie. I felt the heat in my face and hurriedly returned to the kitchen for the coffee. There was more talk about sheriff duty but I heard no details of it. Winston and I knew something the others did not. I had not breathed a word of our misadventure with Jeannie to anyone. It was a secret between us four girls. Jeannie had learned her lesson and we did not need to broadcast it. I hardly remember the rest of the meal. I was in my own little world and I was remembering Grayson's comment that we would need a chaperone. I almost wished the three cousins in the kitchen would start chattering loudly to draw our attention elsewhere.

After dessert, Grayson and his guest went into the parlor and I took more coffee in for them. As I poured the coffee, Mr. Chambers addressed me.

"Miss Merriweather, you look somehow familiar to me. Have we met before this evening?"

"And I have been wondering where I saw you," I said, although I was no longer wondering.

"He is a sheriff in Thackeray Pond," said Grayson. "I doubt you have met."

"Oh. Perhaps you were at the Harvest Festival?" the sheriff asked.

I hesitated only a moment. His comment gave nothing away. "That must have been it. Mystery solved," I said quickly. But I did not look at Grayson when I poured his coffee.

I returned to the three cousins in the kitchen. I now felt safer with them. They were still shouting to each other but I no longer heard them. I was remembering the night we three girls walked the dark streets of Thackeray's Pond. What a night. I hoped the sheriff no longer remembered the details.

When I finished washing the dishes, I decided I would go right to my room. The cousins were now together over in Becca and Lizzie's part of the house. The men were still talking in the parlor and I did not want to meet Grayson this evening. He knew nothing of our midnight excursion through the streets of Thackeray's Pond and I had a feeling he would not think very highly of such unladylike behavior.

When I stepped back into the kitchen, I met Aunt Sarah.

"I am afraid I will have nightmares of our supper tonight. What an embarrassing situation. I don't know what we should do when we have visitors. I am sure Grayson was not pleased with the evening," she said.

"Maybe we must take the food over to their apartment. At least then we would not hear their shouting."

"It would be funny if it were not so embarrassing," she said with a smile lurking at the corners of her mouth.

After the dishes were back in the cupboard, I went up to my room, only to realize I had finished the book I was reading. I would have to return to the library for another book. I was careful now not to go when Grayson was in the house, since that was now part of his apartment. But he was, I hoped, still with his guest. Surely there would be some interesting book to take my mind off the evening.

I hurried down the stairs, glad to hear some low voices in the parlor. I put the book I had borrowed back on the shelf and began searching for another book. The book I looked for, I could not find. After a few minutes of searching, I heard footsteps approaching the door. And before I could think, Grayson was at the open door and before I could escape, he entered the library. I kept my eyes on the bookshelf, but I was not seeing the books. I heard him close the door and come into the room. I was aware that his footsteps slowed. I heard him put another log on the fire. I had to leave. I grabbed a book without looking at the title and headed to the door.

"June, please take a seat here by the fire."

So, he really was upset about the supper. I sat down and prepared to apologize. He turned from the fire and looked at the book I was holding.

"I see you picked up some nighttime reading." I was too busy wondering how upset he was and merely nodded. "Do you often select such reading for yourself?"

"Pardon?"

"I see you plan to read the dictionary." His eyes went to the book in my hand.

I looked in utter mortification at the book I was holding. It was indeed a dictionary. My face turned red. Trying not to smile, he took the book from me and placed it back on the shelf.

"So you knew Winston."

"Winston?"

I should not have said that. Grayson turned and just looked at me. His look was very rebuking.

After a rather painful pause, I realized he would not give me the satisfaction of repeating the question. We both knew who he was talking about.

"Not really."

I could tell Grayson was looking at me, but my eyes focused on the flames in the hearth. "You got so nervous you nearly dropped the pie." I said nothing. "I'd be interested in hearing how you made Winston's acquaintance."

I could not think of anything to say that would save me from saying more than I wished to. My hesitation was too long.

"I think you have a story to tell and I want to hear it." He took a seat close to me, sat back and put one foot on the opposite knee. He could shake me up so easily and now, sitting so close, I was acting so guilty one would think I had robbed a bank that night.

"It wasn't anything, really."

"Your actions suggest otherwise." Grayson's voice had a slight edge to it. We could sit all evening. He was not going to let me go until he heard my tale.

"Jeannie got lost and the sheriff helped us to find her." I said it as nonchalantly as I could. Grayson just looked at me, which did not lessen the heat in my face. In a desperate attempt, I added, "Just because I live here, doesn't give you the right to know all that happened."

"No, it doesn't. But as your friend...."

So he considered me his friend? My surprise at his statement must have been reflected on my face. He was my landlord. I was his charity. But friend? After I spurned him?

"I've always been your friend," he said softly, without letting any sign of emotion on his face.

For some reason, it knocked the wind out of my sails. I looked away from him, trying to gather my thoughts. I had to forget my attraction to him and think about that night in Thackeray's Pond. We girls had promised to keep this experience under our hats. But the sheriff had messed things up for me.

"Did the sheriff tell you anything?"

"No. And I did not ask. I want to hear it from you." Again, that bit of steel in his voice.

With his dark eyes fixed on me, I took a deep breath and began our tale. I did not look at him but instead, fixed my eyes on the blazing hearth. I told him about Jeannie. I said she saw her "boyfriend" with someone else and it angered her and when she was offered a ride by a boy she knew from school, she went, before we had a chance to stop her.

"And then?"

"The three of us went looking for her."

"So you tried to follow her?"

"No, we went to Mary Lou's aunt for the night. And then went to look for her."

He thought a while. "What time was that?"

"Late."

"Really late?"

"Really late."

"You three girls went out looking for her on the streets of Thackeray's Pond alone?"

"We were not alone," I said stubbornly. "There were three of us."

"And Mary Lou's aunt was okay with that?"

"She did not know." Silence.

"And then you went to the sheriff."

"Not exactly." Grayson waited. "He found us." There was a long silence. I heard a clock strike the hour.

"So he put you in his sheriff's wagon and hauled you off to the sheriff's headquarters."

"Yes. No. He was on his horse, so we followed him to the station where he got the carriage."

"Did he lock you up in the station while he went to look for her?"

"Goodness, no. He took us along." I could not tell if Grayson was finding this amusing or pathetic.

"You went hunting with him?"

"We waited in the carriage while he went into the bar to look for her. He was pretty sure where she was."

"And the three of you were locked in the sheriff's wagon?"

I could tell Grayson was actually enjoying the tale.

"Yes." Grayson shook his head from side to side, but said nothing. "And I suppose you all got written up on the sheriff's report?"

I shrugged. I said nothing.

"So tell me about the finding of Miss Jeannie. My guess is that she was a bit drunk...."

"Not drunk. But she was badly scared. I don't think she will do it again."

There was silence for a full fifteen seconds.

"May I go?" I asked.

Grayson looked at me, his face serious.

"I want you to promise me you will never do such a foolish thing again."

"We could not let her out there alone." When he said nothing, I added, "You don't need to feel responsible for me."

"But I do."

"Why?"

"Let that be my secret. I mean it for your good. You girls needed a chaperone. Now find yourself a book that is a bit more readable than the dictionary."

CHAPTER 18

It was Sunday, and Vesta wanted to go to church with us. Becca and Lizzie heard so little they usually did not go, so the pastor came to visit them regularly. It was a nice, mild morning with bright sunlight, which caused one automatically to think of the coming spring. Grayson suggested that I take the carriage and take Vesta and Aunt Sarah and he would ride his horse. And so we did. It seemed more people were at church than usual and I wondered if it was the bright spring-like day. As we took our seats, I saw that Marley was there. I seldom saw him, but I gave him a smile when he looked at me. After the service, as I was walking to the carriage, Marley came up to me.

"Good morning, June."

"Hello, Marley. So the nice weather brought you to church today."

He grinned and looked just a bit sheepish. "No, it was you that brought me."

"Me?" I had no idea what he was taking about.

"How about going for a ride with me this afternoon?"

I think I must have looked shocked. I just did not expect it of him. My thoughts were always centered on Grayson and I did not think about anyone else. But what did I have to lose? It was a lovely mild day and a time to be outside.

"I accept, Marley."

"I'll pick you up at three," he said and strode off with a smile.

I walked a bit in a daze to the carriage. When I got there, I found myself just staring at the carriage while I considered what I had just accepted. Finally, I turned my face to the retreating Marley, but instead of Marley, my eyes locked with Grayson's as he stood observing me from his horse. How much had he caught? I looked away first and searched for Aunt Sarah and Vesta. They were still chatting with the pastor's wife. Seeing Mary Lou coming in my direction, I turned to her.

"Hi June," she said. "I see Marley came today. I have seldom seen him here."

"You won't believe it, but he asked me to go riding with him this afternoon."

"Really? Oh, you lucky girl. I'd love to go riding with him. Do you like him?"

"I barely know him. I very seldom see him."

"How old do you think he is?"

"I think I heard Grayson say one time that he is in his mid-twenties."

We were interrupted by Aunt Sarah and Vesta and without further talk, we headed home.

Grayson was almost never with us on a Sunday noon. Aunt Sarah said once that he met a friend for lunch every Sunday. I was somehow glad.

That afternoon, I watched for Marley and met him outside. I remembered skating with him and I had enjoyed it. Now, I decided I would simply enjoy the ride and not think further than that. He arrived shortly after three.

"Hey, this carriage looks brand new!" I said as he helped me into the carriage.

"It is. Just got it. My other carriage had been my father's old carriage."

"And it still felt like it belonged to him, rather than to you?"

"Exactly."

"It's very nice," I said as we splashed through the ford and up to the gatehouse.

"Thanks."

"How long have you had the horse?"

"Susan?"

"Is that the horse's name?"

He grinned. "When I got the horse I was interested in a girl named Susan."

I laughed. I could completely relax with Marley. We drove to Thackeray's Pond and back, mostly on roads unknown to me, so it was very interesting. I had a feeling that Marley just wanted to drive his new carriage around—maybe show it off to anyone he might know— and I was the one he chose to share the ride with him. We came home around suppertime and I found I had thoroughly enjoyed my time with Marley.

On Wednesday afternoon, Vesta left us. I was a bit relieved although the three cousins seemed to get along well. I did quite a bit of sewing and was at the gatehouse every day. The gown I was making for Mrs. Forbes was ready for a fitting and she came on Thursday afternoon and was happy with the result. I told her she could pick it up on Monday.

The following Sunday, Marley was again at church. During the night it had rained hard and it rained part of the morning. But when we got out of church, the sun was shining although the air was cool. I joined Mary Lou outside the church and we talked of planning another sewing day at the gatehouse. As we talked, I saw Marley watching me and also noticed that Grayson was standing in view of us, but talking with someone else. Mary Lou was watching Marley and when he came toward us and greeted us both, she blushed. But when he again asked me for a drive, she turned away, sad. I accepted the ride, but I knew I was not interested in Marley and I was pretty sure Mary Lou was, so I decided I would not ride with him if he asked me a third time.

When Marley arrived, I walked out to meet him. He was in a good mood and kept the conversation going easily. We could not travel some roads because they were too muddy. The creeks were high, as well as the ford in our drive. But it was fun driving around and Marley was good company. However, as we headed back toward Bluster Hill, I knew I had to say something. Although I enjoyed the ride, I knew that Marley was not replacing Grayson for me. I thought romantically of Grayson, whereas Marley was a great brother. Furthermore, Mary Lou was sad that I was out with Marley and I really did not think that Marley was in love with me. He liked me. I liked him. He would not be heartbroken. I waited for the right moment, then began.

"Marley, I must have a serious talk with you."

"Are you proposing?" His grin was wide as he leaned a bit toward me and I had to laugh. I had a feeling this would not be so difficult.

"I am not proposing marriage, but I perhaps am proposing. I just want you to know that I think you are a great guy and someday you will make someone's life very happy. But it won't be mine. I enjoyed our rides, but this is a waste of your time. I know you are not in love with me, and I am not in love with you. But I have a question for you."

Marley's smile was fading and he was beginning to look more serious. He turned his head and looked at me.

"Let's have it."

"What do you think of Mary Lou?"

He did not answer right away, but looked off into the distance. "Mary Lou? I have not thought too much about her. She is a very nice person. I had fun skating with her last winter. Why do you ask?"

"I think she was sad that you asked me and not her this morning."

"Really? You really think so?"

"I do."

He was quiet for a bit. Then he looked at me and I could see he was very serious. "Now I have a question for you." He just looked at me a few seconds before he spoke. "What do you think of my boss?"

I know my eyes opened wide. "What makes you ask that?"

"Just answer my question."

"He is a good landlord."

"And? You are not going to get away with that for an answer. Is he the reason that you are backing off of me?"

"If he were interested in me, he would ask me out."

"You are having a hard time answering the question. But I have my answer. So this is our last ride?"

"I think so," I said.

I was not sure what Marley was thinking, but I hoped my feelings for Grayson were not written all over my face. We were just coming up to the gatehouse and I suddenly wanted to know what made Marley ask me about Grayson. He had no reason to think that I was waiting for his employer. He hardly ever saw us together.

"Marley," I said as he turned in the lane, "stop the carriage." He did as directed. "What makes you think that I am interested in your employer?"

"I can't tell you." I just looked at him, hoping he would say more, but he was firm. He was not saying it slowly, trying to think just why he suspected it, he just said I can't tell you. Odd.

"What do you mean, you can't tell me?"

Marley looked off in the distance again. "I just can't. Period."

I could tell this was a dead-end street.

"You know, Marley, I feel like walking. I'd like to walk in the lane. You can just let me off here."

He helped me out, and I felt he was studying me.

"Marley, I enjoyed our time together. I enjoyed the rides. Thank you."

He nodded, still serious. "So did I."

As I walked in the lane, I thought about our talk. I just could not figure out how he could have thought I was interested in Grayson. I had given him no clue. But, of course, his boss was a bachelor. And we lived in the same house. We would see each other often. I would have to be satisfied with that.

Just then I heard the clip clop of a horse behind me. I gave a quick glance over my shoulder and then looked straight ahead. It was Grayson. I waited for him to pass me, but instead, he rode up beside me, tipped his hat without a smile and stayed beside me. He paced the horse to my steps. At times I had to skirt the mud, and although he stayed by my side, he did not speak. I was so intent on his manner to me that we were at the ford before I knew it. The water was too deep and I immediately turned to go over the bridge.

"June." I turned to Grayson. "Come here."

I walked slowly to him. "Give me your left hand." I did not. I just looked at him. He silently held out his hand to me and I finally, hesitatingly, held up my hand. Instead of taking my hand, he took my arm above my wrist. "Now, June, you are about to have your first riding lesson." As I pulled my arm back, his hand tightened around my arm. "Put your left foot in the stirrup and as I pull, put your arm around me and you will be sitting right behind me." He would not let go. I did as he said and surprisingly to me, it worked. I was suddenly high up on the horse, now holding on to Grayson for dear life. And although scared of falling, I was loving it.

"Ready to cross the ford?"

I somehow squeaked out a yes. This was fun and scary at the same time. We crossed the stream and the black horse trotted on to the stables, rather than to the door. Once there, Grayson helped me down.

"So June, how was it?" he asked, looking at my red face.

I had to smile. He looked like a naughty boy. "I survived."

"You enjoyed it but would rather die than admit it," he said looking hard at me. "Tomorrow morning I will meet you right here at nine o'clock. Your riding has been put off long enough."

"Tuesday morning."

He looked at me in surprise. "And why not tomorrow morning?"

"I must do something first." I said no more. Let him think what he wanted.

Reluctantly he gave in. "I hope this is not just an excuse to put it off?"

I just shook my head, and he let me go. I knew he would not let go with the riding lessons, but I needed to sew a skirt I would be comfortable in. I heard of a kind of split skirt. I never saw one but I could visualize it. I was sure I could make one. There was fabric enough left in the gatehouse. I just had to get at it tomorrow first thing.

I walked into the house with my mind whirling. A lot had happened this afternoon. Misty, the cat, was waiting for me at the door and hurried in ahead of me. I saw it was nearly six o'clock and supper would be ready. I had no time to digest my ride with Grayson.

We had sausages and potato salad for supper. Grayson was in a good mood and kept the conversation going, mostly with Aunt Sarah. He talked of his first years here and spoke a lot about Uncle Theodore, which was good for Aunt Sarah.

We were just about finished with supper when someone knocked. Grayson answered and told me that Pastor Stafford was in the parlor and wished to see me. That was a bit strange, and I wondered what it meant.

When I entered the parlor, Pastor Stafford shook hands with me with a very serious face.

"What is it?" I asked.

He took a deep breath. "It is Donna Gable."

"What happened?"

"Please take a seat." Once we were seated, Pastor Stafford looked at me with a sad face. "Donna is with child."

"Oh!" I had at one time thought of that possibility, but had now dismissed it. This story was about to get worse. Poor Donna. I could not help but feel sorry for her, in spite of her part in the whole mess.

"Yes, oh," said the pastor sadly. "I guess it should not surprise us, but I am sorry it happened."

"And?" I asked when he just sat in deep thought.

"She says she loves Bud and she wants him to know. Her father wants nothing to do with the boy. The father is perhaps the biggest problem here. There is no forgiveness there. He is a hard man and is furious that Donna is with child." He paused. "I think Donna trusts you. Maybe you can be a support to her at this time. Maybe be the mediator between the father and Donna. Are you willing to try?"

I did not know the father at all, but I felt very sorry for Donna. Surely the father would not care if I came to visit Donna. "Is the father putting any restrictions on her?"

"He does not let her leave the house alone."

"Would he let me take her for a drive?"

"I don't know. You are the one responsible that she came back, so maybe he will trust you."

The pastor left soon after our talk and I was left to ponder my actions.

———————

I went to the gatehouse early Monday morning. I knew there was fabric there left by the woman who had lived there with her husband. I wanted to try making a split skirt. It would make it easier to ride horseback. I wanted something like that if I was to have riding lessons. I was very uncomfortable with my skirt when I was sitting behind Grayson on Sunday. And I could picture in my mind what I had to do. In two hours I had completed what I planned to wear. I was pleased with it.

When I got to the stables on Tuesday morning, Grayson was there waiting for me with a young man that I did not know. He introduced the boy, who was perhaps twenty years old, as Jock, and said he was in charge of giving me riding lessons. I saw Grayson eyeing my skirt, but he said nothing. He then left us and it was Jock who spent an hour with me, getting me on Star and off again, and finally walking around the corral with me sitting on her. At least Star and I were not strangers and Jock was very patient and kind. So much so that

I looked forward to my next lessons, which would take place every morning at nine.

I then hurried to the gatehouse to sew. I had sold the dress in the village and needed to make one or two more for that store. Mrs. Forbes was coming for another fitting and I was excited about the sales that I was making.

It was not until Friday afternoon that I took the carriage and went to see Donna. Her father would not be in the house as he worked in a factory in Thackeray's Pond. When I knocked on the door, Donna's mother came and with a sad smile, let me in.

"Hello, June. I suppose you came to see Donna. Thank you so much for your part in bringing her back to us," she said, taking my hand.

"I was glad to do it. May I see Donna?"

Mrs. Gable called her and soon Donna came in from the kitchen and her face brightened when she saw me.

"How are you?" I asked.

"Okay." But her face said otherwise.

"Can we talk?"

She looked around. Her mother suggested we go to Donna's room, which we did. As soon as the door closed, Donna had tears in her eyes.

"Did you hear?"

"Yes. Pastor Stafford told me."

"I made such a mess of my life. I disappointed my whole family. They are so ashamed of me. But I thought we were getting married." She began to cry and then I remembered something Aunt Sarah had told me.

"Donna," I began, "your life on this earth is a journey. There are things you will do wrong. There will be things you will regret. God does not cast us aside and refuse to love us anymore when we make mistakes. He even knows ahead of time that we will make the mistake. And He does not stop us. He lets us choose our path. But when we are sorry and ask His forgiveness, He gives the forgiveness we need to face the future. The important thing is to learn from our mistakes." I paused, wondering if I could honestly say what came next. "I believe that someday you will look back on your life and see God's loving presence through all the rough places in life, including this."

She was silent for a few moments. "My father is very, very angry. I am almost a prisoner here. I don't know what to do. I want Bud to know about the baby. He has a right to know. I still love him and want to marry him." Her face brightened. "Would you take a letter to him? Or just mail a letter for me?"

This was getting too sticky for me. What did Pastor Stafford expect of me? She saw my hesitation.

"Please, June. I know he really wants to marry me. He needs to know about the baby."

"Where does Bud work?"

"In the shoe factory in Thackeray's Pond."

"What hours does he work? I would like to hand the letter to him personally. What does he look like?"

"You would really take it to him?"

"Do you trust me to do this?"

She thought this through. But in the end, she trusted me.

"He has curly red hair and wears a brown jacket. He works until five."

"And where is the factory?"

"On Merchant's Row. When you come into Thackeray's Pond, you go three blocks past the center of town and turn left at the Carriage Shop. Then you will already see it. He walks home through the park and walks right past where you found me. If you wait there, you will see him."

"Hopefully he will be the only one going by there with red hair," I said.

And so I took the letter and I left Donna happier than I found her. I hoped her mother would never know what I did. But Bud had a right to know that there was a child. A baby that would need a good home with a father and a mother. And I believed that Donna really loved Bud.

I looked at the time. It was already after four. It was already five days since the pastor had asked me to see Donna. I felt I should not put this off for another day. I headed for Thackeray's Pond and eventually found the park. After leaving the carriage, I walked to the bench where I had found Donna. I would have a half hour wait. Hopefully he always came this way and hopefully there were not too many men with red hair. The air was cold today and I walked around a bit until I saw that the factory had let out. As a result there was more traffic and also more people crossing the park on their way homeward. I sat and watched the men and women as they came by my bench. Some looked curiously at me. Probably because I was looking so keenly at each one passing me. About ten minutes after five, a young man with bright red hair came despondently toward my bench. He did not look up. He never saw me. When he was directly in front of me, I spoke.

"Bud?"

He stopped and looked at me curiously.

"I have news of Donna," I said. His face lit up and he was sitting beside me almost before I knew it.

"Where is she?"

"My name is June and I am Donna's friend. Here is a letter for you from Donna. I want you to read it here and then we will talk."

He ripped open the letter and read quickly. I saw the dismay on his face when he read about the child. Then he folded the letter and looked at me.

"Tell me everything you know."

So I did. I did not know what all was in the letter, but I told him what I knew. And the part I had in taking her away from the park.

"I want to marry her."

"It seems you have not thought things out very well."

"I know. It is my fault. But her parents do not approve of me."

"And this did not help. They think you are hiding something from them."

He grew sober. He looked across the park and was silent. "What are you hiding?" I asked. "I cannot help you if you do not tell me the truth. And if you are serious about Donna, you must tell her the truth also."

"Her parents will never let me marry her."

This was getting too deep for me. "Bud, I have a suggestion. I don't know if you ever go to church, but I have a really fine pastor. He is a kind man and very wise. He will be your friend if you are honest with him and if you truly love Donna, I believe he would try his best to make a way for you to marry her. Are you willing to talk to him?"

"I don't go to church."

"How badly do you want to marry Donna?"

Bud hesitated only a second. "I'll go. What church?"

"It is the only church in our village of Cobbler's Crossing. In fact, the name is simply 'The Chapel of Cobbler's Crossing.' The service begins at nine."

"How about if I just come at the end of the service?"

I realized this was a big step to ask of Bud who had never been to church.

"The service ends at ten. I will tell the pastor to look for you. He greets the people as they leave the church."

There was a brighter look on Bud's face when he left me. I heard the town clock strike six. It was time for supper and I was five miles from where I should be.

CHAPTER 19

When I arrived home, I found Grayson and Aunt Sarah still at the table. They both looked curiously at me when I came into the room. Their plates were empty.

"I'm sorry I am late. I hope you left some for me. I'm hungry."

"I was worried about you," said Aunt Sarah. "You are never this late."

I was still rehashing the afternoon and did not want to say too much, although it was not as if either of them would spread gossip. They knew why the pastor had visited me. But I did not want to see any disapproving glances.

"My afternoon with Donna got involved," I said, then went into the kitchen to get warm food from the stove. When I came back they were both sitting there waiting.

"Did you see the parents?" asked Aunt Sarah.

"Only her mother. She was friendly and let me talk to Donna."

"You better walk very carefully. Her father has a bad temper," said Grayson.

Just then Lizzie came into the room. "Where were you? You missed supper," she asked, clearly wanting to hear why I was late.

"I got waylaid," I said and left it at that.

Lizzie then began talking about Becca having a cold and Aunt Sarah went to get some medicine for Lizzie to give her. That left Grayson and me at the table for a few awkward moments, but just then the knocker sounded.

Grayson went to the door and it was Marley to see him on some matter and Grayson brought him into the dining room for a cup of coffee while they looked at some business papers together.

"Hi, Marley," I said as I got up to leave them alone. I took my plate and silverware to the kitchen and came back to get a few other dishes. The two were in conversation, but just before I got to the kitchen door, Marley called after me.

"Hey June, I saw you with your boyfriend in Thackeray's Pond this afternoon."

I looked back in surprise. He was looking at me with a teasing look in his eyes but I saw in my peripheral vision that Grayson looked up equally in surprise. I did not know what to say and so I laughed and disappeared into the kitchen. I was dismayed that we were seen and hoped no more would be said about it.

The next morning I took Star and went once more to see Donna. I wanted to tell her about my talk with Bud. I did not plan to stay long, and when she came to the door, I asked if she could step out on the porch. She did so.

"Donna, I saw and talked to Bud yesterday."

"You did? What did he say?" Her eyes were bright now.

"He knows he went at things the wrong way."

"And? What can we do? My father...."

Suddenly the door opened and out came Mr. Gable. He was not happy to see me.

"Good morning, Miss Merriweather," he said without a smile. "What can I do for you?" His eyes looked black without a trace of friendliness.

"I just wanted to talk to Donna a wee bit," I replied.

"It seems I heard you were here yesterday. I hope you are not interfering with our daughter's life. We want nothing to do with this Bud."

I was so disgusted with his attitude that I did not know what to say. My silence must have told him that what he feared, was exactly what I was doing.

He leaned toward me and continued. "Donna was disobedient and has brought great shame to the family. Now she must pay for her mistake."

"But maybe..."

"Did you hear me? I just said..."

Mr. Gable took a step toward me, his index finger wagging in my face and I instinctively backed up a step and promptly fell backwards off the front porch onto the steps. Somehow, as I fell, I put my arm out to protect my head, but I hit the steps hard and was instantly aware of something cutting my leg in the process. I heard a scream from Donna as I fell. As I lay there in a crumpled heap on the steps, the others gathered around me, wanting to know if I was alright.

"Something is cutting me," I gasped.

"I don't see anything," said Donna frantically. "It must be under you."

"Can you get up? We will help you." This was Mr. Gable talking. He sounded scared.

I hurt badly all over, but, with help, I could get up and sat on the steps. There was blood on my skirt and my leg above my knee hurt badly.

"What is this broken glass doing here?" asked Mr. Gable.

"Jimmy was going fishing and that was his jar for worms," answered Donna. "Oh, that must be what cut her. Her skirt is bloody."

By this time Mrs. Gable was on the scene. She took a quick look at my bloody skirt.

"John," she said, "go into the house, we have to see about this cut."

He left and Mrs. Gable stood over me and pulled up my skirt. Just above the knee was a deep cut with a piece of glass still in the cut. She pulled it out and ordered Donna to get some cloths to soak up the blood. But the cut was too deep and they could not stop the bleeding.

"We must take you to the doctor," said Mrs. Gable. "Donna, go tell your father to get the carriage. And we must wrap this as tightly as we can."

I was hurting too badly to really know what all was going on, but Mr. Gable was the last person I wanted to take me to the doctor. However, he got the carriage and even helped me into it. Because Mrs. Gable could not come along, Donna was allowed to ride with me.

When we got to the doctor, Mr. Gable helped me out of the carriage, but it was Donna who came along inside with me. The doctor asked a few questions and otherwise worked quietly, cleaning my leg, looking for possible broken glass, stemming the flow of blood and finally sewing up the cut.

"Your cut is deep, Miss Merriweather," he said when finished. "You must spend a day or two off your feet. I see bruises showing on your arms and tomorrow you will be hurting as much or more than today. But I don't think you have any broken bones. Keep your leg up as much as possible."

I looked a mess with my bloody dress and I felt faint. Donna seemed to see my weakness and held on to me firmly as we headed to the door. I realized I could not talk to Donna once we were in the carriage, so I stopped just inside the door.

"Donna," I said nearly gritting my teeth for pain, "before we go out, I must finish about my talk with Bud. I believe he will come to church to talk to the pastor on Sunday. He will maybe just come after the service, but I believe he will come."

"But he does not go to church...ever. Did he promise to come?"

"I can't remember if he actually promised, but I think he will do it. I believe he really does love you. Maybe something will work out. I know you probably feel distant from God just now. But talk to God about your situation and pray for a good result on Sunday."

"I will, I will. Oh, you have given me hope. But my father will never allow it."

"Give it time and pray for him also. He will want his grandchild to have a father."

Mr. Gable did not say much on the way home. In fact he said nothing at all. I think he was busy thinking. He had not pushed me, but it was because of his advance to me in an angry manner that I had stepped back. Whether he felt guilt, I did not know. I hoped this would make him realize his own faults and cause him to be more lenient with his daughter.

When we got to the house, he wordlessly helped me down and we walked in the door. As we entered, Grayson and another man came out of his office. I must have looked terrible because Grayson took one look at me and led me to a chair in the library.

"What happened?" I saw his eyes go to my bloody skirt. It was Donna who answered. I was so glad to sit down and lower my head. I thought I might faint.

"She fell down the steps at my house. We took her to the doctor. She has a cut above her knee and has eight stitches in it. Her horse and carriage are at our house."

There was a brief silence. I could not see Grayson, as my face was bent down to prevent fainting.

"Mr. Gable, may I send someone along with you to bring the carriage back?"

"Yes, sure."

"What happened?" asked Aunt Sarah with big eyes. Hearing the voices she had come into the room.

"June has been hurt," said Grayson. "I am going to get a man to go with them to bring back the carriage."

And he was gone. Donna said goodbye and she left also.

"Do you feel faint?" asked Aunt Sarah.

"Yes."

"Keep your head down and I will get you a glass of water."

I managed the glass of water and felt a bit better.

"You must get out of these bloody clothes," said my aunt. "Can you walk?"

I tried to stand but I hurt all over. My leg was not the only problem. All my bones hurt. When Grayson came back in he stood and looked at me a moment. I could see the questions in his eyes.

"We have to get you upstairs and I don't think you will make it without my help," he said. "Go ahead of us Sarah, and I will help her." He turned to me. "Can you stand?"

I needed his help to stand up, but I made it without falling back down. Grayson offered his arm and I took it gratefully. In fact, I leaned very hard into him. With Aunt Sarah going ahead of us, we headed for the stairs. Each step hurt. I had bruised my body badly and I was now feeling pains I had not felt before. I hesitated, hurting.

"June," said Grayson. "Put your arm around my neck."

Any other time I would have hesitated. Now, he was my lifeline. I did as directed and suddenly I was swooped up and was being carried in strong arms up the stairs and into my room, where he laid me down on my bed. Even though he had been very gentle with me, I had to hold my breath to keep from moaning from pain.

"Thank you, Grayson," said Aunt Sarah, "now skedaddle so I can help her out of her dirty clothes."

The bedroom door shut and I closed my eyes as Aunt Sarah found a chair and sat beside me. "What can I do for you first?"

"Do you have something for pain? I hurt all over."

"What happened?"

"I fell down the outside steps and there was a glass jar there and it broke and cut me badly."

"Did the doctor give you something for pain?"

"No. I don't think so."

She hurried off and came back soon with a cup of some tea. "I put a bit of laudanum in it. That should ease the pain quickly. May I see your leg?" I pulled up my skirt. "Hmm. He has it bandaged good. But your leg looks swollen. And your arm looks bruised also." She kept chatting a bit and then asked, "How is the pain?"

"A bit less."

"Good. How about I put you in your housecoat for now? Looks like you got blood on all your clothes."

Aunt Sarah, with my feeble help, finally got my clothes off of me and into my nightgown and housecoat. It was simpler this way.

"What time is it?"

"Way past lunchtime. I will bring you a sandwich. Would you like tomato soup?"

"That sounds good. Skip the sandwich. If I don't move, nothing hurts just now."

Aunt Sarah hurried off. About ten minutes later she came with the soup. I felt better having something in my stomach. I no longer felt like I might faint. I now had time to think about my morning. It certainly had not gone according to plan. I thought again of angry Mr. Gable. He had scared me, coming close to me in a threatening manner.

I heard steps on the stairs. It was Becca and Lizzie. They came in the room with big eyes and serious faces. I almost had to smile, but was touched that they made their way up the stairs to see me.

"We heard you fell down some steps," began Lizzie.

"I did!" I shouted, or tried to shout. I hurt when I put effort into shouting. "It could have been worse, but I'll be okay. I just hurt all over today and have a bad cut on my leg."

"How did you get cut?" asked Lizzie again while Becca stood silent but sympathetic.

"There was a jar on the steps!" I shouted. "A little boy was going to collect worms to go fishing, I am told."

Although it hurt to shout, if she understood the first time I shouted, I wouldn't have to repeat it.

"Well, we hope you are soon better."

And with that they left the room to carefully make their way downstairs again.

I must have slept a bit, because I woke up to hear Aunt Sarah coming up the stairs with my supper.

"Have you slept?"

"I believe I did."

"I hope you are hungry. I made beef stew. You only had soup for lunch and you need nourishment."

"It smells good," I said, trying to get into a sitting position, but hurting badly all the while.

"How did you manage to fall off the steps?" she asked.

I hesitated, remembering. "I just took a step backward and down I went."

She stayed and chatted as I ate my supper. The rest had already eaten. She took my plate and went back downstairs. Not long after she left, I heard steps once more. Heavier steps. I held my breath. He wouldn't, would he? I was still embarrassed about hanging around his neck a few hours before. And then Grayson was standing at the door with a sober face.

"I have Sarah's permission to come up to see you. May I enter?"

What could I say? I felt heat gather in my face. "Come in."

Grayson stepped through the door and stopped. He just gave me a sober look. Then he took a few steps closer to the bed, towering over me. I could see he, too, was uncomfortable. He looked around the room, saw a chair and brought it near the bed and sat down.

"June, I would like to know what happened today."

"I took a step backward and was too close to the edge of the porch."

"I would like to hear the whole story."

I wondered if Aunt Sarah was not happy with my rendition of the incident and mentioned it to him. His eyes were not unkind and there was a part of me that was glad to tell the whole story to someone. I kept rehearsing the incident in my mind anyway. I had acted on my own pretty much and now Mr. Gable was angry with me and that would not help Donna.

"Well," I began, "I went this morning just to..."

"How about we start with yesterday?"

Why did he have to hear about yesterday? "Yesterday? Well, it is a rather long story."

"We both have time."

So I told him about the letter from Donna and meeting with Bud in the park. About the hope I had and how I was convinced they really loved each other.

"And on what do you base that?" His eyes searched mine.

I hesitated. "What do you mean?"

"What convinces you that they love each other?"

I had to think a bit. "When I suggested he talk to Pastor Stafford on Sunday, he said he never went to church. So I asked him how badly he wanted to marry Donna. He immediately changed his mind about talking to the pastor."

When I got to the part of today's experience with Mr. Gable, he interrupted once more.

"You went today, although you knew that Mr. Gable would be home?"

"I hoped he would not be, but I had to talk to Donna. I had to take the chance."

"And what happened?"

"Donna came to the door but before I could tell her much, Mr. Gable came out. He was angry that I was there and feared that I was abetting the relationship between Donna and Bud. He was so angry that when he took a step toward me, I instinctively stepped back and fell."

"Mr. Gable did not touch you? Or push you?"

"No. I do not think he touched me, although he was shaking his finger at me. But I am sure that he did not push me."

Grayson leaned toward me. "I suggest you let the pastor help the Gables from now on. He will know what to do." His face was telling me that this was more than a suggestion. I was silent. "Will you take my suggestion?" His dark eyes were not so far from mine. I still did not answer and his look became almost stern. "June?"

"I will try." He just looked at me a moment. I could not promise more. I was involved in this with Donna and if she needed me, I wanted to help her.

"You always did have a mind of your own," he muttered.

I wondered if he was thinking of our teenage acquaintance. I realized suddenly that I was enjoying this and it made me forget my pain.

"I use the mind God gave me."

He raised an eyebrow. "I am sure you are, but the question is whether you are using it wisely."

He let that sink in a few moments. "How are you feeling?"

"I hurt all over when I move and my cut is aching. When you go downstairs ask Sarah if I can have more pain medicine."

He nodded. "I guess your riding lessons are on hold."

"Grayson."

"Yes?"

"I will not be able to go to church on Sunday. I have not told anyone else the whole story. Will you keep your eyes open for Bud? I will want to know if he comes. He has bright red hair."

Grayson nodded. "Sleep well and consider my suggestions."

And then he left.

———————————

Sunday dawned with sunshine splashing over the world, but I had to stay home from church. Of course, I had no wish to go anyplace. It seemed every muscle and every bone in my body hurt. I was finding more black and blue spots on my arms, legs and shoulders and I was in misery until Aunt Sarah brought me more pain medicine. She offered to stay home with me, but I told her to go. I would be fine for an hour. I just hoped Grayson would have some word for me regarding Bud.

I spent the morning sitting by the window. It was a lovely day and I enjoyed the view to the village. I wondered if Marley was doing any thinking about Mary Lou. Becca and Lizzie came up to see me a short while, since they heard I would not be going to church and so the hour went by quickly. Of course, I would not know if Bud had been to church until Grayson came and he would be gone most of the afternoon. So I had to wait for what seemed like a long time. Aunt Sarah made a pork roast with potatoes and carrots and it tasted wonderful to me. I asked her a bit about church and then I read a book to make the time go faster. I was feeling a bit better and that made me more impatient for news. I was fully dressed and sitting on a chair by the window mid-afternoon when I saw Grayson's carriage come in the lane. My heart started to beat a little faster at the thought of him coming up to see me, but it was another ten or fifteen minutes until I heard his footsteps and voice downstairs. I was eager to see him. I told myself I was eager to hear if Bud had come to church, but I would have been disappointed if he had simply told Aunt Sarah to tell me. After what felt like a long time, I heard his footsteps on the stairs and then he stood in the doorway.

"Am I allowed in?" he asked. I caught my breath. He was absolutely stunning when dressed up.

"If you have news for me," I answered, trying not to smile.

"So I am just a useful item to you. Only welcome if I can give you something."

He was teasing but his look was keen and I hoped I did not blush. I said nothing.

"June?"

"I am pleased to see you."

"And I am happy to bring you news," he said, smiling.

He came in then and pulled a chair up to where I sat by the window.

"I trust you had your own little service here in your room this morning."

"No, I must admit, I did not. But I did pray that Bud would come to see the pastor."

"Then I must acquaint you with the message of the morning. It was 'Trust in the Lord with all thine heart and *lean not unto thine own understanding.*' Very appropriate for you, don't you agree? Your understanding was a bit lacking as well as your trust in the Lord that He could do this thing without you going over to the Gables' when Mr. Gable was there."

I wondered if it really was the text for the morning. Grayson had a nasty sparkle in his eyes.

"Was Bud there?" I felt he was stalling and I could not wait any longer.

"Who is Bud?" He pulled a very blank face.

"Bud! Donna's *boyfriend!* Didn't you see him?"

Grayson chuckled. "You are certainly feeling better today. But you should not get yourself so worked up."

"You work me up!" I said with force and tried in vain not to smile.

He laughed outright now. "I am glad to hear that."

I was amazed at him. This was not the usual Grayson. He seemed happy and free from all restraints. He was almost a naughty little boy. He finally pulled himself together and got serious.

"You will be happy to know, a red-haired young man was standing at the edge of the churchyard when I exited the building after the service. I purposely waited for the end of the line, for your sake, because I thought I might have more opportunity to see him, when most people were done shaking hands with Pastor Stafford."

"And?" It seemed to be taking forever. I wanted to know more.

Grayson shook his head. "I shall have to tell Pastor Stafford to preach on patience very soon. You have great need of patience."

He was enjoying making me wait. I did not comment on the patience issue.

"Did Bud talk to Pastor Stafford?"

"I have every reason to believe he did." Grayson just looked at me.

"And?"

"June," he said condescendingly, "I did not listen at the door. That is beyond my sense of propriety."

This time it was me that laughed. It felt good to laugh and he was looking at me so appalled at what he seemed to think I expected of him, that I first couldn't stop laughing. Meanwhile, he was looking very pleased with himself.

"It is good to hear you laugh, June."

"It hurts when I laugh though." He grinned and said no more. "Is there anything else you can tell me?"

"Actually, there is. But it might be bad news." My laughter flew away and I waited with baited breath. "I hung around my carriage until I saw this Bud approach the pastor. When they walked into the church, I got into my carriage. But before I left the parking lot, I saw another carriage approaching and it pulled into the churchyard." Grayson paused and looked at me. "It was Mr. Gable."

"Oh no! It can't be! Did you talk to him?"

"No, I certainly did not. I left the churchyard and the last I saw of Mr. Gable, he was entering the church."

I just looked at Grayson in dismay. "What do you think he wanted?"

"Whatever it was, it is none of your business. Remember that."

"But Bud was there!"

"Yes, Bud and Pastor Stafford. And, I presume God was also there." Grayson gave me a long look till I nodded in agreement. He was surely telling me to let God handle this. Then he got more serious.

"Who knows? You prayed about Bud. Maybe this is God's answer. Think about it. An unplanned meeting. The pastor is there to be the referee. And this time you are safely at home and not getting hurt."

He studied me as I tried to imagine what happened this morning. "You might be interested in knowing I had my own talk with God about the confrontation as I headed away from there."

"Thank you. I hope you and I are on the same page and were praying the same thing."

"You don't trust me!" Grayson looked accusingly at me and I smiled but gave him no reassurance.

"We'll let God sort it out," Grayson said after while. "How is the cut feeling?"

"It hurts only if I touch it."

"Tomorrow you can walk around. That will perhaps get the stiffness and soreness out of your body."

"I hope so. I am tired of sitting in my room."

"Shall I carry you back down?"

"No, no," I said quickly and looked to see if he was serious and found he was trying to hide a smile. I was embarrassed enough about the trip up, and he could probably read that on my face.

"I really could support you well enough so that you could go down for the rest of the day. I am serious. And we can get Lizzie and Becca over and you can have a wonderful shouting match for the rest of the afternoon and evening. What do you say?"

I had to laugh about the shouting with Lizzie and Becca, but he could see on my face that I was interested.

He stood up. "Come, it will work."

"But can I get back up again?"

"Was it really so bad the last time?"

Now my face got hot, but I had to laugh at the insulted look that Grayson gave me. Why had I even brought that up? I stood. I really was tired of being in my room. He let me put most of my weight on him as we headed to the staircase and with the railing on my left side and his support on the right, we slowly made our way down. By the time we got downstairs, Aunt Sarah was cheering me on and in no time I was sitting in the parlor visiting with my aunt while Grayson disappeared to his quarters.

At suppertime, the shouting began with Lizzie and Becca, but it was just good not to be alone anymore. It was partway through the meal that something was mentioned about church.

"Aunt Sarah," I asked, "what was the text for the message this morning?" I did not look at Grayson.

"Oh, let me think. I forget the exact verse, it was about love and reconciliation."

Now I did look at Grayson. He looked right at me and grinned merrily. Then he winked at me. *Winked!* I quickly looked away. His wink nearly undid me. I reached for my glass of water and I almost lost my grip on it and in trying to keep it from falling over, water sloshed out on the table. Not a huge amount but enough for all to see. And enough for Grayson to know he rattled me.

"Oh dear," I said.

O dear, indeed.

CHAPTER 20

Aweek went by. I got my stitches out and I was back to riding lessons. My body was recovering its normal color and I was busy sewing for a new client. I had finished the second gown for Mrs. Forbes and thanks to her, I had a new client, Mrs. Hoydt.

Aunt Sarah came to me one evening just before supper with a curious glass container that she found in the basement. The lid was of glass also and seemed glued on.

"What is that?" I asked, wondering why she brought the dirty container to me.

"I just saw this down in the basement and thought of that note written about the money. But I must look at the paper to see if this is the right shape."

The container was a bit odd, but I was not surprised when she said it was not the right shape. However, it proved to me that I was not the only one keeping my eyes open. She went to the sink and cleaned the outside of the jar, and when it was clean, the lid came off, but it was simply an empty container and we had no clue what it had been used for. When Grayson came in and heard what Sarah had found, he laughed.

"I am sure everything was checked out very good. If it still exists, it will be where no one has suspected it to be." And the subject was dropped.

I had heard nothing more of Bud from anyone and my curiosity was getting the best of me. On this particular morning I walked briskly to the gatehouse after my riding lesson, hoping to finish another dress for Mrs. Hoydt. The birds were beginning to be heard again and I saw a few daffodils blooming by the side of the creek when I crossed it. Spring was here and I was ready for it. When I got to the gatehouse, I quickly found my way to my sewing room and was happy for the bright sunlight coming in the window.

An hour later, I heard a distinct knock on the door downstairs. I had heard no carriage, but when sewing, I blocked out everything around me. When I got to the door, there stood Pastor Stafford.

"Come in," I said, "I am so happy to see you."

"Thank you, June, and I am happy to see you again. I should have come to see you when you were laid up, but I have only so many hours in the day and so many needs to see to."

"You are forgiven, but now I am all ears. I need some news of the Gables."

Pastor Stafford took a seat on the couch and I added a log to the fire. The house was cool and it would take a while for the cold of winter to leave its walls.

"Can I make you a cup of coffee?"

"No, thank you, I've had my quota for the morning already. Just sit here and let me tell you what is happening."

I sat down gladly and waited as the pastor got serious.

"I had quite a Sunday. Bud really did come, although not to the service. But he introduced himself to me at the end of the service. He wanted to talk to me about Donna and so I took him into my study. We had barely gotten started, when someone else knocked on the door. I told whoever it was to come in, and in came Mr. Gable. I think for about ten seconds we all just looked at each other. I finally got my wits together. I thought this had to be God's timing and so I accepted it as such. I invited Mr. Gable to take a seat. The two men knew each other and at first I thought Mr. Gable would leave. But he did not, and I don't know why."

Pastor Stafford stopped his narrative and looked at me. "I am curious. Just how was it that you fell? You were not pushed, were you?"

"No," I replied. "He did not touch me, but he took a threatening step toward me and I instinctively took a step back. Into space."

The pastor nodded. "Good, I am glad he did not push you, but I think the fact that you fell as a result of his step toward you, scared him. He did not know what you would say. However, he said nothing of this, but I found him not so aggressive as I expected, and I suspect he was frightened by your fall. Maybe it made him look at his own actions more closely. At any rate, he did sit down and I sat there a bit, hoping maybe one of them would start talking. They did not. So I just started praying out loud for our unplanned meeting." The pastor paused again. "And after praying, I talked. I can't tell you what I said, but I believe God gave me the right words. They listened. The tension diminished. I pleaded for peace. I pleaded for the unborn, innocent baby. I talked of forgiveness, of God's grace and redemption. When I finished, it was Bud who spoke first. He said he did not know much about God. Before he left, I gave him a Bible, a strong suggestion that he start attending church, and offered him time for Bible study with me. He accepted all three."

"And Mr. Gable?" I asked.

"Mr. Gable took a good look at Bud. Finally, he asked him about his family. Bud took a long time answering, but he talked. He said he is a foster child, has no knowledge of his parents. He ran away from the last foster home and has been on his own ever since. He got into the wrong gang and was involved in the burning of the covered bridge, and stole some tools with a buddy. For that he landed in jail for a short time. He then said that was the worst he did and there were tears. He really does love Donna and quite frankly, I think there is hope."

"Oh, I am so glad. So you think Bud is sincere?"

"I do. We have set up a meeting with Donna and the Gables in one month. After Bud has time to learn about God and show up for church and Bible study." He paused. "We have much to be thankful for. And much to bring to God in prayer." Pastor Stafford looked at his watch. "But now I must get going. I just wanted to let you know what came as a result of your efforts. We work together as a church. Each one does his part and I thank you for the part you played. Keep praying for them. Prayer changes hearts."

———————

I spent the rest of the day sewing. That evening, I shared a bit of the pastor's visit with Grayson and Aunt Sarah.

"And then you sewed all day?" asked Aunt Sarah.

"I did." I turned to Grayson. "I have a guilty conscience. I need to start paying rent."

"I love it when you have a guilty conscience," he replied, trying to hide a smile. "It happens so seldom."

Aunt Sarah chuckled and started clearing the table.

"But I have a suggestion," he continued. "I would like a new jacket to go with the vest you made me. Will you do that? It will take care of the rent for now."

"I would love to," I said, thrilled that he trusted me to be able to do it. "But I will have to know what fabric you want."

"I'll take you along on my next trip to town and we'll pick it out."

"Let me know when." I was already excited about making a trip to town with Grayson.

"But first, I must take a trip to Lemock on business."

"Where is Lemock?" asked Aunt Sarah, who came back for more used dishes.

"About a half day's journey. I expect to spend the night there. If there are any problems, contact Marley."

———————

The following day was the day for our gatehouse party. The day was dreary, but I looked forward to being with the girls again. I spent the morning sewing for Mrs. Hoydt. She was evidently a close friend of Mrs. Forbes and she came one day bringing the fabric and the patterns for two dresses, and although she barely condescended to enter my humble abode here, she was semi-friendly. I hoped she would be happy with my work, but she spent so much time complaining about her former seamstress that she made me nervous. However, today as I sewed for her, I was daydreaming about shopping for fabric with Grayson. Actually, it was the time spent with him that I was looking forward to, and not the shopping. I came home for lunch and returned to the gatehouse with cookies for our gathering. It started raining just before the girls arrived and they came running and splashing through the rain, glad to be out of the wet. It took a while to settle down with everyone chattering but we eventually got to enjoy our cookies and tea and only after that was done, did we get down to knitting, crocheting, or stitching or whatever we had to do.

"Do you need wood today?" asked Mary Lou soon after we started sewing.

"Not that I know of. I think I have plenty and summer is coming. You just want to see Marley again," I teased, wondering if he ever got around to asking her out. "I saw he was at church on Sunday," I added.

"He was," said Mary Lou. "He even talked a bit with me. Of course Jeannie and Annelie were standing there, too, so I don't know if he was really there for me."

"One of these days he will get up the nerve," I said, although I never told her that I mentioned her name to him. If he did not ask her, it would be better not knowing I had suggested her to him.

"Hey, what is going on with Donna? She sure looks sad these days," said Annelie.

I hesitated. Let someone else comment. I did not want to be the one to spill the beans about her situation.

"She is probably pining away for that guy that took off with her."

"Did any of you see the redhead that was at church last Sunday?" asked Mary Lou. "I did not actually see him in the church, but I saw him outside, back at the horse sheds. He was sort of cute."

"Yes, I did," said Annelie, "and now that I think about it, I wonder if it was Donna's boyfriend. I saw her with him one time and he had bright red hair. Just like this guy."

"Wow, and now he is hanging around the church to get a glimpse of her? I hear her father does not let her out alone. I bet he was mad if he saw this guy hanging around. Did you see him, June?"

"No," I replied. "I was not there that day."

"Where were you? Oh, you fell off the porch and cut yourself. Someone said you were over at Donna's. Is that where it happened?"

"It did. I stepped back and lo and behold, no more porch, just air." I hoped they would not ask anything else. "But it is just about completely healed now," I added. "Jeannie, is Marvin completely out of your life?" I wanted to change the subject.

"Yes. I don't trust him out of my sight. Who would want him?"

"I thought I saw him husking corn with you."

"Well, he came and started husking corn beside me. I couldn't push him away."

"But he found a red ear," said her sister.

I stopped sewing and looked at Jeannie in time to see her blush.

Just then we heard a carriage coming up the road and all three girls jumped up and hurried to the window. It did not interest me. I knew it would not be Grayson. I took the opportunity to take the teapot, which was still on a table in the room, out to the kitchen, and as I passed the staircase I accidentally bumped against the post and again the top came loose. Maybe I would say something to Grayson anyhow, but I hated to.

Mary Lou came back smiling. "It was Marley and he looked in. I hope he didn't see us all at the window."

"Well, if he saw anyone, I hope he saw you. Maybe he will have the nerve to ask you out."

"I don't know why you think he might."

"Well, you said he came and talked to you last Sunday."

And so the afternoon passed. There was a heavy mist all afternoon and by the time the girls left, it was looking foggy.

Because we spent so much time talking, I did not get much done when the girls were here, but now I had an hour before suppertime. I cleaned up the dishes, then ran upstairs and sat down at the sewing machine. I worked a good hour and then noticed that I had made a mistake. I had to correct it and the whole process took much longer than I thought. When I next glanced out the window, it looked like thick fog had descended over the whole countryside. I looked at my watch. I had missed supper. Oh dear. I hoped Aunt Sarah did not worry. Ever since being caught here in the snowstorm, I had brought some essential foods to keep in the gatehouse, as well as a nightgown, washcloth and towel. I told Aunt Sarah about it one morning when we were discussing the snowstorm. I told her that if for some reason I did not show up sometime, she should not worry. I had all I needed there. She reminded me what Grayson said and I told her that I would make an effort to come back, this was just for an emergency. Now I thought of my provisions. I walked to the door and opened it. I held the lantern. It was not real cold, but the road was muddy from all the rain and there was a dense fog so that I could barely see. And the good news was that Grayson was gone for the night. I smiled to myself and closed the door. I would be in my cozy little house, out of the fog and mud and could sew all night if I liked.

I went to the kitchen and made more tea. I opened a jar of home canned tomatoes and a jar of canned sausages from butchering the pigs last autumn. I would not starve. I was suddenly humming a song while heating my tomatoes and sausage on the kitchen range. I heated more water for tea. I even had cookies left over. What a feast! I tried not to think of Grayson. He was very insistent that I realize he was renting this house to me for daytime only. Well, he would understand that I could not walk in thick fog and muddy roads in the dark. I hoped.

I put another log on the fire. The house could feel damp very quickly in this weather. I had lamps burning in the sitting room and upstairs in my sewing room. I enjoyed my supper by the fire, and then hurried upstairs to sew. It was harder at nighttime. I had three lamps burning, but it was not the same without daylight. I finally realized I was tired and saw it was nine o'clock. I would call it a day.

I fixed the fire for the night, ate two more cookies and put out the oil lamps. Then I returned upstairs and went on up to the little bedroom above the entrance. It usually was a great view from up here. Tonight, there was only fog and blackness when I looked out. But I felt secure in my little gatehouse and was enjoying spending the night here. I prayed that Aunt Sarah would know I was safe and also hoped that should Grayson ever discover I had stayed here overnight that he would be understanding about it. But there should be no reason for him to find out. Then I crawled into bed. I felt rather alone, out here at the end of the road, in the house wrapped in fog, but at the same time I felt wonderfully independent. I had done it. I soon slept.

I do not know what woke me. Maybe some sound that I was not used to. Or maybe the bed, which was not all that comfortable. I opened my eyes and to my surprise, I saw the moon out the window. The fog had cleared. I was very thirsty from the cookies I had eaten, so I lit an oil lamp and made my way down to the kitchen for water. I was so proud of myself. I thought maybe I would be scared here, but I was not. I felt right at home. I got my glass of water and drank it, then took my lamp and went back up the stairs. Just as I was about to put out the lamp, I heard a carriage come down the road. Who was out so late? I looked at my watch. It said eleven-thirty. I put out the lamp and crawled into bed. I listened for the carriage. I did not hear it anymore. Did that carriage go past? I went to the window by the light of the moon and looked out. The countryside looked awash in the moonlight with no trace of the fog. I had just snuggled under the covers when I heard a loud banging at the door. My heart stood still. What on earth?

I just froze. Whoever it was, would soon go away. The banging continued. My heart in my throat, I went to the window. I could see no carriage. If there was a carriage, it must be *directly* below me. The knocking did not let up. It was very loud. I lit a candle, hung a small blanket over my shoulders in place of a housecoat, and slowly made my way down the first set of stairs. I walked through the sewing room and was slowly descending the second stairs when the banging stopped. I almost thought I heard someone call my name. How could that *be?* Had something happened to Aunt Sarah? I now hurried to the door but did not unlock it.

"Who is there?"

"Open the door, June."

My eyes popped and my heart felt like it was jammed into my throat. It was *Grayson's* voice I heard. It could not be. It took all my courage to open the door and I knew I had to, but my hands were trembling.

Grayson, holding a lantern, just looked at me. He did not enter. After a long, hard look, he spoke.

"What are you doing here?" I stood transfixed. This could not be happening to me. As I tried to come up with the right words, he added, "I am waiting for an answer and I hope you have a good one."

I was so nervous, the candle fell from my fingers. Grayson quickly picked it up and handed it to me. As he relighted it for me, I tried to explain my clumsiness.

"You scared me badly."

"I am glad I did. You should be glad it was me and not a stranger."

"I can explain." The words came out with difficulty, as if my tongue were stiff.

"Please do so." He made me so nervous I could not think straight. His words were clipped.

"I...worked late."

"That is no explanation. It is an excuse. Go get dressed, I am taking you home."

"Now? I was already sleeping."

"Or do I take you as you are?"

I suddenly realized I was standing in my nightgown, the small blanket hanging haphazardly over my shoulders, and I was talking to Grayson! I moved quickly then, sensing his patience had run frightfully thin with me. My legs felt like water and I thought the candle might slip from my fingers again. My heart thumping, I somehow got to the staircase where the top of the post wobbled in my hand, then I stumbled badly up the stairs. Once in the bedroom, I quickly put on my clothes, trying to comprehend what was happening. I had been *sleeping!* My brain was highly befuddled. Before I went back down the stairs, I heard something happening at the hearth. He must have come in to make sure it would not be a fire hazard. By the time I got downstairs, Grayson was standing by the door. I did not look directly at him but instead I looked at the door as I walked toward him. He took the candle from my hand and extinguished it and set it down by the hearth. Then he stepped out and held the door open as I walked numbly through it. I felt his eyes were burning holes in me, but he spoke not a word.

I realized that Grayson was angry. Very angry. And I just better not give any resistance to his commands. My first thought was that he would never marry someone he could not trust. My second thought was fear that he would take the gatehouse from me. He wordlessly helped me into his carriage and then we sat side by side, dead silent as he drove down the moonlit, muddy lane and across the ford. I hoped he would let me off at the house. But he had no mercy for my interrupted night. He took me along to the stable and helped me down from the carriage. Afraid of what I would see in his eyes, I did not look at him. When I made a move to go to the house, he stopped me.

"Stay right here."

I stayed. If he would have ordered me to stand on my head, I would have attempted it. I was complete obedience. Too late. I watched as he took care of the horse and the carriage. And then, lantern in hand, he came to me. I dared to look at him. His eyes were dark and there was not a bit of a smile on his face. I quickly looked away.

"Take my arm."

I took it and we walked silently to the house. I was feeling worse all the time. By the time we got to the house, I found I was fighting tears. I could not go to bed like this. I cleared my throat and took a deep breath.

"Please let me explain." My voice gave out. He held the lantern up and looked at me, probably seeing the moisture in my eyes. But he remained hard.

"You will have ample time to explain tomorrow morning during your riding lesson."

Riding lesson? But he was not the one giving me the riding lessons. One of the hired men had that task. I did not answer. He opened the house door, bade me a curt goodnight and we went our separate ways. I sneaked up the stairs like an intruder. I did not want to wake Aunt Sarah. I did not want to tell her about angry Grayson. Sleep evaded me for the first hour. I had a lot to think about. Most important being how to explain my sleeping in the gatehouse to an angry Grayson.

———

Morning dawned bright with sunshine. At least there was that. Aunt Sarah had breakfast on the stove and it should have smelled good to me. But eating was a chore.

"You have me confused," said my aunt when we began eating. "I thought you stayed in the gatehouse because of the fog."

"I did. The road was muddy and the fog so thick I could not see."

"But you just came down the stairs." She looked totally confused.

"Grayson came home last night anyway."

"Oh." Aunt Sarah looked at me, not eating. She wanted to hear more.

"And he made me come back with him."

"Oh my. What time was it?"

"Very late."

Aunt Sarah said nothing for a few minutes. "But he certainly understands. Because of the fog and all."

"By then the fog was gone and the moon was shining brightly."

"Oh dear." She said no more about it and the silence hung heavy in the room.

By nine I headed out to the stable. I took in deep breaths of the fresh air and let the sunshine kiss my face. Certainly Grayson would not tolerate me being late. I did not rush, but I did not think it wise to be even a minute late.

A sober Grayson was at the barn waiting for me. I followed him to the corral and ten minutes later we were riding slowly out into the sunshine. I wondered if our whole riding lesson would be in silence. I was still feeling chagrined at last night's episode. He had been really angry and his silence made me think he was still angry. Or at least very displeased with me.

Finally, Grayson asked me what Jock had taught me. He listened as I told him all I could remember, while riding beside him across the meadow. I wished last night had not happened. I had been on better terms with Grayson in the last week. This could have been fun. Besides that I had pretty much lost my fear of falling, although Jock said I was still too tense while riding. I saw Grayson give my skirt a look when I got on the horse, but he said nothing about it. I wondered if he had ever seen such a skirt that was split in the middle.

When we had crossed the meadow, he opened a gate that led to a winding lane. The leaves were small and bright green on the budding trees and I tried to concentrate on the beauty around me and not my morose riding partner. Finally, we came to the eastern entrance to the estate. I had never come in this way. Our fastest way to town, to church, and to many of our acquaintances, was by the other entrance. Here, we were on a knoll overlooking large fields where farmers were plowing with their horses. There was a brook flowing under a bridge right at the entrance. Grayson called a halt, got off his horse and tethered him to a tree. Then he came to me.

"I would like to see you get down from your horse alone." He made me very nervous, but I did it. "Now tether Star to that tree," he said, pointing to the same tree that his horse was tethered to.

While I tethered Star, he walked to the road, crossed it and put one foot up on the wooden rail and looked out over the landscape. Birds, chirping happily in the tree branches over our heads made me wish to be a bird. I would fly away. I did not know where I would fly to, but I would fly away and stay for a full week. I walked across the road and up to the fence, but not too close to Grayson. I saw in my peripheral vision his head turn, and then he took a few steps in my direction.

"Were you ever here at this entrance?"

"No. But it is a lovely view."

Silence. Why couldn't I think of something to talk about, to extinguish his anger? But my brain failed me. It seemed completely empty—devoid of anything even remotely suitable to this landscape. I was much more aware of the masculinity of the man I had angered, now standing close beside me.

"I am now ready to hear your explanation for last night."

I had almost relaxed. Now I took a deep breath and watched a bird soaring in the blue sky. "I stayed because there was very thick fog, a very muddy road and it was dark."

"Fog?"

"Yes, a thick, soupy fog, but by the time I went to bed, it had lifted."

"Of course it never crossed your mind to leave before dark?"

"I had work to do on a dress."

"And you conveniently had all you needed for a night's stay."

"I had that there before. After we both got stuck there in a snow-storm."

I added the "both" to remind him that on that night it was much worse than me staying alone. We had to be careful that no one knew that we had spent the night together in the gatehouse. He did not answer right away. I mentally thought maybe I had scored a point. But he was not done.

"Look at me, June."

I tore my eyes from the lovely spring landscape and met those smoldering dark eyes.

"Would you have stayed if you had known I would return yet last night?"

He had now turned and was watching me closely. I tried to keep looking at him but could not. I once more looked out over the fields, watching the farmers and their horses. I knew well the answer to the question and when I hesitated too long, he put one finger under my chin and gently turned my head so I had to look at him. He did not smile, but looked so intently at me that I felt the heat rushing to my face. I looked at him a moment only. I never answered him.

"Your silence is answer enough."

He took his hand from my face and stared out over the fields and I wondered what was going on in that head of his. He would not dare to take the gatehouse from me. I think maybe ten minutes elapsed before he spoke.

"June." He waited for me to look at him. "You know I am only concerned for you. That could well have been someone else at the door last night."

I saw something different in Grayson's face as he said that. It was a mixture of frustration, concern and something else. I could not sense the anger anymore and I relaxed.

"I'm sorry." It came out easier than I expected and sudden moisture threatened my eyes. I *was* sorry for the anger and frustration I had caused him. "I shall try not to let it happen again."

His look baffled me. "Thank you." A blue jay flew screaming over our heads, chased by smaller birds. He remained standing there a moment or two.

"Is your sewing career all that you hoped it would be?"

I was surprised at the change of subject. "Oh, yes. And Mrs. Forbes has talked to two of her friends and they have also shown interest in using my services."

"And you are happy when they look down their noses at you?"

I laughed just a bit. "You are right. They are snobs and they do not let me, even for a moment, think I am on their level."

"And you are content with that?"

I thought it through before speaking. Yes, for the time, I was content with that. I was just so happy to be doing what I loved.

"I like to sew," I answered simply.

There followed a pause.

"And if that young man, I think his name was Gerald, who came to the corn husking shows up and wants to marry you, what will you choose?"

I gave Grayson a quick glance and smiled. "Oh, that would be easy. I would choose my sewing."

He had been searching my face. Now he glanced over the fields before us.

"And if you learned to know someone else whom you really liked, would you still choose to sew?"

Although he was leaning on the fence, I knew Grayson was watching me. I did not look at him, but kept my eyes on the busy farmer going back and forth across his field with his team of horses.

"If I did not love him, I would choose to sew," I said slowly.

"And if you loved him?" The question, though asked quickly, was asked in a softer voice and Grayson turned a bit more, his keen eyes on me. I turned my head ever so slightly away from him.

"That is a hypothetical question."

"Is it?"

I tried my best to think of something to say. I drew a blank. I had tried to sound nonchalant with my answers. Like they were not important questions. But if I had to choose between a husband that I loved and the sewing I loved, I knew I would choose the husband.

When I remained silent, Grayson backed away from the fence.

He walked slowly back across the road and I followed. He watched as I went to Star and got on her without help. Then we rode off and suddenly I was very happy riding with Grayson. It was fun and I wanted to keep on riding. We talked a bit on the way home, but I don't remember what we said. It must not have been of any consequence. When we reached the stables, he watched as I dismounted.

"Are you still scared of falling off?"

"No, not really. But my riding has been fairly slow. I'm in no hurry to race," I added, daring to smile at him.

He replied, "Next time we'll race. Just a short one." Then he grinned at my look of dismay. "Well, maybe we'll wait a while. I'll have Jock riding with you on a daily basis for another couple weeks. Can you say you enjoy it?"

"Actually, I do."

"Good. That is what I wanted to hear."

CHAPTER 21

It was a warm Sunday in May and the drive to church was very enjoyable. I liked summertime and it was almost a year already that I had lived here at Bluster Hill. Now I could not envision leaving it, but that was because of the owner, not my aunt. I knew that I wanted to marry Grayson and the memory of our last conversation as teenagers made me determined not to show him how badly I wanted him. He was not indifferent to me, but for some reason he was making no moves in my direction. He had taken his carriage this morning as usual and Aunt Sarah drove with me.

"Where does Grayson go every Sunday?" I asked her, as we passed the gatehouse and were out on the road.

"He never says much, but I think it is to a good bachelor friend of his. Someone he has known ever since he moved here."

"And they meet every Sunday?"

"I think so. I am glad he has a friend to talk to. A male friend. They probably just eat in an inn someplace."

We pulled into the parking lot and soon entered the church. I nodded to Mary Lou as we went up the aisle. A short time later, Grayson came and sat beside Aunt Sarah. I usually went up the aisle first and therefore, I never got to sit beside Grayson. One Sunday I managed to get Aunt Sarah up the aisle first. But that Sunday Grayson chose to sit elsewhere. I had not tried it again.

A month had gone by, and Bud had come to church every Sunday. He never sat with Donna and her family. Instead, he sat near the rear of the church. Mr. Gable seemed to steer his family as far from Bud as possible, but there was a slight change in his behavior and I was still hopeful. Today, I saw that Bud came up the aisle to the Gable pew and sat down next to Donna. I nearly gasped out loud. Mr. Gable looked straight ahead as if he had not noticed. During the service, my eyes went again and again to the pew where they sat.

After the last hymn, the pastor stood and looked out over the congregation. He cleared his throat and we waited expectantly.

"I am pleased to announce the coming marriage of Donna Gable and Charles, better known as Bud Russel. Next Sunday, Bud will be baptized here and on June 15th they will be married at the Gable home at four o'clock in the afternoon. The church is invited to a potluck reception following the marriage."

I was overjoyed. I looked over to the Gable pew. Mr. Gable still sat unsmiling, but Donna and Bud looked very happy. I was excited for them. Immediately after the service, Donna came to me.

"June, I need to talk to you," she began, just beaming. "I want you to be my maid of honor. Will you do that? We will have a small, private wedding and Bud has a friend who will be best man. Will you do that?"

"I would love to be your maid of honor," I replied, just happy for this wonderful ending to their botched elopement.

Bud came and stood by her side, looking relaxed and happy.

"Bud, I am so happy for you," I said, turning to him.

"Thanks lots for what you did for us," he replied. "I am trying to do things right."

"This is a good beginning," I assured him.

"So Donna and Bud are getting married," said Grayson at the supper table.

"They are, and June is to be maid of honor at their wedding," announced Aunt Sarah proudly.

Grayson gave me a steady look. "Does that mean shopping for dress fabric?"

"Yes."

"Could we look for my coat fabric at the same time?"

"Yes, I suppose we could."

"Are you in overload with your sewing?"

"In a way I am, but I enjoy it. Do you need your suit coat by a special time?"

"No. When do you want to go shopping?"

"Soon."

Grayson was silent a short while. "Tomorrow afternoon?"

"What time?"

Because I was going shopping in the afternoon, I went early to the gatehouse to sew in the morning. I had a dress to deliver to the store where we would shop and I needed to work on another dress that was ordered. Halfway through the morning, I got a visitor. Donna. I suddenly realized she may need someone to make her dress. I was not wrong.

"June, could you please make my gown? Mama says she has no time and I am not good enough to sew my wedding dress. An everyday dress is one thing, but I want this to be very nice."

And so I put my sewing aside, took measurements while she was there, and she gave me the choice of fabric.

"My father says I may not wear white."

I understood what she did not say. "What color would you like?"

"I love lavender."

"Do you care what color my dress is?" I asked her.

"Oh, are you going to have a new dress, too?"

"I think so. If I can, maybe I can get a darker lavender to go with yours."

"That sounds wonderful. Oh, June, I am so happy."

"I am happy, too. Now, if I can't get a darker shade of lavender, I will try to get something that looks nice with lavender."

"Oh thank you. You are such a good friend."

I got nothing else done that morning. I had little time to get excited about my trip to town with Grayson. As it turned out, he came in for lunch, which he generally did not do, but I assumed because we would leave right after lunch, it made sense.

"Well, Grayson, how is Dusty?" asked my aunt.

"Dusty? Is the dog sick?" I asked.

"He got kicked by a horse," replied Grayson, "but I think he is alright. It happened yesterday. This morning he seems to be walking okay again."

I looked at Grayson. "Remember that dog you had...." My voice trailed off. Aunt Sarah looked at me, confused.

"This is the only dog we had since you were here."

I just sat there, looking at Grayson and Grayson looked at me. I had goofed. There was nothing ever said that we should not say we had known each other before, we just never had.

"What did you mean?" asked my aunt.

"Oh nothing."

Now Aunt Sarah was studying us both. "That was a strange statement and now you say nothing. What am I not understanding? Or knowing?"

I was pretty sure all was lost, but I made one more attempt.

"I knew a fellow by the name of Conrad that had a dog."

"But how would Grayson know that?" Aunt Sarah looked at Grayson. "Your name is also Conrad isn't it?"

"It is," said Grayson, still not giving anything away.

"But you two did not know each other until you met here."

It was a simple statement and neither one of us commented on it.

"Grayson," said Aunt Sarah. "Did you know June before you met her here?"

"I did," said Grayson, not cracking a smile.

"What?" The look on her face was so funny that we both burst out laughing. Now she looked at me. "You knew each other before coming here?"

"Yes." I know my face was red because looking back was painful. I did not want to repeat it.

"Now I think I deserve an explanation," said my aunt, looking at me almost sternly.

"Ask Conrad," I said.

Grayson immediately looked at Aunt Sarah, smiling. "I must leave. June, I shall pick you up in fifteen minutes at the portico."

"Well, I'll be!" said my aunt as Grayson exited the room. "I wonder if Theodore ever knew that?"

"I never told him," I said.

"Why *didn't* you tell us?"

I took a deep breath. "I was in shock at finding Conrad at the door when he came for supper that first Friday night. I did not know he was the estate manager. And added to that, we had traveled on the same train and coach when I arrived. I eventually learned that he recognized me, but I never saw him close up and did not know it was Conrad."

"So you knew him as Conrad. I forgot he has a double name. Yes, I have seen his name as Conrad Grayson Everleigh. But how did you know him? Did you live in the same town?"

"Actually, yes, at least for a time. And we casually dated while very young. I was only fifteen and he was seventeen. We were very immature and we parted with angry words. I do not like to think back on that time. Conrad is a different person now, and I hope I am also."

Aunt Sarah just looked at me a long time, processing what I had told her.

"God's ways are amazing," she murmured. I did not ask what she meant.

When Grayson and I left for Thackeray's Pond, I was a experiencing a certain sense of relief. It was out in the open. We were both aware of our parting, and thank God, we were on better terms now. Soon after we were out on the open road, Grayson turned to me with a slight grin.

"How did you make out with Sarah?"

"You ran out on me. Now you can just wonder."

He chuckled and it was good to hear him laugh. I felt like this was Conrad now, but a mature Conrad. I sensed him glancing at me now and again, but I did not meet his look.

"Can we bury the past?" he asked finally. His words were sincere.

"Of course." I wondered if he remembered his last words to me. But I would not remind him of them. He seemed in a good mood and was talkative. I did not want to spoil it.

"So the wedding takes place," he said as the horse clopped along the country road.

"Yes, and I pray that all goes well before and after the wedding. My main concern is Mr. Gable, but it seems he is at least not standing in the way."

"He probably will need to see some positive action from Bud for a while. Mr. Gable's pride was hurt pretty badly."

"I hope the baby will help mend the problem. This will be the first grandchild."

Grayson did not comment and we rode in silence for a while. I was enjoying the drive with him. There were fluffy white clouds floating above fields of cows who curiously lifted their black and white faces to watch us roll by, grass hanging out of their mouths. A bumble bee flew past my nose and made me jerk back. But it was a glorious day and I had springtime in my heart.

When we got to town, we walked together into the fabric shop. Just as we entered, I thought we probably looked like a husband and wife going shopping together. And then he opened the door for me and I caught the curious stare of Mrs. Kent, whom I knew now rather well, after buying so much from her.

"Good morning, June. How can I help you?" Her eyes went to Grayson.

"We need to see fabric for a suit coat for Mr. Everleigh here," I said.

She led us to the fabrics and told us about them. Finally, it was up to Grayson. He made his choice and then, while he walked around the store, I made my choices for fabric. I did find a lavender in organdy, which I bought for Donna's dress and I bought a mint green organdy for myself since they only had the one shade of lavender. Donna had said nothing about a veil, but I wanted her to look like a bride, so I bought gauze for a veil and decided that would be my wedding gift to her.

In a short time, we were once more on the sidewalk. Just before we got to the carriage, we met Lillian, the girl from church that had never warmed up to me. I felt sure she had her eyes on Grayson and I was a threat simply by living on the estate he worked on. Now she stood and stared openly at us.

"Hi, Lillian," I said. She did not answer me.

"Hi Grayson," she said.

"Hello, Lillian."

There was no more said and we were soon on our way home. I guess I was a bit put out that she so rudely ignored me. At any rate, when we were out of town, I took the plunge.

"Lillian never warmed up to me."

"No? How is that?"

"I think you know."

Grayson pulled a very innocent face as he turned to me. "How should I know?"

Did he really not know? I hesitated. Maybe it was all in my head. And it was showing my own feelings. But no, had she not just ignored my greeting and greeted Grayson instead?

"I live too close to you."

Grayson just looked at me.

"I don't understand."

"If you don't understand, you are very ignorant when it comes to girls." I was talking like I was talking to Conrad, not the owner of the estate where I really lived on his charity.

There was a pause. I wanted to see his face, but did not want to be too obvious.

"I may be," he finally answered. "I don't have too much to do with girls."

This was my chance to ask what I had been curious about for a long time.

"Are you saying you never dated since we knew each other?"

Grayson gave me a long look. I was embarrassed for asking. "Did I say that?" he asked.

I did not know where to go from there without coming across as just plain nosy. And I had a feeling I would not get an answer anyway.

We were getting very close to home when a carriage came toward us and Grayson stopped. The other carriage stopped also. It was Marley. He gave me a smile and a nod. The smile was a "I told you so" smile.

"Are you going for the fence posts?" asked Grayson.

"Yes."

"Add six more to the number I gave you. If he does not have them today, we can pick them up later."

And then we were once more on our way and the conversation was at an end.

CHAPTER 22

I am not sure anymore when I first noticed it, but Lizzie was not her usual self. True, I was not seeing as much of her anymore, but I always saw her at the supper table, unless Grayson had a guest, which happened sometimes. But Lizzie was grumpier than usual and looked sad.

"I think she is missing her niece," said Aunt Sarah to me when Lizzie was out of hearing. "She lived with her niece a long time but did not want to move to Ohio with them. Maybe she regrets it. I heard her talk of Ohio recently to Becca."

"Does she ever hear from her niece?"

"Yes, she does. And she just got a letter and I think that is why she is sad."

"Do you think she would like to go back to live with her niece?"

"I do. I really do, but I have never suggested it. Maybe the niece no longer wants her. But I could write to the niece and ask her. Maybe Lizzie tells her things she doesn't tell us."

"But what would happen to Becca if she left?"

"I don't like to think about it. Becca would really miss her."

My days flew by. I had two dresses to make and a suit coat to make for Grayson. That was what interested me the most and scared me at the same time. I did not want to botch it. But the dresses and veil came first. I also had a gown in progress for a woman named Mrs. de Frappe. So far, I did not have a good impression of her. She was a snob in the first degree, but I determined to think of the money I was making and to try my best to please her.

A week before the wedding, Donna came for the fitting. When I showed her the dress, she got tears in her eyes.

"Oh, it is so beautiful, June. I am so excited. And you made a veil! I did not think I would have a veil."

"All brides need a veil," I said as I adjusted it to her head.

Before she left, she gave me a hug. "You are the best friend I have," she said.

"I am proud to call you my friend," I replied.

When I finished the bride's dress, I worked on mine. I liked light green and was pleased with the final outcome. I worked on Mrs. de Frappe's gown and had her come for a fitting. I think she thought it a bit beneath her to come up to my little sewing room, but she came, looking at the room like a spider might jump out and bite her.

"I don't like the way these pleats look," she said, after seeing herself in the mirror.

I showed her the pattern that she had picked out.

"Yes, I know," she said, "but I think I would like it like this." She then began explaining to me how she envisioned the gown.

"Well, Mrs. de Frappe, I can try to change it to your specifications, but I cannot promise what it will look like."

"Please change it."

"I will not get to it until next week since I have a wedding this weekend."

"Well, just get it done as quickly as you can."

There was no apology and no thanks.

———

Donna's wedding day was hot, but not humid. The ceremony would take place at four in the afternoon. The wedding was private, but the reception would be on the lawn as a pot luck. I spent the morning with Aunt Sarah making fried chicken and potato salad. During breakfast, Grayson came in for a few minutes and told me he would take me to the Gables'. I had been told that Mr. Gable would pick me up, but secretly, I was pleased by Grayson's offer, knowing he could not stay because the ceremony would be private.

I was excited and wished I had a sister to help me get ready. Or someone to enjoy this day with me. I had made the two dresses and the veil and was quite happy with the results. Donna had cried with joy when she saw herself in the finished dress. Because my dress was for a wedding, I had added lace and buttons to the puff sleeves. It was the nicest dress I ever owned. Now I gave myself time to get ready, and at three-thirty, I went down the stairs. Partway down, I realized Aunt Sarah, Lizzie and Becca were all standing at the bottom to see me. And behind them stood Grayson.

"Oh, you make me nervous!" I said to the four of them, embarrassed but pleased at Grayson's presence.

"You look like a bride yourself," said Aunt Sarah. "I just hope to see the day you come down the stairs in white. I just don't understand why it hasn't happened yet."

I said nothing because Becca and Lizzie were both shouting their approval of my dress. Once down the stairs, I looked at Grayson, who came to me and offered his arm. I took it, feeling like a queen. When we got to the carriage, I saw he had thrown a robe over the seat and floor to protect my gown. He helped me up and then took his seat beside me. Then he looked at me with a twinkle in his eyes.

"Where shall we go?"

I blushed. "You know where we are going, and we better not take the long way around."

We did not talk much on the way to the Gables'. I thought he drove slowly and hoped we would get there on time. But I enjoyed the drive. I somehow felt good by his side. Today I did not feel the need to talk. Strange. I was just enjoying being in his presence.

When we arrived at the Gables', Donna's father came out and shook Grayson's hand and thanked him for his offer to bring me. I thanked Grayson also, and went into the house with Mr. Gable. The wedding would be performed by Pastor Stafford who was waiting in the parlor of the Gable home. A friend of the groom stood by him and I waited in line with them as Donna came down the staircase. She looked beautiful. I stole a look at Mr. Gable and was pleased at the look he gave her. He thought her beautiful, too, and his look said he was proud to call her his daughter. Thank God for a good resolution to this situation. Bud looked nervous, but happy. His buddy looked more nervous. He did not know anyone and I could tell he was very ill at ease. After the ceremony, we went out on the lawn where tables for the food were set up under big shade trees by people from church. As the people were still arriving, I took the opportunity to talk to Bud's friend who looked anxious.

"Hi, I'm June."

"I'm Nevin," he said.

"I think you look a bit lost and I know what it is like to be the new person here. I went through the same thing about a year ago."

He smiled. "Yeah, I do feel lost. I don't know anyone."

"Well, the people are friendly and you will find others to talk to. Are you a relative of Bud's?

"Just a friend. But we work at the same place."

At this point, Nevin and I were told to sit at a table with the bride and groom. I had been keeping an eye open for Grayson and Aunt Sarah and now I saw them not too far from me. After the meal, I walked around a bit visiting with others. It was not a large crowd, but we had a nice time together. Mary Lou was there and she loved my dress. Later, three men played instruments and the bridal pair danced. As they danced, Grayson came and stood beside me.

"You look lovely, June. The dress is beautiful and so is the person in it." Grayson looked directly at me as he spoke and looked so sincere that my heart began pounding. To get such a compliment from him was better than all the compliments I had gotten that day. And there were many.

"Thank you." There was a bit of a pause as we watched the dancers.

"Are you envious of the bride?"

I couldn't believe he asked me that. I hesitated and looked away, but he did not look away.

"A little." It was hard to be so honest, but what was the sense in telling a lie? "And you?" I couldn't believe the words came out of my mouth.

He, too, looked back at the bride and groom before answering. "A little."

The dance was ended and there was clapping and then Donna's bouquet was thrown and Mary Lou caught it. With Grayson at my side, I was glad I did not catch it. I did not want to be teased and have Grayson feel uncomfortable.

After the dance, I talked quite a while to Donna and Bud. They thanked me again and again for my help in making this day a reality. Donna was young, but she would mature fast in the coming months. Her mother also talked quite a while to me and the evening passed quickly.

Nothing had been said about going home but I suddenly realized that Aunt Sarah was no longer there and neither could I see Grayson. Just when I thought there might have been a misunderstanding, I saw Grayson coming my way.

"Are you ready to call it a day?"

"I am. I couldn't find you or Aunt Sarah and thought I might be here for the night."

"Hardly," he grinned. "Aunt Sarah is already home."

I did not ask any questions. We said goodbye to the bride and groom as they headed to the inn for the night, and then we headed home.

"It was a lovely day," I commented as the horse clopped down the road. "I am truly happy for them. I think all will be well."

"Where are they going to live?"

"For right now, with the Gables, but in a week or so they expect to be able to move into an apartment in town. He has a pretty good job and they have high hopes for their future."

The night was still young and daylight lingered. I suddenly realized that Grayson was not taking a direct route home. I said nothing. I was enjoying the ride.

"How is the sewing going?"

"In general, good. Oh, I guess I have time now to make your coat. I just have to redo a dress for Mrs. de Frappe. She is not an easy customer. I made the dress according to the pattern she gave me and now she does not like it and wants me to change it."

"And it is all your fault."

"Exactly. Do you know her?"

"I know her husband. He is a nice man but I was never impressed by his wife."

"How do you know her husband?"

"He is on town council." I had to assume that Grayson was also on the council.

"You will have to deal with more Mrs. de Frappes in the world you are stepping into."

"They pay well," I said with a grin.

He grunted and turned his head to me. "You are getting more materialistic all the time." I laughed out loud. I loved sparing with Grayson. "What are you going to do with all your money?"

"I am going to buy the gatehouse from you."

"It is not for sale. Not now or ever to you."

"Oh dear, does anyone else have a gatehouse around here?"

"No, you are stuck here." He paused. "Do you ever wish to go back to Trinkels?"

"No, never. Oh, it would be nice to see some friends again, but I have many sad memories from that place." I paused, remembering the death of my parents, being stood up by Gerald and the broken engagement with Alan. And I was not forgetting the breakup with Grayson and being sorry about it later.

"So you have been here a year now. Has it been a good year?"

"Yes. Mostly, except for the death of my uncle and the horror of coming for you through that wild storm."

We were coming in the lane past the gatehouse. The sky was now dark and a nearly full moon was hanging above us. It was a wonderful evening and I did not want it to end.

Grayson turned to me with a grin. "Do you turn into a pumpkin at midnight?"

I giggled. "I haven't yet. At least not that I am aware of. I don't know if pumpkins can think. If I turn into a pumpkin I might not know it."

He was so handsome as he looked at me.

"Well, if you are missing tomorrow and Sarah makes a pumpkin pie, I will know. I'm sure you will taste good."

We both laughed and he drove on to the stables and then helped me out of the carriage.

"Wait, while I take care of the horse," he said.

I waited in the moonlight. The night was bright in its light. When finished, Grayson stepped up to me, took my hand and walked me down to the pond. The fireflies were dotting the meadow with their lights and the evening was enchanting. The moon was reflected in the pond and I heard a frog croak nearby. We stood in silence a few moments, hand in hand each in our own thoughts.

"Shall we give our relationship another chance?" Grayson asked softly.

My heart stood still. I could barely breathe.

"Yes," I answered. But I could barely hear my own voice.

CHAPTER 23

The letter from Ohio came two days later. Aunt Sarah read it out loud to me when neither of the sisters were around.

Dear Sarah,

    I was glad to hear from you about Lizzie, since she does not write. Even though she is sometimes very grumpy, I miss having her around. I have a proposition to make. We have a big house that has ample room for not only Lizzie, but if Becca wants to come to live with her in Ohio, she too, is welcome. They are used to living with one another now and it would make the move easier for both of them. I do not know how you feel about this.

    I do not want to take Becca from you if you want her there with you. But you are not getting younger and you no longer own the house. I thought this might be a good solution for you. Let me know how you feel, and if you are agreeable, you can talk it over with Lizzie and Becca. Then we will have to work on how to get them here. I will be waiting to hear from you,

                        Love, Fanny

"How do you feel about that?" I asked when she finished reading.

"To tell you the truth, it is a relief to me. I will miss them both, but I am getting older and stiffer and so are they. Besides that, I no longer own this place and we are all sort of living on Grayson's kindness. I have been wondering what we would do if he suddenly married."

My heart was full. He was now courting me, but I was not going to say anything. Let it just come out.

"What do you think Becca will say?"

"I don't know, but I shall talk to them both within the next couple days. But first I must get used to the idea. And God only knows how we will ever get them to Ohio."

I left Aunt Sarah to her musing and hurried up to the gatehouse. I now had the wedding dresses behind me and needed to change Mrs. de Frappe's gown and then get started on Grayson's coat. I was disgusted with Mrs. de Frappe and her attitude toward me and all others "beneath her." But I was able to make the necessary changes, although it took up most of the afternoon, and then I at least got to cut out the coat fabric. That evening, at the supper table, Grayson suggested a ride after supper. I noticed Aunt Sarah give us both a quick look and then busied herself with the dishes. I helped her and since she asked nothing, I told her nothing, but instead chatted of other things. The early apples were nearly ripe and we would have applesauce to make and apples to sell. We discussed how many we would keep and how the tomatoes were doing in the garden and how the carrots and cabbages and potatoes were growing.

The evening ride became nearly a ritual and I loved it. Grayson and I found lots of things to talk about and to learn about each other. One evening when we came back, Grayson had work in the barn and I sat outside and helped Aunt Sarah, Becca and Lizzie who were all taking the heads and tails off of green beans that Aunt Sarah would can the next day. When it got too dark, the sisters went in and Aunt Sarah and I chatted.

"You are enjoying your landlord's company," she said with a knowing smile.

"I am."

"So you are giving it another chance."

I nodded and smiled as Misty came and rubbed against my legs. I was so in love with Grayson I was afraid if I started talking about him I would not stop.

"I hope it works out this time. You could not find a finer man."

"I agree."

———————

The next day, I told Grayson he could come and get his coat fitted. When he came, he seemed a bit ill at ease and I suspected it was because we were here alone. We talked only of what needed to be said in regards to the coat. My fingers trembled as I pinned and worked at getting it just right. Grayson just stood there, not talking, but I could tell he was pleased with it. And when I said that I was finished, he abruptly left.

That afternoon, Mrs. de Frappe came to see her gown, now with the changes. I let her alone while she got into the dress. I had a long mirror in the room for her to see herself.

"It is not like I envisioned," she said when I entered the room. "Not at all. You will have to change it back to the original pattern."

I could not believe my ears. I tried to keep calm and tried to encourage her to keep it as it was, but she was not at all interested in what I had to say. Her mind was made up.

"You did not tell me what I would look like in it with the changes. You as a seamstress should have known that. No, it must go back to the former plan. When will it be done? I have a big party coming up and it has to be done by that time."

I promised her to do it. I just wanted her out of the house before I exploded. There was no thought of the work in changing it in the first place and now again. She was used to giving orders and thinking only of her own skin. I was disgusted and for the first time, I wondered if I really wanted to sew for the rich. They had money, but that was all. And money was not everything.

At supper that evening, Lizzie told me with a beaming face that she was moving to Ohio. I looked at Aunt Sarah.

"I talked to them both this afternoon and even Becca seems to want to move so she can be with Lizzie."

I looked at Becca. She smiled. Maybe this was an adventure for her.

"How and when will they go?" I asked.

"We shall see. I have a letter written to be sent tomorrow. Then we must work on when and how."

Grayson said not a word, but he looked curiously at both the women, then at me. I wanted to know what he was thinking.

A week later, we received word from the niece that anytime was good. Now it was up to us.

Grayson was busy with the early apple harvest and came late to supper. When the sisters were out of the room, he called Aunt Sarah and me to the parlor.

"There is no way we can send them to Ohio on their own," he said. "And I cannot free myself from the work here just now. I wonder if Fanny would come to pick them up, if I picked up the train fair for her."

I suddenly had the urge for an adventure. I had never been to Ohio.

"I'll take them."

Grayson gave me a long look. I could tell he did not like the idea.

"Really, I could take them. But I need perhaps a week to finish your coat and the gown for Mrs. de Frappe."

"I thought you finished it," said Aunt Sarah.

"I finished it twice. I will take no more work from her. But don't ask me about it or I won't sleep tonight."

Grayson grinned at me. "She really ruffled your feathers, didn't she?"

"She did and I get no thanks from her. Let's get back to our subject before I say anything more about that woman."

I tried not to see the "I told you so" expression on Grayson's face.

"I could go along," said Aunt Sarah, "but that leaves Grayson alone. And I don't know how long we would be gone and there is the garden work and the men are all picking and selling apples."

I thought of Mary Lou. We could have a ball going on this trip together.

"Let me ask Mary Lou if she will come with me."

Grayson made no comment, but Aunt Sarah thought that a possibility.

"When could you leave, if you go?" he asked me.

I thought a while, considering the work I had to do. "Give me one week. We could leave in one week if that suits Becca and Lizzie. But not sooner."

"In that case, I will check train schedules. Once we know the schedule, maybe you, Sarah, can write and say when they will arrive."

So it was settled and I had a lot to think about. I found that I was not as eager to leave as I would have been a few weeks ago. I would miss Grayson. True, he was working long days, but still, I saw him every day at some time. I sent a note to Mary Lou in the mail. We would talk about it Sunday.

Mrs. de Frappe came two days later to see the finished dress. I held my breath when she tried it on. It was accepted without fanfare. We had agreed on the price of the gown before I made it. She did not offer more for the extra work and I did not ask for it. I was afraid she would not give it to me anyway and I just wanted her out of my life.

The following days were a bit hectic. Surely Becca would never move back here, so her things, as well as Lizzie's, had to be packed and sent on ahead by train. Nettie was cleaning the house as we worked in the addition where the sisters lived.

"It looks like fun," said Nettie, watching us throwing things into the trunks. "I wish I were going on a train trip."

"Oh, Nettie, I think sometime you will. You and your husband-to-be will maybe go to Niagara Falls for your honeymoon."

She laughed merrily and went her way, mopping the floors and dusting anything within sight.

After two busy days of sorting, throwing away and packing Becca's things in a trunk as well as a trunk for Lizzie, Grayson hauled the trunks off to the railway station and things calmed down a bit. I expected Becca to be sad, but both Lizzie and Becca seemed eager for the adventure. Becca had seldom, if ever, ridden on a train. The plan was to get the evening train at eight-twenty at Thackeray's Pond, which would take us to Watchman's Tower about an hour away and there we would transfer to the Pullman car, which would take us all the way to the town in Ohio where we would be picked up and taken to the niece's house. It was Grayson who suggested the Pullman car and the sleeping berth just to cut down the wake time, which we all knew would be stressful. I had visions of all four of us being thrown out of the train for all the shouting. I was so looking forward to my time with Mary Lou and counted on her to keep me sane.

I managed to finish Grayson's coat and brought it along home with me two days before the trip. I was happy with it and when I handed it to him, I told him to also put on his vest so I could see how they looked together. He was accommodating and I could not hide my admiring look as he stood before me.

He grinned widely at me. "Do I pass muster?"

"You exceed it," I said, feeling generous as I contemplated leaving him for a few days. But I blushed as I said it.

The following day, I did my own packing. I stayed home helping Aunt Sarah and also helping Becca and Lizzie do last-minute things. I did not want anything to mess up our plans. It was scary business taking these two women all those miles. I sensed a sadness in Aunt Sarah in spite of her relief that they were both going. I did not know how long Becca had been here, but life would be a lot quieter without the two sisters.

At suppertime the evening before we would leave, Becca and Lizzie were shouting to each other and Grayson caught my eye.

"Are you sure you are ready for this?" he said in a low voice.

"Mary Lou will keep me sane," I answered. "It will be an adventure."

Five minutes later, someone knocked and Grayson went to answer the door. He came back with Mary Lou's father.

"Have a seat," Aunt Sarah offered after greeting him.

"Thank you, I will, but no supper. I've already eaten."

He looked serious and I wondered what had happened or who might have died. And when we had chatted a bit, we waited to hear why he had come. It was then he turned to me.

"I am sorry, but I bring you bad news. Mary Lou cannot accompany you to Ohio."

His words were like a death knell. I felt myself go pale.

"Why not?" I croaked.

"She was sick all week and now the doctor says she has pneumonia. She has been in bed the last two days but kept hoping she would get better. She wanted so badly to accompany you."

I could not think of what to say. I was dumbfounded. There was no way I could take Lizzie and Becca to Ohio by myself. We all sat completely quiet while we digested this news.

"What happened?" shouted Lizzie. "Why is no one talking?"

No one answered right away. Then Aunt Sarah said, "Mary Lou is sick."

"Is she going to die?"

"Certainly not," said my patient aunt. "But we must find someone else to go on the trip."

Yes, I thought to myself, but who in all the world? Not Aunt Sarah. Not Grayson. Not Jeannie or Annelie. There were various reasons why we had eliminated them all before.

Grayson was looking at me soberly. I hoped he was thinking of a solution, but he said nothing.

And then I thought of Nettie. She wanted a train ride. She thought it sounded like fun.

"Nettie," I said.

"Nettie?" Aunt Sarah looked at me.

"She would not have been my first choice, but she was envying me yesterday because of the train trip. I believe she would go."

I looked at Grayson. He was looking at me in deep thought. But he was not saying no.

"Who is Nettie?" asked the pastor.

"The girl who cleans for us," said Aunt Sarah. Then she looked at me. "Do you really think she could do the job?"

"She knows both Becca and Lizzie and she does her work well. I think I can count on her to be a help and not a hindrance."

Nettie lived quite close to us and I would have to go talk to her immediately. Hopefully, she could go.

"We'll ride over there," said Grayson, looking at me.

"Can we leave right now?"

We left for Nettie's house before Pastor Stafford even left the house. But I had to have help and who would I get if Nettie could not?

When we knocked on the door at Nettie's house, it was quickly opened by two young children who just stood and stared at us. Then Nettie showed up. Her face looked at us anxiously as she invited us into the house.

"Is something wrong?" she asked.

"Yes, Nettie, I have a problem and I hope you can help me."

"How can I help *you*?"

"Mary Lou is sick and cannot go with me to Ohio. Could you go in her place?"

Nettie's eyes lit up. "Go on the train with you to Ohio?"

"Yes."

By this time Nettie's whole family was standing in the room listening, including her mother and father.

"Oh, Mama and Papa! May I go?"

They looked pleased that I asked her. "How long will you be gone?"

"We leave tomorrow evening and we will sleep on the train. We get to Ohio in the morning and the following morning we will board the train to return," I said.

Permission was granted and Nettie was so excited that if we had been planning to leave that night yet, she would have still said yes. She was the oldest in the family and surely had learned responsibility and her parents were proud that we asked her.

Grayson and I rode back to the house slowly. The crisis was past. What the morning would bring was unknown, but we could relax for now. I just hoped Lizzie and Becca would sleep well.

We walked together to the house after taking care of the horse in the stables.

"So, tomorrow the adventure begins," he said.

"Yes, and I shall miss Mary Lou but Nettie will be alright."

"Do Lizzie and Becca know that they must change trains at one point?"

"I don't know, but I will try to get that information in them as soon as we begin the journey. I think it is good the change of trains is just one hour into the journey. If it were one hour before we arrive it might be harder to get them back into the train."

"And you have your return ticket?"

"I do."

"You won't want to stay there longer than one day?"

"No. I will probably be so sick of Becca and Lizzie's shouting that I might take the next train back that day yet."

Grayson laughed. "Just remember to come back."

We were at the door and he opened it for me. I was hoping maybe he would give me a hug or even a kiss. After all, I was going all the way to Ohio the next evening. But there was no kiss and no hug. But he did look at me with his beautiful dark eyes as he wished me a good night.

CHAPTER 24

It had been a strange day. I think Becca finally realized that she was not coming back to Bluster Hill. Aunt Sarah was fighting tears all day, but Lizzie was excited about going. I had mixed feelings myself and felt very sad for Aunt Sarah who would most likely never see her two sister-in-laws again on this earth. Grayson brought the carriage with two horses to the portico. Aunt Sarah wanted to go along to the train station and that made five of us, plus our bags. It would seem strange to Aunt Sarah to return home with just Grayson.

We got to the station in plenty of time and it is good we did, because we needed all that time. Nettie was already there, excitement on her face. By the time we had shouted instructions to the two sisters and gotten them to the track, we could see the train coming in the distance. Grayson placed our bags close by and seeing the train coming, Aunt Sarah immediately began saying goodbye to her husband's sisters. She and Becca cried and even Lizzie had tears in her eyes. I quickly said goodbye to them and then I felt Grayson's arm around my waist. The train came to a hissing, screeching stop and as the others were grabbing their bags and looking at the people coming off the train, Grayson gave me a long look. I suddenly had tears in my own eyes. I did not like to say goodbye to him. Seeing the moisture in my eyes, he put his arms around me and gave me a wonderful, prolonged hug. I hugged him back and did not want it to end. But of course, it had to.

"I'll be praying for you," he said. "I think you will need it with Becca and Lizzie. Just don't lose them on the way." He grinned. "Enjoy the adventure."

I was fighting tears and couldn't get a word out, but I am sure he got the message from me.

And then we were boarding the train while Grayson talked to the conductor and finally I was waving to Grayson and Aunt Sarah for as long as possible.

And then I looked at Becca and Lizzie. They were sitting quietly and wide-eyed, looking out the window. I hoped the quiet would last the whole trip. I took my seat with Nettie. She was so wound up I thought a spring might pop.

"I've never been on a train before," she announced. "Do they always go this fast?"

"They do," I assured her, "and we better be glad they go so fast so it does not take us a week to get to Ohio."

I then turned around to Becca and Lizzie who were seated right behind us. "This train only takes us to a town called Watchman's Tower. There we will get another train that will take us all the way to Ohio."

"When do we go to sleep?" asked Lizzie.

"On the next train."

I was speaking very loudly but it was the only way to get the message to them the first time. I did not want to shout more than I had to. I saw a few people turn their heads and heard a little boy ask his mother why we were yelling at those ladies. I repeated the message regarding the change of trains in one hour so there would be no confusion, but that took a lot of explaining and a lot of shouting. I did not look around at the other passengers. I did not want to see their curious looks or their frowns of disapproval.

The trip was just beginning and Becca and Lizzie were pretty quiet that first hour. Nettie kept commenting on the scenery and simply chatted about anything she saw from the window. I would have liked to have had a break, so I could think about Grayson's hug, but I was grateful for her. I would need her help when we changed trains.

It was dusk by the time the train pulled into Watchman's Tower.

"Nettie, I would like you to be responsible for Lizzie and I will try to take care of Becca. Just see that we stay together, since this is a much bigger station, and see that Lizzie has her small bag and her purse."

Nettie was looking out the window. "June, there are a lot of trains here. Which is ours?"

I was scared myself. "I'll ask the conductor when we leave the train."

We got the sisters out of the train with a bit of prodding and a lot of shouting, and then I showed my ticket to the conductor, who was very helpful in pointing the way to our next train.

"Just walk through the station and out the other side. Your train will arrive there in about ten minutes."

We made it though the busy station with little problem. We discovered there would be a ten-minute wait, which was fine, although it seemed like an hour. Lizzie thought we should not have gotten off the first train and Becca kept wanting to go back to see if it was still there. Finally I could hear the train coming.

"Can we sleep on this train?" Lizzie shouted to me.

"Yes!" I shouted back, my voice now getting lost in the screeching and hissing of the train. "This one will have a sleeping car. Now let's just stay together and don't stumble when we go up the steps. Nettie, can you carry Lizzie's bag until she gets up the steps? I'll do the same for Becca."

"Give me your bag!" shouted Nettie to Lizzie.

"Why do you want my bag?" she shouted back.

"Just till you get up the steps!"

The bag was handed over a bit grudgingly. Becca gave her bag immediately and without question and the conductor was very helpful.

Our tickets had the berth number on them so we had to find our seats. Grayson had chosen berths across from each other, for which I was thankful. We found our seats and sat down.

"I thought these were going to be beds," grumbled Lizzie as we pulled out of the station.

"The seats we are sitting on will become beds!" I shouted.

"How can that be?"

"You'll see. They will be bunk beds. Look above you. My bed is hanging up there above us and that will flip down. Nettie will sleep up above you on the other side."

"Never saw nothin' like it," grumbled Lizzie, not convinced it was possible.

It wasn't long before a porter came through. "Are you ready for me to make up your beds?" he asked.

"Yes, I think so," I replied.

It was now dark outside and the lanterns in the car were not very bright. He suggested we go to the far end where we could sit while he prepared the beds.

"Are we going to bed now?" shouted Lizzie as we made our way up the dim aisle.

"We are going to sit and wait while he changes our seats into beds!" I shouted back.

Ten minutes later, we were allowed back in our seats, which were now beds.

"Well, I'll be," said Lizzie. "I can't believe it."

Finally Becca spoke. Till now she had been quiet, letting Lizzie do most of the talking. "I don't think I can sleep with the train moving."

"Oh, you will," I said, silently praying that she would. I did not want to be awake all night sitting with Becca. "It will be fun, sleeping in a moving train."

"What?" she asked, looking wide-eyed at me.

"It will be fun!" I said much too loudly for the other passengers.

"Sun? What about the sun?"

"Fun!" I shouted. "Oh! I just remembered that Aunt Sarah sent some cookies and crackers along. Anyone want a bedtime snack?"

"Did she send any sandwiches? I would like a sandwich," said Lizzie.

"I believe she did," I said, digging into Aunt Sarah's bag. I passed over the cookies and crackers. Sure enough, there were four sandwiches. No one had been too hungry at supper.

"Here we go. A sandwich for each of us."

"What kind?" asked Becca.

"Bologna. All the same."

And for a few minutes, all was quiet as we ate our sandwiches. I found I was hungry, too, and in the bit of silence, I wondered what Aunt Sarah and Grayson were doing. Were they thinking of us?

It seemed to take a long time till we got everyone into bed. We pulled the curtains and sat on the bed to change into nightgowns. This was a huge job for Becca and Lizzie. They both needed help and Lizzie grumbled loudly.

"Why can't I undress in the aisle?" she shouted for everyone to hear.

"Because you don't want to undress with other people watching, do you?" asked Nettie who had her hands full with Lizzie.

"Why do they want to watch?"

Why wouldn't they? I thought to myself. But I did not say it out loud.

"Where will you sleep?" asked Becca as I tucked her in.

"I will sleep up here." I pointed above her.

"Oh my," said Lizzie, listening in. "I hope you don't fall out, June. And I hope the bed does not collapse on Becca."

"I have to go," said Becca.

"Me, too," said Lizzie.

I sent Nettie up the hall with Lizzie and when they came back, I went with Becca. I hoped they would not have to go during the night, but I had to expect it. I just hoped no one else was up at the same time. We brought no housecoats, just nighties.

We finally had the two in bed. Nettie looked at me. "Do we go to bed now, too?"

"I think so. I just hope there are no disturbances during the night. Do you think you can sleep in a moving train?"

"I think so. It is so exciting."

I was so thankful for Nettie's attitude. Being the oldest in a large family had given her a lot of practice in being responsible and I knew I could count on her. Nettie and I climbed up on our respective bunks, pulled the curtains, and lay back on our beds while the train rolled over hill and dale on our way to Ohio. I did not sleep right away. My mind went back to Bluster Hill. To Aunt Sarah and to Grayson. I hoped all was well. I was missing Grayson's dark eyes and remembering his admonition not to forget to come home again. And I was reliving the hug.

The miles ticked by. Always the clickety-clack of the train going over the tracks. But finally sleep claimed me.

I woke up to someone talking. I opened my curtain carefully. It was Lizzie grumbling. Rather than shout down to her, I slipped out of my bed and was soon standing in the aisle. The lights were so dim, I could barely see.

"What is it Lizzie?" I leaned very close to her and spoke directly in her ear.

"Becca is gone," she said.

"What do you mean 'gone'?" I looked in Becca's bed and sure enough, no Becca.

"She must have gone to the lavatory," I assured Lizzie.

"She did, I went first, but she isn't back yet."

"Well, let's give her a little time yet," I said, but rethinking it, I decided to go look and decided I could use the lavatory myself since I was up anyway. "Go back to sleep," I told Lizzie. "I'll check on her."

I headed out through the curtained beds. I heard some loud snoring as I passed one bunk and some sighing from another bunk where I presumed someone could not sleep. It seemed a much longer way now at night going through the car. It felt like I must have gone the whole length of the car a few times till I finally got to the lavatory. Someone was inside and I waited a short time. Did Becca fall asleep in there? How long had she been in? I tapped on the door.

"Becca?" I called, but of course she was too deaf to hear. However, I heard a grunt, which did not sound very much like Becca. And then the door opened and to my surprise, a big fat man came out.

He pushed past me and I quickly went in and did my business while I tried to figure out what had happened to Becca. I was out again in a very short time and looked around where I stood. She could not go to the next car and she was not in bed. Just then, down the dim aisle I heard a disturbance.

"Help, there's a man in my bed!"

My heart nearly stopped. That voice sounded suspiciously like Becca's voice, but I had never heard it screech as it did now. And it came from the far end of the car, which is where we slept. As I made my way down the aisle as quickly as I could in the dim light, I accidentally brushed open a curtain where someone slept. The person must have already been awake and I instantly got scolded soundly by the person who was sleeping there. Or trying to sleep. I quickly pulled the curtain closed again and hurried on until I got to a blockade. The fat man, complete with a long white nightshirt, was standing in the aisle.

"That happens to be my bed you are in," he scolded. "What are you doing in there? What kind of loose woman are you?"

If there was anything Becca was not, it was a loose woman. I hoped for once she really could not understand what was said. I heard curtains opening and hoped the curious passengers did not think that I was the one in the wrong bed. I looked across the aisle to see if Lizzie was in the opposite bed. She was not. So if Lizzie was not in that bed, Becca was in the wrong one. The man was right. It was Becca who climbed into the wrong bed. No wonder we could not find her. She must have gone in the first bed she came to with an open curtain. She had likely passed the man in the aisle. I tapped the man on the shoulder.

"Excuse me sir, I know who that is. She is very deaf and cannot hear you."

He slowly turned and looked at me. He had a scruffy beard and a big nose and bulging eyes. Of course, who wouldn't have bulging eyes after finding an unknown somebody in one's bed in the middle of the night?

"It is your mother?" he asked, a bit calmer. Giving me a look-over.

"No sir, but she is my responsibility on this trip and I am sorry for the disturbance. I am sure it is all a mistake. She went to the lavatory and got into the wrong bed."

"You better believe she got into the wrong bed."

Then he snorted as if he was finally seeing a bit of humor in the incident. He finally moved out of my way and in the background I heard other people talking about the disturbance and getting irritated.

"Hey!" called one man. "What kind of shenanigans are going on out there? I want to get some sleep." A bit farther up the aisle I heard some giggles.

By this time Becca, her eyes wide open and looking frightened, was cowering in the bed. I coaxed her out and took her by the arm.

"Come, Becca, you got into the wrong bed. Your bed is the next one."

Becca said nothing, but she came willingly. I got her into her bed as quickly as possible and closed her curtain. I hoped she would sleep.

"Did you find her?" asked Lizzie.

I put my mouth next to her ear. "Yes."

"Where was she?"

"She got lost. I'll tell you in the morning."

Then Nettie leaned out of her bunk. In the dim light, I could see her grin. "Isn't this the funniest thing you ever heard of?"

Lizzie was the first one awake in the morning and soon made

herself heard. One by one we got up and I was glad to note that Becca said nothing of the night's adventure. Perhaps she thought it was a bad dream. But Lizzie remembered.

"Where were you so long last night?" she asked her sister. "June had to go looking for you."

Becca gave her a confused look and then I could see her beginning to remember.

"I got in the wrong bed," she said simply, as if it happened every night.

"What do you mean you got in the wrong bed? Whose bed were you in?"

"Shh," I said, my finger to my lips. "I'll tell you later."

Lizzie was not finished. "You could have gotten into a man's bed."

"I did," said Becca calmly. "What do we eat for breakfast?"

My eyes went wide and I looked at Nettie. Was Becca going to dismiss her misadventure so simply? Nettie snorted in her hand and I bit my lip. I guess I would ignore it, too.

I looked at my watch. "It is eight o'clock and we are in Ohio. According to the schedule, we should be at our destination in less than an hour. And Fanny said she would have breakfast ready for us when we get there."

The time went quickly. The landscape was much flatter in Ohio. We were used to hills and valleys. Here it was just flat and we could see for miles. And we saw a lot of sky, which was clear this morning. None of us had ever been to Ohio before and we quietly enjoyed the new scenery. And then, suddenly, it was time to get our things together. The next stop was announced and it was ours. As the train slowed, we looked out to see if Fanny was there to greet us. She was not, but I was sure her husband Mark would be waiting. Just then I saw a man looking at the train and I believed it must be him.

"There is Mark to pick us up. Nettie you go first and lead the way out and when you are all out, I will hand Lizzie and Becca's bags out to you or Mark."

The fat man next to us gave both old women a long look as they got up to leave. He was probably wondering which one was in his bed. He seemed to be traveling alone and I wondered if he was a widower. Catching me watching him, he grinned at me. I grinned back.

———————

Mark and Fanny were a very special couple. I had never met them before, but they seemed genuinely happy to see both women and I was so happy to hand the responsibility over to them. He introduced himself and got us seated in the carriage and we were off. It was not long before we were seated in Fanny's large kitchen and eating a wonderful breakfast of eggs and bacon. And I am afraid we gobbled everything up they offered us. We were hungry. Of course, they asked how the trip went and although I would not have said anything in Becca's presence, Lizzie had no qualms about it.

"Becca got in a man's bed during the night," she announced loudly. Mark and Fanny looked at me with wide eyes and open mouths.

"She got lost on the way back from the lavatory during the night," I said more quietly, hoping Becca was not catching on. But Lizzie had spoken loudly and Becca looked up from her breakfast.

"He made me get out again," she said before putting a forkful of egg into her mouth.

I am sure she did not mean to say what it sounded like, but Mark guffawed loudly and the rest of us finally let loose with our own laughter over the unfortunate incident. To my amazement, Becca looked around the table at us all laughing and when she joined in, we nearly lost it.

After breakfast, which was getting on toward noon, we got the sisters in their own rooms. As we worked, I asked Fanny if she was sure this was what she wanted to do.

"I do. The children are grown and out of here. I enjoyed having Lizzie with us and I will enjoy having Becca as well. It is something we can do for them and we see it as a service to them and to God."

"Well, all I can say is God bless you both. You are God's gift to them. I hope all goes well."

"Thank you for bringing them to us. It saved us a trip. Do I understand that you are returning tomorrow morning?"

"Yes. Nettie must get home and I have work of my own."

I then told her of my sewing business and then she took me to the room that Nettie and I would share that night. Later in the day we walked around their neighborhood and then chatted on their porch in the evening. I surely enjoyed my relaxed day with Fanny. I quietly thanked God again for her and Mark and for their commitment to the two sisters.

It was just as we were going to bed that Fanny somehow made a misstep going up the stairs and slipped back down a step and hurt her ankle. She was obviously in pain, but tried to make light of it. She insisted it was nothing serious. But the next morning, she was still hobbling so I decided I would send Nettie home alone and I would come when Fanny could walk easier. I could not let her here with two women who did not know their way around the place and could not do the cooking. She made a big fuss, but finally agreed and I could tell she was relieved. I talked to Nettie and she was not afraid to make the trip alone.

In the meantime, I went along to the train station to see Nettie off. She was rather excited at making the trip alone. It was an adventure for her and would maybe be the only such adventure in her whole life. Furthermore, this time it was by daylight and no sleeping berth. But the trip would seem longer. I wrote a quick letter to Aunt Sarah, explaining why I would come later. I said unless she heard differently, I would plan to come in two days, at the same time.

And so we waved goodbye to Nettie and I went back to spend the next two days helping Fanny. By the third morning, she was again fit and Mark took me to the train station. The trip seemed longer now and I was eager to get home. I had missed Grayson more each passing day and could hardly wait to see him again.

When I finally got off the train at Watchman's Tower, I still had an hour to wait for my next train. I checked which track my train would come in on and then still had a lot of time left. This hour would go slowly. I was so close to home and here I sat. Seeing an inn across the street, I went over for a cup of coffee. When I returned, I found a bench at the far end of the station platform where I would be out of the hurry and bustle of the train station. I even sat with my face slightly turned away from the station and gazed at the track that would take me home. And to Grayson.

"June?"

I looked up and for just a split second I thought maybe Grayson had come for me. But I was dismayed to find Gerald walking up to me, all smiles.

"Gerald? What are you doing here?"

"Probably the same as you. Waiting for a train. Luck seems to be on my side."

I did not say so, but I was thinking it certainly was not on mine. Without asking permission, he sat down by my side. Too close. I inched a bit away from him.

"Where are you headed?" I asked, hoping he was headed in a different direction than I was.

"Thackeray's Pond. And you also?"

I nodded and looked away. Why did this have to happen? There was enough drama on this trip without Gerald's company. He had to sense my coolness, but it did not deter him.

"I live now about twenty miles from here, but I am going back to my brother for a few days. He is building a new stable and needs my help. So I will be close to Bluster Hill for a few days."

I did not like to hear what he had to say. I did not want him talking to me now and did not want his company on the train.

"It will be nice to see my brother and his family again. I miss family. I don't know if I will ever have a family of my own." There was a slight pause. "What is going on with you by now? What does your future look like?"

I looked straight ahead at a train that was just leaving. "I don't know. It isn't in my hands."

"Oh, yes it is," he said quickly. "It is more in your hands than you realize."

"Gerald, I do not want to discuss it. That is finished." I paused and added, "And for your information, I am being courted by Mr. Everleigh."

He gave me a long look, then pulled out a cigar and stuck it in his mouth. I hate cigars and the ugly smell and I was tired of Gerald. I wanted to dream about my reunion with Grayson.

"And if you plan to light that cigar you must sit elsewhere. When did you ever start that filthy habit?" There was a barb in my words and I was immediately sorry for it.

To my amazement, he put the cigar back in his pocket. I would have rather he lit his cigar and went elsewhere to smoke it.

"We can at least talk together as we wait for the train." His voice almost held a pleading note in it and I was embarrassed at the way I was treating him. I melted a wee bit.

"Tell me about your life now," I said.

He talked for the rest of our waiting time. I realized that Gerald was a lonely man and I was a bit kinder to him. I mostly looked down the track while he was talking to me.

And neither one of us noticed a handsome gentleman who came toward us, stopped, stared for a long moment and then turned and walked away.

CHAPTER 25

When we boarded the train to Thackeray's Pond, I found a spot at the rear of the car and sat at the window. I could hardly believe it when Gerald came and sat next to me. I was tired of fighting him and did not comment. He managed to keep up a running monologue and I did not do more talking than necessary. We were on the home stretch and I hoped that Grayson would be there to pick me up. I could not wait to see him again. It seemed like weeks had gone by since we said goodbye. When the train began slowing for Thackeray's Pond, I got my things in order and breathed a sigh of relief. I looked out the window, eager to see if Grayson was there to pick me up. Of course, if something came up, it might be Marley. But I saw neither one of them.

"If your ride is not here, I'll take you home," said Gerald. "My brother is coming to pick me up."

"No thank you, I am sure someone will be here."

"It was nice talking again."

"I wish you well," I said, still looking out the train window as I stood up. "Goodbye."

I did not want to talk to Gerald when I was hoping to see Grayson in just seconds. I stepped into the aisle and was one of the first out of the train. I looked around, not seeing anyone and just when I thought maybe there was a miscommunication, I saw him. Grayson. He was standing on the platform just looking at me. He did not come toward me, but in my moment of happiness at seeing him, I did not notice that.

"Grayson!" I cried and walked toward him as quickly as I could with my bag. In return—I received a very reserved half smile. It was more like a formal nod from a complete stranger, but he came to me and took my bag. I remembered very well the hug he gave me when I left and now I waited eagerly for a welcoming hug. It did not come. I tried to hide my disappointment. And since it seemed he had lost his power of speech and asked me no questions, I did the talking.

"How is everything at home?"

"Fine, as far as I know." He had nothing more to say. Was he upset that I stayed longer?

We got the stagecoach to Cobbler's Crossing. The coach was full and two men were talking the whole time so it was not the place to find out what had gone crooked in our relationship. We sat side by side like strangers, not speaking. I was confused. And I was devastated.

At Cobbler's Crossing, Grayson had to hire a carriage to take us home. Once we were on the way, and alone in the carriage, I hoped Grayson would tell me what was wrong. He remained silent.

"Did Nettie get my letter to Aunt Sarah?"

"I believe she did." Wow. This man was not just cool, he was chilly.

"And you heard why I stayed longer?"

There was a bit of a hesitation. "Why *did* you stay longer?" He finally looked at me.

"Didn't she tell you?" I was amazed that he did not know. "Fanny hurt her ankle and I could not let her hobbling around there with Lizzie and Becca just having arrived."

No comment. He looked away. I tried one last time.

"Did Nettie stop by and tell you of the hilarious night we had on the train with Becca getting into the wrong bed?"

I glanced at him then and he gave a half smile.

"Yes, she told Aunt Sarah about it."

Again no more than those few words. I finally got it. Light broke through. Grayson was displeased with me. Something was very wrong in our relationship. I looked away from him where the sun was sink-ing low in the sky and blinked back tears. What had happened? I wasn't even home for something to happen. And then I thought of Gerald. Had Grayson seen him exit the train just before me? But if I remembered correctly, another man got between us before we left the train, so I was not even right behind Gerald. He could not possibly think.... No, it was not Gerald. He would not get that upset because we were on the same train. But something was definitely wrong and somehow I could not bring myself to ask what it was. Frankly, by now I was so upset that I was afraid if I asked him what was wrong, I would start crying. I had to brace myself because we were just heading in the lane past the gatehouse.

We splashed through the ford and then we were at the portico and somehow Grayson helped me down, but I did not look at him because I was fighting tears. He opened the door for me and I went in without a word. And there was Aunt Sarah!

"June, it is so good to see you again! Come let me give you a hug!"

It was what I needed to boost my morale and I willingly went into her arms as I blinked the tears away.

"I am glad to be back," I replied. "It was quite the journey."

"And you had a nice surprise at Watchman's Tower."

I looked at her confused. She surely did not know that Gerald... she did not even know Gerald. And he certainly was not a nice sur-prise.

"What do you mean?"

The door opened and Grayson came in with my bag.

"Well," said Aunt Sarah with a wondering look in her eyes, "Grayson, meeting you there to ride the last leg of the journey with you."

I looked at Grayson, who stood silent. But his steady, sober look said a whole lot. I felt the blood drain from my face and for a moment I thought I might faint. Even Aunt Sarah knew something had gone very wrong. She simply turned and walked away. Grayson and I stood there a moment just looking at each other.

"I never saw you," I finally croaked.

"No, you never did," he replied, not blinking an eye.

And then he turned and went out the door.

I stood there in shock, staring at the closed door. And then I suddenly realized that he must have also been riding in the same train with me that last hour. Was it in the same car? Now I knew who stood between us. Gerald.

Aunt Sarah made me a late supper, but there was no Grayson. Thankfully. I could not have eaten a bite had he come. After supper, I went in the kitchen to help Aunt Sarah with the dishes, but I was so distracted, she stopped me.

"Sit down, June. Tell me what happened between you and Grayson."

I was glad to share it with someone and she had a compassionate ear. I told her the whole sorry tale.

"I never even saw Grayson at Watchman's Tower Station. He must have seen me with Gerald and assumed the worst. How could he? I would have been thrilled to have come back with him. I am so angry at Gerald for staying with me. He knows I am not interested in him and I told him I am dating Grayson. Or was."

And then I started crying and Aunt Sarah wrapped her arms around me.

———

The next day Nettie came to clean and we spent time talking about her ride home alone and we laughed together over Becca crawling into the bed of a stranger. However, it was Grayson I wanted to talk and laugh with. But he stayed out of my sight. I was learning something about Grayson. He could keep his hurt to himself and would give me an icy reception, rather than ask for an explanation. I was so intimidated by his manner, that I was scared to approach him. Afraid of what might be said.

That afternoon, I went to sew in the gatehouse. I told Aunt Sarah that I would stay and sew and eat a sandwich when I came home. I would not be home for supper. I never asked her if he came for supper. I saw nothing of Grayson that whole day. I was hurting badly.

The next day, I stopped in our village store to see if my dress had sold. It had. And someone had left a message for me to come see her. She lived in the village and I stopped in immediately. It was a Mrs. Charles and she was interested in a gown for her daughter who was going to a wedding and she needed a new dress for the occasion.

"Do you have the fabric and the pattern?"

"No, but she likes some fabric that we have right here at the mercantile. Do you have time to go with me now? I don't know how much we need?"

And so my day was filled with what I liked to do best. At the end of the day I was missing Grayson so much that I went home at suppertime and sure enough, Grayson was there. When I saw him, I wanted to feast my eyes on him, but instead I gave him a stiff smile and greeting. He responded in like manner. It was our first meal together and Aunt Sarah tried her best to keep conversation going for which I was grateful.

"Grayson, isn't this the time for the Summer Fete?"

"I believe it is. Did you get an invitation? I did not."

"Not yet, but it will come. I shall not go this year. It gets too long and I mind the night air after sundown. It starts late and ends much later. And Theodore is not here to go with me." She sighed.

"I could bring you back."

"No, you must be there. You get out socially little enough. Let the ladies admire you. There are so few bachelors."

Grayson harrumphed and I looked at my food.

"And June, you will be invited also," she added.

"Where is it?"

Grayson gave a quick look at Aunt Sarah and spoke.

"Oh, at a wealthy estate not far from here."

"Is this an annual thing?"

"Yes," said Aunt Sarah. "Probably the biggest fete of the season. They do it up big. All landowners and political people and those holding some sort of office in the village or surrounding area are invited, plus others that I do not know and I suppose they are somehow friends or relatives of the family. How many people do you think come, Grayson?"

"I'd say a good hundred."

"And what do you do there?" I looked at Aunt Sarah.

"Sit and talk and eat. There is a pig roast and some rather exotic foods. And they have some musical entertainment and I think some dancing. We never stayed long enough for the dancing."

"I am sure I will not be invited," I said. "If it is a wealthy person throwing the party, I have enough bad memories of Mrs. de Frappe to last me a long time and she might even be there. I am sure she does not like me and has probably made me look bad to her friends."

Grayson and Aunt Sarah exchanged glances.

"Oh," said Aunt Sarah, "you are too hard on yourself."

"I really have no wish to go if Mrs. de Frappe is there. She does not like me," I repeated.

There was silence at the table.

"Or do you not like her?"

The question came from Grayson. I looked at him in surprise. He just gave me a long, sober look. But he had at least spoken to me. Even though it sounded like a reprimand.

"I am disgusted with her. She is the one that I changed the gown for, and then she decided she liked it better as it had been and I had to redo it again."

Grayson was studying me and he opened his mouth to say something and closed it again. It made me wonder what he was going to say. I hoped so much that at the supper table we could at least talk like old times. It was not to be. Soon after this conversation, he abruptly left the table.

As I helped clear the table, I was fighting tears. Aunt Sarah said nothing, but a little later, she came up to my room where I was staring moodily out the window, listening to the katydids and crickets singing in the meadows and fields.

"June, I have an idea."

"Shall I move away?"

"Of course not. My observance of men is that when there is a problem to be solved, it is the woman who has to take the initiative. Neither one of you is happy. You live too close together to let this hang between you. He is in the library. Go talk to him."

"What? What would I say?"

"You will know when you face him."

I had had a couple days to stew about our relationship and I had a feeling that Grayson would not come to me. Did I dare? Could anything get worse between us?

"Think about it," said my aunt, as she left the room.

I could not go on this way. I sat for another fifteen or twenty minutes and then I washed my face, brushed my hair and almost changed my dress. No, that was too much. And then I took a deep breath and went down the stairs. My heart was pounding. But when I knocked on the door, I knew I had gone beyond the point of no return.

"Come in."

I opened the door slowly. Grayson was standing by the window, his hands in his pockets and when he saw me, our eyes locked. When I hesitated, he spoke.

"Close the door." I did so and slowly walked toward him. He motioned to the sofa facing the hearth. "Please have a seat."

When I had taken my seat, he remained standing, his eyes on me.

Aunt Sarah had said I would know what to say, but when I opened my mouth, I felt tears slide down my face. I brushed them off and tried again.

"Why are you angry with me?" I heard my voice tremble.

He took his time answering. "You really don't know?" His eyes were dark and I could not look away.

"No. I don't," I said with some force. Silence. When it got too long, I continued. "I went away and all was fine. I came back and..." I had to get a hold of myself "...you don't want to talk to me." The tears in my throat caused my last words to be a mere whisper.

There followed a long silence. Grayson turned and looked out the window and I thought maybe he simply did not want our relationship to go any further for some other reason that had nothing to do with my trip...and Gerald. Had something happened here while I was gone? I began to fear he was going to refuse to answer, but finally, as the clock ticked loudly in the quiet room, he turned once more to me.

"When I came to join you at Watchman's Tower, I found you in conversation with an old boyfriend." He paused. "I do not know what your conversation was, but in my mind, I did not see Gerald. I saw you eleven years ago, walking toward me at the fountain, laughing and talking to your neighbor, not even looking for me. And if you remember right, that ended in disaster."

I just stared at Grayson. That exchange must have been more traumatic for him than it was for me. And we had never addressed that conversation until now. He was waiting for a response. I thought back to that evening and I could only blush in memory.

"Grayson, I am very sorry for that evening. I was young, silly, and immature. Please forgive me for my words. I often regretted them, but you were gone. I was only ever friends with the boy. I can't even remember his name anymore." I paused. "But how could you ever think I could be interested in Gerald?"

"I stood in full view of you, but you were focused on Gerald. You never saw me."

"I would have been so *happy* to see you. It was a *wonderful* gesture to come to ride the last hour with me. I would have cherished it." I wiped the tears from my face. "Instead, Gerald once more just took a seat beside me."

"You could have sent him elsewhere."

I was silent, remembering. "Yes, I could have. I had said some not so nice words to him earlier. And I told him we were courting. But somewhere in our conversation, I realized Gerald was a lonely person. I do not know much of his personal life. I did not ask. But after I convinced him I was not available, he just sort of chattered on about anything in general. He just seemed contented to have someone listen to him. I had no real reason to make him move elsewhere."

Grayson just looked at me, listening and weighing my words. I had no more to say. Now it was up to him. The hardness was gone from his eyes and I hoped for peace about the past as well as the present.

Grayson moved from the hearth and took a seat beside me on the sofa. And then he took my hand in his.

"I seem to be the one who is at fault here. I seem to have a problem with trust, which maybe originated back in our earlier years." There was a long pause. "Will you forgive me for my own harsh words back then?"

"Of course. We were both young and immature."

He sat silent a few moments. "And perhaps I struggle with jealousy. I judged wrongly and you were the compassionate person who saw Gerald's need. I apologize again for my judgment."

"Of course."

"I feel like I can breathe again," he said, absently using his finger to brush a strand of hair from my face. "What do you say we go for a ride?"

"Now?"

"Now." He stood up and reached for my hand. "It is just twilight. Star will be glad to have you back. As am I."

I looked into his eyes and wished for a belated hug, but instead he headed for the door.

"Let me change skirts, I won't be long."

I ran past Aunt Sarah who, seeing my beaming face, muttered something under her breath, and I have every reason to think it was a thank you to God. I, too, was thanking God.

———————

"I think we have time to take a trail that you have not been on," said Grayson as we headed out. "It is not much farther than we've gone before, but we can climb a hill and get a nice view of the estate."

"Are we headed to the other entrance?"

"To begin with, but a trail goes off of it, across a meadow and we'll jump the fence on the far side of the meadow."

"We will *what?*" Grayson laughed and his laugh put healing oil on my wounds. "Maybe *you* will jump the fence, but there better be a gate for me."

"I must teach you to jump. You would make a good jumper."

"It is not me that has to jump. It is Star and she says she wants nothing to do with jumping."

"You have a vivid imagination."

There followed a comfortable silence as we headed to the bright sky where the sun had already gone down.

"I only heard the Becca story second-hand. I'd like to hear it from you."

I chuckled. "Becca surprises me sometimes. We don't always know what is going on in the heads of these old people."

And so, I told the tale about Lizzie's concerns, and me going to hunt for Becca. "And then, down the aisle, I heard a woman shouting for help because there was a man in her bed. And I knew right then where Becca was. And then the man loudly accused Becca of being a loose woman! Now it is funny. Right then I did not have time to enjoy the humor of it."

"I'm sure Becca was upset over that."

"The funny thing is, she did not act upset. Maybe she did not hear what the man said. When we talked about it in the morning, she passed it off as if getting into the wrong bed happened all the time."

Grayson chuckled. "Maybe she enjoyed it. Nothing terribly exciting happens in her life."

I laughed with him. "Fanny beware. You may have a Becca you did not expect."

Grayson laughed and seeing a gate ahead of us, I slowed down. To my surprise, Grayson and his horse suddenly picked up speed and they sailed over the fence with ease and then he came back to open the gate.

"See, it is easy," he teased as he opened the gate for me.

"Forget it. I have no interest in sailing over fences and neither does Star." I patted the mare. "Do you, Star?" We both laughed as she nickered.

When the gate closed again, I found we had a nice hill not far ahead of us.

"This is the hill!" shouted Grayson. "Let's race!" And off he went.

I never meant to let Star race, but somehow she seemed to take her cue from Grayson and soon I was hunkered down, hoping I would not fly off her back. Especially since we were going uphill. It seemed a long way to the top, but I stayed on the horse. Grayson was there ahead of me and was laughing heartily.

"There, don't tell me Star did not want to race. Her nicker was saying the opposite."

He tied his horse to a post that was probably put on the top of the hill for that purpose. Then he turned to me and helped me down.

"Where on earth did you get the idea for this skirt?"

"It was not my idea, but it was a good idea and I am sure any woman that rides will be switching to this kind of skirt."

"You could make a lot of money just selling them."

"I shall think about that."

"Look behind you."

I turned from the darkening sky and looked behind me and caught my breath. A full moon was coming up over the horizon. I just gazed in wonder, saying nothing as I watched it rise until it was a big orange ball just hanging over the edge of the earth. I did not want the moment to end. Especially when Grayson draped his arm over my shoulder and pulled me gently against him. Why is a full moon so romantic? I do not know. But I just wanted time to stop. I was as happy as I had ever been. All was right in my world. No words were necessary and finally the spell was broken by Grayson taking his arm away.

"We must head back."

And so we rode back in the last of the daylight and in view of the full moon. It was an evening to cherish.

CHAPTER 26

"Here is your invitation to the Summer Fete," said Grayson at the supper table the next day as he handed Aunt Sarah the envelope.

"Oh, my. I used to enjoy the food and meeting everyone, but now without Theodore, it just does not interest me. I shall beg off."

She opened the envelope and looked at the invitation. "Oh, but you are invited, June, and you must go. It is on the fourteenth. That is..."

"Next Saturday evening," said Grayson, giving me a meaningful look. "We will go together."

I just looked at him a moment. I really did not want to go to a party of the wealthy. I did not belong with them. And if Mrs. de Frappe was invited that would be reason not to go. However, when I looked at Grayson, I wanted to be with him and he was going. If we went together it would not be so bad.

"Thank you," I replied. "Now tell me about it."

As the dishes of food were passed around, Aunt Sarah told me about this celebration.

"It is an annual celebration. Or, I should say gathering for the closest neighbors and the town council and other important people. You must go. You will enjoy the pig roast and the exotic dishes that will be served and you will meet people you maybe never met before."

Grayson soon changed the subject and by the end of the meal I almost forgot about it. It was the next day when I was sewing another gown for someone that I remembered the invitation and wondered what I should wear to the big party. I had my mint green gown from the wedding and another blue dress that I had worn to church a few times that would probably do also.

Grayson still would not take any money from me, but asked instead for two new shirts. I got the material in the village and planned to work on them next.

My afternoon was interrupted. I heard someone call my name and looked out the window. It was Mary Lou.

"May I come in?"

"Of course."

She came running up the steps. "I thought I would save you a trip down both flights of steps. I can talk up here. I always like to see what you have going here."

"Well, I am about to make two shirts for Grayson and I have a gown to finish for a lady from the village."

As it was, we spent the rest of the afternoon talking. There was a lot to discuss. I told her all about the trip to Ohio and the few days of agony before talking things out with Grayson.

"So things are good between you?"

"Very good."

"Guess who asked me out." She was smiling big.

"Marley?"

"Marley himself. We were out riding about a week ago and now he has asked me to go to Thackeray's Pond for some celebration."

"The Summer Fete?"

"Oh help, no. That is for the big shots. Not for the parson's family. No, this is a town thing. I forget what he called it."

"What do you mean the Summer Fete is for big shots?"

"Well, you know who puts it on."

"No. I don't think I heard the name."

"It is the de Frappes."

"No!"

"You did not know?"

"No, I did not. And neither Aunt Sarah nor Grayson told me the name of the people. Are you sure it is my client that made me spend two whole afternoons changing her dress and then changing it back to its original state?"

"The same."

"Then I am not going."

"You are not going?"

"Not now. I am suppose to be going with Grayson. I guess the Bluster Hill estate has been big enough to get an annual invitation, but Aunt Sarah is not going without Theodore but Grayson is going....Oh dear. They never said where it was and I remember now that Grayson changed the subject rather abruptly. I even mentioned being afraid I'd see her there and he knew I would not want to go. Oh, Mary Lou, I am tired of the snobbishness of the wealthy. I like real people. Ordinary people."

"Well, I have something else for you to think about. Another invitation," said Mary Lou.

"What is that?"

"My cousin Jeff is getting married. The wedding will take place about ten miles from here. Jeff's father is my mother's brother. His mother's family is quite large and some of the relatives live far away. They can't put everyone up at their house, but a friend of Jeff's just bought an old inn just perhaps a mile from where they live. And although the inn needs repairs that will have to be done before he officially opens it, his friend has offered free lodging for those who need a bed."

"And where do I come in?"

"There are five girl cousins who will stay there and that includes me. But I need a roommate. That is where you come in. I missed out on the trip to Ohio, but maybe we can make up for it now."

"That sounds exciting. When does this take place?"

"This Friday. We come home Saturday. We can pick you up and bring you back."

"Wow. Let me think this through."

"Please come. I think it would be so exciting sleeping in this old inn."

I talked it over with Aunt Sarah and the next day, rather than sew, I helped make applesauce. The apple picking was at its peak. We had a lot of applesauce yet from last year and now with neither Becca nor Lizzie here, we would use even less. But we canned quite a few jars the next day and made a couple apple pies. I felt a bit guilty about Aunt Sarah. She was missing Lizzie and Becca and now I was going away again for the night. Life was changing for her. She was slowing down since Theodore was gone, but mostly her health was good. But I knew she was lonely. I was glad she had the cooking and laundry for Grayson. And Nettie would still come and clean once a week and with all her chattering, she would be good for Aunt Sarah.

Grayson had men taking apples to town and some were sold right here on the estate. I told him that if he needed help for sorting I would help, but he knew that I was sewing and so far had not asked me. Nothing more had been said of the fete, and I hoped it would be forgotten.

CHAPTER 27

The bright, summer sun shone hot on my face as we began our trip to the wedding. But I enjoyed the ride through the countryside. Butterflies fluttered above the wild flowers growing along the road and birds chirped from the trees we rode under. We saw busy housewives working in their gardens and someone was selling strawberries at a little stand in front of their farmhouse. Cows were lazily chewing their cuds under trees that gave welcome shade and a mother duck and her ducklings crossed the road slowly ahead of us. There was lots of chatter on the way and the ten miles went by quickly.

We drove directly to the church in the village where the marriage would take place, but the reception would be held in the barn on the farm. By the time we arrived at the church, it was nearly time for the four o'clock wedding. It was a bit strange, being at a wedding where I knew none of the bridal party, but it was fun to observe. There were quite a few people there, but then, Mary Lou had said there were many relatives. And then the church bell began to ring and and a middle-aged man began playing the organ. The groom and best man entered the church from the front and took their places. Then the maid of honor entered and finally the bride came up the aisle. It was a nice looking pair, but the best man caught my eye and I found my eyes focusing on him. He was a tall man with what I suspected, were blue eyes and a short beard. He looked like a gentleman.

The service was soon over and we went back to the house where we were invited to a reception in the barn. There were tables set up on the upper floor of the barn where large platters and bowls of food were being placed. There were a few simple decorations setting around the interior of the barn and a table for the bride and groom and their attendants. A table laden with wedding gifts stood in a corner. We were invited to eat and sit where we found room. There were a few tables set up, but most of the young cousins and friends of the couple sat on bales of hay that were placed around the barn floor for seating. It was a fun time and I learned to know the four other single girls that would be sleeping in the inn with us. They were Esther, Jane, Verna and Jennifer. All cousins or sisters.

We had just begun eating, when a girl came up to me.

"June?"

I took a good look at her. She looked familiar. "Are you Grayson's sister?"

"I am. Brenda. I thought it was you. Nice to see you again. What is your connection here?"

"None, to tell you the truth. But I was invited to come with Mary Lou. It seems there is an overflow of people needing beds and a friend has offered room in an inn he just bought. I came to be her roommate at the inn."

"Oh yes, that is Maxim. I heard that some girls are sleeping in the inn tonight. That sounds like fun, but it might not be in the best repair. In fact, I'm told it has a haunted look. Maybe you will see a ghost."

I laughed. "I doubt it, but there are enough of us to keep a ghost at bay."

"How is everything at Bluster Hill?"

"Good."

"And my brother is still single?" I felt her scrutiny as she asked.

I smiled. She did not know. "The last I heard he was."

"He must be blind in one eye and can't see out of the other. But I think my own father was thirty before he married."

And off she went with a wave of her hand. She was so different from Grayson I could hardly believe they were from the same family.

There was a great deal of laughing and joking among the guests as they conversed with the bride and groom, but since I did not know them, I did not pay much attention. After the meal, cake was distributed by the bride and groom, who then took time to talk to the guests while a small group of men took up their instruments and began playing in a corner of the barn. And for a while there was just a moving around and visiting among the guests. It was at this point that Esther, one of the cousins, came to Mary Lou.

"We asked Maxim if he could quickly take us to the inn now, before the games begin, so we can put our bags in our rooms and get an idea of the place before we go there for the night. Do you want to come along?"

And so we trooped outside and stood waiting for the man who owned the inn. To my surprise, when the man came out, it was the best man! He was quite friendly and shook my hand since I was the one he did not know.

"Maxim Cullensworth," he said smiling at me with his blue, blue eyes.

"June Merriweather." I thought he hesitated a bit and did not let go of my hand for a moment.

"Are you from around here?"

"I live in Cobbler's Crossing."

"Close to Bluster Hill?"

"That is exactly where I live," I replied. "You have been there?"

"I've...seen it. Nice estate."

"It belonged to my uncle but he is now deceased."

We spoke no more and when he had helped us all up in the carriage, we headed down the road a short distance where I got my first glimpse of the old inn where we would spend the night. The building stood at the edge of a small village. There was nothing extraordinary about it, other than the fact that the whole place needed a coat of paint. It was white plaster on the outside with black shutters. It definitely had a look of neglect. There was an upper and lower porch and a very small strip of lawn between the inn and the sidewalk. Hanging out nearly over the sidewalk was a sign that read "The Teacup Inn." The sign needed paint also and now creaked a bit in the evening breeze.

It was nearly dark by now, with just a half of a moon, giving us its meager light as we climbed the well-worn wooden steps to the front door. Maxim led the way inside and told us to wait by the door, while he went and located a lantern, which he lit and then hung on a long chain hanging from the ceiling right at the foot of the stairs. Then he bade us come and we walked through a small lounge area and past the reception desk to where he stood.

"I'll let this lantern lit so you will have some light when you come in later. It will go out by itself during the night. I did not put that much oil in it. I will also put an unlit lantern by the front door with matches under the wooden box setting there. You can light that when you return and take that along upstairs with you, where you will find candles and matches," he informed us. "There is only one bedroom downstairs, so we will have to climb the stairs, which are a bit creaky." As we began following him up the stairs, he added, "And beware of the post here at the bottom of the stairs, because it is a bit loose. Just don't lean on it. I am sorry the inn is not in better shape, but I just bought it and have not been able to make any repairs yet."

"It is fine, Maxim," said Esther. "It is better than sleeping under the stars. I think it is exciting staying here in this old battered inn."

We all agreed, and after putting our bags on our beds in three adjacent rooms, we trooped downstairs again and Maxim placed the key in Esther's hand. Then he took us back to the reception where there was music played by three fiddlers.

"You better get in there, Maxim, before the maid of honor thinks you have abandoned her," teased Esther, who seemed to know Maxim.

There was a different atmosphere now. The fiddlers were playing and the bride and groom were about to be entertained by their guests. This continued for a couple hours as games were played, songs were sung, poetry was recited and skits were performed.

There was also a type of charades played and in this, I was chosen to be in a team of which the best man was leader. We were to choose a well-known book and act out an event in the story. We chose the quadrille in *Pride and Prejudice* by Jane Austin. In the end, Maxim was Darcy and I was Elizabeth. We included the snobbish behavior of Darcy, Elizabeth's obvious hesitation to dance with him, and then the quadrille where there is much stilted conversation between the two. I did not really know Maxim, but he seemed to be able to act out the proud Darcy and I did my best to act out Elizabeth's role in my disgust at his prejudices. Of course, all was in silence as Maxim and I simply made mouth movements as we twirled, touched hands at times and then twirled out of reach again and again among the other dancers. All the time I was looking into those blue eyes that seemed to be studying me. Fortunately, they soon guessed what we were acting out and we were finished.

It was nearly midnight by the time the party broke up and the happy couple headed off for their wedding night. Our first plan had been that we would walk to the inn. It was late, but there were six of us. The moon would have given enough light, but now we were tired and Esther's father did not want us walking. So he drove us to the inn and waited as we went up on the rickety porch, lit the lantern standing there, and unlocked the door. Then he left, and we trooped in, following Esther, who led the way with the lantern. Now, it seemed, there was something spooky about being in this old inn late at night. No one really knew the inn and I was so glad that Maxim had taken us to our rooms beforehand. As we walked through the furnished lobby, the light of the lantern cast strange shadows on the walls around us.

"Remember not to lean on the post," said Esther as she led the way up the stairs.

The steps creaked in the stillness as we climbed them and then we arrived to a completely dark upstairs. The first room, right at the top of the stairs was given to Mary Lou and me. The other girls waited while we each lit a candle. Then they went on to the other rooms that were just up the narrow hall from ours. I was glad they were adjacent to one another. This was not a big inn, but it felt big and spooky now. No one was talking as we got to the rooms. Just as the last door closed, Mary Lou looked at me.

"I have to go to the outhouse."

Oh, brother. Why had we not thought of that beforehand? Of course, we all needed to go. Had he even told us where the outhouse was? If he did, I did not remember. We took our candles and went to the other two doors. Finally, all six of us headed downstairs to find the outhouse.

"Actually, Maxim told me it was out back but we have no key to the back door," said Esther, as we all gathered in the hall. "So we must exit the front door and go around the inn."

It was a scary excitement and once we made our way down the creaking stairs, we walked through the lounge and finally, out the door. We still had only the one lantern, and we let Esther lead the way. It was not completely dark, since there was a moon. There were also houses close by on one side of the inn, but all was dark in those houses. Once out back, we looked for the narrow, small building that would be the outhouse. Sure enough, we could see it and we cautiously made our way to it. Halfway across the lawn, a dog began barking in the neighborhood. He had good ears and I am sure we were the reason he barked. Just as we got to the outhouse, a small animal ran out from behind it, scaring us badly. In fact, one of the girls let out a muffled scream, which really got the dog barking. We never did know what kind of animal it was, but it was as scared of us as we were of it and we did not see it again.

Our mission accomplished at the outhouse, we found our way back into the inn safely. Once inside, we hurried through the lounge and wasted no time getting up the stairs to our rooms. I did not know how late it was, but it was time to sleep. We were soon in our nightgowns and turning back the covers to crawl in.

"When do we get up?" asked Mary Lou getting in bed ahead of me. "What time is Esther's father picking us up? I think we are all suppose to eat breakfast at the bride's grandparents' house."

"I'll go ask," I said, although I was not at all eager to leave the room again. "My candle is still lit." I hurried to Esther's room and called through the door.

"You still awake? When do we get up?"

"Breakfast is at eight, came a sleepy voice. Papa will pick us up around quarter to eight."

"Thanks. I knocked on the next door to inform the others and then headed back the hall with my candle in my hand to Mary Lou. Just before entering our room, I paused, and glanced down the stairs. I do not know why I looked down the stairs. I think maybe to see if the lantern had gone out, but I don't really know. But I did glance down the steps and saw the lantern was still burning. I looked away and with my hand on the doorknob, turned and gave the lantern a second glance. My heart went into my throat.

The lantern was swinging.

Not wildly, but it was definitely swinging, as if someone had touched it. And it was creating very spooky shadows as it swung back and forth.

I just froze, looking at it for a moment, not quite believing what I was seeing. Then my heart started pounding and I remembered Brenda mentioning a ghost. My eyes went to the dark areas around the swinging lantern and then I really got spooked and I tore into the bedroom and slammed the door. I just looked at Mary Lou and somehow could not even get the words out.

"What is wrong?" The noise of the slamming door had her sitting up in bed and just staring at me.

"The lantern at the foot of the stairs is...swinging!" My mouth was so dry I could hardly get the words out.

"What lantern?" She looked at me like I was dreaming.

"The lantern hanging at the foot of the stairs."

She did not immediately answer. Just looked at me. Finally, comprehending, her eyes widened and she whispered, "What do you mean, it is *swinging?*"

"It is swinging all by itself."

"Did you see someone?" I just shook my head. "Tell the others," she whispered.

If it took nerve to open the door before, it was doubly scary now. But we had to tell them, because there had to be someone in the inn. Someone besides us. Before I could get too scared to go out, I cracked open the door. I heard no footsteps. Lantern in hand, I opened the door and hurried to the next room and flung open their door.

"Girls!" They sat up in bed and looked at me wide-eyed.

"The lantern downstairs is moving!"

They just looked at me for a few seconds. "What?"

"The lantern at the foot of the stairs is swinging. Someone must have…"

The girls were out of bed.

"Are you sure?"

"I'll tell the others," I said as I ran to the next room. I just walked in. This was Esther and Verna.

"The lantern downstairs is swinging!"

They looked at me like I was out of my mind. "It is *what?*"

"There must be someone in here. The lantern is swinging."

They got out of bed without a word. Esther had the courage to come and look down the stairs with me. The lantern was not swinging nearly as badly, but enough to convince her that I was not hallucinating. Almost without talking, we all just got into the room that I shared with Mary Lou, and we closed the door. No one wanted to go back to their rooms. We now talked in whispers as we planned what to do. In the end, Mary Lou joined me in my single bed, Jennifer and Jane got in Mary Lou's bed, and Verna and Esther dragged a mattress from one of their beds to our room. There was barely room to walk. But we would stay together. And there was no way that the door could open with the mattress in front of it. No one could possibly get in. The person who had touched the lamp for whatever reason, could not get in our door.

And we all knew that lantern had not swung back and forth on its own.

Just as we all got settled in our beds and I was about to blow out the last candle, there was a loud bang downstairs, like a door slamming. In seconds we were all sitting up in bed, looking at each other, wide-eyed.

"Whoever it was, must have gone," said Jennifer.

"Well, no one can get in here," whispered Esther.

"I talked to a girl today that knows Maxim. She said there were stories about the inn being haunted," I said.

"Well, I'm beginning to believe it," said Verna.

I wanted badly to reassure them that we had nothing to fear. But that lantern had not swung by its own strength and *someone* had been in the house. I did not believe in ghosts. I did not sleep right away, but we were so exhausted that we eventually did fall asleep and knew nothing at all until, sun streaming into the room, we wakened to loud pounding on the front door.

"Oh, we overslept," said Esther. "That must be Papa at the door."

We had indeed overslept and we moved as fast as we could, once the mattress was set on edge and we could unlock the door. That done, Esther grabbed a sheet to wrap around her in place of a housecoat, and ran down to assure her father we would soon be ready.

Thirty minutes later, we were seated with Esther's parents at the breakfast table at the home of the bride's grandmother. It was a young grandmother and she was very happy to give us breakfast. As we ate, we told the old couple and Esther's parents about the swinging lantern and the loud bang. But although they listened with sympathetic ears, I got the feeling they did not quite believe us. Just thought we were scared girls imagining things.

I arrived back at home around noon and was greeted warmly by Aunt Sarah. I could tell she was lonely without Lizzie and Becca and I felt a bit guilty for having gone for the night. Grayson was not around and I was disappointed. I was eager to see him again. I did not go to the gatehouse to sew, in order to keep Aunt Sarah company. She wanted to know all about the wedding and was horrified when I told her about our night in the inn.

"Did you tell the owner of the inn?"

"We did not see him this morning and at the breakfast table, no one seemed to take us seriously. I think they just thought we were hysterical girls."

Mid-afternoon, Mary Lou's father stopped by.

"Pastor Stafford, it is good to see you," said Aunt Sarah, offering him a seat in the parlor. "I don't see you as often since Becca and Lizzie are no longer here."

"You are right and I have a feeling you are missing them. Are you not?"

"I am. I even think I am missing the shouting," she replied smiling. "They were company, even though they lived in the little house, I could go over to talk at any time."

"That is the reason I am here," said the pastor. "But first, it is good to see you, too, June. I hear you had an exciting sleepover in the inn."

"Scary," I said, laughing, "but we all hunkered down in one bedroom and we were so exhausted that we soon slept."

"Well, I am glad that God protected you. Now Sarah, I have something for you to think about."

The pastor gave my aunt a serious look. "I know someone who needs a home. Not permanently, but at least for a few weeks. And I thought of you, because Becca and Lizzie are gone."

"Who is it?"

"You do not know her, but her name is Rachel Montgomery and she is a sister to Jean Lindsey from church, whom you know, and she was recently widowed and has to leave her home. She is looking for a place in this area, but must move within the week and so has no time to look. Jean still has two boys at home and cannot offer her even a room to herself. I do not know the woman, but if she is anything like Jean, I think she would not be a problem. And you might enjoy the company. I realize you would probably have to cook for her. Is that a problem?"

"That is not a problem. I am used to cooking for Becca and Lizzie and it will be no different. I think I may have met Rachel at some time. I can give you my answer right now. She is welcome to come. But you should really say something to Grayson. It is his house now and he has the last say."

"Of course. I just knew that you would be the one around her the most and wanted to see that it was alright with you."

After the pastor left, I had a good talk with my aunt. She was lonely and I was glad for this possible solution and I had a feeling there would be no problem with Grayson.

I did not see Grayson until suppertime. I was so happy to see him that I am sure I left no doubt in his mind that I had missed him. He smiled broadly at me and he suggested a ride to Thackeray's Pond where there was a concert that he thought I would enjoy. We left right after supper and because it looked like it might rain, we took the enclosed carriage. It was nearly dark when we left and sitting in the enclosed carriage with Grayson suddenly felt very intimate. I loved it when our sleeves touched or a bump in the road would throw us against each other.

"Tell me more about your weekend," he said as we passed the gatehouse and got out on the main road. "I don't think I got the whole story of the mystery of the swinging lantern either."

"You are laughing at me. You think we are just hysterical girls."

"I did not say that."

"That is what everyone else thinks."

"I'm not everyone."

So I told him all I could remember of the wedding and then I tried to describe the inn and then my scare when I saw the swinging lantern.

"In what village was the inn?" he asked when I had finished.

"I forget."

"And it was not open to the public?"

"Not yet. It had just been bought and needed repairs."

"And who did you say owned it?"

"The best man. He took us to see it during the reception."

"He left the reception to take you to the inn?"

"It was just down the road. Less than a mile. In the time they were setting up for the games. We were soon back again."

"Does the best man have a name?"

"Let me think. Maxim something. Maxim...Maxim...I forget the last name."

Grayson gave me a slanted look. He was silent just a moment. "Was he good looking?"

I laughed, pleased that Grayson might be jealous. "He was a real gentleman and he had the most beautiful blue, blue eyes."

For a split second Grayson gave me a funny look and then grinned. But he did not comment.

"And just who saw the swinging lantern?"

"I did."

"You saw it first and set off the alarm?"

"Grayson, we were in an empty, run-down inn all alone."

"Six girls is not 'all alone.' In fact, I would say six girls is something to be reckoned with. Even for a ghost."

"And what are six girls to think about a lantern swinging on a chain? It certainly did not swing without some outside help."

"Was a window open?"

"Not that I know of."

"You said you had all just been outside. Was it windy?"

"Not in the least."

"How much was it swinging?"

I thought a bit. "I am guessing now, but I would say at least..." I held my hand up and measured. "At least six inches on each side. It was swinging good. And besides that, there had to be someone in the inn because later we all heard a door slam."

"So what did the best man say when you told him?"

"We did not get to tell him. We did not see him again. That is why he took us ahead of time. He probably had to take the maid of honor home after the wedding. I don't know where he lives. I think Esther knew him the best. Maybe she got to tell him, but she was not from that area either, otherwise she would not have stayed overnight. The only people we saw the next morning were the grandparents of the bride and Esther's parents."

We drove a bit in silence. After a while, I looked over at Grayson. He was just driving along and grinning to himself.

"What are you grinning about?" I was scared he was not believing me either.

"You."

"Why?"

"I'd rather not say. But here we are at the concert."

We did not talk about it again. On the way home we talked about the concert and other things and I put the mystery of the swinging lantern aside.

———

I drove Aunt Sarah to church the next day. Grayson always took his own carriage, and since we were courting that did not change. I was curious whether this Rachel Montgomery would be at church. The pastor had not said if she was here right now. I always sat with Aunt Sarah and now that Becca and Lizzie were gone, Grayson sat on our bench also. I liked sitting next to Grayson in church. He had a lovely tenor voice. In my own imagination, I envisioned us sitting here with a bench full of cute little girls and mischievous little boys. But I kept that to myself.

Rachel Montgomery was not at church, but I talked to Donna and Bud after the service, who were looking happy to be there, but when I looked for Mary Lou, she was busy talking to Marley and I did not want to butt in on them.

I spent the afternoon walking with Aunt Sarah around the meadow and pond. I enjoyed the pond and there was a bench under the weeping willow tree and we sat there awhile. I wondered if Aunt Sarah had sometimes sat here with her husband on summer evenings. I sensed a bit of sadness in Sarah, and I was happy for this Rachel that was coming. I knew my aunt would be happy for her company.

"Well, I'd best go in and get supper on the table," she said as we turned toward home. "Grayson said he is bringing someone for supper."

"Today?" I was surprised. He had men in for supper during the week sometimes, but he was always gone Sundays. I wondered if perhaps one of his family was around. "Oh, that reminds me," I said, "Grayson's sister Brenda was at the wedding."

"Oh? I wonder if she has a special friend just now?"

"I think she mentioned a boyfriend, but I did not meet him," I said. "Is supper at six?"

"He asked for supper at five."

"That is early for supper. I'll help you," I offered. So I made biscuits and Aunt Sarah made a delicious vegetable soup. Just before five, I saw two carriages come in the lane. I was curious who Grayson was bringing. Not that a guest was odd. Just odd that he had someone here on a Sunday, when he spent most of the day elsewhere.

Grayson and his guest walked into the dining room just as I was setting the vegetable soup on the table. When I looked up, my mouth dropped open.

"How did you get here?"

There was laughter from both Grayson and his guest. They had expected my surprise. I was completely baffled.

"Sarah and June, I'd like to introduce you to Maxim Cullensworth. And Maxim, this is Sarah Morgan and June Merriweather."

Maxim offered his hand to Aunt Sarah and then to me. But as he clasped hands with me, he was laughing at my bewilderment.

"I don't get the connection," I said.

Grayson answered me. "June, this is the friend that I visit every Sunday. And when I heard your story, I knew I had to bring him here today."

I looked at Maxim. "And you had no clue who I was?"

He hesitated. "I thought I recognized the name."

Grayson was watching me. So he had told Maxim about me. "But you did not say anything."

Maxim just looked at me and grinned.

We sat down to eat and we had an enjoyable supper and talked of an assortment of things and then when we were all finished, Grayson asked me to tell Maxim what happened at the inn that night.

"You did not tell him?"

"I want you to tell him."

I looked at Maxim. His blue, blue eyes were fixed on me, his face sober.

"Well," I began, "we had a really big scare. Esther's father took us to the inn after the wedding was over. All went well, but when we were safely in the house, and found our way upstairs, we realized we needed to visit the outhouse before going to bed. So we turned around and came back down the stairs and out the front door because we had no key for the back door. Fortunately the half moon helped us find our way. Then we came back in and Mary Lou and I had the room at the top of the stairs. She was already in bed when I checked on the other girls to see when we had to get up in the morning. You told us the lantern did not have much oil in it and it would go out by itself. As I came back to our room, I just happened to look down the stairs. I did it without thinking. Maybe I wanted to see if it had gone out yet. I don't know. But when I looked down the stairs," I looked at Maxim and hesitated before finishing, "the lamp was swinging."

I expected him to register shock. I expected his face to get very sober. What is it about men that they can't show fear? He looked a bit concerned, but he remained calm. After a short pause he replied with possible solutions.

"Were you running around in the inn? The building is old. Maybe the floorboards above the lantern were shaking."

"Remember, it was late and we were too tired to think. We just wanted to get into bed. There was no running around. And it was not windy and I saw no open window. Do you know of an open window? And besides that, just as I blew out the last candle, we heard a loud bang. It sounded like a door slamming."

He shook his head and I saw just a hint of a smile on his face.

"You don't believe me," I said accusingly. "No one believes us. They think we were just a bunch of hysterical girls, scared to be alone in an old, empty inn without a man."

I think my frustrated outburst amused the men. They both began laughing and did not stop right away.

"Did it keep swinging?" asked Maxim, finally his blue, blue eyes looking curious.

"No," I replied, glad that he at least thought it worth questions. "But it was swinging good at first. By the time the girls saw it, it was still moving but not nearly as much."

"What do you think it was?" Maxim asked, his blue eyes still intent on mine.

"I have no clue. I was hoping you had one. Do you think a tramp might have been in the inn? It gives me shivers to think of it, but the lantern was swinging good...just like someone had bumped against it. But it was too high for someone to accidentally do that."

"Well," said Maxim, "there certainly have been tramps in my life, however, I do not live in that village, so I can't say anything for sure about that."

"Grayson's sister said there were ghost stories about the inn. I can believe it."

"Brenda said that?" asked Grayson.

"She did."

"Do you believe in ghosts?"

"I think I do now." I did not really, but I wanted them to know this was no joke.

"I don't," said Grayson and then his face turned serious and he looked at Maxim.

"What about that man that escaped from prison recently?"

My eyes got big and they both saw my reaction and then both of them spontaneously burst out laughing. Hard laughter. I stood up and began clearing the table. They were laughing so hard it was a bit hard not to laugh with them. But their laughter proved to me that they did not really believe me. I was a bit hurt and also disgusted that they obviously thought so little of women. Did all men believe that women are that stupid?

"You don't believe me! But it was real and it was scary!" I turned to take some dishes to the kitchen.

"Sit down, June."

I looked at Grayson in surprise. It was a command. He was still smiling, but now he was serious as he locked eyes with me.

"Sit," he said again when I made no move. I sat.

"I do believe you," said Maxim. "And I am sorry for your scare."

He was serious now and I looked back and forth at the men, surprised now at their admitting they believed me. I looked back at Maxim.

"I caused the lantern to swing."

Now he was trying to calm me with an untruth.

"How?" I said, unimpressed. "You were not there."

"Yes, I was." I just looked at him, dumbfounded. No words came to mind. He paused a moment and then continued. "I planned all along to sleep in the downstairs room, but thought it better if no one knew I was there. I just did not want anything bad to happen. When you were all in the house, I just drove around the inn and left the carriage and the horse in the inn livery. When I'd done that, I went in the back door and into my room. I planned just to wait till all was quiet upstairs, and then extinguish the lantern. I did not count on you all trooping down the stairs again, but when I heard you, I quickly extinguished my candle and sat quietly in my room. I guessed where you might be heading. When you were all back upstairs again, I waited just a few minutes and then made my way to the foot of the stairs to put out the lantern. I did not think any of you would be coming out of your rooms again. I had just reached up and taken hold of the lantern when I heard a door open upstairs. I jumped back, but you fortunately must not have looked down, because you would have certainly seen me. But when I jumped back and let loose of the lantern, it swung. I did not go back to my room, expecting all to get quiet again. But someone had seen the swinging lantern and called the alarm."

"It really was you?" I had to digest this information.

"It was. I am sorry for the scare." I just looked at him for a few moments.

"We all slept in one room. Two in each single bed and two on the mattress on the floor. No one could get in."

"I heard the moving around and guessed what was happening."

"And the loud bang?"

"Later, when I returned to my room, I accidentally bumped the open door and it slammed. Sorry for that, too."

"Were you gone when we got up?"

"I was out of the inn by six in the morning."

I took a deep breath and then looked at Grayson. He just grinned at me.

"Mystery solved."

CHAPTER 28

On Wednesday afternoon, we girls had what we called a gate-house party again. Actually, it was Mary Lou that suggested it and I think she just wanted to be close to where she just might see Marley. She was smitten. So we gathered to talk, eat molasses cookies and drink apple cider. Jeannie and Annelie came, too, and we were all into crocheting things for winter. Annelie was knitting a scarf, Jeannie was knitting a shawl, and Mary Lou was knitting a sweater and I had a feeling it was a man's sweater and I suspected it was a Christmas present for Marley. I was not knitting or crocheting. I had buttons to sew on the two shirts that I had made for Grayson.

"You will never guess what I found out," said Mary Lou when we finally got done eating and settled down to the business at hand.

"What is that?"

"Remember you went out driving with Marley a couple times?"

"Yes."

"Well, did you ever wonder why he never asked you again?"

I thought for a while. "I think we had a mutual understanding that I was wasting his time. And I remember telling him that you liked him."

"You said that?" She looked at me wide-eyed.

"I did. Aren't you glad?"

She almost looked disappointed. "I wish it had been his decision."

"It was his decision. I just told him you liked him. It made it easier for him to ask you. And he certainly is not going out with you now because I suggested it. He is going out with you because he is interested in you."

"Did you like Marley?"

"Yes, I still do. But quite frankly, I had my eye on Grayson." We laughed.

"Well, Marley said he liked you, but he didn't know you too well yet, but in some conversation with his boss, Grayson hinted that you were off limits to Marley."

"What do you mean?"

"I don't remember just how Marley said it, but he felt that Grayson was saying he had a claim on you. If it was not said outright, it was insinuated."

"I can't believe it. I would love to know just how he said it. And it took him a long time to actually ask me out."

I sat silent a bit, thinking about what Mary Lou told me. I wanted Grayson, but I could hardly believe that he told, or at least hinted to Marley that I was off limits.

"What do you hear from Becca?" asked Annelie. "I nearly split laughing when I heard she crawled into the wrong bed on the train. Becca of all people."

We all burst out laughing just thinking about it and I was wiping tears from my eyes till we were done. "Becca has some hidden talents," I said and then we all laughed again. "By the way, Aunt Sarah got a letter from Becca. She wrote a nice letter, thanking Aunt Sarah again for all she did for her and it seems she is adjusting well to life in Ohio."

"It is nice the sisters can be together," said Jeannie.

"Yes," I agreed. "And what is new with you, Jeannie? Oh, did I ever tell you about the sheriff that came for supper and it was the sheriff that found you for us in Thackeray's Pond?"

"No!"

"And it took us a while to recognize each other—at least for me to recognize him—and then later I had to confess the whole story to Grayson. No wonder it took him so long to ask me out."

"Do you have anything else to hide from him?" asked Annelie.

"I have a feeling he already knows the worst about me." And then I told them about having dated him ten years earlier. And about telling him to get lost and his telling me that someday I would come crawling back to him.

"I can't believe it!" said Mary Lou. "All this time and you never told me."

"I just thought it was better not said. It was our secret, but I finally told Aunt Sarah also."

"But you did not crawl back to him. He asked you out on his own."

"At least that," I said. "And when it is safe to remind him, I shall remind him of that."

"How is the sewing business?" asked Mary Lou. "What you are sewing now sure does not look like anything for one of your wealthy ladies."

"These are shirts for Grayson. Whenever I remind him that I should be paying him rent for the use of this building, he gives me something to sew for him."

"Just think, if you marry him, you don't ever have to think of rent," said Annelie.

"Huh," said Jeannie, "she'll be sewing for a dozen children and for him. What have you sewn so far for him?"

"A vest that was a gift from Aunt Sarah and me for his birthday, and then a jacket to go with it and now these shirts."

"Next comes the pants," said Jeannie.

Just the way she said it made everyone laugh and then there was a knock at the door. We quickly quieted down and I went to the door. It was Grayson and I am sure we all looked guilty having just talked about him.

"Am I intruding?" he asked, looking somehow stiff and formal as if he knew we'd been talking about him. All I managed was a shake of the head.

I got a long look from Grayson and I am afraid I blushed as

the girls looked on, not missing a thing. He then handed me a small shopping list.

"Sarah would like you to go to the village and pick this up for her. I am leaving now for a meeting in town and won't be back till after supper. She has been informed that Mrs. Montgomery will be here today yet, and in time for supper."

"I'll do that."

With a nod at the girls, he left.

"He is one handsome man," said Jeannie, looking out the window as he left.

"I agree," I said, smiling.

"But so sober. He would make me nervous," she said.

"And I never quite know what he is thinking," I added. "It keeps me guessing what is behind that sober face."

"You know what time it is girls?" asked Annelie. "Time to head home."

Mary Lou had brought the girls today as her father did not need the carriage. So in no time they were out the door and I cleaned up and headed home. I had walked to the gatehouse, so I had to go get the carriage before I would head out.

Driving to the village was always exciting because I would always take time to see if they got any new fabric in the store. Of course, there was a much bigger selection in Thackeray's Pond, but that was a lot farther. Now, as I drove, I enjoyed the scene before me. I heard a crow flying overhead and I nearly ran over a ground hog running across the road. The sun was warm with a light summer breeze.

Once in the village, I picked up the items that Aunt Sarah needed. Then I headed to the fabric shop. However, I was disappointed to find nothing new there. Going out the door, I saw two ladies talking close to my carriage. Too late, I saw it was Mrs. de Frappe and another woman whom I did not recognize. I went to the carriage but looked at Mrs. de Frappe. She had to have seen me, but chose not to. In the village one greets those one meets.

"Good afternoon," I murmured, as I walked by them. The stranger looked at me, but Mrs. de Frappe did not so much as turn her head. And neither one responded.

I do not know why it irritated me so much. Yes, I guess I do. I had worked so hard on the gown for Mrs. de Frappe and I really think she was not happy with it. I made it according to specifications, but maybe it was not the right dress for her. But it was her choice. It was not my sewing. And I was invited to the fete? I really had no wish to go. In fact, right then and there, I decided I was not going to go. Why should I go to a party hosted by someone who on the street did not recognize me?

By the time I got home, I was not in a very good frame of mind. However, Rachel Montgomery had arrived. I took Aunt Sarah's parcels to her and she informed me that Rachel was over in the small house where Becca and Lizzie had been.

"She is very nice and feeling very lost," said my aunt. "Come with me and I will introduce her to you."

I followed Aunt Sarah to the connecting door and she knocked.

"Come in."

The voice was friendly and when we entered, Rachel Montgomery was standing by the window where she was probably getting acquainted with the view from her house. She was a slight woman with a friendly smile but sad eyes. I hoped Aunt Sarah would be able to help her in the adjustment she had to make.

"This is my niece, June Merriweather," said my aunt. "And June, this is Rachel. I don't know if you have met before or not."

"I think I did see you in church one time," I said. "You were probably visiting. Your face looks familiar."

"Yes, I was here to visit about six months ago," she responded. "And you live here, too?"

"I do, for over a year now. My mother died and I needed a home."

"Well, you aren't the only one needing a home. But I do hope to move on within a few months."

"In the meantime, you are welcome here. My aunt is happy for your company."

That evening at the supper table, Rachel joined us. She already knew Grayson because she had talked to him about renting from him. They chatted a bit and then somehow the fete was brought up again. It was to take place in three days.

"Are you making yourself a new dress for the occasion?" asked my aunt.

"No." I said no more, but I saw Grayson look at me, trying to read into my quick, abrupt answer.

"I received a letter today from my mother," said Grayson, after a few moments of silence. "She informs me that my father hurt his back and is on bed rest for a week. I talked to Marley and he is willing to take charge for a few days and I think I will go check things out with my parents. I don't see them very often and it might be a good time to visit with them."

"When will you be back?" I asked, hoping maybe we could skip the fete.

"In time for the fete," said Grayson, giving me a steady look. "Probably the afternoon of the fete." He knew I was dragging my feet. I did not want to make too big a deal of it, but I really did not plan to go.

"You don't really want to go, do you?" he asked me.

"I would rather not."

"Why not?"

I thought a bit. "She does not like me."

The silence lasted too long. I knew my aunt and Rachel were watching us with interest.

"Or do you not like her?" asked Grayson softly.

"Well, her manner is always stiff and unfriendly," I said quickly in my defense, "but then the whole thing with the gown that she made me do over two times just because she did not like the pattern anymore, did not endear her to me."

No more was said.

After supper, I went for the two shirts I had made for Grayson and gave them to him before he disappeared in his rooms.

"Here are your shirts, I thought maybe you would need them for your trip."

"Thank you, June. I appreciate your work even if there are those who do not. Don't worry about Mrs. de Frappe. She will soon be coming for more gowns from you. You do good work."

"I really do not want her business."

Grayson gave me a sober look, but did not comment.

"I expect that all will go well while I am gone, but in case you need help, you can ask Marley. I have put him in charge."

I thought of what Mary Lou had just told me about Marley feeling that Grayson did not want him to go out with me. I must have been looking at Grayson as I remembered that. He gave me a curious look.

"What is it?"

"Grayson, I went riding a couple times with Marley. Remember?"

"Did you?"

I almost said no more. Maybe it was not true. But I was this far and something in his face told me that he knew very well that we had gone driving. I took the plunge.

"Did you tell Marley not to date me?"

Grayson gave me a blank look. Then he said, "Why would I say something like that? Now, are you going to say goodbye to me now or will you get up early in the morning?"

I just looked at Grayson. He had abruptly changed the subject. And there was a spark of something in his eyes. But I did not have the nerve to ask again.

"What time are you leaving?"

"At first light."

"Then it is goodbye now."

Grayson shook his head. "You won't sacrifice a little sleep for me."

"If you want me to get up, I will."

He grinned his wonderful grin.

"That won't be necessary. Don't get in trouble while I am gone. I will pray that all goes well here." And then he put his hand to my face and let his finger slide down my cheek and I nearly melted at the look in his eyes. I stood at the bottom of the stairs and watched him until he entered his room.

My cheek felt hallowed. But I had rather had a kiss.

CHAPTER 29

The next morning, Grayson left early and I missed him before I even went downstairs. Not that I ever saw him in the morning, I seldom did. But just knowing he was not even on the estate gave me a very lonely feeling. I went to the gatehouse and lost myself in sewing, knowing that if I were sewing, the day would fly by. And the day really did fly by. That was one day gone. On Friday, I went to do a bit of shopping for thread for myself and yarn for Aunt Sarah and took Rachel along so she could acquaint herself with the shops in Cobbler's Crossing. Rachel was a pleasant woman and we chatted all the way to the village. As I climbed down from the carriage, I was trying to forget my last trip here when I had encountered Mrs. de Frappe, and as if on cue, there the woman was again. We were not even out of the carriage when I saw her and as I looked at her in dismay, she turned and saw me. She was again talking to a woman just outside the store. Actually, two women, and I really truly believe she changed the subject when she saw me. Rachel and I had to walk right by her to get into the shop. As we approached, I decided I was not going to even look at her. Instead I looked in the shop window and made some off hand remark to Rachel about something in the window. But my ears were standing straight up like a mule's ears and I could hear every word Mrs. de Frappe said.

"I was so disappointed in it. She took it apart and then put it back together because...."

I was furious. She *planned* that conversation when she saw me coming. She *wanted* me to hear her complain. And I had done *nothing* wrong. Fortunately, Rachel had no clue what was happening and her attention was immediately on the shop and its contents. But an elephant could have been standing in the shop and I would not have noticed. I saw nothing. But I knew one thing. I was not going to any fete put on by this terrible woman. No way. Grayson could go, but I would be angry if he did. He should stand by me in this. I don't know if Rachel sensed my mood or not. I tried to be friendly to her and tried my best to forget my enemy. Fortunately, Mrs. de Frappe was gone when we left the shop. My day dragged after that, but finally, I had two days behind me. And tomorrow was the fete and I was not going.

On Saturday I baked bread for Aunt Sarah and made an apple pie. In the afternoon, I should have gone again to the gatehouse to make the day go faster. Instead I cleaned my room and studied some patterns I had bought, but my mind wandered. I was obsessed with my dislike of Mrs. de Frappe and the whole thing hung like a black cloud over my head. This was the night of the fete and I had to face Grayson when he got home. I was suddenly torn. I wanted to see Grayson, but what would he say when I told him I would certainly *not* go to the fete. The more I thought about it, the more I found that I was more scared for Grayson's return, than waiting eagerly for him.

I sat at the supper table with Rachel and Aunt Sarah. I had told my aunt about my new encounter and my decision not to go to the fete. She was quiet. I wished she would say something, confirming my decision. Her silence worried me. Surely she understood. I just picked at my food. I knew why I was not hungry. We expected Grayson any time now. My hands were cold and my stomach in knots. How would he react? When I came home from the village yesterday I was so brave. No way was I going to the fete. And he would have to understand. I thought back to our shaky relationship just a couple weeks ago. Would this jeopardize it again? I did not want to lose Grayson because of this terrible snob.

Just as we stood up from the meal, I heard the carriage. Now I did not know what to do. I was not dressed for the evening and he would be coming in to make a quick change. We were already nearly an hour later than the time set for the fete, but not everyone could come so early. In my indecision, I stood still a moment and then I just helped clean off the table as if there was no fete that evening. And then the front door opened and moments later, Grayson strode into the dining room. He stopped short and stared at me. Dead silence reigned and my heart started thumping.

Grayson had a very sober, confused look on his face and there was no smile in sight. I took hold of a kitchen chair and almost sat down because my legs were suddenly weak. But I knew I could not challenge him sitting down. I don't know what happened to Rachel or Aunt Sarah. I was only aware of Grayson. He came very close to me. So close, that I was tempted to take a step back. But I did not want him to know I was scared. He just looked at me in silence a moment or two, our faces just inches from each other, before speaking.

"Why are you not dressed?" He spoke quietly but there was force behind each individual word.

"I...I'm not going." The words barely came out. My tongue felt thick.

"What do you mean you aren't going?"

"I..." Oh dear, now my thoughts were going in all different directions. When he looked at me like that I could not think. "I can explain."

"Please do." He spoke almost before I was finished talking.

"I had another encounter with Mrs. de Frappe..." I saw Grayson look toward the open kitchen door to where Rachel and Aunt Sarah had fled. He interrupted me.

"Wait." He put a heavy hand on my shoulder and walked me to the library and shut the door. Then he turned to me.

"What is this about Mrs. de Frappe?" I had a hard time looking into his dark eyes, challenging me.

"When she saw me in the village yesterday morning, she began complaining about me to the two women she was talking to." I had to talk fast and now I was on a roll. "I am sick of her and her snobbish friends and I do not want to go and have to be polite to her. I don't even want to see her tonight. She either ignores me on the street or talks about me. She will be happy if I don't come. I am sure I was only invited because I live here."

Even to me, my words were sounding rather petty and I was so nervous that I felt tears behind my eyelids. I could not cry and make a compete fool of myself.

I got a very long, studied look from Grayson. I swallowed hard. I could not read his thoughts.

"Go get dressed."

"Grayson…" A tear trickled down my face and I stopped.

He hesitated, and then I saw the sternness go out of his eyes. He placed a hand on each side of my face. He opened his mouth to speak and then closed it again. He just looked at me a moment more.

Then he spoke very gently. "June, I know how snobbish Mrs. de Frappe can be. I have been to their fetes often. However, I happen to believe as Christians we should not treat people the way they treat us." He paused, to let that sink in. "We should rise above their snobbishness. For most of the last ten years, I have been a good friend of Mr. de Frappe who, by the way, is a very fine gentleman. I do not know what he sees in his wife, but love sometimes makes strange partners." He paused, still looking intently at me, speaking slowly and deliberately. "I would like to go to this fete tonight because of my friendship with Mr. de Frappe. And I would like you by my side." He let that sink in, and with him so close and talking so gently, all my defenses took flight. "Now June, will you please go to the fete for *my* sake?" He was looking so kindly at me and his voice and touch was so gentle that at that moment I would have hung upside down from a tree, had he asked me to.

"Yes," I whispered, just wanting to be with him.

I think he almost kissed me. He bent down just a bit, then drew back. "You have ten minutes to get ready. Go!"

As I flew out of the room and up the stairs, his voice followed me. "And wear your green dress!"

On the way to the fete, Grayson told me all he knew about Mrs. de Frappe.

"Her husband, George, told me that she is actually from royalty. French royalty. I do not know how far back, but she has probably been trained to behave as she does. She is, in her estimation, a class above us and lets us know."

"She is not a class above us! She is below us with her personality."

"June, June," said Grayson and I heard the smile in his voice.

"Who taught you to be so kind to the snobs?"

"Believe it or not, your Uncle Theodore. Your uncle changed a lot after his first heart attack. I believe his close shave with death made him more aware of what Jesus asks of us. He used to talk about Mrs. de Frappe's snobbishness. Then one day he told me he pitied her."

"*Pitied* her?"

"Yes. He said anyone with her personality cannot be happy. Not the happiness that we know. You cannot look down your noses at others and have God's peace in your heart. Neither the peace nor the deep joy we can have in spite of circumstances."

I did not say anything. I was feeling like I was hearing a sermon. Maybe from my uncle. Maybe from Grayson. And the words were true. But that did not take away my resentment. I took a deep breath as we headed in the de Frappes' lane. It would soon be dark, but there were lanterns along the lane and up around the house, as well as the barn. There was light also coming from inside the barn.

"Is the fete in the barn?"

"Mostly, but people are inside and out. Mr. de Frappe has some horses, but otherwise the barn is not used. And this way, there is no problem if it rains. You see the bonfire behind the barn? Probably that is where they roasted the pig and now it is a place to warm up if you wish to be outside. The night will turn cool."

There were a lot of carriages in the field. We found our way and parked alongside the last one. As we walked toward the barn I saw another carriage come in the lane. So we were not the last ones to arrive. Just before we entered the barn, Grayson took my hand. I loved him for it and hoped Mrs. de Frappe saw him holding my hand. Maybe he thought I might run, but I think he wanted to give me confidence. I was bracing myself for when I would have to face my enemy. As we entered the barn, we stood just a moment to get our bearings and see what was going on.

"Grayson, welcome." To our right, a tall man with a black mustache came toward us.

"Good evening, George. Looks like you have a house full."

"Barn, actually," he laughed. "And it is the way I like it." His eyes came to me and his eyebrows lifted in surprise. "A special friend?"

"June Merriweather," Grayson answered. George offered me his hand just as his wife made her appearance.

"Grayson! It is so nice to see you again! And I see you have brought a friend."

"And I believe you know her," replied Grayson smoothly, as I put my sweaty hand in Mrs. de Frappe's cool, dry hand.

"Of course, I know her. She made the gown I am wearing." I took a closer look. It was the gown that caused me so much stress.

"And you probably made the lovely dress you are wearing," she said, giving me a big smile.

I nodded and smiled. But I was thinking, what a hypocrite! Maybe Uncle Theodore was right. They need pity when they can change faces so easily.

"Please help yourself to food and drinks. There is plenty for all," added Mr. de Frappe.

For the next half hour we walked around as Grayson greeted people he knew. Then we helped ourselves to a plate full of food, as Grayson continued to meet old friends. Seeing all the curious glances, Grayson introduced me and I realized this was perhaps the wonder of the evening. Grayson with a girl. I stood proudly beside him and tried to look at ease.

The food was Grayson's interest now. He was having a late supper and who knows what he had eaten for lunch. He had piled his plate with roasted pig, roasted potatoes, coleslaw, and then looked at me. "I'll eat this and then go for the clams and the oysters."

My plate was not as full, but I was making up for the supper I could not eat two hours ago. We found some chairs to sit on and counted ourselves fortunate. Many people were sitting on bales of hay. We tried to hold a conversation, but were continually interrupted. Mr. de Frappe came by with glasses of cold tea for us.

"So you got yourself an estate," he said to Grayson.

"Seems so. I did not deserve it, but God was good."

"You deserved it as well as anyone. You worked hard and were an honest laborer. They don't come easily."

Mr. de Frappe then gave a long history of all the workers in his shoe factory and how many he fired. Grayson was having such a good time that when he finished his food, he just kept talking to Mr. de Frappe. I decided to go get him some clams and oysters. As I was walking over to the table with his plate, a man stood in my path. He said nothing, and in the dim light, I did not recognize him right away. When I did, I gasped out loud and nearly dropped the plate.

"Alan!"

He grinned. "You still know me."

I stood there in shock. This was the man I nearly married. The one I had *promised* to marry. And then he could not wait for me.

"Of course, I know you." There followed a silence. I was in shock, seeing this man with whom I had expected to spend the rest of my life. "But how is it that you are here? Have you moved?"

"No. I am here on a visit. George de Frappe is an uncle to my mother. A relative of theirs died and I brought my mother here for the funeral."

"I see."

Again, a silence as we studied each other and remembered our time together.

"By the way, you look beautiful. Better than ever. This place must be good for you."

I hardly knew what to say. I cautiously looked around for my old girlfriend who had married Alan.

"I hope I did not hurt you too badly," he said quietly.

I looked at this man that had caused me many, many tears during a very hard time of my life. Yes, he had hurt me badly. Instead of standing by me as I watched my mother in her last months on this earth, he had abandoned me and had chosen a close girlfriend of mine.

"I would be lying if I said I was not hurt." I looked at him boldly but dry eyed.

"Well, I just..."

"You need not explain," I interrupted, not wanting to rehash what was long past and no longer my interest. "I hope you are happily married. Did Janice come along?"

He hesitated. "No, she couldn't come. She is expecting our first child and is not feeling very well."

"I'm sorry." I found that I could honestly say I'm sorry. She had been a good friend. I no longer had any yearning for Alan. I much, much, preferred Grayson. There was more to Grayson. Character. That was it. And there was a goodness in him that Alan did not have.

"June?" Grayson was by my side.

"Oh, Grayson, I took your plate and meant to bring it back with oysters and clams." I noticed that Alan and Grayson were taking good looks at each other. "Grayson, this is Alan, a former close friend of mine. Alan, this is Grayson Everleigh."

I said no more. I did not feel the need to tell him of our relationship.

"Tell Janice I said hello," I said to Alan and then turned to Grayson. He was still looking at Alan as he walked away.

"A special friend?"

I nodded. "We were engaged."

Grayson turned and looked again at Alan as he walked away. He then bent his head to me. "And he married your girlfriend?"

"Yes." He was still looking at me. Looking for hurt. "They can have each other. I don't wish for the past."

"In that case, let's look for the clams and oysters."

I was not interested in either clams or oysters and decided to check out the desserts. By the time I had my grape pie and a small piece of chocolate cake, I had again lost Grayson. I looked around and saw he was standing not too far away, talking to a tall, willowy girl who was smiling broadly into his face. And much too close. I had never seen her before, but then nearly everyone here was new to me. I saw two empty chairs and went and sat on one in full view of Grayson, hoping he would see me and come to me. But I evidently had misjudged the intensity of the conversation. At least the girl was intense. I saw Grayson glance at his plate of fried oysters, but the girl, eating nothing, did not seem to notice.

"Excuse me, is this seat taken?"

I said no before I thought. The speaker was a gray-haired woman and she needed a seat. But now I had given Grayson's seat away.

"I was standing too long and now my back is hurting," she told me. "Be glad of your youth. We get old too fast. Yesterday I was a young girl flirting with all the young boys and today I am an old woman that no one looks at anymore. I should not even come here anymore, but I enjoy seeing everyone and my niece brings me."

She did not come up for breath and I decided to eat my grape pie while she talked. The pie was wonderful and I savored each bite.

"But you don't know who I am," she continued. "I am Matilda Groat and I was born on the next farm and have been there ever since. But I believe you are new to the area."

"Not really. I am here a year already. My name is June Merriweather and I live with my aunt Sarah at Bluster Hill Estate."

"Oh, I know your aunt and uncle quite well. Although, he passed on recently, did he not?"

"It is almost a year."

"Is it that long? They were a fine couple. Didn't your aunt come tonight?"

"No, I think it is just too hard to go to some of these events alone. She was always with Uncle Theodore, you know."

"Of course. My Harvey died just two years ago. Worked like a horse he did, and then died of lung disease. Nothing to do for it. Now I live in the same house but with my son and his wife. The grandchildren keep me on my toes. I don't get a moment's rest until they finally go for a nap...or go to bed for the night. Whew! I am ready for bed by then also." I smiled.

"I hear your uncle left the estate to his manager. What a generous gift. I know him, too. My niece always hangs around him at such parties, but so far he has not succumbed to her charms. To her dismay."

I did not reply, instead I enjoyed my last bite of my pie, but the woman kept talking.

"I think one of the first times she was here, my niece talked to Mr. Everleigh the whole evening and now she always claims him at this fete."

I looked over in Grayson's direction.

"Is that your niece talking to him right now?"

"Where? Oh there she is. What did I tell you? She'll be with him all evening."

"I hope not," I said, tired of the chattering woman.

"Pardon?"

"I said I hope not, because *I* came with him."

"You...? Oh dear, are you...?"

"Courting? Yes." I decided that girl needed to know, but I saw, to my relief, Grayson looking for me. And then he spied me and walked over. Seeing no place to sit, he stood and ate his oysters and clams.

"I lost you."

"And I you. You should try the grape pie. It is delicious."

"Mr. Everleigh," said the woman by my side.

"Good evening, Mrs. Groat."

"Congratulations."

"On what?"

"A couple things. You got yourself a farm, actually more than a farm. A lovely estate."

"Thank you. I am truly grateful."

"And congratulations on your girlfriend, although my niece will not be happy to hear of it."

Grayson laughed. "She already knows."

"Oh, I am sure she is heartbroken. So you told her?"

"Well, she saw us together and then asked me about June." He looked at me. "Are you going to show me the desserts?"

"Gladly."

But before we got there, Grayson again got side-tracked by a group of three men. I believe they were all bachelors. A bit younger than Grayson. I don't remember quite how it happened, and I know he introduced us, but the men wanted to show him something or someone and I was interrupted by someone else at the same time. He went with the three men and my conversation with the woman who wanted to ask about Aunt Sarah soon was at an end. I decided to stroll outside to see what was going on at the bonfire. I was no sooner there, than someone called my name.

"June?" I turned. It was Brian and he seemed to be the one tending the fire.

"Brian! Were you here all evening?"

"I was. I work part time for Mr. de Frappe and tonight the bonfire is my job."

"It feels good now that the sun has gone down."

"That is partly the idea. Hey, did I see you come in with the big boss?"

I grinned. "If you mean Grayson, yes."

"Hey, I like that. He's a good guy. I thought he was immune to girls."

"I hope not!" Brian laughed with me. "Do you enjoy working for Mr. de Frappe?"

"Yes. He is a good man." Brian looked around to make sure no one was listening. "But I would not work for his wife."

I laughed. "I know what you mean."

"By the way, your old flame Gerald moved away again."

"Oh. Any particular reason?"

I remembered Gerald telling me he moved twenty miles away, but I wanted to know why.

"He just did not feel at home here and I think he started writing to someone and moved closer to her."

I was relieved. I did not have to worry about meeting up with him again.

"June?" Grayson walked up to me.

"I am here talking to Brian."

"Hello, Brian. You here working?"

"I am."

"Can you help with the early apples? We'll start picking next week."

"I'll be there."

Grayson looked at me and then back at Brian. "I keep losing June and I still did not have any dessert. See you Monday."

We left perhaps an hour later. There were still many people walking around outside among the hanging lanterns and some were gathered around the fire. But Grayson was ready to call it a day.

"Let's just say goodnight to the de Frappes," he said.

I was hoping that would not be necessary, but he was right. We came and enjoyed their food and the company of friends. They deserved a thanks.

On our way to find the de Frappes, I saw the tall willowy girl standing somewhat in the shadows, watching us. I felt sorry for her. But I was not about to offer Grayson to her.

And then we were standing in front of the de Frappes.

"Thank you so much," I said, giving my hand first to Mr. de Frappe, who was closer to me and then to his wife.

"We were glad to have you," said Mr. de Frappe.

"Grayson," said his wife, "you are wearing a very interesting vest. I never saw stitching like that. Where did you get it?"

Grayson grinned and looked at me.

"It is the work of the best seamstress in the area. She also made my shirt and jacket."

Mrs. de Frappe gave me a long look. "She did a good job."

"I think so, too. Goodnight."

We grinned all the way to the carriage.

CHAPTER 30

The next morning I amused Aunt Sarah with the tale of our evening at the fete.

"So did you have a good time?" she asked.

"Yes, I enjoyed it. But mostly because I was with Grayson."

She smiled. As always, she did not comment on our relationship. She would not play matchmaker. At least not in the open. But she was a woman of prayer and I had a feeling she was praying for the success of our courtship. I was, too.

Rachel was also at the table with us. She was getting more talkative and I enjoyed her and was grateful that she was here with Aunt Sarah. However, this morning she had news.

"I got a letter from a friend who never married and she lives in a big house and has offered me the possibility of living with her in a separate apartment. The apartment would not be available for another six weeks, but I have decided to accept."

"I am happy for you," said Aunt Sarah. "But I will enjoy your company for as long as you can stay."

After breakfast I walked up to the gatehouse to sew. I was working on a gown for another woman who was very nice, but I began to wonder if gowns for wealthy ladies was really my love. I did not want to deal with the snobs. Maybe I was too sensitive, but I could use my creativity for other things. Children's dresses, men's vests and much more. I knew some of my change of thought was the hope that maybe, just maybe I would marry Grayson and have children who would need clothes. Would I be happy with that? For the first time, I thought I just might be. As long as Grayson was in the picture.

When I got to the gatehouse, I headed to the kitchen and up the stairs, and, as always, placed my hand on top of the post. It moved. Like always. The top was loose and I don't know why, but today it irritated me. I took a good look at the post. It was nothing special. In fact, the top looked like it did not quite belong there. Maybe the top had broken at some time and it was replaced. And it was a bad fit. Someone who was not really good with wood repairs had tried to fix it. I pushed down on it as hard as I could, but though it helped, it did not fix it good enough. I pounded with my hand, but I only hurt my hand. It had it be pushed down harder. Frustrated, I looked around the kitchen for something to use. I wanted this to be a tight fit so I would no longer have to deal with it. I wished for a hammer, but that of course would damage the wood. My eyes finally fell on a big iron frying pan hanging by the stove. Now there was a possibility, but I could not slam that down on the bare wood. I found a tea towel and draped it over the post. It stayed. Then I grabbed the pan. I took good aim and I slammed it down on the post. Wham!

The lid of the post that did not want to go down far enough to be tight, went down inside the post as the sides of the post began to bend outward, nearly breaking. I stood and looked at it in horror. What had ever possessed me to slam a frying pan down on that post? My hand hurt and the post was wrecked. How had I managed to destroy part of my wonderful gatehouse? I could not believe what I was looking at. And how would I explain it to Grayson? I could not fix this myself. I would have to tell him what happened. This romantic house that he let me use to sew and did not charge me rent, was now sadly damaged by me. I stood a long time just looking at the post. My first thought was to quickly push it back together. It was not splintered. But alas, the top was now wedged so hard down in the hollow post that I could not get it out. For a full ten minutes I just sat and looked at the destroyed post. How could I ever tell Grayson that I used a frying pan on it? I would offer to pay for damages. The post was strangely made anyway. And the top did not fit. He should not be too upset. But that I used a frying pan....

I had things to sew and I could not fix the post anyway, so I would try to forget it for now. I was not going to go to Grayson immediately. It would wait. No one ever came here anyway. In spite of my anxious thoughts, as always, I lost myself in my sewing and the afternoon flew by. I was doing what I loved and, for the moment, the damaged stair post was forgotten. In fact, I was so involved with my sewing that I stayed longer than planned. When I finally took my leave, I quickly went down the stairs but when I saw the post, my heart went back in my throat and my appetite vanished.

At supper that evening, Rachel was talking about her husband. It was good for her to talk about him and she talked most of the meal and into dessert. I was glad that Rachel was talking, and I concentrated on eating my food. I barely looked at Grayson and tried to concentrate on what Rachel was saying. But it was hard, because all the time I was wondering how I was going to tell Grayson about the stair post. It seemed it would not be at the supper table, although a part of me wished to tell him when Aunt Sarah and Rachel were there also. He would not dare to get too angry. I should not say angry. I did not expect anger. The angry Conrad I had experienced, seemed under control, if not gone.

But I just did not want to see that look that said "How can you be so stupid?" But I did not want to push it off, it would just eat away at me and I wanted to get it off my mind.

Once during supper, my thoughts strayed and I found myself pushing my food around on my plate in deep thought. I looked up to find Grayson looking at me curiously. After supper I took the dishes to the kitchen and washed them. Then I dried them. After that, I took a deep breath and walked up the hall and knocked on Grayson's door.

"Come in."

I opened the door to find Grayson sitting at his desk in the library. When he saw who it was, he sat back and just looked at me. And he waited for me to talk. I was sorry that I was scared. He was a fine gentleman, but I had acted so stupidly.

"Grayson, I have a confession to make."

"That sounds interesting. Sit down. What kind of confession?"

"I don't need to sit, it won't take long."

But Grayson stood up, motioned to the couch and soon we were sitting side by side, Grayson sitting a bit front and looking at me.

"Now, let me hear your confession. You messed up someone's dress. A dress for Mrs. de Frappe."

"Oh, don't mention Mrs. de Frappe. I do not plan to sew for her again."

"Then what? You burned down the gatehouse."

He did not really mean that. He was trying to make me relax.

"Not quite. It's not quite that bad."

"What did you do?" His face became sober.

"Promise me you won't think I am really stupid."

Grayson got still and looked at me too long. I was sitting too close for this confession. Finally he spoke.

"I shall reserve my comment till after I hear what you did." No smile.

I swallowed. "You know the stair post in the gatehouse? How it always wobbles?"

"Yes, it always has, if I remember correctly. So it fell off complete-ly for you."

"No...well, sort of. No, not quite."

Grayson's face was a study.

"Please continue."

"I have tried so often to push the top of the post down to make it a tight fit and it just does not quite fit or it would not keep wobbling. I mean, it looks like it fits and the next time it gets loose again."

"And?"

"Well, today I got tired of it always wobbling when I put my hand on it."

I kept looking away from Grayson while I talked. I would look at my hands, or even at his hands but now I looked at his face to see how I was doing. His eyes never left my face. Silent waiting.

"So I looked around for something to push down on it...well, slam down on it." I stopped and tried to read his face again.

"And? Don't keep me in suspense."

"I knew I could not use a hammer because it would damage the top, although I don't think the top was any real work of art."

"What did you use, June?"

"Well, I put a cloth over it to protect the wood." Grayson's eyes were looking more interested all the time.

"And then?"

I hesitated. This was it. "You know that big iron frying pan hanging on the wall at the stove?"

Grayson bit his lip for just a moment or two. "What did you hit with the frying pan?"

"The post."

"Did the lid go down?"

"Yes. I mean, the lid went halfway down the inside of the post."

Grayson hung his head down so far I could not see his expression. I had really done it this time. And then I saw his shoulders shaking. I held my breath. Finally Grayson came up for some air, but he was still laughing, his mouth wide open and his head now thrown back. What a relief. Thank God he saw some humor in it.

"Grayson, you don't understand. I destroyed the post."

He finally got himself under control and even managed a very serious face.

"June, right now I want you to promise me something."

"Anything."

He raised an eyebrow at my ready answer. He had barely stopped talking. "Anything?"

"Anything." He gave me a very contemplative look.

"You should not make such hasty promises."

I said nothing in reply. "What must I promise?"

"Promise me that you will never come after me with a frying pan."

Finally I allowed myself to laugh and he joined me.

"I promise. But what about the post?"

"I can't wait to see it."

Grayson said he would look at it sometime the next day. At breakfast I told Aunt Sarah and Rachel the story.

"You mean the top that always was loose went down *inside* the post?" she asked.

"Yes, the post was made with four pieces of wood probably glued together. I did not know they made them like that. But that is the way this one is made. It is hollow on the inside."

Aunt Sarah sat a bit just thinking. I guessed she was trying to envision it and I did not think it was so hard to describe.

"You know, June, I remember something about that post. It must have come apart once before, because I remember now that Theodore asked someone to make a new top for it. Probably just one of his men, because it never looked as good as the other one. I wonder...I almost think the other top broke in half at some point and I don't know why. Maybe that one never fit right either and someone else slammed a frying pan down on it before."

"I can't imagine anyone else doing such a thing," I said. But Aunt Sarah was still thinking.

"Sometime or other, when I was at the gatehouse, putting something in the cupboard in the corner, I think I saw the old broken top. I really think that is where I saw it."

"Well, Nettie would have maybe seen it when she cleaned after Grayson moved out. It was probably thrown away. What we need is a new top, not a broken old top. We have two of them now."

I went to the gatehouse soon after breakfast. I considered waiting until after Grayson saw the smashed post. I was not sure he would still find it funny when he saw the damage. The whole post needed replacing. But I had no idea when he would take the time to check it out and I did not want to waste valuable time here at the house when there was sewing to do. So I walked down to the ford, which was almost dry just now, and enjoyed the shade of the trees before hitting the slightly upward stretch that was open to the hot sun and cloudless sky. I went into the gatehouse and tried not to look too hard at the post as I passed it, but halfway up the stairs, I remembered about the top of the post that Aunt Sarah talked about. I doubted I would find it, and I don't really know why I went back down. Just curious. Had someone else had trouble with the top of the post—enough that it, too, was damaged?

I walked to the kitchen cupboard. It was old also, and although the top shelves were open, there was a door or two at the bottom. I knelt down and opened the first one. In there, I found a couple old tin bowls and an object I could not define. I tried the other door and thought it was empty, but peering deep inside it, I found that which I sought. The top of the post. The original, I presume. And although it was not split in two pieces, it was cracked open so wide and maybe warped, so that it was not usable. I just gazed at it for a moment, wondering what kind of tale it could tell if it could talk.

And as I gazed at it, I noticed something that nearly made me stop breathing. I looked at the shape of it. How it must have looked before it was damaged. I tried to remember what the shape was on the piece of paper that I had looked at with Aunt Sarah and Grayson. Was it possible I had found the last hiding place? Is this why the post was unusual? And why the top did not fit? Had the first been damaged when they replaced the post so it would be hollow?

I went back to the post, all my sewing forgotten. I looked at the post top pushed down into the hollow. Was something really under this? I tried my best to look. It was too dark. I got a candle, but the light did not go down into the tiny spot around the jammed post top. I looked for something long and narrow, but before I found anything, I heard a carriage. I ran to the window. Grayson. I had to think fast. I was so excited, but I had to play this right.

Before Grayson got to the door, I raced to it. If I had found a treasure, I did not care about the damage anymore. I waited for

Grayson. He saw me standing at the door and I think he expected me to open it for him. I did not. He opened it. I did not move.

"May I come in?" He looked at me, surely wondering why I did not step aside for him.

"On one condition." For that I got a surprised but sober look.

"Do you have a frying pan in your hand?"

"No."

"What is the condition?"

"Finder's keepers."

He looked at me, trying to understand. But said nothing at first. "Finder's keepers?"

"Yes." I could not keep the excitement out of my eyes.

"Have you found the treasure?"

"I don't know. Maybe. Finder's keepers?"

"No, my lady," he replied firmly, a stern look on his face, "but if you do not let me in soon, you will be spanked for being disrespectful to the owner of this property."

He looked so serious, I put all playing aside. I let him in.

"I must show you something," I said. I took him into the kitchen and showed him the top of the old stair post. "Isn't that the same shape as the drawing on the note?"

Grayson studied the shape of the post. "Looks like it, but that does not mean it has to be this. I somehow assumed that the other things were containers of some sort."

"See if you can get the post top out of the post."

"You are really looking for treasure, aren't you?"

"I'm just curious."

"Well, before we unearth any hidden treasure, I want to remind you that although I own the property, thanks to the generosity of your uncle and aunt, I would certainly consider any treasure found in this post to belong to your aunt."

"You are very generous."

"They were more than generous to me."

"Let's look." I could hardly have it that we were talking and not getting to the business at hand. I think Grayson thought I was an impatient child. He smiled indulgently and we turned to the post.

"Where is the frying pan now?" asked Grayson.

"It is not damaged. I hung it back on the nail."

"I forbid you to touch it while I am here." He looked very serious, but I saw the sparkle in his eyes. "Do you understand?"

"Yes sir. Now to the post."

Grayson was stronger than I was, and he somehow pushed the sides of the post apart enough to get a good grip of the top and pull it out. It, too, was cracked. Thanks to me. Grayson handed it to me. The hollow post, we discovered was not hollow all the way down. Just the top half. And then Grayson reached in and pulled out a cloth bag. It was not terribly big, but when he pulled it out, I knew we had found the treasure. Someone, presumably Theodore's father, had cut the post in half and made a new top half that was hollow on the inside. And this he used as a place for his last treasure.

Grayson looked at me, as he held the bag. "June, I want you to go sit on the couch."

"Do I have to?"

"You do."

I did so. Then he went into the kitchen and looked into the contents of the bag. In just a minute or so, he came back into the parlor with the bag and sat next to me.

"June, you have indeed found a treasure. I do not know how much money is here, but you will not find out from me the monetary amount. This belongs to your aunt and you and I will speak of it to no one. Do you understand?"

"I do," I said solemnly. But I did wish to know what was there. I understood his reasoning. The less said the better, but I wanted to know badly.

"If your aunt tells you how much is here, that is up to her, but we will be silent," said Grayson again, looking soberly at me.

"It is enough to fix the post, I hope."

"I think we can safely say yes to that." Then he grinned.

By the time I came home for lunch, I knew that Grayson had handed the bag to Aunt Sarah. I met her in the kitchen and Rachel was not yet there.

"You made quite a find this morning," she said quietly to me.

"It was so exciting," I replied happily.

And then Rachel arrived and we took our food to the dining room to eat and no more was said.

And nothing was said at the supper table either. I caught Grayson looking at me with a hint of a smile on his face while I was trying to make conversation of other things when he knew what I really wanted to talk about.

"Did you sew today?" asked Rachel of me.

"Yes, I sew nearly every day. I love sewing."

"I hear that the Forbes firm is holding a contest," said Aunt Sarah to me.

"What kind of contest?"

"A contest for dressmakers. The applicants create an original gown and the best one gets to have their design manufactured in the firm and there is a monetary award. I forget all the details, but I thought of you right away. I think the last time they did this, they were looking for a new designer."

"That is exciting news!" I said, automatically looking at Grayson, but he was not smiling. "Do you think it is a bad idea?"

"The contest, or you being a part of it?"

I hesitated. "I did not say I would take part."

Grayson laughed, but not very merrily. "You don't need to say a thing. Your eyes tell the whole story."

"You don't think I should take part?"

Grayson did not answer right away. He just looked at me. "You do what your heart desires," he said finally, but he was very sober.

Aunt Sarah had read about the contest in the newspaper and as soon as supper was over, I went looking for it. I gave it a quick glance, and then, after the dishes were cleaned up, I sat in the parlor to read it again. I knew I was interested and I wanted to read all the rules so I would know what was allowed and what was not allowed.

Later, I sat and daydreamed about what I would sew. While sitting there, my head swirling with ideas, Grayson came in.

"Have you seen the newspaper? Oh, I see you are reading it."

"You may have it. I am finished, but don't throw it away when you are done. I would like to cut something out of it."

Grayson nodded and left without another word. I was wishing he were as excited about the contest as I was. But why should he be? He knew nothing of sewing.

The next day I went to the village mercantile. I wanted to see what the fabric woman knew of the contest. She had a poster in the window of the shop that gave the date of the show and the time. She was very excited about it and encouraged me to try for it. I looked through patterns for ideas, but the design had to be my own. I did discover that the contestants would be modeling the gowns at a special show in the Town Hall in about two weeks.

I really did not take time to think about the consequences of my involvement in this show. I just knew this was my chance. Sewing was my life. At least it was something I loved to do. And now I could show my work to a large crowd and if I did well, I would be known as a good seamstress. I would have opportunity to earn well. Maybe. I did not really think beyond that. I was too busy planning. I only had two weeks and I had to plan my pattern and I had to buy fabric. And then sew. I looked at patterns there at the mercantile. I looked at the fabric. Then I went home.

I ate lunch with Aunt Sarah and Rachel, chattering the whole time about the contest. After lunch, I took the carriage and went to Thackeray's Pond. There I looked at fabric. By the time I left the store, I knew what I was going to make and I had bought the fabric, lace and buttons—all what I might possibly need for my gown.

That night at the supper table, I suddenly realized that Grayson was rather quiet. Not that he was a great talker, but I wanted him to be as enthused as I was about the contest. He said very little and when he did talk, it had nothing to do with the contest. When no one was talking, I was busy seeing my gown in my imagination and did not really hear what the others were talking about. Once when I was staring off into space, thinking about my gown, I looked up to find Grayson just quietly looking at me. It gave me a jolt and I realized I was barely talking to him. He looked so sober, almost sad, somehow.

"Grayson, how was your day?"

"You really want to know?" He did not smile.

"Yes," I replied with a bit of hesitation. "What did you do today?"

Grayson just gave me a long look, then spoke. "I spent the morning helping a hired man to mend a fence. I gave instructions to Marley about a pregnant mare, and told him I may be gone for a week or so to help my folks."

"What? You are leaving?"

"Will you miss me?" Somehow it sounded like a loaded question and he seemed to be studying me.

"Of course, I shall miss you."

It was at this point that I noticed that Aunt Sarah and Rachel left the table. Grayson leaned back in his chair and made no move to leave the table.

"Are your parents well?"

"They are, but a few days ago a storm did a lot of damage to their stable and my brother and I hope to rebuild it. It may take a week."

"When are you leaving?"

"That depends on my brother's schedule."

I just looked at Grayson. There was something wrong, and it

bothered me. "It comes at a good time," he added. "You will be so involved working on your gown that you won't know I'm gone."

"Oh, yes I will," I said. But quite honestly, it really was a good time for him to leave. I would be too busy to miss him much. Except evenings at the supper table. I knew that the gown could be modeled either by the seamstress or by someone of her choice. And I had already decided this would be my gown and I would model it at the contest. This was not a big city contest, and I would not be terribly nervous. I hoped. Although it was the gown that was being judged, it was my talent that counted. But I wanted Grayson to be there.

As it turned out, Grayson did not leave as soon as he thought, and just five days before the show, he received a letter from his brother. He would leave the next morning, at daybreak.

I cleared the supper table with a sad heart. I would miss Grayson. In fact, I missed him already, just knowing he was leaving. And it seemed we were not having really good discussions just now. But maybe that was my fault. All I thought about was the contest. Before I was finished cleaning up the dishes, Grayson came into the kitchen.

"June, I am saying goodbye to you now."

"Grayson, if you just leave now, you will not be here for the show."

"Does it mean that much to you?"

"I would like you to be here, but I know your heart is not in the show like mine is and your parents need you. But don't stay a day longer than you need to stay."

He just looked deep into my eyes and I knew I never, never wanted to lose this man. I had the feeling he was looking for something when he looked at me so intensely. I felt already that I was wearing my heart on my sleeve and did not quite understand his look.

"Goodnight, June," he said softly. "Search your heart. Is this really what you want?"

And then he turned and walked away from me. Grayson neither

hugged me nor kissed me. I was disappointed. I would not see him the next morning because he would leave at daybreak. I fell asleep with tears in my eyes.

I had a restless night. I did not feel good about Grayson leaving, but could not put my finger on why. At some point, I don't know if I heard a door close or if it was something else, but I got awake and thought there was some light in the east. I thought immediately of Grayson and I got out of bed and went to the window. Although I had a view of the distant village from this window, I did not have a very good view of the lane. So I opened the window and leaned out a bit and strained my ears. Sure enough, I did hear the clip-clop of a horse. I leaned out as far as I could. There were some trees along the drive, but in between the trees, some of the drive was visible. I wanted to see Grayson yet before he was gone. I heard the clip-clop come closer and I watched between the trees and sure enough, I saw him ride down past the house. Then he was hidden until just before he crossed the ford. I watched carefully and then I saw him for a brief moment. But in that moment, he turned and looked toward my window. I quickly waved. Had he seen me? The horse kept racing down the drive but just before the trees swallowed him up, I saw Grayson raise his hat. He had seen me! Happy tears ran down my face, and then I saw him no more.

CHAPTER 31

By the time I rose, an hour or so later, I was already feeling lonely. It was not a good feeling to know that Grayson was traveling away from home and from me. I felt sluggish and reminded myself that I had hard work to do on the gown I was creating. That gave me a push. I ate breakfast and told Aunt Sarah I had actually seen Grayson leave and she was happy for me. Amazingly, the week actually went by quickly because I had so much to think about. So much to do. Mary Lou came by to see my creation. I asked her to be my helper at the show. To help me get into the gown and see that everything was in order—my hair, my dress, my whatever.

On the application I had filled out, it gave instructions regarding the time, the place, when to get there and what to expect. I was looking forward to the show, but there was always this hole in the program. I knew that Grayson would not be back before Sunday at the earliest. The show was on Friday night.

When Friday arrived, I began to get very nervous. My dress was a cream satin and I had layered sleeves, a slight bustle and a full skirt. I had heavy lace on the sleeves and on parts of the skirt. Some of the narrowest lace was a dark brown, the wider lace was mostly cream. I knew that my own dark hair and eyes would accent the bit of dark brown lace on the gown, and hoped for the best. I was happy with the dress. Aunt Sarah had come to see it on Friday morning. She, of course, said it was beautiful. She said it was nice enough for a wedding gown. I just wanted the judges to like it. Somehow, it was very important to me to win this contest.

As I got ready to go to the show, how I missed Grayson. I wanted him to be there, too, but when I thought about it, he never acted excited about the show. And when we said goodbye he said I should follow my heart. What did he mean by that? Somehow, when he said that to me, it sounded like he meant me to follow my passion. That was my heart, was it not? I hoped then that he was encouraging me in my sewing. He knew how much I enjoyed it. But now I began to wonder. What was he really saying? And what was my heart really saying about the contest? This show was so important to me, but it was not as important as Grayson, and he would not be there. I could always sew, but I could not do without Grayson.

At six o'clock, Marley came with the carriage. He would drive Aunt Sarah, Rachel and me to the Town Hall. He probably hoped to see Mary Lou there, because she was coming to be backstage with me to help me get into my gown.

It was a lovely summer evening. The sun was already setting earlier and the days were a bit shorter. However, it was pleasantly warm this evening and I was very excited. We stopped at the gatehouse where I picked up the dress, first wrapping it loosely in a sheet. In the carriage, we held it on our laps to keep it from getting wrinkled. The show would start at eight, so Aunt Sarah and Rachel would have a bit of a wait, but they did not care. They were there to cheer me on.

By eight o'clock, I was dressed and waiting with about fifteen other contestants, ready for our time on the stage. They would take us one by one and we would not only parade back and forth on the stage, but we would walk later, the whole group of us, down the steps of the stage and down the middle aisle and back. I looked at the other gowns around me. No one had much to say but we were eyeing each other's gowns, wondering whose would be chosen. There was an assortment of colors but mine was the only cream-colored gown. I had extra frills on the sleeves and ties hanging down at the elbows. My hands were sweaty and one half hour before it began, Mr. Forbes came back to take a good look at each one of us individually. He looked pleased, but did not look at any one gown longer than the next.

And then the show began. Mr. Forbes first went out on stage and made a speech about the contest and how the winner's creation would be made by the company and the girl who won would be paid a certain sum for the pattern, which would then be Forbes property. He then announced that the winner would be offered a designing position in the company. I looked around at the other young girls.

This was news to all of us. They showed their surprise and excitement. They were all dreaming of the position. For myself, I could not quite see me in that position. Somehow, it did not quite fit into my lifestyle, but I did not need to think about that now. I had not won. At least not yet.

I was number nine in the line up. I watched the girls go out and a bit later they came backstage to the accompaniment of applause. One after another. I wondered if they looked at the crowd or at Mr. Forbes. Was Mrs. Forbes here? She certainly would be. And probably Mrs. de Frappe. I had not thought of that until now.

And then, my name was being called and the man directing us motioned for me to come forward. I took a deep breath and stepped out into the bright lights of the gas jets. The room was crowded, but I had no time to really look at the audience. I had to watch where I walked and how to walk. There was a soft murmur of approval as I walked across the platform, turning clear around once or twice to show off the gown. I walked slowly, turned and walked back and all the time someone was describing my gown to the audience. I fleetingly wondered what Grayson would have thought. He was so quiet over the show. Too quiet. What had he said? Search my heart, that is what he said. And was this really what I wanted?

It was a long wait behind the curtain, but finally the last girl made her way across the stage. And then we all walked out on the stage and down the center aisle where we turned and walked back up on stage where we lined up for the announcement that we were all waiting for. Mr. Forbes, who had been down in the center of the audience with his wife, stepped up on stage and conferred with three other men for a short time. Then he turned to the audience.

"Ladies and Gentlemen," he began, "you have now seen the gowns that have been created for this show. I think they are all very well done and I congratulate each one of the creators of the gowns for their accomplishment. It is hard to choose one above the rest, but that is what I must do tonight. I had other judges looking at the dresses from the audience and they have turned in their top three to me. I myself had one chosen and I discovered that each one included that gown in the top three of their choice. That makes it easier for me. I would first like to give honorable mention to the runner-up before announcing the winner. Miss Josephine Larkins, please step forward."

A girl just two persons from me stepped forward to much applause. She was terribly excited and looked very pretty in her blue silk gown. When the clapping ended, Mr. Forbes continued.

"The winner of this contest this evening is Miss June Merriweather. Please step forward."

I felt myself go pale as I stepped forward. There was much applause and my heart was beating hard in my chest. I had done it! I had won! But somehow, all I could think of was what would Grayson think? Could he be happy for me? If I continued to sew for Mr. Forbes, or design clothes for them, what would this do to my relationship with Grayson? The glamour of the moment was dulled a bit by the thought. However, I smiled and turned to show off the gown amid the applause and finally I had to go down the aisle the second time, this time alone and then, finally, the show was over.

I went backstage where Mary Lou met me. She was so excited. Mr. and Mrs. Forbes also met me backstage.

"Congratulations, Miss Merriweather," said Mr. Forbes. "I would like you to see me in my office on Monday at two-thirty in the afternoon to discuss plans. Is that acceptable to you?"

I caught my breath. What had I gotten myself into? Right this moment, I was glad the show was over and I was looking forward to going home to relax. And think.

"That will be fine," I replied.

The ride home was a ride of triumph as far as everyone else was concerned. I was thrilled to have won. My creation had been the best, according to Mr. Forbes and the judges. I had a huge sense of accomplishment. But at the back of my mind was Grayson. Somehow, I did not think that Grayson would be as excited about it. He was courting me. Women were to be at home. And honestly, I had no wish to be in Mr. Forbes' factory designing clothes. But this proved to me I could do it. I did not know yet what I would say to Mr. Forbes on Monday. I would have time to think till then.

I waited all Saturday for Grayson's return. He had promised nothing, but I still hoped. He had not promised to even come on Sunday. In fact, when he left, it seemed there were less than usual words exchanged between us and I hardly knew exactly what he had said. But still I hoped he would come on Saturday.

But I hoped in vain. This show had already done its work in our relationship. I wanted to ask Aunt Sarah if she knew exactly when Grayson was returning, but was embarrassed that I did not know. She should be asking me. So I said nothing. Sunday was a lovely day and I hoped for Grayson's return. Marley and Mary Lou were going out driving in his carriage. I wanted to do the same with Grayson, but Sunday afternoon came and went, and Grayson did not come.

In the meantime, I had time to think. I walked out the lane and back. Then I walked to the pond and sat down and tried to get my thoughts together. Tomorrow I was to meet with Mr. Forbes. The whole show and prize was fast losing my interest. It was Grayson I wanted. I had the satisfaction of creating a winning gown. I could sew for private persons if I wanted to. But what I really wanted in life was to marry Grayson. I thought back to his angry words to me so long ago. "Someday," he said, "you will come crawling back to me." If he only knew it, in my heart I was really doing just that. I wanted him that badly. But I would not stoop to that. He was not the kind of man that would give in to a girl that easily. He would make the decision.

I found myself talking to God. I too often tried to think everything out by my own wits. Now I felt this was something bigger than I could handle. I should have talked to God right from the start, and now I was getting desperate. I was anxious and I was fearful. Now I began telling God everything. I went into detail, just as I might have with Mary Lou. I told Him my fears and my hopes. I told Him about Grayson, and although I knew I was not telling God anything new, I found a certain relief in just voicing my troubled thoughts, putting them out in the open, rather than just having them swirling in mass confusion in my tired brain. Gradually, a sense of peace settled over me. My troubles were not past, but I finally was certain what I would say to Mr. Forbes.

When I went down to breakfast on Monday morning there was good news. It was evident that Grayson had returned and had eaten breakfast. He had been gone for days and he would have lots to catch up on and I doubted I would even see him till evening. But he was home! I was so eager to see him. I wanted to tell him I had won the contest. Just maybe I would see him during the day. I wished my bedroom faced the back of the house. Maybe I could catch a glimpse of him. Just a *glimpse.* I wondered what he would say if I went out to the barn to see him? Or wherever he was working. He might even be in the library, but I doubted it. And the more I thought about it, the less inclined I was to go search for him. Our relationship was a bit strained when he left. I was not sure where I stood with him at the moment. I would let him take the lead.

I was not surprised when he did not show up for lunch. He almost never came for lunch. But I was disappointed. After all, he had not seen me for how many days. Didn't he want to see me? But he would come for supper. I would have to wait for that.

At two o'clock I walked out to the stables. My heart was pounding. Would I see Grayson? I kept my eyes wide open and looked in every direction. No sign of him. I was very disappointed as I entered the carriage and rode out the lane without seeing him.

At two-thirty I was at the factory that Mr. Forbes owned. I was nervous, but I was sure now that I knew what I wanted in life. And it was not working for Mr. Forbes. I did not want to be out of my home. I wanted to have a family, if I ever got married. When I knocked on his office door, Mr. Forbes greeted me as any busy executive would. He was politely impersonal.

"Miss Merriweather, let me again congratulate you on your achievement. I have money here for winning the contest and another one hundred dollars for the sale of the pattern."

"And here is the pattern," I said, handing it to him.

"Now," he said, "I would like to know your answer in regards to becoming a designer in my firm. It is a lucrative offer. It pays well. You would have your own workspace here. You obviously have a talent for creating gowns and I am offering this to you."

I took a deep breath. "I am very grateful for your gift of money and also for the opportunity to work for you. However, I do not think I would be happy working here in the factory. I am not looking at a career in dressmaking."

"Ah, so you have marriage in mind."

I hesitated. "I do."

"Well, if you are not interested, there will be other girls who will be more than happy to claim the position."

And after another ten minutes, I was heading away from the factory, my brain in a whirl. I thought I would be relieved to have this behind me. But all I could think of was Grayson. Instead of going straight home, I stopped at the mercantile. I needed some lace for a dress I was making. As I left the mercantile, I passed a millinery and displayed in the window was a hat that caught my attention. It was the perfect hat for my gown. None of us had worn hats. Mr. Forbes was interested in the gowns and our creativity. Now I stopped and stared at the large brimmed hat. I just admired it for a few minutes and then got into the carriage to go home. But I was not quite ready to go home yet. I wanted to talk to Mary Lou. I headed to the parsonage and Mary Lou saw me before I had tethered Star and came to meet me.

"Are you driving around enjoying the weather?"

"No, I just am on my way home from the Forbes Company."

"Did you get your money?"

"I did."

"Are you going to work for them?" She looked anxiously at me.

"No."

"You sure?" Was there disappointment in her voice?

"Yes."

"What does Grayson say?"

"Oh, Mary Lou," I began and then had to fight tears.

"June, what is going on?" Mary Lou came and put her arm around me.

"I haven't talked to him since he left."

"Didn't he come back yet?"

"Yes, but I have not seen him. He doesn't seem to be in a hurry to see me. He came home last night after I was in bed and I still haven't seen him. I can't wait to see him and he evidently doesn't care to see me." I was crying now.

"What happened?" Mary Lou gave me a hug, and I tried hard to get control of myself. I did not want her family to see me.

"I did not mean to cry. I am just worried. He had very little to say about the show. When he left, I said something about it and he said I should search my heart. Or follow my heart. I forget the exact words. You know, I don't even want to work for Forbes. I had the fun of winning, but it is not fun without Grayson."

"You will see him at supper and all will be well," comforted Mary Lou. "I would feel the same way about Marley."

"I hope to see him at supper although I think we have things to sort out beforehand. I don't want a strained supper in front of Aunt Sarah and Rachel."

"Oh, tomorrow this time all will be well. Just hang in there."

I stayed another hour with Mary Lou. I don't know why, but I was suddenly scared to meet Grayson. What if it was all over between us? I felt like I needed Mary Lou and so I showed her the lace I bought and told her about the hat I saw and she thought I should go and buy it. As a consolation for Grayson's attitude toward me. She even got me laughing a bit. As a result, it was suppertime till I got home. My heart was pounding as I rode to the stable but I saw no sign of Grayson. Marley met me and took care of Star. I walked to the house, trying to figure out how to act when I would see Grayson. I was all worked up, wanting to see him and yet scared, somehow.

But Grayson did not show up for supper. I was terribly disappointed. I was nearly in tears, but I put on a brave smile as I told Rachel and Sarah about my afternoon in town and about my visit with Mary Lou. I wanted to ask why Grayson was not there, but could not bring myself to ask. Later, after doing the dishes, I finally broke down and went to Aunt Sarah who was already in her room.

"Have you seen Grayson today?"

"Barely," she replied. "He came in shortly after you left and said he would not be here for supper."

I said nothing. Did he purposely wait till he saw Star was gone? But he did not know I would be going anywhere. Perhaps he thought I would be sewing. I said no more to Aunt Sarah. I went to my room a bit early. This was not typical Grayson. Something was very wrong.

I went to bed and cried myself to sleep.

I woke up hopeful. At least I would see Grayson today. He could not hide forever. Had not Mary Lou told me that by this evening, all would be well? Please God, may it be so. But at breakfast I saw a note on the table in Grayson's writing. I brazenly picked it up and read it, although it may not have been meant for me. It read: *I will be going to a meeting at six o'clock in the village and won't be here for supper.*

My hopes crashed. I nearly cried. But I ate my egg and bacon and tried to think of something to talk about to Aunt Sarah. She came to the rescue. She had the last of the garden to bring in and was happy for a nice day to do it. I went to the gatehouse and sewed. I was glad for an order that I had gotten in the mail and expected the woman to come by with the fabric in the afternoon. I knew if Grayson was going to a meeting, he would come out the drive. I thought of standing in the drive and forcing him to stop and talk to me, but thought better of it.

Around four o'clock, the woman came with the fabric and we chatted a while and she seemed to think she needed the dress for the weekend. I said I would do what I could. It was not a difficult dress. Just as she was leaving, a carriage came out the lane. I wanted to look up and at least see him wave to me, but as she stepped across the threshold she stumbled and nearly fell and when I looked up again, all I saw was the back of the carriage as it turned down the road.

I never even saw Grayson on Tuesday.

When I got to the kitchen on Wednesday morning, Aunt Sarah was churning butter and Rachel was talking about the house she would be moving into and was looking forward to settling down in a permanent place. I was not feeling cheerful, but I did try to take part in their happy conversation. I was slowly getting frantic about seeing Grayson, but if he did not seek me out after all this time, something told me to let him be. He was his own boss and would not take to a sniveling female. And I was not going to "crawl" back to him. I could be strong, too. So after breakfast, I headed to the gatehouse to sew. I came back at noon and left again. I caught Aunt Sarah looking at me with a question in her eyes, but true to form, she did not get involved in my relationship with Grayson.

As I headed back for supper an hour early, my heart started its usual pounding. As far as I knew, he would be here for supper. I changed my dress and brushed my hair before going down to help Aunt Sarah.

"Grayson is bringing a stranger for supper. A business associate," she announced as I gathered plates and silverware to take to the dining room.

I stopped in my tracks. There was a mixture of happiness that I was finally going to see Grayson again, and disappointment that there would be no reconciliation, if needed, this evening. A stranger would be at the table. On top of that thought, I had to wonder if he planned it so we would not be able to talk. But I would at least finally *see* him. My heart pounded and I promptly set down the stack of dinnerware so I would not drop them. Did Aunt Sarah have any idea how nervous I was about meeting Grayson? I set the table after putting my favorite tablecloth of Aunt Sarah's on the table. My hands wanted to tremble as I set the tumblers next to the plates. When I put the silverware down I dropped a fork on a plate and it made such a clatter I expected Aunt Sarah to come to see what had broken. I was just glad it did not break the plate.

When I heard the door open from the portico, I knew that the two men had arrived. I nearly stopped breathing. And then I heard Grayson's voice and it was such music to my ears, I stopped and listened. But the two men went into the library. I think Aunt Sarah knew very well what was wrong with me because she asked Rachel to put the gravy on the table and I was given the bread. Not much could happen if I dropped the bread, but no one wanted gravy all over the table or floor. Aunt Sarah also asked Rachel to fill the water glasses. I was beginning to wonder if I really was this bad. But I was. When all was on the table except the butter, I took that in to set on the table. At the same time, I heard the men emerging from the library and coming up the hall. I quickly put the butter down as the men came into the room. And then I looked up and locked eyes with Grayson. I could not look away and he did not look away either for a long moment.

"June." It was just one word, but he still knew my name.

"Grayson." I at least gave a full smile. I would act like nothing was wrong. Like he did not take days to say hello to me. Before we sat down, he introduced us to his companion.

"Our guest is Mr. Elliot from close to Allentown, and Mr. Elliot, this is Sarah Morgan who lived many years here with her husband Theodore. Next to her is Rachel Montgomery, who is temporarily living with us and this is June Merriweather, a niece to Sarah."

He introduced me last, but maybe it was because I was the youngest. At least his eyes lingered just a bit again. And then we sat and he said the prayer and the meal began.

I don't know what I expected from the meal. Grayson talked with the guest. The rest of us made little effort to talk and although I was on Grayson's right, the only thing we exchanged during the meal was the food that was passed from one of us to the other. And I did not look at him when I passed the food to him. One time our fingers touched just a bit and I almost blushed just from that! Whatever I had, I had it bad.

I was the one to clear the table and bring in dessert. Aunt Sarah had made apple dumplings and we served them with cream. During dessert, Mr. Elliot, who was a nice looking man with a blonde mustache and blue eyes, looked at me.

"The dumplings are wonderful. Did you make them?"

"I wish I had, but I must give my aunt Sarah credit for them." I purposely smiled big at the man.

"Mrs. Morgan, you did a splendid job. My mother made them, but my wife has never attempted making them."

"Thank you, Mr. Elliot. My late husband always liked them, too, and we have many apple trees so we have many apple desserts."

The two of them chatted about apples for a bit and it led to other foods and somehow Rachel joined in the conversation also. I, now that Grayson was not talking, could hardly get my dumpling down, even with a good amount of cream. Inwardly, I was shouting to him to *"talk, talk, talk!"* But Grayson did not hear me and my mind was a complete blank. I was not really focusing on the conversation around me, but I did hear Rachel explaining her reason for living here with Aunt Sarah. And that may have been the reason the guest again turned to me.

"And June, have you lived at this lovely place all your life?"

"Oh, no. Just for the last year. My folks died and...I needed a home."

I did not know what more to say. He was probably wondering why I was sponging off others rather than making my own living. That is what spinsters had to do.

"June is an accomplished seamstress," said Grayson to Mr. Elliot. I looked up in surprise at Grayson. He was actually talking about me! "Just last week she entered a sewing contest for the Forbes Dressmaking Company and ran away with the prize."

I was in shock. So he knew. Well, it did make the papers. I just stared at Grayson, eyes wide.

"Well, so congratulations are in order," said Mr. Elliot.

"Thank you," I stuttered.

Mr. Elliot then turned to Grayson. "And I suppose you were there to cheer her on?"

I almost croaked. I looked down at my dumpling swimming in cream.

"I was there," Grayson said softly.

Shocked by his words, I jerked my head up and looked at Grayson. He was lying! He was definitely not there! But when he turned and looked at me, I knew he was there. Grayson did not lie. His look was void of any deceit. I am sure that Mr. Elliot could see my surprise, but I did not look at him. I forgot to look away from Grayson. Only when Grayson turned to Mr. Elliot, did I look away.

"I think we can retire to the library," he said.

And supper was over.

The men left the room. It was my job to clean up since I did not help with the meals but I was in shock. I stayed sitting while everyone else got up from the table. Aunt Sarah hung around a bit, surely seeing my reaction to Grayson's revelation.

"Do you think Grayson was really at the show?" I asked as I finally stood and began to gather the dirty plates.

"If Grayson said he was there, he was there," she replied with a smile.

"Did you see him?"

"No."

I washed up after the meal without being aware of what I was doing. Then I went to my room. I had a lot to think about. I had finally seen Grayson. Although I sat literally next to him at the table, he had spoken not one word directly to me. But he announced my accomplishment. I was so happy he was willing to tell his acquaintance of my success. But was he proud of that? Did he care? And amazingly, he was at the show and had seen me in my gown! And that meant...how did he manage to come and then go back to his parents' home again? It was a mystery to me.

But just when I was feeling good about that I had to remind myself that he was just about ignoring me now. What had I done wrong?

CHAPTER 32

I woke up Thursday morning with the same wish I had entertained since Sunday. I wanted to see and talk to Grayson. How much longer would this go on? If only he would stop in at the gatehouse to see me. There we could talk in private. However, on this day I would stay around the house and help Aunt Sarah. She wanted me to make sticky buns and I had promised to do it. When I looked for molasses, we were out. So I headed first to the village for molasses. I also stopped for the mail and found we had a letter from Ohio. Not from Becca, but from Fanny Bender, the niece they lived with. When I went out the door of the post office, I met up with Nettie. She still came to clean for Aunt Sarah, or rather for Grayson, but I was often in the gatehouse, which I tried to keep clean.

Nettie was beaming. "Guess what, June, I am engaged! Oh, I am so happy I can hardly keep from jumping up and down! I can't hardly wait to get married and settled down with my own family."

"I am so happy for you, Nettie, you will make a wonderful wife and mother. You have had a lot of practice with your siblings."

"But now with my boyfriend...can you imagine? Living with my boyfriend!" Nettie's eyes danced. "And I want six children. Not more."

I was laughing. Nettie was not only happy, she was ecstatic.

"May all your wishes come true, Nettie," I said as we parted.

She was very, very happy and I must admit, I was envious of her. Why couldn't Grayson talk to me? What was wrong? It had something to do with my winning the contest. I was now sure of that. But he had proudly announced my accomplishment to his friend. I was baffled.

I let Star set the pace on the way home. My thoughts were so jumbled as I just tried to figure out what happened between Grayson and me. He liked me enough to come to the show, but now he did not want to talk to me. I was hurting badly. How could our relationship go downhill so quickly? I somehow felt stuck in the mud.

Actually, I felt like I was in the "slough of despond" as John Bunyan put it.

———————

I was working the dough for the sticky buns, when someone knocked on the door. Since I had my hands in the dough, Aunt Sarah went to see who had come. It was Marley and I could hear their voices as they drifted down the hall and into the kitchen.

"Hello Marley, what can I do for you?"

"Is June around?"

"She is, I will get her."

"Just tell her that Grayson wants her to come out to the stables."

I nearly fell into my dough. Grayson wanted me in the stables? Whatever for? He was actually *asking* for me?

"Here," said Aunt Sarah, coming into the kitchen. "Marley says you are wanted in the barn. I'll finish kneading the dough."

I quickly washed my hands and was soon out the door. If Grayson was finally calling for me, I was not going to doddle. As I walked briskly across the lawn, Misty came padding after me, but she soon got distracted with a butterfly that was dancing above Aunt Sarah's zinnias. As I approached the stables, I looked for Grayson. No sign of him. I entered the stables, walked past Star's corner, but it was empty. Star must be out in the meadow. As I walked farther into the stables, I heard a cat crying. Insistent crying. Just then I saw Grayson standing about ten feet in front of me.

"Good morning, June. Do you hear the kitten?"

I stopped before I got to him. The crying kitten was somewhere to my right.

"I hear it."

"I put it in a box. Maybe you can take it under your wing."

I walked over in the direction he pointed. In a corner of the stall was a small box and when I looked into it, the little gray kitten just looked up at me, mouth wide open, and mewed loudly and continuously.

In that instant, I realized this was not going to be the meeting with Grayson that I had hoped for. Again. And, I noted, he was not coming closer, to show the kitten to me.

"The kitten seems to be alone, frightened and hungry," he added from where he stood.

"So am I," I said softly, the words just slipping from my tongue. "We will make good companions."

I did not look at Grayson. I was already embarrassed for my brashness. Had I no self-pride at all? I was begging for pity! How had I slipped so low? Would he interpret my words as my crawling to him? I took the kitten in my arms and without a backward look, headed back to the house. By the time I got to the house, I was kicking myself in embarrassment and not wanting to ever see Grayson again. Only when I got into the kitchen, did my thoughts go to the kitten in my arms.

"Guess what?" I said to Aunt Sarah. "We got us a kitten."

"Oh my. That is how we got Misty. Only one?"

"Only one and it needs food badly."

While I held the scared kitten, Aunt Sarah heated a bit of milk on the stove. Just enough to get the chill off of it. Then we put the dish on newspaper and I put the kitten down. He was a hungry little kitten and walked right into the dish before starting to lap up the milk. I spent most of the next hour with the kitten, petting it, calming it, and loving it. Then we put a blanket in a box and with its full belly, it slept while I worked again on making the sticky buns.

At lunchtime, I remembered the mail and gave the letter to Aunt Sarah. It worried me a bit that Fanny had written the letter. Was something wrong with Becca? Aunt Sarah read the letter out loud.

<blockquote>
Dear Sarah,

I don't know when you last heard from us, but I just wanted you to know that Becca had pneumonia and was very sick. She is still recovering, but it is a slow process. Lizzie keeps her company and as always, it is shouting rather than talking. We are so used to the shouting around here, that sometimes my husband and I even shout to each other without thinking! We are very busy, but Lizzie does the laundry for me which is a huge help. We have canned lots of beans, peas, corn and fruit that we will be thankful for this winter. I am sure Becca would be very happy to hear from you.

God bless you all,

Fanny
</blockquote>

"Oh dear," said Aunt Sarah. "I guess Fanny has her hands full. I am glad to hear that Becca seems to be recovering. But can you imagine the shouting? And now Fanny and her husband are shouting to each other! That must be comical."

"I'll try to send her a note, too," I said. "Becca will know we are thinking of her."

As I put the sticky buns in the oven for baking, I tried to think how I was ever going to face Grayson at the supper table? But I need not have worried. As it turned out, the men were harvesting the oats and would keep working until they were done, as rain was expected. I found a book in the library and took it to the parlor. I would wait up for Grayson. Maybe he would come in the parlor for some reason. Or eat late and find out I was in the parlor. This had gone on long enough. I was ready to face the enemy, no matter what.

I tried to read, but the kitten was on my lap and kittens like to play. I finally put the book aside and played with it. When the kitten was tuckered out, it fell asleep on my lap and I then picked up my book again. I heard the door around eight o'clock. It was dark by then. He could not know I was in the parlor but I heard him go upstairs to the washroom. Later, when he came down, I heard him in the kitchen. I did not go to him. He would see the light in the parlor. I do not know what I read, but about twenty minutes later, when I heard his footsteps come toward the parlor, my heart jumped into my throat. And then he was there, standing in the doorway. I looked up and our eyes locked for a long, silent moment.

"I see the kitten has found a home."

It was not exactly what I wanted to hear from him first, but I would not be choosy now. His voice was music in my ears.

"It has."

Grayson came slowly into the room and stood not far from me, but he did not sit down. There was something in me that resented the fact that he had ignored me so long and now he was not staying long enough to sit down. There had been no talk of the show except that which was exchanged when his guest was here. And he had said nothing of his time with his parents.

"Welcome back," I said, perhaps with just a hint of sarcasm and saw his eyes widen. He had been home days already.

"Thank you." There was no smile.

"How are your folks?"

I had the impression he was changing gears. He had not come into the room to talk about his time away. But I was interested in hearing about his time there and about his parents' welfare. Actually, I would have been ready to talk about the garbage in the garbage bucket, anything to exchange words with Grayson. At least we were *talking*.

"My parents are well and send you greetings."

"Thanks." How long was he going to wait to give their greeting to me? "Did you get the shed built?"

"I did, with the help of my brother."

He was not wasting words but he was studying me as he answered my questions. Again silence. It was like pulling teeth to get him to talk.

"Why did you come to the show?" I surprised him with my change of subject but the answer slid easily from his lips.

"To see you." It caught me a bit off guard.

"I did not expect you to come. I would have liked to have seen you."

"You were too busy to see me. And I had a train to catch."

"You returned to your folks yet that evening?"

"I did."

I had to give him credit for caring enough to come. I would not have faulted him if he had not come. In fact, I had not expected him at all.

"Are you happy I won the contest?" I did not know I was going to ask that question. But it was in my heart and just slipped out.

"I am proud of you." Again the answer came quickly, sincerely. But he had not really answered my question and somehow I wanted to know.

"But are you happy I won?"

There was a slight hesitation and a shifting of his feet but he did not look away. "Yes, for your sake."

Ah! Therein lay the problem. Up until now, I was determined to find out what was wrong. Why the distance between us. Now my mood shifted and a sadness came over me.

"You didn't want me to win?" My voice trembled ever so slightly.

Grayson never took his eyes from me. But he did not answer. I suddenly fought tears. Was my winning the contest going to separate us? Grayson saw my struggle. He finally spoke.

"Are you really lonely, scared and hungry?"

He shocked me with his words. He remembered the words I had spoken earlier that day. I had said them softly, but he had heard them. And they were true. I was very alone ever since he came back from his folks and I was scared about our relationship. And I was hungry for his love. But now I was too choked up to talk. I only nodded, trying not to let the tears fall.

Grayson took a step closer to me and bent down and took my hand. I blinked back the threatening tears. His words were spoken softly, but firmly.

"June, I want you to listen carefully to what I have to say." He paused, as if to let those words sink in. "You won the contest. You were the most beautiful girl in the show and you wore the prettiest gown. Your passion is sewing. You are offered a place in the Forbes' Company. Take it. Work for them. This is what you want. You are creative and I won't stand in your way." He hesitated. "I'll even rent the gatehouse to you and you may live there if you wish."

It was sinking in to me that he was giving me my freedom to do my thing without him. The tears were swimming in my eyes.

"Grayson, I don't want...."

He dropped my hand and held his hand up to stop me from talking.

"Search your heart, June. Make sure of what you want."

And then he turned abruptly and walked away from me as my tears ran down my face and fell on the kitten.

CHAPTER 33

The weekend was long. I did not know if Grayson ever planned to discuss the topic with me again. He seemed to think he knew that I wanted to work for Forbes and he never let me tell him anything different. Was he using this as an excuse for ending our relationship? Had he met someone at his parents' place? The idea made me almost sick to my stomach.

On Sunday, Grayson did not sit beside me at church. I heard his tenor voice somewhere behind me. In the afternoon, I took a walk out the lane and back, needing badly to do something other than sit morbidly in my room. But I did not wish to be with anyone. Except Grayson. I probably chose the lane, hoping I would see him when he returned from seeing Maxim. I was always hoping for an opportunity to talk to him in spite of circumstances.

When I came back across the ford, I was still restless and although it was now late afternoon, I finally took Star and rode to the hill where Grayson and I had raced our horses. Once there, I tethered Star to a tree and I sat on the grassy hill and let my mind rove where it would. I watched a hawk riding the air currents above me and wished for the freedom it was enjoying. As I sat there, I found myself talking to God again. I was discovering that when I deliberately took time to sit quietly, simply to converse with God, just as I would a good friend, a peace descended on me. My troubles were not over, but somehow I began to believe that God was really there for me. That He cared and that my life was indeed in His hands. In fact, I was enjoying this time with God so much that I did not notice the time going by.

And then I heard someone coming up the hill behind me on a horse. I turned, just a bit frightened, as I was very alone here. I was relieved to see that it was Grayson. He rode right up beside me where I was sitting, before he stopped. He gave me a quiet, sober look.

"Are you alright?"

"Yes."

"Sarah sent me out to look for you."

"What time is it?"

He looked at his time piece. "Nearly six."

As he spoke, there was a rumble of thunder. How had I never noticed the clouds coming? I quickly got up and walked to Star. As I did so, Grayson rode his horse over to me and gave me a helping hand to get up on my horse. And then the raindrops began to fall and without a further word, we gave the horses freedom to run and we raced side by side on our horses all the way back to the stable. By the time we got back, we were both soaked. Grayson, the water streaming off his face, slid off of his horse and reached out a hand to help me.

"Run to the house, I'll take care of the horses," he said.

I wanted to linger, but I did as he said and ran through the rain to the house. Both Grayson and I had to change clothes before we sat down to eat. We ate supper together, but it seemed Grayson still held back. We talked. All of us, but it was not the Grayson I had known. And I did not like the new one.

I, Rachel, had gone to the kitchen for something after supper and happened to see Grayson and Sarah talking softly in the parlor. There was something about the serious look on Grayson's face that caused me to stop and watch. I was too far away to hear any words. He had not been himself for days and poor June looked like she was fighting tears far too often. I did not know what was wrong, but I felt sorry for June. I somehow thought it was Grayson who was causing the problem. But now he looked like he was seeking help from Sarah. They both stood silent for a moment, then Sarah's face brightened. She said something to Grayson and he just looked at her a long moment without talking. He did that often. He was not quick to talk. Then he nodded and turned, barely giving me time to look busy in the kitchen.

It was certainly not a good time to have a birthday, but I could not change the date and Aunt Sarah, clearly noticing my somber face, said we had to celebrate. She was talking about it for two days already and seemed to have everything already planned.

"You must see that things are very strained between Grayson and me and I just don't feel like a party," I said. It was the first I admitted the bumps in our relationship, but she was well aware of that.

"We cannot ignore such a day that comes only once a year," she replied. "Who knows, maybe this is just what you need."

"Well, at least, let's have the girls here, so Grayson will feel outnumbered and will perhaps not stay long," I said. "Maybe he will find an excuse to not be here at all. He has managed it quite well recently."

I realized I was showing my frustration and perhaps anger, but I just could not imagine having a party with a man I wanted so badly, who was willing, finally, to let me live in and rent his gatehouse, just so I would be out of his way. I fought tears every time I thought about it.

The three girls were invited for a birthday supper the evening of my birthday. I did not invite Grayson. I am sure Aunt Sarah told him about the party at some time when I was not around. I did not know if he would be there, and I did not ask. It was a full week since we had talked in the parlor and I had rarely seen him since. Of course, there was harvesting going on and he was working long days. I think I was almost hoping he would not be there. It would be less of a strain. I would have more fun with just the girls.

Sarah did not let me help with the meal. She said she and Rachel would make it, so I went to the gatehouse and did what I loved. I sewed. I could forget my problems when I sewed. I had put more dresses in the village shop and also in the shop in Thackeray's Pond. I was making dresses, rather than gowns, but I was adding lace, buttons, frills and anything I could possibly think of, to make them appealing. And since I had gotten good publicity in the paper from the show, the dresses seemed to be selling.

"June," said Aunt Sarah, the day of my birthday, "I told Grayson to invite Marley also. That way he won't feel so outnumbered and Mary Lou will be happy to see him."

I thought about her suggestion. It was probably for the best. We couldn't tell Grayson he could not come. And Marley was a good idea. Too bad I could not flirt with him and try to make Grayson jealous, but I could not do that to Mary Lou.

"That is a good idea, Aunt Sarah. With these girls one never knows what topics will be brought up and this way Grayson and Marley can talk of things that interest them. I hope you told Grayson I do not expect a gift from him."

"I said no such thing. That will be his problem."

I had to smile. It was the closest thing she came to getting involved in our problem. I was happy that Marley would be invited. I considered him a friend and Mary Lou would be happily surprised to see him. As for the menu, there would be roast chicken, root vegetables from the garden, pickled beets, and applesauce. Rachel was making a cake that I was not to see until the party. I appreciated both my aunt's and Rachel's attempts to make it a happy party, because they, too, knew of the tension between Grayson and me.

As planned, I spent a good part of my birthday sewing. I was happy with that. And Aunt Sarah and Rachel wanted me out of the house anyway, so it worked well for us. I did not return to the house until one hour before the party. Even then, the women did not want me around. I stayed up in my room and was surprised to find both

Misty and the kitten curled up on my bed. I was glad to see that they got along.

At six o'clock I saw a carriage come in the lane and I went downstairs. It was a rather dark evening, rainy and a bit gloomy, but the women had the house looking very bright with lamps, candles and someone had even gathered some late zinnias and placed them on the table. When the knocker sounded, I went to the door and Annelie, Jeannie, and Mary Lou tumbled inside to get out of the rain that was now coming down hard. I took their wraps and put them on hooks in the hall and soon thereafter Grayson and Marley came in the door. It was fun to see the surprise on Mary Lou's face. I was wishing I could be as openly happy to see Grayson.

It wasn't long until we were seated at the table. Aunt Sarah took charge, putting Grayson at the end where he always sat and to his left, Marley. She said she had to keep the men together. Then came Mary Lou next to Marley and then Rachel. At the other end sat Aunt Sarah, then Annelie and then me and Jeannie at the end next to Grayson. Aunt Sarah said I, as the birthday girl, had to sit right in the middle of the gathering.

Before Grayson said the prayer, introductions were made for Rachel's sake, and then the meal began. The aroma from the roast chicken was tantalizing and Aunt Sarah had made mashed potatoes as well as stuffing. There there were salads and vegetables. It was a feast and I was grateful for it. I was nervous that Jeannie was next to Grayson. And Marley across from her. Who would she talk to? I decided I better keep her occupied.

But the conversation seemed to flow easily. Something was eventually said about the new kitten.

"Where did you get the kitten?" asked Annelie, who also loved cats.

"Grayson found it in the barn," said Marley.

"Is it his birthday gift to you?" asked Jeannie, making me cringe. I did not expect a gift from him and this comment made it awkward.

"It is simply a stray that needed a home. Now Misty has taken it under her wing and the kitten is no longer alone."

Marley and Grayson did talk a bit at the table but Annelie was talking at the same time and I did not hear what they said. I was just glad they were talking. We girls got talking about the food and our own experiences at cooking.

"Jeannie, tell the others about your white cake," said Annelie.

"Which cake?"

"You know very well which one," answered her sister.

Jeannie for once looked a bit embarrassed. "I had this beautiful cake baking and I wanted to see how it looked, and when I opened the door it looked like a pancake."

"She forgot the baking powder," said her sister.

"Was it edible?"

"For the pigs only."

"Do you have pigs?

"Yes, two, but they turned up their snouts at it," said Annelie laughing.

"Impossible."

"They had just been fed and were too tired to get up to see what we threw in the pen," said Annelie.

"I heard once of someone who made a pie out of dried currants and did not soak them first," said Rachel.

"I bet they broke their teeth on them," laughed Jeannie, glad to be out of the limelight.

I don't remember just how we got on the contest subject, but it came up and I instantly cringed.

"Oh June, you looked so beautiful in your gown at the show. Wasn't that the greatest evening of your life?" asked Jeannie.

"Well, I am sure I will never have another night like it," I replied. But I was thinking it was the biggest mistake of my life.

"I'd love to see you in the gown again. This time close up. Do you have it here?"

"Yes," I said a bit reluctantly, guessing where this was headed.

"Oh, will you put it on for us? After supper?"

The girls all joined Jeannie. I hesitated. It seemed this was the problem between Grayson and me. Would it spoil the evening?

"You don't get any gift until you put it on for us," threatened Annelie.

I finally agreed, glad that Grayson was not across the table from me. I did not want to see his face.

Soon the birthday cake was brought in, and shortly thereafter we went into the parlor to open gifts. I thought maybe the two men would not come along, but they did. Aunt Sarah said we would open gifts first before I put on the gown.

I received a vase from Annelie, a quilt from Aunt Sarah, handkerchiefs crocheted around the edges from Rachel, a crocheted doily from Jeannie and a fancy glass bowl from Mary Lou. There was no gift from Grayson or Marley, but under the circumstances, I did not expect any. Then the girls made me put on my gown.

"Well, the girls are invited to my room to see my gown," I said as I headed out of the room.

"No such thing," said Aunt Sarah. "We all want to see it. Put it on and come down here."

Did she have any idea how difficult this was for me? Would Grayson stay in the parlor until I returned?

"In that case, just Mary Lou can come with me to help me," I replied.

Ten minutes later I came downstairs again. The others had remained in the parlor and I felt self-conscious as I entered. I wanted to look at Grayson, but forced myself not to. I stood quietly as the girls especially, gave it a good look. At one point, my back was to Grayson, and I felt, rather than saw, that he left the room at that time. I did not expect to see him again that evening.

"Now let us see the back of your gown," said Aunt Sarah eventually.

As I turned, Grayson came back into the room with a hat box that he handed to me.

"Happy birthday, June." His words were soft. I just stood and looked at him. I did not take the box. What was I to think? He was ignoring me most of the time. Now he had a gift for me. Because I just stared at the box, he set it down, opened the lid and took out the hat. I gasped. It was the exact hat that I had admired in town. I could not believe my eyes. I am afraid my mouth stood open in surprise. I was simply dumbfounded. And then, since I made no move to take the hat, Grayson gently placed it on my head, his eyes steadily looking into mine. I know I blushed badly. Then he stood back and smiled.

"Looks good."

"The hat is perfect for the dress," said Annelie. "Where did you find it, Grayson?"

"I'm afraid I can take no credit for it. June found it and thanks to Sarah, I found out about it."

And with that, he once more took his seat.

"Thank you so much," I said, when he looked at me, but I felt the moisture in my eyes.

When I was once again out of my gown, we had a lot of fun playing charades. I could hardly take my eyes off of Grayson, who stayed and helped play. It was the old Grayson again.

The one I loved.

CHAPTER 34

We were now into September and Sunday was a lovely warm day. But I was restless. Grayson attended church, but as always, he was meeting with Maxim for lunch. He was not expected until suppertime. I could not stay in the house. The balmy weather lured me outside. The sun was warm and there was a certain feel of autumn in the air. I headed down to the pond, a blanket under my arm and a book in my hand. Both cats followed me and when I spread out the blanket, both cats joined me. I tried to read, but Buff, the kitten, gave me no peace. He wanted to play, so for the first half hour, I had to play with him. When both cats got interested in something down by the pond, I lay back and relaxed in the sun. And although my mind kept replaying the events of the previous night, I somehow managed to fall asleep. I do not know how long I slept nor do I know what woke me. I just opened my eyes and gazed at the puffy white clouds in the sky. I was trying to see a ferocious lion in one of the clouds when I heard a voice.

"Do you always talk in your sleep?"

I sat up in a blink. "Grayson! How long have you been here?"

"You did not answer my question."

"I *never* talk in my sleep!"

I was embarrassed at him finding me asleep and I tried to rub the sleep out of my eyes, pleased that he was back early and hoped it was for my benefit.

"How do you know you do not talk in your sleep? You sleep alone."

"I just know it. Anyhow, what makes you think I talk in my sleep?"

"I heard you." There was something about the way he said it that made me pretty sure he was teasing. "Were you dreaming?"

"Not that I remember."

"You must have been."

Now I got a bit scared. Had I really talked in my sleep?

"What did I say?"

Grayson was sitting just to my left, not quite within reach. There was a bit of a breeze that made his dark hair blow across his forehead.

"Are you sure you want to know?" His eyes were challenging and I hesitated at the intensity of his look.

"No, I don't want to know."

"Aha, June is scared. Interesting."

"How long have you been sitting here?" I asked.

"Maybe ten minutes."

"You are back early."

"I wanted to talk to you."

Again I stilled. He was finally ready to talk! And now his teasing seemed to take flight. He was beginning to look serious. He leaned a bit forward.

"Did you really tell Forbes that you did not want to work for him?"

"I did."

"Why? This was a golden opportunity for you. You won the competition. You had the chance to do what you love to do and to make good money doing it."

Did he really want me to work for Forbes? Most men thought women should be at home. And I wanted to be at home as long as I could sew. I was a bit unsettled and hurt when he urged me to work for Forbes.

"It is not what I want for my life," I said slowly. My voice trembled just a bit, feeling suddenly rejected again.

"What *do* you want?"

His eyes never left my face and his voice was soft. I knew very well what I wanted, but could I tell him? His eyes were keen, reading me.

"That is a very personal question."

"That is what it was meant to be."

He was not budging. He had turned toward me, and I looked deep into those searching eyes.

"You are scared to hear what you said in your sleep. We are honest in our dreams."

"I am not scared. I think you are making this up."

"You are afraid of what you may have said."

"If it makes you feel better, tell me what I said."

"You sure you want to hear?"

I still thought he was bluffing and I did not really think he would know what to say.

"Yes, I want to hear it," I replied, although my heart was beginning to pound.

"You said I love you, Grayson."

I blushed. He was leaning closer to me and I had to get my breath.

"I don't believe you," I said, hardly looking him in the eye. "You are making this whole thing up." He said nothing, just grinned at me.

"I presume you also know what you answered," I suddenly challenged him.

Grayson stood up and pulled me to my feet. He just looked at me for a long moment.

"I said I love you, June." I suddenly knew this was not about me talking in my sleep. I found I was holding my breath. "But you have not yet answered my question. Why did you turn down Forbes' offer?"

"Because I am very happy right here. I can do my sewing in a lovely, romantic gatehouse. I have an Aunt Sarah who loves me and is company for me."

"And?" He was waiting for more.

"I...also have a..." I stopped but I could not look away from the handsome face so close to mine, urging me to speak. "I have a friend that I...like very much."

"Wrong. Try again." His dark eyes nearly melted me.

"I have a friend that I...love very much." It was barely a whisper, but it was heard. Grayson's eyes went to my lips and then he slowly pulled me into his arms and kissed me. Even before he assured me of his love. And he just held me close for a very long time.

"This is where you belong. In my arms," he said. He paused just a bit. "It is time for Aunt Sarah to move in where Rachel is living. Do you know that Rachel leaves next week? And you and I are going to live in the house. Not in separate rooms on separate floors. But all over the house. We'll paint and paper the main bedroom and make it ours. And...." His voice drifted to silence.

"Don't stop now, I could listen to you all day."

He laughed. A deep, joyful laugh. "And you already have your wedding gown, complete with hat so we really could get married in... two weeks."

"Grayson!"

"What? How long do you need to get ready? You already live here. We'll get married on the lawn with the falling leaves swirling around us and Mary Lou and Marley can be our attendants. Wait a minute. I can't let Maxim out of it. You will have to add a girl to the picture."

"Annelie. Annelie and Maxim," I said, getting carried away with the plans. "But you haven't asked me to marry you yet." His face registered shock and he fell to one knee and suddenly his face was completely serious.

"June Elizabeth Merriweather, will you marry me?"

"Have you told me you love me? You were talking about the imagined dream."

"I think I did tell you."

"Tell me again to make sure." I heard that wonderful rumble again.

"I love you, June. I think I have loved you ever since...that time long ago. Will you marry me?"

"Of course I will marry you. Today yet, if you would insist on it." I had never seen Grayson so animated and I was caught up in his joyful mood. "But I must remind you of something that you declared so long ago."

"If you are referring to my declaration that you would one day come crawling back to me, you fulfilled that statement."

"I did not! Never! You are imagining things again."

"Well, it was close enough to it for me, when you saved my life in the snowstorm."

"What do you mean?"

I really was not sure what I had said in that frightful moment. What had I said as I pleaded with God? What had I said to Grayson?

"You knelt by my side and pleaded with me to wake up. You were crying."

"How did you hear me? You were unconscious."

"I was nearly frozen but my hearing was good and my brain, though sluggish, still worked. Just why did you want me to survive so desperately?"

"I wouldn't want anyone to die by freezing."

"Would you cry and plead with God for them? Just tell me, did you love me even then?"

"I'm not telling," I said, but I had to smile.

And then I was in his arms again, his lips on mine.

And we barely noticed when the cats started rubbing their furry bodies around our legs.

EPILOGUE

It was a lovely day in mid-October when we got married. October seemed a long time for both of us to wait, but apples had to be picked, Rachel had to move out, and Aunt Sarah had to move to the little house. And that house needed a small kitchen built onto it. But Grayson got his men on it and not only did they get that finished, our bedroom got painted and papered. And finally, the day before the wedding, Grayson moved out of his room and we both moved our things into the main bedroom. It was a breath-stopping experience.

The wedding took place on a Saturday morning on the front lawn where we could look down past a clump of blazing sugar maples and over the harvested grain fields to the village below. The big, yellow leaves of a maple tree on the front lawn drifted down over our smiling guests during the ceremony, which took place when the sun was the warmest on the front lawn.

When Mary Lou, Annelie and I walked out the front door, the crowd's backs were to us. But Marley, Maxim and my beloved Grayson were facing us. I just stood a moment on the porch and looked out across the gathering of our friends. It was a day to savor and I did not want to be rushed. And then I looked at Grayson, standing tall and handsome and sober and for a moment we locked eyes. This was it. The day God gave us. The day He was giving us to each other.

The church choir sang and we were married by Pastor Stafford. The cats, I was told later, sat primly on the front porch and silently observed the whole ceremony from start to finish. I had to blink back tears when Grayson held my hand and said his vows to me, and my voice trembled as I said mine to him. But my heart was overflowing with love for Grayson and for my God who ordained this marriage.

After cake, coffee, and bite-sized sandwiches, we opened our gifts. And then our bags were placed in the carriage and my husband and I waved goodbye to a group of well-wishers. Maxim drove us to the village, where we got the stagecoach to a little cabin, sitting by a lake. It was not so very far away from Bluster Hill and this would be our home for the next week.

By the time we arrived at the cabin, it was dusk and the air was decidedly chilly. We took our bags into the cabin where Grayson immediately started a fire in the hearth. Then we made hot tea and ate a hearty supper that was packed and sent along by Aunt Sarah. Cold fried chicken, potato salad, pickles and apple pie. I was very hungry, but halfway through the meal my appetite dwindled and suddenly I was timid and unsure of myself. Grayson, his eyes ever seeking mine, sensed my mood and pushed his food aside also. His eyes were dark and soft. We put the food away and then stood on the porch of the little cabin and watched the moon come up over the water. Once the moon was completely over the horizon and reflecting in the pond, Grayson's arm tightened around me. And then he turned and kissed me and just held me awhile.

"Ready to go in?" he whispered.

I nodded.

THE END